CASCADE

“Finally, something to make the hope-punks shut the fuck up.

“A near-perfect blend of implacable horror, gallows humor, and ecological apocalypse. It seems almost absurd that a novel about chaos magic and bureaucrat magicians (even if they are embedded in the sociopathic morass of Canadian politics) can somehow feel more viscerally relevant than all the earnest mainstream novels and Suzuki-Foundation bulletins you could stuff into a ballot box. Pay attention, people: all magic aside, we're far closer to this future than any of our rulers will ever admit.

“Rachel A. Rosen is some kind of twisted genius. I wish I had even half her moves.”

— Peter Watts, author of *Blindsight*

* * *

“Finally, an urban fantasy that kills the cop — and the rest of the government — in your head. Relentlessly radical and often hilarious, Cascade will change the way you look at magic, and the state, forever.”

— Nick Mamatas, author of *The Second Shooter*

* * *

“*Cascade* is an excellent introduction to the imaginative prose of Rachel A. Rosen. Her debut novel takes us to a futuristic North America filled with vividly realized characters surrounded by magic and the possible end of the world. One of the few novels I've read recently in a single weekend. Sharp and thought-provoking, with thrilling moments and crackling with compelling ideas, I wouldn't miss this one. I'm looking forward to her next instalment!”

— Bryan Thao Worra, author of *Before We Remember We Dream*

* * *

MORE PRAISE FOR

CASCADE

"Rachel A. Rosen's *Cascade* is one of the best books I've read this year. She brings a unique blend of magic environmentalism, Canadian politicking, and indigenous and queer rights to the table. I never thought I would be so interested in the near-futuristic Canadian political process!"

— Marsha Altman, author of *The Darcys and the Bingleys*

***

"Full of magic and social commentary, Cascade is never so witty that it hides its anger or so angry that it sacrifices wit. This is a brilliant exciting debut by an author that will have a long and fruitful career if there's any justice in the world."

— Tim Lieder, author of *Sugarplum Zombie Motherfuckers*

***

CASCADE

The Sleep of Reason
Book I

The BumblePuppy Press

Ottawa, Canada
2022

The BumblePuppy Press

This book is a work of fiction. Any references to historical events, real people, or real places are used fictitiously. Other names, characters and events are products of the author's imagination, and any resemblance to actual events or people, living or dead, are strictly coincidental.

Cover by Rachel Rosen, www.rachelrosen.ca.

Cascade is published by:

The BumblePuppy Press
Station E, P.O. Box 4814
Ottawa ON K1S 5H9
Canada

National Library of Canada cataloging in Publication Data:

Rosen, Rachel, 1979 -
Cascade / Rachel Rosen

ISBN: 978-1-7770944-5-4

An electronic edition of this book is also available. 978-1-7770944-4-7

First edition

For Reccia. You taught me how to read, so this is technically your fault.

And to Cocoa and Sabot, who ensured that my keyboard was warm while I wrote it.

FUTURE RUSSIA
OIL & MAGIC
THE COUNTRY CURRENTLY KNOWN AS CANADA
CFA
NEWFOUNDLAND
CFA
CFA
VANCOUVER ARCHIPELAGO
WINTERPEG
OTTAWA
AMERICAN TRADE ZONE
AMERICAN RUMP STATE
SILICON VALLEY AUTONOMOUS REGION
AN ATTEMPT WAS MADE
THE FREE STATES
GUNS, GOD, & GENOCIDE
MEXICO
N
W
E
S

Don't expect anything you do to be glamorous or interesting. Legally speaking, everything has to be catalogued and registered to comply with the Banff Accords, so think 50 pages of paperwork per spell, minimum. And since I am not the only MAI in the office, nearly all of my day is spent doing the paperwork for someone else's spells, which go into some kind of highly classified top-secret vault guarded by three-headed dragons, as far as I can tell. Or a shredder. Probably that, but you still need to type them up for some reason.

If you think you're going to be blessing beer or DJing synesthesiac orgies with your newfound mystical power, please remember that those are hobbies, not careers, and like your mother told you when you said you thought your Soundcloud was going to get you signed to a major label, always have a backup plan. Mine involves extensive research this weekend into what constitutes business casual.

— *Sujay Krishnamurthy*, https://not-your-chosen-one.tumblr.com/

Book I

The Blip

1

On a blistering September morning, four months before magic tore the country a brand new asshole, Tobias Fletcher stood in front of his wife, a dizzying array of choices before him, all of them wrong.

It wasn't idle nerves. Tobias had shot for AP in Aleppo, where the click of a shutter separated a clear, placid day from a maelstrom of bone and rebar. It was about preparation. Whether a combatant or not, you wore a flak vest in a war zone. Tobias was about to ride into battle against Ian Mallory, the federal government's resident wizard, and he needed the right armour.

Or some means of disarmament. Tobias was a jocular Golden Retriever of a man, slow to anger and quick to forgive. He prided himself on moderation in all things. He ate sensibly, watched his salt, and cycled to work. He did not bring up politics unprompted; when asked by new acquaintances, he described himself as "socially liberal, fiscally conservative," and switched the topic to hockey.

He did not speak of magic. It didn't touch his life, except in this one particular way. He was, in short, an unlikely man to provoke a revolution. But the gentlemen's agreements that held civilization together only worked when everyone agreed to be gentlemen. And when they didn't, it became the duty of gentlemen to get a little uncivilized.

Lucy, his wife, was a perfectionist who understood the impact of a flourish. She'd unearthed a pile of ties from the walk-in closet that Tobias had set up as a darkroom—now colonized by wardrobe overflow—when they'd moved to Ottawa. She held four ties between her fingers, and he squinted at them. The blue felt partisan, the red, politically confusing under the present mercurial landscape.

"The green works best with your complexion," Lucy insisted. Tobias considered whether it looked garish against his charcoal suit. "The grey will bring out his eyes, not yours."

Should he even wear a tie? Dress had taken a turn for the dishevelled up on the Hill since the cocaine socialists had taken over. But that really was the problem, wasn't it? The rabble wasn't just at the gates; it had invaded the palace, smashed the Qing vases, demanded and received the heads of the aristocracy, and was, figuratively if not literally, shitting on the tables. And at the centre of it all, Prime Minister Patrice Abel slouched on the throne with his stolen golden crown, drunk at the feast with Mallory, his shrivelled, skulking vizier, at his side.

The election might be called any day now. When it was, the *Post*'s editorial board had been quite clear about its desire to see Canada's three-year experiment with magical governance end. Tobias was there to observe, to document, not to editorialize. If his camera happened to catch Mallory leading a cabinet minister around like the Pied Piper or performing telekinesis on the press gallery, so much the better.

Tobias reached for the green one, holding it up to his collar in the mirror. "I didn't even know I owned so many ties," he admitted.

She tilted her head to one side. "It's Cynthia's profile, not yours. He won't even be looking at you, let alone making you cluck like a chicken."

"If that was the worst thing he'd done, I'd forgive him." Tobias looped the tie into a Windsor knot. "This is about democracy. It's one thing when two gangs of bastards murder each other with regular weapons like normal people. It's quite another when the enemy is hexing the

Opposition and all their descendants. That isn't supposed to happen in Canada. Anyone who thinks democracy and a tiny minority of wizards can co-exist is a fool."

"I think they prefer MAI." Like so much else, terminology was a lost cause. Magic had returned to the world too late, long after the mass media had established a vocabulary for it. That vocabulary sat uneasily with the gravitas of Serious Politics. Magic Affected Individual was about as anodyne and euphemistic as it got, but that was Editorial's problem, not Tobias'.

"You're right about the green," Tobias said. He checked his armoury again, gauged battery levels and cable connections. The padding in his messenger bag was more than adequate for his Nikon D7000 and the microdrone nestled in its tiny foam casing. "I might just be the photographer, but if I can play a role in ending Ian Mallory's reign of terror, I will."

He expected her dulcet laugh in response. Instead, Lucy straightened his tie. She watched him with the same seriousness as she had, two decades ago, when she'd been an ambitious young music student at McGill, during the heady days when the Cascade's magic had remade the world.

"Great," she said. "Now go do it."

• • •

The Septembers of Tobias' childhood were bright and crisp, carrying in them the cool premonition of autumn. But that was Before. Now, the grass had baked to parched yellow and brown. The official end of summer was marked only by the return to Parliament Hill and the retreat of schoolchildren to the century-old brick fortresses that kept the public safe from them. Even at a leisurely roll through residential streets, a thick sheen of sweat settled over his skin.

The *Post*'s Ottawa correspondent, Cynthia Tan, was meeting him on Laurier Ave. West, in front of the office that housed Mallory and his staff.

No one had been exactly sure where to put the consultancy department that insiders called the Broom Closet. Public Safety had, ominously enough, seemed the best fit.

Cynthia emerged flustered from a cab, six months pregnant, smoothing her hair back into place, and only five minutes late. She was a good choice for the Ottawa desk—photogenic, soft-spoken, and non-threatening enough to catch her subjects with their guard down. And, courtesy of parents who'd fled Hong Kong just before reunification, she was possessed of an allergy to anything that carried the faintest whiff of socialism.

"You ready to nail this guy?" she asked, already walking briskly ahead of him despite her shorter strides.

Tobias shifted the camera bag at his side and nodded.

"Cool. I'm looking forward to this. It'll be like the time Jordan trapped Titania with the salt circle and got her to spill the name of the Last Guardian."

He blinked. "Like what?"

"I always forget you're the one person in the world who doesn't watch *Night Beats*. You really should take in some fiction made in the last millennium, Tobias."

Always chivalrous, he swallowed the dig at his pop cultural savvy, and held the door open for her.

Outside Mallory's third-floor cement cell, the reception desk was staffed by an intern with a coffee stain on her sleeve. The downward hunch of her shoulders told him she'd noticed, and lived too far away to run home and change. He smiled sympathetically, but she didn't look up from her computer screen.

Tobias peered past her desk. There was another, short corridor, and then the office itself, the door ajar enough to be an invitation. A cursory look at the desk revealed the girl hadn't been and wouldn't be there long enough to accumulate many personal items. There was a printout that might have been a locket around a woman's neck, and a strange, dilapidated lineup of rubber stress toys. They were grubby, as if someone had given them to her as an office-warming gift and unpredictably, they'd proved more useful than expected.

If she hadn't been on the enemy's side, he would have felt just a little bad for her.

"You're from the *Post*," the girl said. She adjusted her thick, black glasses over the bridge of her nose. Mallory's empire was built on the ashen corpses of eager-to-please young women. "He's expecting you. Go right in."

"You sure?" The girl might be as corrupt an ideologue as her boss, but she was just as likely punching a clock or trying to complete university co-op hours. Not beyond redemption. Empathy was the better tactic. "From what I hear, he's a bit—" The gesture was supposed to be teeth and claws or—something. "Prickly."

The girl reached for a well-used fidget spinner that lit up with a flick of her wrist. "Hmm," she said. "Don't know where you'd get that impression. Go on in before he turns you both into toads."

Tobias rapped his knuckles on the doorjamb, just in case.

There was no sweat on Mallory. For all Tobias knew, he came to work in an armoured car, flanked by flunkies with old-fashioned handkerchiefs. Maybe wizards didn't sweat at all, had found some supernatural means to avoid the myriad liquid humiliations of mortal flesh. Mallory wore a suit—and yes, a tie—grey, as Lucy had predicted. He leaned backwards from his desk in a tall leather chair, waving them both inside.

The teenage Tolkien aficionado in Tobias whined in disappointment that Mallory hadn't actually opted for a wizard's staff and robes. He supposed that would have been a little much to ask. Lanky and ragged, with hair the colour of rust shot through with grey at the temples, there was nothing overtly mystical about the man. Tobias' own personal Saruman was fraying around the edges and, for all his legend, was just another bureaucratic drone in a swiftly bloating state apparatus. Last election, when an unexpected conflux of economic catastrophe, personal scandal, and—Tobias could only assume—magic dark as Vantablack had swept the Party to power, Mallory had been all charm, but he'd aged decades in the years that followed.

If Tobias turned the right way, he saw something more than physical weariness. Desiccated grey flesh clinging to bone, a grim, taut-lipped death's head. Izzy, his microdrone, wouldn't capture that Dorian Grey degeneracy—it was just too new to react properly to magic—but the older generation DSLR might, if he got lucky.

"Ah, good. The legacy press's arrived," Ian Mallory announced, barely looking up. Even the craggy stone of his Newfoundland accent, exaggerated and parodied in countless editorial cartoons and comedy sketches, had eroded into a muddy, undifferentiated Toronto grumble from his years of living there.

"Cynthia Tan." She put out a hand, which he shook, bemused. "This is my photographer, Tobias."

It took more than Mallory's crushing grip to throw him off his game. He waited for the feeling to return to his fingers, and set up his gear while Cynthia attempted rapport.

"Do you prefer Magic Affected Individual, or—"

"Patrice calls me his court sorcerer,'" Mallory said. "My preferred term is 'charmer,' if it matters to ya." Small mountains of crumpled paper littered his desk, marked with intricate labyrinthian designs. Tobias caught one and unfolded it. What he'd taken for black pen, maybe graphite, was a series of precisely etched scorch marks.

Cynthia, serene, took a seat across from Mallory. Tobias framed the shot, letting Cynthia's questions drift into the background. The lens kept going out of focus. The edges of Mallory's thin lips curved upwards in something less a smile than a wolf's snarl. Was he flirting with her? Stranger things had happened, though if that were the case, he was barking up the wrong tree.

"Anyway, I never refuse a good character assassination. How's old Reid Curtis these days? Still rulin' the newsroom with an iron fist?"

"You've stated in the past that you see the country on the precipice of crisis—environmental, social, economic—and that magic is the solution. Would you say that the Party is any closer to solving these problems?"

"I'll get the obvious joke out of the way first. My vision of this country's political future is so preposterous that it takes magic to make it work in practice. Fortunately for all of us—" Mallory's fingers sparked white where they tented. One stray ember burned a moment on the polished mahogany of his desk before fizzling out. Tobias abruptly remembered that while Ian Mallory might be a cog in the machine, a cog could still grind you underneath it. "—I happen to be a fucking magician."

• • •

Mallory existed in a Terry Gilliam fantasy of analog minutia: faded manila envelopes, stacks of papers that mysteriously bent at the corners the moment they entered his presence. Throughout Cynthia's questions, he fidgeted. A skinny knee bobbing up and down here, a shifting of typed pages there. Every molecule in his body seemed irritated at having to keep still while there was a country to run into the ground. It was an open secret on the Hill that Ian Mallory's septum had about as much structural integrity as the De la Concorde overpass, and Tobias wondered if he was high now.

"Just a second." Mallory swung out from behind his desk, stalked across the room, and threw open the door. His intern blinked up, startled. Tobias hadn't noticed it before, but under those glasses, she was breathtakingly pretty.

"Quit fucking around and get back to work."

The air, for a split second, shimmered around the girl. The slightest shift as her head dropped, and no, not pretty at all, kind of plain, actually, funny how the same person could look entirely different depending on the light and angle—and then he realized that what he was seeing was magic.

"Where were we?" Mallory asked brightly. Tobias caught the admonished intern's brief shudder before the door closed.

"We were talking about the cancellation of the Applegate Ridge Extension. At the cost of—" Cynthia paused, as if she hadn't memorized the backgrounder, "—$2.5 billion to the taxpayer, and almost a thousand jobs. Cancelled, based on one report, from you."

"And an open vote in the House. I don't sits here, behind a desk all day, castin' spells for votes," Mallory said. "That's not how this works, despite what the troglodytes in your comment section think."

"Was this a strategic decision to pit Quebec voters against Albertans? The provinces against the feds?" Her intonation rose, and she tucked a long strand of black hair behind her ear.

"It was a democratic decision to respect Indigenous sovereignty," Mallory replied coolly. "And because the pipeline went right through a thin place. There would have been an explosion that killed half a dozen workers and poisoned a river for a generation."

The truth was, no one had managed to pinpoint exactly what Mallory was capable of doing. He could walk through walls. He could turn people into brainwashed zombies with a particular ringtone. He could see the future, chart out the course that had won the Party, against all odds, a minority government in the last election. And when he said a project was a bad investment, the great minds steering the great ship of state listened.

So did Cynthia, leaning forward almost eagerly as Mallory pontificated.

"We know what caused the Cascade," he was saying. "You gots a couple hundred years of human industry. We melted the ice caps and thawed the shit frozen in them. Can I say shit in your paper? We spewed carbon and we fracked and we drilled and we cracked the world wide open."

Cynthia didn't seem to notice that he was wandering off topic. She was entranced. Izzy continued to hover, slavishly recording everything.

Tobias pushed down a groan. For fuck's sake. What was he supposed to do? Grab her and shake her? Stomp on her foot? He couldn't slap her, mind-controlled or not. Smelling salts, but where would you even get something like that these days?

"The world changed," Mallory was saying. "I am part of that evolution, but the human imagination, b'y, that's still quite limited. For the first hundred thousand or so years of history, magic was hypothetical. We could imagine it, as wielded by humans, to be as finite as humanity is. We envisioned the magician as kindly but weak, or powerful and evil. It's always easier to envision a dystopia than a paradise."

Mallory met Tobias' gaze as Tobias crouched to catch him looming over the desk. Cynthia, in his shadow, looked enraptured.

"Sorry—" She swallowed. "How does your government intend to make the new Externality Assessments transparent to the taxpayer?"

"Every time I cast a spell," Mallory said, "I gots ta fill out 30 pages of paperwork and Sujay—my intern—has to process it. That transparent enough?"

It apparently was for Cynthia, award-winning journalist that she was, nodding along to whatever Mallory had done to her. Tobias shuddered.

"Who appointed you?" he heard himself say before he could stop himself.

Mallory turned, as if seeing Tobias for the first time. "Wah?"

That's right. Whatever mojo you pulled on Cynthia isn't working on me.

"Who appointed you, Mr. Mallory? Who gave you the power to decide for the rest of us?"

The pebble he'd tossed barely made a ripple. "Are you a photographer or an editorial columnist, Mr. Fletcher?"

"What you're doing," Tobias said. "It's the death of democracy, of individual freedom and choice."

"Hmm," Mallory said. "In which case, you're still free to think that. There's the hard limit of what I do." Now he spoke directly to the microdrone, a rehearsed speech. "What this administration has done, on the other hand, is improve transparency, improve access and equity, close the gap between rich and poor, repair some of the damage that your bunch has been inflicting since the '80s. I'll go to my grave knowing that whatever gifts I'm given are after makin' the world a better place. Can you say the same?"

The flash, this time, bounced off the cactus on the desk. Tobias flicked back to the preview, and yes, the shadow of two arms fell perfectly behind Mallory's head and bent towards the ceiling. He could work with it.

Mallory said, "What concerns you more? That I can somehow control the minds of 34.58% of the country's population—including hers," he indicated Cynthia, "—or that all this might have been what they wanted all along?"

"I'm just the photographer." He glanced at Cynthia.

She cleared her throat, collected herself enough to say, "How accurate are your predictions, Mr. Mallory? How far can you see into the future?"

"Far enough to see what happens to both of you," Mallory said, deadpan.

"I still believe in free will," Tobias said, earning a warning look from Cynthia. He was being toyed with. Tobias was a mouse thinking that the cat would let him escape were he only fast enough, clever enough.

"If you asks me, b'y, you're focused on the wrong things." Izzy hovered closer to Mallory, and he flicked at it. Aggrieved, the drone buzzed and darted back. The technology had come a long way since the experimental camera Tobias bought as a Hollywood-obsessed teenager, but it was still persnickety, and more so in the presence of an MAI. Technology and magic coexisted uneasily. "We woke up the world." A tiny explosion burst from his palms. "And it's pissed."

Mallory squinted at Tobias, no doubt assessing, like everyone of a certain generation did, whether Tobias was old enough to remember the beginning of the Cascade. Tobias was, though it was easy to forget the boy he'd been, enraptured by the early, grainy footage of Pandora City like a mirage above the Mumbai skyline. The little squat figure of Vasai Singh, the first human touched by magic, raising her arms to build cities in the air. Tobias nodded. Their experiences were close enough for common ground.

"And you, alls you, are worried about the point-zero-zero-zero-zero-five of the population with some control over it. The little kid in the splash pool blowin' bubbles when a tsunami's about to hit. Shriekgrass, demons, the whole planet-wide fuckening. The real question ain't what I want." Deliberately in Izzy's blind spot, Mallory said, "It's what magic wants."

• • •

After the shoot, Tobias had no desire to go back to the office with Cynthia. He felt like he'd gone the distance in a heavyweight bout, wrung out and too concussed to be sure of who had won. Instead, he climbed on his bike and rode alongside the Rideau Canal, the afternoon sunlight glinting over the surface of the water. The sun was descending but the heat felt even more oppressive than it had in the morning, a stifling weight pushing down on his shoulders and legs. Even the steady tick of the chain as he pedalled, a rhythm that he associated with content, aimless weekends—back when he'd had them—did little to still his unease.

What does magic want?

He could normally lose himself in the pure sensation of his body's movement through space, the steady rise and fall of his legs, the faintest hint of the breeze against his face, but his own thoughts sabotaged him. The prickles of anxiety that reminded him of the passing of time, of the inconstancy of opportunity, burst in, unbidden.

Tobias leaned his bike against the barrier, draped his arms over the railing and watched the river. The City That Fun Forgot dreamed in manila envelopes. It lacked the frenetic energy of Toronto, the poetry in every brick that had marked his youth in Montreal, but it had its own calm, staid virtues. Or should have had. Instead, the long summer—not quite long enough to be officially a supersummer, yet—had drained the rivers to their bones. The water levels were low enough to expose stained cement retaining walls. He thought of the hunger stones along the Elbe, a solemn warning to generations long inured from famine and hardship. No one had placed such a memorial in the Rideau. Never in the history of human settlement here had there been a summer with so little rain.

The noise of the city followed him, the whir of electric cars, the roar of an airplane overhead. Tobias put on his headphones. Montserrat Caballé's soprano filled his ears, soaring impossibly in twirling flights above the orchestra. A prayer for peace that teased from within it the scream of a lovesick priestess, the aria leapt and eddied. He marvelled at the heights to which a human voice could soar, unaided by any magic beyond pure virtuosity, how perfect each note, inked by a human hand two centuries ago. There could be no *Norma* today, though the doomed Druid might well have mourned for a world as lost as her own had been.

"Casta Diva" was one of Lucy's favourites, and she had been known to methodically torture particularly talented students by making them attempt it. Like Tobias, she was driven to greatness and perpetually dissatisfied by anything less. But while the MAI had yet to produce a photographic shard of glass that would wrench itself into the depths of the viewer's soul, the impact of magic-affected singers was inescapable. And so it would never be her voice recorded, lilting in front of rich orchestration, that drove him onward. A part of him liked it that way. Her singing was for him alone. But the rest of him mourned for a world of masterpieces unpainted, arias unsung.

But what else was music, except the sound of human potential bashing up against its limitations? What was more magical than that?

Meanwhile, creatures like Ian Mallory had emerged wholesale out of mankind's primordial nightmare. Humanity had lived too long assigning didactic morals to fairy tales when their purpose was to remind children that the world was hostile and capricious. One almost had to laugh at the irony. Centuries of backbreaking progress towards more progressive, more humane modernity, and it turned out that the medieval villagers huddled before a fire had been closer to the dark truth at the heart of the universe than any number of enlightened thinkers.

He took the crumpled paper out of his pocket and turned it over to reveal the sinuous lines etched in ash over its surface. It felt warm, though that might have been his body heat, and vibrated softly in his palm.

What does magic want?

Tobias' intuitive reaction to the question was that it was a distraction from the real issues at hand: Abel's corruption, the threat to the entire social order posed by Ian Mallory and his ilk. Magic wasn't sentient, any more than an avalanche was sentient. It was merely a world lashing out at the abuse to which humanity had subjected it. It didn't have a will of its own.

But, dear God. What if it *did*?

He tried to imagine a force, awakened from a long slumber, reaching with its invisible tendrils to touch a chosen few to enact its will. Smoke whispering over unsuspecting sleepers until it enveloped one, cocooning them, before they awoke as something else. Deciding on the avatars that would shape its presence in a world transformed.

He tried to imagine such an entity settling on a foulmouthed young man in a godforsaken Newfoundland shithole and propelling him to infamy. That Mallory existed for some supernatural purpose, a plan meant for the knowledge of gods and wizards.

Tobias had always credited himself with an open mind; even he couldn't take the thought experiment that far.

His phone vibrated in his pocket. Before he saw the number, he knew who was calling. "Hey."

No one ever used his patron's name over the phone, least of all the man himself. Reid Curtis cultivated such an air of mystery that, had he not known better, Tobias would have suspected the *Post*'s owner of being an MAI himself. But no, he was part of the old guard, both a literal and spiritual descendent of the Family Compact. His wealth, hidden in various offshore pockets, was directed toward restoring a battered country to its historical greatness. Despite the struggle of any paper to stay afloat, let alone employ full-time photographers and videographers, he'd taken an interest in Tobias' career. Market realities were no match for the Old Man's bullheaded determination.

"Are you free?" The Old Man's voice murmured in his ear, deep and rich.

"Do you want me to come in?"

"To the office? Fuck no, Fletcher, I'm at the pub. If I'm going to hear all about your little date with Mallory, we'll do so over a drink or three."

There was something to be said for tradition, Tobias thought, as he swung a leg over his bike. And, magic or not, some things never changed.

2

When the government's jackbooted thugs rolled up in a black car to take Jonah Augustine away, he didn't make it easy for them. The car plowed through kilometres of unpaved road, its glossy paint job scratched by the bramble that sprouted beneath the lush verdant cover of old growth forest. Mud leftover from the last rain splashed in violent brown sprays across the tires and undercarriage of the vehicle. The young functionary, Eric Greenglass, dispatched from on high to perform this questionable public service, twitched in the back seat, watching his phone lose bars the deeper they drove into the woods.

Eric hated nature. He recognized, in the most abstract and intellectual terms, its value. He'd briefly joined the Green Party as a youth delegate before the Cascade had smashed together the tectonic plates of the political landscape. Eric liked the *idea* of nature, but preferably far away from him. He suspected that in every soul lurked an ancestral mistrust of the woods, honed over generations of fairy tales. A finely tuned process of natural selection favoured those who did not stumble, for some obscure pleasure, into the territory of a wide variety of flora and fauna that hungered for human flesh.

Jonah Augustine—on whom Eric's political future now depended—had managed to survive to adulthood devoid of such self-preservation instincts. He had ensconced himself deep in the Incomappleux Valley, at the mouth of a Canfor logging operation. The car stopped at a dirt lot and the security goon, without asking, opened the door to let Eric out.

"It's on foot from here."

"Oh goody," Eric said. "A hike." He'd had to buy new boots for the dubious privilege of hauling Jonah out of the wilderness. A small group of mainly Secwépemc protestors were holed up at the logging site, some of them chained to the old growth trees. The security guard, Adams, brought bolt cutters, just in case Jonah had joined them. They'd held out for months, through the long, dry summer and attempts to starve them out. Now, they ran the risk of simply being forgotten. Eric's boots, top of the line from MEC, were monstrosities, brown nubuck leather that pinched at the sides and did nothing to disguise the mud that streaked them from the instant he stepped out of the car.

The rain began in earnest 40 minutes in, just as the last of the bars on Eric's cellphone stuttered and evaporated, leaving an ominous "No signal" in the top left corner. Horror stories start this way, in the thin places where the vestiges of civilization crumble. He found himself scanning for shriekgrass, demons, but the forest was an older, more primeval predator. It wanted to devour him, certainly, not out of the pseudo-sentient malice that the Cascade had unleashed, but because everything in nature was parasitic. Everything fed upon everything else and in turn was fed upon. Trees were patient farmers of animals, of human beings, supplying their oxygen and tending them until they inevitably fell to decay in the dark, rich soil.

Daylight still scattered blotches of pale green over the rain-glimmering leaves. The coat of moss blanketing the thick tree trunks glistened, viridescent. The driver, whose name Eric had already forgotten, appeared to be enjoying himself up until the raindrops exceeded the point of tolerance. Adams remained stone faced, as he had during the entire 12 hours of their acquaintance.

Eric, miserable, shuddered and pulled the hood of his windbreaker over his head too late to avoid the accumulated dampness trickling down the back of his neck. Minutes later, it barely mattered. The rain was all but a solid mass, sliding over the jacket to soak his jeans, seep into the tops of his boots, slick his face with ice. He cursed, in order, Nature in All Her Glory, the Cascade, the Party, and most of all, Ian Fucking Mallory.

The protesters had erected a blue tarp around the surveying markers, and were damp but energetic enough to be surly as he approached. Eric raised both hands and allowed a burly man with a sleek black ponytail to frisk him for weapons. He noticed the driver and the security guard subjected to the same scrutiny a few feet away.

"I don't know what you think we have planned here..." he started, but the glare in the other man's eyes cut him off. The permit had been approved by the previous government, and cancelling it required a delicate negotiation and likely millions of taxpayer dollars. Not that this man would have cared. Every government was a government of colonizers as far as the protestors were concerned, Haitian-Canadian Prime Minister or not. They were right, but he had to quash his impulse to protest his own innocence.

"I'm just here to talk to Jonah Augustine," he said. "That's it."

From somewhere high above him, a voice replied, "So. Talk."

Eric had to crane his neck to locate the source of the voice. Rain sluiced over his face. Through the spots of water on his glasses, the tarp slung between several of the wide branches was a thick smear. A lookout post; the tarp kept Jonah, squatting beneath it, dry enough to smoke a cigarette.

Eric loathed him on sight.

"Why don't you come down here first?" Eric had to shout. He wasn't even sure how Jonah had gotten up there. A rope ladder he couldn't see, or maybe the guy was an MAI and had flown up. He was mostly sure that Ian would have mentioned if the person he was supposed to extract was a flying wizard. Mostly.

Jonah flipped him off.

"Mr. Augustine, this is serious," Eric said, as if there was anything serious about arguing with a man who was up a tree. And was possibly, though probably not, a wizard. Eric was a serious man, with a serious job—albeit not one his parents could be particularly proud of, what with the conservative leanings of most of their friends and relatives—and it was pissing rain and he was cold and muddy but he was *not*, under *any fucking circumstances*, about to lose his composure.

"Laura," Jonah said. "Something's happened to Laura."

Right. There was a daughter, age 11, back in Victoria, with an ex-wife, Blythe.

"Laura's fine. This is a business proposition. A few hours of your time. And better coffee than you have here." He glanced at the folding table off to one side of the camp, where an industrial-strength coffee urn hooked to a generator belched acrid smoke.

It was the offer of coffee, it seemed, that weakened Jonah's intransigence. He shouted something at one of the other protestors. They must have reached some kind of agreement because Jonah descended from the canopy on a rope. Not an MAI, then, but nonetheless possessed of an easy athleticism that Eric immediately resented. Jonah presented himself, a scruffy little hand grenade of barely contained hostility.

"It better be some fucking great coffee," Jonah said.

• • •

It took Eric ages to locate a coffee shop that wasn't Tim Hortons. In recent years, the surge of indie cafés had receded, driven into bankruptcy by the shrinkage in coffee-growing regions. There was distinctly less glamour, and taste, in the cheap robusta harvested by prisoner labour in the Free States, which in turn drove up the cost of the good stuff higher than even the most discerning hipster could afford.

Still, a few indies hung on, and the hand-drawn wooden sign, ironic needlepoint mounted on exposed brick walls, and chairs upholstered in burlap told Eric that he'd found one of them. He took one table, Adams and the driver another. Jonah slid off his rumpled, ugly windbreaker, and shook it out over the floor. The drink prices, too, had yielded to the New Normal. Jonah's old-fashioned drip coffee, black, was twice as expensive as Eric's caffè gommosa. In the forest, Eric might have guessed him for late twenties. At a closer glance, he was probably old enough to have formed memories of a pre-Cascade world order in which his tastes would have been frugal rather than pretentious.

"You want me to move across the country to go work for the government." The flat tone betrayed incredulousness, but he scrolled through the e-contract on Eric's tablet anyway, dark eyes widening at the salary. "Why?"

"*I* don't want that." In retrospect, a caffè gommosa was far too small to stretch into an awkward negotiation. He was going to finish it before he got to any of his more compelling arguments, and then he'd have nothing to do with his hands. He settled for watching the rain hammer, then still, against the front window. "Mr. Mallory says you're the guy we need. There's a map of wellsprings and thin places that the government wants to quarantine, and he doesn't want to step on any land claims when they do it."

Jonah snorted, pushing a wave of black hair from his face. Eric thought he heard him mutter, "*Mr. Mallory*," under his breath before taking a long sip of coffee and declaring, "Land *title*. This one of his predictions? Thirty-eight percent chance of Indigenous protestors shutting down the rail lines versus the usual point-gazillion-zero percent chance that an asteroid wipes us all out anyway?"

Eric shrugged. "I'm not party to that kind of—look. I'm Patrice Abel's liaison to the Broom Closet, and they're offering you twice what I make, and I found you *up a tree*."

"I'm needed here."

"He said you'd say that. Exactly in those words."

"Well," Jonah said, "he *is* the all-knowing, all-seeing eye, eh?"

Drinking extravagantly expensive coffee, the latest katajjaqwave mix on Spotify droning from speakers mounted on the wall, Jonah couldn't seem to sit still. He watched his phone, face up on the table by Eric's, like the two devices were carrying on their own, parallel conversation. He tapped a foot on the floor. He checked the supply of hand-rolled cigarettes in the pocket of his red flannel shirt. Eric refused to let the other man's obvious signs of annoyance faze him. He'd trekked through the mud at the behest of a lunatic wizard for the privilege of begging a scraggly anarchist to chop off his hair, stuff himself into a suit, and put his resource management degree—oh yes, Eric had read an entire dossier on the guy—to some practical use.

"Anyone can block a bulldozer," Eric said, though of course, the problem wasn't that anyone *could*, it was that not enough people *were*. "For what it's worth, I—I'm totally on side here. A hundred percent, no one supports the environment, or Native land cl—*title* more than I do—"

"Not even the actual Natives."

"It's not just the money—though kids are expensive—it's a place at the table. Not just for you. For your friends out there, for whatever the next fight is. It's an opportunity to make real change."

"You sound exactly like him," Jonah said. "And he's an asshole."

"He said you were his best friend."

"That's just a measure of how much he hates everyone else." He drained his coffee fast enough to activate Eric's caffeine-deprivation migraine. "But he's not *that* kind of asshole. There must be a deal on the table already—he wouldn't hold unceded land hostage just to get to me."

Eric wasn't sure about that. His transfer from Gaby Abel's office was so fresh it stung, and he hadn't worked with Ian long enough to determine exactly *what* variety of asshole Ian was. He wasn't about to rule any of them out. He'd sent Eric *here*, after all.

"He really didn't tell you what he saw?"

Eric shook his head. Wondered if Jonah was looking at him with pity, or whether he was projecting. "Just that it was important. And that it had to be you."

"The fucking surveyors have to be gone."

"I can't promise—there's a contract, it's not simple..."

"Gone. Equipment, vehicles, the whole deal. And I need a week, at least, to get my things in order. Tie up loose ends. That sort of thing."

It sounded enough like agreement that Eric was momentarily lost in a fantasy of gaining Ian's approval, a blossoming of one successful deal after another, words like "senior" and "chief advisor" added to his job title, so much that he almost missed Jonah's quiet, "You know he's completely insane, right?"

"Huh?"

"He can't not be. Shit he's seen, it'd drive anyone a bit... They tried to simulate the prognostication process at an MIT lab and it crashed the whole system for six hours. The human brain wasn't meant to continually witness the end of the world."

"That's what you think this is about?"

"That's what it always comes down to, with Ian. That's the problem. The world is always ending, for someone."

It *was* pity, Eric decided. Just maybe not directed at him.

"I've been fighting this fight for a long time," Jonah said. "I guess that's useful now? But I can't speak for the Secwépemc."

"No one's asking you to."

"There are treaty experts out there. I'm not one."

"I know," Eric said. "This isn't about treaties, it's about—" He let the sentence trail off. Environmental stewardship? Justice? He'd worked for the Party long enough to know how inadequate any of those would sound.

"Ian sure as fuck doesn't need the can of worms that hiring a token Métis would open without a token First Nations for balance. "

Eric nodded along in a way that he hoped signalled that he was knowledgeable and not that he knew more about *Night Beats* lore than the legal and historical contexts of Indigenous nations.

"I'm sure there's an emergency, because there always is, but look. Ian doesn't want my expertise. He needs a friend. And that should worry you." He grinned, manic and humourless. "Thanks for the coffee. I'll be in touch."

Eric didn't have time to ask how he planned on getting to wherever it was he was going before he'd gone. Maybe he *could* fly. He'd heard of weirder MAI abilities than that. When he reached the door, there was no sign of Jonah, or anything but a slate-grey rain cloud, sliding towards him like a punchline.

3

The steady spike of pain between Blythe's eyes presaged an oncoming storm.

The soccer field was a war crime in emerald, a stark contrast to the drought-parched grounds of the school. The sky was crystal, unblemished. But Blythe's migraines were an unfailing augur of barometric pressure, the way her ward tattoo—a stick-and-poke job on her shoulder that Ian had done, way back when they'd all been young and stupid—went off in the presence of magical activity. It hummed now, in the way that the world had always been magic, that spirits and monsters pressed into the tangled skein between worlds until it ruptured to allow them passage.

The kids, oblivious, shrieked and thrashed their way across the field. Blythe followed number 5, searched out the long black ponytail when she couldn't see her daughter's face amid a sea of red and yellow uniforms. Few battles were as bloodthirsty as a soccer match between prepubescent girls, and Blythe dug her nails into her palms, convinced Laura would be trampled by the horde.

"What'd I miss?"

The scent of tobacco and campfire clung to Jonah even in the city, announcing his presence before he sat down beside her on the bleacher. Her body tried to lean into him before her brain caught up and reminded her that the ink had dried on the divorce papers months ago.

He'd only come to say goodbye.

"The sports ball went in the sports hole," Blythe said, "A few times."

Laura hadn't hit her preteen growth spurt yet, and she was easy to overlook. She darted out from the mess of uniforms to mount an assault on the goal, one skinny leg jutting out to kick the ball. Jonah leaned forward, despite being only slightly more interested in sports than Blythe. His hands gripped the knees of his jeans. His sleeves covered most of his tattoos but were rolled up to reveal Laura's tiny handprint inked on his wrist.

The ball glanced off the goalpost. That was what Laura got for having walking disasters for parents. At least her grades were usually good.

"So," Blythe said. "You've done something stupid again."

Jonah watched the ball instead of answering. He'd been fucked up, in order, by the Millennial Scoop, the Catholic Church, and the Cascade. He'd spent his life at war, standing between the truncated wilderness and the mining and logging companies that would pillage it, mapping out the thin places created by the eruption of magic from the earth where human life was increasingly untenable. Canada had always been three resource extraction companies in a trench coat, and it was Jonah's life's work to make sure that magic didn't become another excuse to relocate communities, and rob their people, and people like them, of what little they had left.

"Probably," Jonah replied. "It involves the feds."

"And Ian." She could only assume. Most, though far from all, of Jonah's bad decisions had involved Ian.

"And money. Which the Secwépemc could use, let alone Laura's college fund—"

"I'll give you this much," she said. "When you sell out, you sell out spectacularly."

That was the thing about knowing someone for over three decades. There were few secrets left between them. She'd stolen his lunch money in third grade, and he'd cheated off her tests in high school. She knew—though she'd never confront him on it—about his Grindr profile. He knew about the geas-armoured shoebox in her mother's closet, with a birth certificate, school awards, and the other relics of her pre-Cascade life, long before a charmer had buried both their birth names in the snow beneath the Northern Lights.

"You could come with me," he said. "It'd be less disruptive for Laura."

Blythe was a Prairie girl, born to plains and big skies and the Red River, but the ocean had called, and she'd followed. She had no intention of leaving. And only in Jonah's bizarre worldview was packing up and moving across the country, away from her school and her friends, less disruptive for Laura. "I have work."

"Go remote. You can crunch numbers from anywhere."

"You could look at maps from anywhere," she fired back. As if that had anything to do with him taking the job. "I'm doing field work tomorrow. I can't do that from a screen."

"I can't get the government's ear from one either." Laura was momentarily lost in the stampede of other girls, chasing the ball from one corner of the field to the other. She swerved, nearly colliding with a taller girl on the other team, then rolling into a near-somersault with a yelp of pain.

Jonah rose to his feet at the referee's whistle, and Blythe yanked him back down. "She's hurt."

"Let her do her thing." The ref was leaning over Laura, head bowed, and flashed a yellow card at the other girl. Laura climbed to her feet. She had Blythe's light colouring but her cheeky, v-shaped grin was all Jonah's.

The game resumed, and Jonah picked up the thread of their earlier argument. "Ian will listen to me. And the Prime Minister will listen to him. Do you know what this means? We can be *effective*."

It was a low blow. Her work, a vast and aimless prayer breathed over vanishing corals, eroded coastlines, seldom garnered more than a nub of a news article well below the fold. At least Jonah managed to piss off the right people.

"Just because it's reformist," Blythe defended, "doesn't mean it's effective."

Laura slid out from under the girl marking her, feinting to one side to jump up and smack her head into the ball. It just skirted into the corner of the goal, and she threw her arms up in victory, her round little face beaming.

No one else saw. Even the ref had turned to look upwards, at the slate clouds roiling over the tops of the firs, a cold shroud edging over the grass.

"There it is," Blythe muttered. Laura ran for her and Jonah shielded an arm over both of them as the downpour scattered the players and their families.

"This field work you mentioned," Jonah said. "You'll wear a lifejacket, right?"

Laura, deflated by the game's abrupt end, backed away from him. The rain's onslaught turned the ground soft and treacherous under her feet. Blythe reached to steady her, but Laura was already under the cement overhang by the school, arms folded across her chest. "What do you care?"

"Laura," Blythe said.

"He's leaving," Laura said. "He said yes."

Jonah toyed with the wooden crucifix around his neck, lighter in places where, over the years, he'd worried it smooth. That was the problem with faith. When you lost it, you faced the prospect that there might be no one to absolve you and you might be left having to forgive yourself.

"Yeah," Jonah said. "I fly out tomorrow morning. I was thinking—"

Blythe shook her head. No one would drive him, no one would see him off at the airport. If he was hellbent on abandoning his family to serve at the right hand of power-mad, coke-addled wizard, he could call a cab.

"I'll be back in a month. Maybe two. It'll be worth it."

The truth was, the moment Ian had asked for him, Jonah was gone. When Ottawa called, with benefits and a moving allowance in its back pocket, you picked up the phone. Blythe wanted to believe she'd be more principled than to say yes. Jonah might have been ideologically pure enough once—but Ottawa, Patrice Abel and the Party, making the world a better place and halting the slide into scorched-earth dystopia, blah-de-fucking-blah, were one thing, and Ian Mallory was quite another.

There were some things no amount of magic could bury.

• • •

Blythe circled the bathyscaphe, squinting at its apparent fragility. She told herself that the porthole was thicker than it appeared, the reinforced steel casing tested under conditions only slightly kinder than the ones to which she was about to subject it. Still, she would have preferred titanium and live cameras, though it would hardly match the thrill of personal observation. Blythe shivered in her wetsuit, trying to summon back the elation of departing from shore with the ocean spray on her face.

The vessel was officially—and disappointingly—dubbed the *Nemo* after a crowdsourced naming campaign had come up, predictably enough, with *Sinky McSinkface*. The team, slightly less predictably, had christened it the *Love Craft*, though anyone higher up than Edgar Yip, her group leader, refused to call it that.

Blythe didn't trust it.

"Does it creak? I bet it creaks."

Dahlia West, deep sea pilot and her fellow lunatic in this endeavour, eyed the vessel with the same skepticism. It had to be older in order to not fail the moment little Celene put the recorder to her lips. A state-of-the-art piece of equipment could potentially give up its shit and crack apart at the slightest whiff of magic.

But this thing was right out of Jules Verne, and it creeped her out almost as much as Celene did. It hung on a massive crane over the deck of the ship. The float was a squashed steel cylinder housing the air and gasoline tanks, dwarfing the sphere at its base that housed the observation cabin. A single round portal watched the ballast and the floodlights like an unblinking eye.

Celene sat with her back to the railing by the crane, alone, her fingers slowly moving up and down the instrument. Blythe hadn't interacted with her much, either at the observatory or during the voyage out. Her own purpose on the expedition had nothing to do with her particular area of expertise, which was more typically run-of-the-mill data processing, safely done from behind a desk. She'd been voluntold because she was the only researcher on the team who was also a parent. Funny thing about climate scientists; since the Cascade, none had been too eager to bring children into the world. But the kid, a year or so younger than Laura, unsettled her. Blythe was there to reassure the child if things went pear-shaped 6000 metres underwater, or to serve as a translator to determine if the girl's behaviour was normal kid weirdness or pants-shittingly terrifying MAI fuckery. Getting too close made her tattoo itch. The twinge was an unnecessary indication that Magic Was Happening. But there it was, nonetheless.

"Put it this way," Blythe said, "it's probably worse if it's quiet and all we can hear is the recorder."

"Guess we're lucky we got us a waterbender." At her side-eye, Dahlia added, "Well, what else are you gonna call that?"

Blythe rubbed at her arm, frowning.

"You okay?" Dahlia asked.

"Yeah. Just an old scar." They both watched the girl, who seemed oblivious to their presence, the boat, the bathyscaphe—everything but her instrument. "It'll be even worse," Blythe added, "if we *can't* hear it."

She'd heard Celene play once, on a video—she hadn't so much as *seen* a VCR since her own childhood, they'd probably dug it out of the storage closet at an underfunded elementary school—during the briefing. The water coiled and bubbled out of the swimming pool in time to the music. She'd watched it filtered through the tracking lines, jerking between frames, a piss-poor special effect if she hadn't known it was real. She didn't look forward to hearing it a second time. Recorder was a terrible instrument anyway. Blythe still recalled Laura's grade-school years, and her unspoken relief when her daughter had gravitated towards drama as her means of artistic expression.

The entire operation was rickety and jury-rigged, a shambling Frankenstein of anachronistic machinery and unproven hypotheses. A narrow hatch separated the single cramped observation cabin from the hulking gas tanks and ballasts. Even their OBS and camera equipment was at least thirty years old, though that had more to do with chronic underfunding than deference to the hard limitations of magic. But they would be able to directly observe the newly deepened gulf where the Juan de Fuca plate met the Pacific through the porthole itself, illuminated by an LED ring, for a fraction of what it would have cost to develop something streamlined and cutting edge. And, if Edgar's theory was correct, it would be far less likely to explode.

So. Okay. With another backward glance at Celene, she braced herself for strapping into the thing.

There were dangers beyond ocean pressure and engineering failure; they were in contested waters, and the Silicon Valley Autonomous Region ran unofficial pirate vessels nearby. Blythe was only half-convinced that their magitech hybrid could handle the crushing pressure of the ocean floor and even less convinced that they could tackle hostile libertarians with advanced weaponry that pillaged for the SVAR. She ran a hand over the cold casing, willing it to bear them through the day.

The crane's arm floated, as if by magic itself, towards the bathyscaphe.

"Ready?" she asked Dahlia.

The other woman gave her a thumbs up. "For science!"

There it was, that thrill of discovery. "For science!"

• • •

The *Love Craft* did, in fact, creak. It made an infernal symphony of other noises, a susurrus of hissing and spitting, the slow drip of water from some imperfect seal. Dahlia, steampunk enthusiast and unrepentant nerd, was enjoying every minute of it as she navigated the long descent with the occasional "Yee-haw!" The schools of fish thinned and the last dregs of sunlight grew murky, then vanished altogether.

It was only in the darkness that Celene began to play.

Blythe, like everyone else in the world, had heard MAI musicians perform before. If music was their focus, they were usually good, and magic did the rest. And the girl *was* good. It wasn't her fault that her recorder was plastic, all the family could afford, their savings and investments wiped out in one cruel blow during the recession. A rich family would have never allowed their only daughter to get aboard a vessel older than everyone on the mission put together and destined for the bottom of the ocean. It wasn't Celene's fault that while she hit every beat, glided through improvised pauses and grace notes, the nine holes allowed for only so much range and depth. The songs were simple, reed-thin and tinny, the broken cry of a dying loon. Tears sprung to Blythe's eyes despite that. Woven through the melody was pain too deep to belong to a nine-year-old child.

Outside the window, she saw the water around them swell and part, the crushing grip on her skull ease despite the depth. The shell of the ship rippled, alight with a pale spiderweb of green and gold. A feathery sea star, the colour of rust, bobbed past her face. She touched two fingers to the glass, its surface oddly warm, soft, like human skin.

Blythe hummed, the tune familiar, the lyrics, conjuring images of white kids in feathered headbands around a campfire. She had no idea that kids still learned that song.

Land of the silver birch
Home of the beaver
Where still the mighty moose wanders at will
Blue lake and rocky shore, I will return once more ...

Dahlia craned her head towards Blythe, whose lips involuntarily mouthed the words. "Don't sing along," she hissed. "You don't want to get an MAI-induced earworm, trust me."

Blythe touched her shoulder again. "I'm protected. You?"

The pilot grinned and gestured at the orange plugs in her ears. "Never venture into the unknown without a prophylactic."

Blythe, hunched to avoid the low ceiling, shuffled to the back of the ship to adjust the camera equipment and deploy the OBS, cranking the winch until it loosed from under the belly of the craft to drag along the ocean floor behind them. The image through the camcorder's viewfinder was startlingly clear, the dust and specks parting to reveal drifting jellyfish, glittering in the arcing gold light, a forest of coldwater corals lining the seamount. Dahlia pushed them past a plume venting from the floor, surrounded by yellow, pillow-shaped skate egg cases, into sparser waters, a long plane stretching as far out as she could see.

For long minutes, Blythe could see nothing, then a shoal of longfin dragonfish, eyes and thick threads of teeth glowing, wriggled towards them, attracted, then quickly repelled by the light from the *Love Craft*. She managed to catch a few precious split seconds of film before they vanished into the shadows, hideous Cheshire cats whose villiform smiles were the last thing to fade away.

"Fuck me," Blythe whispered, awed, then covered her mouth, though she was certain the kid was too preoccupied to hear.

"Hold onto your hats, folks," Dahlia called back from the controls, "I'm takin' us in."

At last it came into view: the great cleft in the seafloor where the plates had met, ground together, and inexplicably parted, leaving a chasm that even the most agile unmanned submersibles hadn't been able to map. The ROPOS had beamed back strange flickers of shape, nothing discernible, before its camera systems had fried. Now they were going to try it. Her stomach gave a little flutter at her first glimpse of uncharted territory, the wound in the earth that the three of them would be, for a time, the only humans to view.

"It's beautiful," Blythe said.

"It's fucking *amazeballs*."

The sea floor cracked and buckled upwards by the periphery of the chasm, and the seismometer's readings ticked more rapidly. In the gold spotlight of the ship, the shelf might have been the dunes of the Sahara, scattered with the rugose corpses of corals and the tiny bones of dead fish. Nothing stirred, no ghoulish, eldritch-lit lantern fish, no blind and heavy-jawed atrocities of the deep. Closer still, even the graveyard vanished, an empty stretch of desert in which nothing had ever lived, where the current itself died, the ship nearly becalmed and suspended in a cloud of particulate matter.

The opening looked too narrow, at first glance, to fit even a vessel as small as the *Love Craft*, but under Dahlia's control and Celene's protective bubble, the bathyscaphe nimbly dodged the jagged outcrops of rock, plunging into the depths. Blythe checked the viewfinder, then the porthole. She'd expected, with the light cast by the ship, that the lower plate would be only a few metres down, but the chasm didn't seem to have a floor, at least as far as she could see. The porthole, and the wall, was edging from warm into hot, and she would have moved over to check the instruments, to see how far down they'd already gone, approaching the bottom of the Earth's crust, except that, just then, the OBS readings spluttered violently and Celene's song skipped a beat.

It happened so fast that she almost doubted herself, except that something rippled through the compartment in time with the child's stumble, and her shoulder ached. Not the itch of magic this time, but a stabbing, relentless pain, every line of the labyrinth come alive as a conduit for white phosphorus, burning through her skin. Blythe choked back a gasp.

"Hey, Blythe. You cool back there?"

On her knees, braced against the porthole, she ground her teeth together. "Fine," she gritted. "Keep going. The OBS is going nuts."

"But there's not even a current."

The tattoo throbbed viciously in response.

She wasn't an idiot; she'd spent enough time around the country's most infamous MAI to at least guess that the pain was a warning. She could all but hear Ian as if he was there in the ship beside her, fingers sharp as a hawk's talons digging into her shoulder, shouting at her to turn back, for fuck's sake. Worst of all, he was *right*.

Well, fuck him. He'd sold out anyway. *He* wasn't the one here, making history.

"Holy shit, Blythe. You getting this on camera?"

There was a floor after all, much lower than it should have been, than they'd estimated from the submersibles' sonar. Dark, so dark even the ship's light was paltry next to its immensity. As her eyes adjusted, the specks of marine snow suspended in the murky black became distant, gold and green stars of an alien galaxy, speckled bokeh in her blurring vision.

And below them, impossibly huge, something bleached and ancient, a twist of cartilage spiralling out from the dust, rib-like structures branching from its trunk.

"Whale skeleton?" Dahlia asked. "It might have drifted down here, after the earthquake ..."

Clutching her shoulder—*fuck*, but it *hurt*—Blythe rolled her eyes. Dahlia might have *wished* it was a dead whale, so did she, but if wishes could manifest reality, they'd all be goddamned MAIs. This was a small part of a much larger *something*, the rest concealed beneath the floor of the chasm, and even what she could see of it was bigger than any whale she'd ever seen.

Her gorge rose, and she had just enough time to flail for a sample jar before she was heaving, vomiting an acidic burst of coffee and last night's takeout curry into the container. The music was wilder now, a tortured scream vibrating off the walls of the compartment, too many notes at once to be coming just from the instrument. She heard Dahlia gagging in the pilot's seat.

She had to stay conscious. She had to keep her eyes open. She was going to die otherwise. Spikes of pain burned across her retinas.

Celene was vibrating. Her fingers lengthened, sprouted sideways into dendrites, moving rapidly over the plastic recorder. Crackles of light consumed her hands. Her face was placid, frozen, eyes fixed at some spot past Blythe, past the fragile metal carapace that separated them from the hole that something ancient and unfathomable had punched in the world.

Bile smeared across her lips, Blythe crawled to the front of the cabin. Dahlia was slumped in her chair, the veins on her neck bulging in and out with her rapid pulse. Blood trickled down her orange earplugs—not much of a prophylactic after all—pooling at her jawline. When Blythe turned her face towards her, the pilot's eyes were rolled up to the whites.

"Dahlia." Blythe shook her, gently at first, then harder. Dahlia groaned. Blinking, she strained towards the porthole. "Jesus Christ, don't *look* at it."

The other woman coughed. There was blood on her lips too, maybe she'd just bitten her tongue, maybe they were still going to make it through this intact. And then she brought her hand to her ear. There was more blood, and a clear liquid. Dahlia stared at it in dull fascination.

Calmly—that would be the shock—Dahlia said, "I think you're going to have to take the wheel, Blythe."

"I don't—"

Her hand, dripping with cerebrospinal fluid, closed over Blythe's on the control. "Up," she said. "Just...up." And toppled sideways out of the chair.

The scream died in Blythe's throat. Paralyzed, Blythe didn't catch Dahlia in time; she lay crumpled on the floor in a pool of blood and vomit and the unprocessed Jello that used to be grey matter. Blythe's stomach roiled again.

Don't puke, don't pass out, you need to get out, if you stay here you're dead, you and Dahlia and the creepy little kid, and Laura will. Never. Know. Why.

She barely avoided tripping over the pilot's prone body as she stumbled to cut the OBS loose. The ship rocked as she hit the release and they were freed of the system and its anchor, sending Celene sprawling and Dahlia sliding towards one wall.

"Keep playing," Blythe hissed. She and the girl were obligate ram ventilators; if they stopped swimming, they were both going to die. She slammed her hand on the controls that Dahlia had been working. She firehosed prayers out to whoever and whatever would listen—St. Joseph, Li Bon Jeu, to a Creator who might guide a daughter who'd returned to her only reluctantly and inconstantly. She sent the ship jerking up towards the ceiling of the cavity. The motion threw her to the floor, smashed her face into one of the portholes.

The humping coil of white lay below them, took up most of the window even as they pushed away from it. There was a hint of the biological in it, the anatomical, but her mind balked at imagining the layers of muscle and sinew and skin that had cocooned it. Was she looking at a spine? An appendage? What had the creature looked like in life?

Was it even dead?

The bathyscaphe's trajectory swung a circle of light over the sea floor and she could have sworn that the husk, whatever it was, was textured, not with the random pockmarks of age and injury, but with *intent*, a ridge of geometric lines and spirals too defined, too planned to have grown by chance. Here was something ancient, unearthed by spasming tectonic plates, but the structures carved into them implied consciousness, a pattern marked out by human hands in a place no human had ever been.

Her skin was boiling. The water outside the ship bubbled, knocking them up a column of air, hurtled them towards the mouth of the chasm. She retched, and sobbed, and the scream of the recorder was the last thing she heard before everything went white.

• • •

Blythe dreamt of drowning.

There was blood in the water, a call to sharklust, salt and copper frothing from her nose as every wave reached up to throttle her. She kicked, but a bleached-white spine snicked around her ankles, pulling her downwards, her eyes burning as the bony tendrils whipped through the depths, sliced the sea into jagged shards.

Each time she breached the surface, something small and dark bobbed farther away from her. She knew it was important, the most important thing in the world. She thrashed, pinwheeling her arms to gain traction, but with every inch she gained, it drifted further, until she sank, her lungs filling with seawater, and she saw it tossed and twisted on the furious waves, until her last sight of it was her daughter's head wrenched towards her, wreathed in kelp and screaming for her.

• • •

Three days after nearly drowning in a deep-sea sciencing misadventure, Blythe opened her eyes to the bright lines of fluorescent tube lighting. She groaned and turned her head to the side. Her shoulder itched, an intricate configuration of tiny needles prickling at her skin. Her right eye throbbed from brow to cheekbone, but she could breathe, at least, and there were no monitors, no IV lines or catheter, tying her to the bed. Small mercies, Blythe decided, and slid backwards to sit up.

She had always been athletic, aggressively healthy. The last time she'd woken up in a hospital bed was after giving birth to Laura. The first person she'd seen was Jonah, their impossibly tiny, sleeping daughter swaddled in a pink blanket in his tattooed arms. He had raised his head to look at her and she had seen the deer-in-the-headlights bafflement of a stranger in the face of a man she had known for most of a lifetime, unexpectedly transported into the room against his will and handed a ticking time bomb to hold instead of his own infant.

There was a card; she pawed at it. An octopus, holding balloons in each limb out to a fish with a bandaid on its head. She opened it, smiled at the "Get Well Soon" and Laura's scrawled message "and try not to get eaten" beneath it.

Neither Jonah nor Laura were here now. Instead, it was a doctor and Edgar at her bedside, frowning as though she were a particularly troubling data set. Blythe worked her jaw open. Her mouth was parched and her first words emerged soundless through cracked and broken lips.

A good mother would have asked where Laura was, whether she was safe, who was taking care of her.

A good colleague would have asked how Dahlia was, whether she was even still alive after the horror they'd both endured.

A good person would have asked about Celene, and what had become of the little girl whose safety had been entrusted to Blythe, who had, instead, witnessed unfathomable horrors and who had come close to drowning herself. No one in their right mind would have put a child—not even an MAI child, barely regarded as human in certain circles—in such perilous circumstances in the first place.

All of these thoughts rose in her simultaneously, fought over her dry tongue for dominance.

But what Blythe actually said was, "I need to go back down there."

• • •

Beyond the three days of missing time and a blistering headache that no amount of aspirin would touch, Blythe was physically fine. It took hours to confirm—Edgar reassured her that Laura was staying at her friend Kara's house—the hospital unwilling to release her without an X-ray and a lengthy and irritating interview to determine if she'd given herself a concussion. Celene was fine, though the family had withdrawn consent for her to participate in any more experiments.

Dahlia was not fine. Dahlia was in a medically induced coma, on a ventilator, in ICU. Dr. Park wasn't sure if she'd wake up again, or the extent of the damage.

No one blamed Blythe. It would have been better if they had, if she had someone to share the bezoar of self-loathing coiled in her stomach. Instead, she was an innocent near-miss, there but for fortune, with no one but Celene to attest to how she'd urged Dahlia on in spite of her better judgment.

Edgar ordered her to take a few days off, rest, take care of a daughter who'd been no doubt worried sick about her. He insisted she didn't need to review the footage now, and no, he couldn't email it to her—while she'd been unconscious, the whole affair had fallen under government purview. The Impact Assessment Agency, no doubt under an order direct from the Broom Closet, had declared the entire project classified, and designated the chasm, along with a kilometre in each direction, a no-go zone, the marine equivalent of a wellspring. It was now in the hands of a higher authority, and there was nothing more to be done.

"It nearly killed you," Edgar said.

"But it didn't."

Three of them had been there, and Celene—well, Blythe wouldn't have said that she was *untouched*, but the girl retained consciousness throughout the entire experience, while Blythe had dodged the worst of the chasm's effects.

Blythe's tattoo, the wobbly fragment of the universal pattern she had carried with her for nearly twenty years, the clumsy work of a kid stumbling his way through magic, had *warned* her. It had reacted, and when she'd ignored it, it had shielded her, just as Celene's own magic had lifted them out of the chasm.

There were dimensions, spiritual, cosmological, but those could be explored later, in safer ways. They were questions for Senators and Elders and philosophers. But right now, it was the scientist in her that kicked out at her constraints. Results were inconclusive if they weren't replicable, after all.

This wasn't the old days. She couldn't just take a set of bolt-cutters to the layers of bureaucracy surrounding the dive site, hop a fence and explore the depths of the ocean in a black balaclava and a hoodie. There were perfectly sensible regulations in place, and she almost agreed with them.

No amount of red tape would put the dreams—nor the spikes in the ocean temperatures that followed, nor the echoes and moans that the observatory continued to record, nor the footage salvaged from the *Love Craft*'s doomed mission, distorted despite the precautions they'd taken—to rest for long.

• • •

Five days after the ocean had nearly swallowed her, Blythe would visit Dahlia in hospital. Her condition would be unchanged. Blythe would strain to hear, in the quiet of the room, the backbeat of Celene's song, but there would be only the steady beep of the heart monitor, the tidal wave of the ventilator.

Six days later, Laura would go back to school, and Blythe, still officially on leave, would stand outside the playground of the middle school that Celene attended, hoping, and failing, to catch a glimpse of the child or the strain of her recorder.

Seven days later, in Toronto, a bomb would rip through the first few floors of a Bay Street office tower, spewing shattered glass and nails across a three-block radius, grounding planes and stopping transit in the fog of war that followed. The evacuation would be last-minute but effective; the only injuries a security guard who hadn't gotten the memo, and the bomber himself, once the authorities caught up with him. It would be barely a spike in the line of violence and death that rose steadily with the oceans. Cities shrunk and turned inward, restless, crowded, and straining against their confines, as if much worse did not loom, undiscovered, over the horizon. Barely a blip against a background of grief and pain.

4

There are three types of people who enter electoral politics: naïve idealists, doomed to be chewed up and shat out by a system incapable of accommodating them, cynical opportunists disguised as ideologues, and rancid bowel movements that had somehow evolved the ability to walk upright. Jonah spent approximately fifteen minutes of his first afternoon in Ottawa—jetlagged, underslept, and thoroughly cranky—cementing his opinion that Eric Greenglass, the latest piggie in the government's abattoir and the liaison to Ian's not-quite-functional-office, was firmly in the last category.

Everything about Ian's office was temporary. Squeezed into a nondescript tower between various security agencies, it was a labyrinth of boxes and recycling bags, though whether the Broom Closet—he smirked at the thought of just how much Ian must *hate* the moniker—was on its way to a more permanent home or whether Ian was about to be kicked to the curb over the latest series of foreseeable scandals was anyone's guess.

He'd expected—though, *why should he have, fuck?*—to meet up with Ian right away, given the urgency of the last barrage of emails from him, but instead the pasty, tousle-haired young fuckboy in a cheap suit who'd dragged him out of the woods informed him that Ian was busy in meetings for the rest of the afternoon. Jonah caught the eye of the girl at the desk and she gave him a strained smile and a head-tilt towards Eric that told him everything he'd suspected. His ward buzzed a faint note of warning under his sleeve.

"Who's that?" he asked Eric, who was in the midst of relaying what sounded like a soap opera recap of a minor but complicated expense scandal, except less coherent.

"MP for Yorkton-Melville, but it also implicates—"

"No." He jerked his head back at the girl. "Her."

"Oh," Eric said. "That's, uh, that's just Sujay, I think. Mallory's latest intern. Don't get attached."

Yep. Fuckboy. "She's a magician."

"Er," Eric said. "Is she?" The kid stared at him, as though he suspected Jonah of possessing some sort of mysterious wizard-detector ability. Which wasn't inaccurate, but he hadn't meant to advertise it. "How can you—"

"Same way I can tell you're a pederast," Jonah said cheerfully, brushed off Eric's belated protests, and winked at the girl. "Don't worry, your secret's safe with me."

Sujay, apparently unflappable, steadfastly ignored the two men. He wondered what it was she could do. He was between levitation and murdering a man with her brain—only if she *could*, why *wouldn*'t she, close enough to the blackened, beating heart of government to wipe the slate clean for good?—when the door behind her finally opened. Jonah shivered, a gooseflesh rush that traced the contours of the tattoo on his left shoulder before fizzling out.

"You're here." He had a brief glimpse through the inch gap of copper hair and pale eyes. The last five years had thrashed Jonah's life around like a dying salmon and the years previous, where they'd danced just outside of each other's orbit, had left Ian unscathed. *Fuck*, Blythe was right, Blythe was always so fucking right about him. "Eric, why didn't you tell me he was here?"

"You said—"

"Fuck off. Joe. Get yer scrawny ass in here, b'y."

Jonah glanced back at Eric—blinking owlishly, but unfazed by Ian's mood swing—then at Sujay, and edged around her desk.

The door opened just enough to admit Jonah through. "By whose standards am I *scrawny*? Because it can't be y—"

Ian spoke around him, to Sujay. "You can drop it the second the door closes."

"Seriously?"

"Yeah. Eric, don't you have somewhere to *be*?"

As the door shut behind him, Sujay sighed ever so slightly. *Oh*, Jonah had time to think, right before the glamour dropped, *she's an illusionist*.

At first he thought it was his own eyes failing before the rest of him started aging, the colour draining from his vision. But the office—the obligatory flag and formal photo of the Prime Minister, the brass lamp on the desk, the neglected but nevertheless tenacious cactus—didn't change, nor did the robin's egg of Ian's tie. It was just Ian himself, unglamoured, hair grey, irises grey, skin and lips, all that same dreary monochrome. If he could still smile, his gums would be grey.

"Fucking hell, Mallory," Jonah said. "What the fuck did they *do* to you?"

"Whadda y'at?" Ian shook his hand, his grip as vigorous as ever, then collapsed back into his chair. Without the glamour and the veneer of colour, the lines in his face were more pronounced. Politics, as the good Doctor Hunter S. Thompson had put it, was a drug, and magic an even more potent one. It wasn't exactly surprising that Ian had become a self-destructive speed freak in the five or so years since Jonah had seen him last. He looked like he hadn't slept in centuries. A handshake was all Jonah would be allowed; anything more and Ian would no doubt crumble to ash.

"That," Jonah gestured vaguely at the closed door, "is not an intern."

"She's my apprentice." His accent was thicker when the door closed. "Talented girl. Probably keeping the entire country from falling apart lest they behold the monster I've become. I got lucky when she turned up."

"How much are you using your powers that you've gone all *Fifty Shades of Grey*?"

"Didn't hire you to be my fuckin' mother, Joe." He rubbed at his eyes. Even the bloodshot was grey. How did that even *work*, scientifically speaking? "We're talking Instapot levels of pressure. It's the fucking Siege of Stalingrad up here. They're out for blood this time."

"Saw your interview."

Ian slid a paper under the mess of folders; Jonah caught only the slightest glimpse. A Pattern, the continuation of the ward labyrinth on his shoulder, drawn over architectural plans. "Tan's nothing. I liked the picture though—it's on my fridge at home."

"You're losing it. Losing them. The people who voted Abel in."

"The fuck I am." Ian picked up a pen on his desk and twirled it. There was no natural light in the office, because of course there wasn't, but the metal clip caught the lamp and scattered gold over the gleaming wood. There was a thousand times more colour in those few little bright sparks than anywhere on Ian. "No one wants to be governed by fucking wizards. No one even wants to worry that they might, in some remote, abstract, indirect way, be governed by fucking wizards. You'll all happily surrender every bit of autonomy to data mining companies who use your private information to force you to buy shit you don't need, but the *thought* of someone influencing your opinions through magic is a massive subversion of democracy?"

"Well..." Jonah started, then, "you're preaching to the converted here."

"They're not wrong. It's just too late. The genie's out of the bottle, and if the other side doesn't already have someone like me, you can bet it's not for lack of trying. And when they do, they'll use him the exact same way the Party uses me. They're just not going to be all open about it like I am."

"Yeah." He studied the dips and speckles of light. Ian had freckles, he remembered, that first summer up at the reclam-ation camp. He could, he thought, drag Ian out of this drab little office, into the sunlight. They could get in the car, and drive, and drive, until they were out of the city, its fecal toxicity, drive until the colour returned to his face. They could, but Ian wouldn't. "You're just a regular open book, aren't you?"

"The worst thing," Ian said, "is that I'm the most honest fella in this massive shitehole of a city."

"Now that *is* terrifying."

"You good?"

"I have some crazy Newfie wizard barking orders at me. Otherwise—"

"Blythe good? The kid—"

"Laura," Jonah reminded him. "Yeah. Sure. Everyone's good. They're just not, you know. Good with me in the picture."

"I'm sorry." It fell just short of convincing.

"They're using you."

Ian laughed. "You've been aways a long time. You suddenly got too pure for this game, b'y?"

"You're the nuclear option. They were sinking in the polls, otherwise they'd never—"

"I knows that. Of course I knows that."

That was—and he'd had to travel most of the length of the country to be reminded of it—the worst thing about Ian, a man not so much born as spat, vindictively, into the world. He was as big a bastard as the exposé suggested, and then some, corrupt and drug-addled and vicious. None of those were exactly rare qualities in a bureaucrat, even in the newest and most idealistic configuration of political parties. None of them were enough to command the sort of train wreck fascination that orbited Ian like a midge swarm. No, the worst of it was that despite all of it, he believed in what he did to the point of martyrdom.

For nearly half his life, Jonah had loved him for that, and hated him in equal measure.

"And Canfor?"

"Fled for less fraught pastures than Secwépemc territory."

Jonah's eyes narrowed. "That was fast."

"I can predict the fuckin' future, Joe. That's why they pay me. I knew I'd needs ya and I knew you'd needs this. I might have advised them that it was on a wellspring and if they don't wants the entire region choked out by shriekgrass and anything downstream turned into a play-ground for demons, they may want to look at relocating to a nice ski resort that happens to sit on the very same mineral deposit. It's favoured by the MP for North Okanagan–Shuswap, apparently. Her Majesty's Loyal Opposition, of course, not one of ours."

"Is that true?"

"Do you want to be the CEO holdin' the bag if it was?" He winked. "What's the point of unchecked power and influence if you can't call in favours for a friend? Sorry—I mean if you can't be a responsible ally committed to building a nation-to-nation blah-de-blah."

At least he was using his mendacious tendencies for good these days. Jonah could live with that.

The job itself was straightforward. Talk to Dina Koustlolious in Environment, who was currently plotting out which areas of the country were soon to become shriekgrass-ridden, demon-infested hellscapes if the current trends continued. Figure out how much money was needed to move anyone living there. Make sure the terms of any agreement were acceptable to the Indigenous nations that held title there, and didn't make the government look like assholes to the voters. Hope to fuck he was more than just a token appointment.

"In that case," Jonah said, "let's get to work."

• • •

It took nine days for the wave to crash into them. In truth, Jonah knew that holding power always meant drowning, that every second in office meant fighting for oxygen, with one's enemies baying like hunting dogs on the shore.

Ian, with the treacherous sea in his fisherman's blood, must have been used to drowning.

While Ian amused himself with the fallout from the *Post* exposé, Jonah assessed how far off base the Ministry of the Environment had drifted.

The interview was damaging, but the news cycle moved on: a record breaking donation by the reclusive Toronto philanthropist Alycia Curtis that would send the National Ballet on a coast-to-coast tour, the preparations being made in Victoria to restore a concert hall damaged in the last flood in time to host *Swan Lake*. There was the story of a girl in Iqaluit with the power to communicate with whales who'd driven a calf, in danger of beaching, from the shore with her song. Not everyone was obsessed with Ian Mallory as the *Post* was, at least during peacetime, and Patrice's approval ratings were soon limping back out of the gutter.

And then some fuckhead breaking ground for a subdivision in Alberta found another goddamn wellspring, and everything went to shit.

Predictably enough, Cynthia Tan was all over it, Tobias Fletcher at her side, breaking off from the press gallery to dog Patrice Abel at a hospital ribbon-cutting. They were deflected by Eric, who made a good case for Jonah's continued indulgence of allowing him to survive, somehow miraculously un-punched. For a half-hour, all was well. And then finally, fatefully, Tan found Dina Koustlolious outside the women's washrooms. Whereupon the Minister, in crisis-mode, running on two hours' sleep, made an off-the-cuff remark that might, if you twisted it just the right way, have implied that the government might be open to an extraction operation, which was exactly the kind of thing Jonah was getting paid to prevent.

He had the misfortune to be with Eric the exact moment that the tweet went viral, mollified slightly by the look of abject horror on the kid's face.

"You're seeing this too?" Eric said.

Jonah snarled, "You have. One. Job."

"I can't be everywhere."

"Prove you're useful for something beyond using up all the office Kleenex. Get out in front of a camera, any camera. The Minister misspoke. The PMO's line is, and it has always been, no fucking extraction. Shit stays in the ground until we know what we're dealing with, magic can't be monetized, Indigenous sovereignty, blah blah fucking blah. Keep saying it until it sounds like you actually mean it."

Eric's shellshocked expression didn't fade. "The press gallery is all over this."

"Putting out fires is your job. I'm not your babysitter."

"What *is* your job?"

Jonah glared and started walking. He could feel Eric tailing him, but he didn't turn. "Cleaning up the Ministry of the Environment, apparently."

• • •

"I'm supposed to be looking at land surveys." Jonah's protest was fainthearted at best.

"Yeah, but I can't put 'spying on Cabinet ministers' on the expense account," Ian said.

"You could just send Sujay disguised as a tree." Koustoloious rented the second floor of a stately Glebe three-storey. The branches of a thick oak nearly made it to her bedroom window.

Ian flicked the brim of Jonah's baseball hat. "She's a good person," he said. "We're not. C'mon, it's just like old times. Minus the crowbar."

Ian had donned a grey hoodie and a minor illusion for the occasion. It was nothing like Sujay could muster, but without her glamour, he was a pallid ghost in the failing light. They approached the house, dark but for one bedroom window, unseen.

Jonah climbed the trunk. He heard Ian behind him, cursing age and gentrification, though he hadn't been mouldering in an office for so long that he couldn't pick his way across the branch to the balcony.

"Of all the things the Party could use a precog for, they chose threat assessment. And that—" Jonah tracked Ian's gesture to the two figures moving inside the bedroom. "—is a threat."

Koustoloious reminded him of the girls he'd known in the campus environmentalist groups, fresh-faced and confident and quick to volunteer for thankless tasks, like running in a hopelessly traditional, wealthy riding, or taking over a portfolio in perpetual crisis. She seemed okay, as far as politicians went.

So what was she doing with the Prime Minister in her bedroom?

But there she was, horizontal slashes of black lingerie and white skin visible through the venetian blinds. Patrice's unmistakable linebacker's build blocked the bedside lamp, its light gleaming over his bald scalp.

"Patrice has your attitude towards monogamy," Ian said.

"You knew?"

"There ain't a lot I don't knows. Get a picture and I'll practice my 'I'm not angry, I'm disappointed' face."

Jonah hoisted himself up the pillar to reach the overhang. The shingles bit into his palms and fingers where he caught their edge. The last pull up burned the muscles in his arms, reminding him that he was too old for this shit, that he was a legitimate consultant with a government contract and not a twenty-something hippie breaking into a construction site, and he lay a moment, sucking in short, rapid breaths, before reaching for his phone.

"We needs to nip this in the bud," Ian said, crouched on the roof. "Before it fucks Patrice."

They were really going to end someone's political career on top of her apartment like two delinquents. Jonah contemplated the photo, stark in 20 megapixels.

"Why?"

"I need Dina out," Ian said. "Gaby's been in the wilderness long enough. Time to put her back in Environment."

"Like a chess piece."

"Nah, like a good soldier." For a reputed political genius, Ian was startlingly oblivious at times. He could have drawn the right labyrinth, found exactly the right words, and had Jonah dedicated, as fervently and passionately as he'd once believed in the vengeful, omnipotent, and prurient Father, to doing Ian's bidding. But that was what everyone, especially the *Post*, got wrong about Ian. He didn't want control; he wanted to be acknowledged, freely and without the interference of supernatural means, to have been Right about Everything All Along.

Jonah shook his head and before he could talk himself out of it, texted the photo to the hapless MP's phone and measured the gap between the rooftop and the tree. "You should come to dinner at my place."

"Dinner." He said it like someone for whom dinner was a foreign concept, and for how emaciated he'd become, maybe it was.

Anything to drag his old friend out of the gutter. "Order pizza, hate-tweet the Opposition from a burner account." He had no idea what Ian did for fun these days. If he even remembered fun.

"I'm a bit busy right now."

"After." As if there would ever be a time that Ian *wasn't* busy, a time when those in power wouldn't be waiting in line to drain him dry. "Say you will."

Stupid, really; Ian as he'd been, once, with his ridiculous battered old truck and his hand-drawn protest signs was a different man entirely from this slick bureaucrat. Even back then Ian had been the guy who brought the obligatory marked-down hummus to the potluck, too focused on the unseen menace just out of frame to pay attention to the present.

"Okay," Ian said. "Yeah, dinner sounds good. I, uh—beer? Wine? You haven't given up drinking, have ya?"

"I still drink."

"Good. You're the only bastard in this crapsack wasteland of a city I'd drink with. Did Blythe come with you?"

"You do know we got divorced, right?"

"Still. 'S better for the kid."

"I can't ask Blythe to leave the coastline." He sucked in a breath and made the jump back down to the fork of the tree. "Why, do you know something? Did you *see* something?"

But Ian had already moved on. "They wants to destroy me," His voice was quiet and distant, like he'd already acquiesced to his own assassination plot. "There's money behind this, big money. Bad enough that there's a Black PM, a *philandering* Black PM, a-course, but these *Post* fuckers won't rest 'til we're all out on our asses, and preferably in prison for daring to sit in their chairs."

"No shit," Jonah replied, sitting down beside Ian. "I've known that all my life."

"But you're here." Jonah had the sense that Ian was speaking more to himself than to him. "You're fucking ten times the wizard I'll ever be. They'll be choking' on their own ashes."

"Battle stations, eh?"

"Battle stations," Ian said.

5

Outside Ian Mallory's office, his intern and apprentice, Sujay Krishnamurthy, bent forward in her not-quite-ergonomic chair. She craned her neck towards the single, grimy window, down to the street, and—though her conscience begged her to do otherwise—willed the cars below to crash with her mind.

That was something you could do with magic, making cars crash, turning metal to gnashing teeth. It wasn't something that she could do with her magic, or that Ian could do with his, much as the media liked to portray him as an uncontrollable force of nature possessed of terrifying godlike powers. But because it was something that could theoretically be done, it was a common preoccupation amongst a startlingly large segment of humanity. There was even a term for it: *cacoethes*, an irresistible urge for something terrible.

Jamila had given her a stress toy when she'd gotten the job, and it was already well worn. It was a round head, and the ears and eyes and nose all popped out when you squeezed it. It came in a box that proclaimed it Panic Pete, and right now, it was a distraction from thinking about the cars.

Sujay rolled the head over her palm. Squeezed, one-two-one-two, the rhythm quickening, iterating outward, until her hand began to glow.

She pictured a veil between herself and the world, a luminous, translucent screen around her desk. Outside, an onlooker might see a young woman—her hair, unlike Sujay's, neatly styled, her makeup, unlike Sujay's, flawlessly applied, her blouse, unlike Sujay's, perfectly fitted and flattering. This young woman, though she had Sujay's eyes and Sujay's mouth and Sujay's fingers, was—unlike Sujay—intensely focused on her work, sharp and quick and efficient.

Inside the veil, Sujay pushed back in her chair and pulled up her blog. The masthead, "Not Your Chosen One," in beveled, solemn serif type, glowing over a background of mystical forest. *Awesome.* A lot of people angsted about being cursed with the burden of magic, but she wasn't one of them.

The door opened. Ian Mallory's head poked through the illusion field.

"Better," he said, snatching the rubber head out of her hand. "But still kinda shite. I can *hear* your glamour through the fuckin' door. Dial it back."

And the mirage of the ideal intern collapsed in on itself like air in a punctured balloon, dissipating into quantum particles.

• • •

So low in the pecking order was Sujay, even in the cloistered, obscure corner of the vast network of 3Ps that was the Broom Closet, that the earliest whispers of new wellspring activity in Alberta registered first to her only as a grim piece of trivia.

Ian had been on the phone or lurking in cabinet meetings most of the day, sending out first Jonah, then Eric Greenglass, on various mysterious errands. It was only as she gathered her purse from the locked drawer under her desk that he deigned to summon her at all.

Sujay wasn't allowed to talk about anything that happened in the Broom Closet. She'd had to sign a standard NDA, but this was government work, and leaks and rumours abounded despite a veritable fortress of paper. Woven on top of it was a low-level geas, the best Ian could manage given that his talents didn't exactly extend in that direction, but enough to make her spout gibberish whenever her mother or Jamila asked too many questions. It made for a depressingly lonely workday, and she hated the little senpai-noticed-me thrill of anticipation that came every time her *real* work—that of learning from him how to fix the world—began.

She didn't show a reaction when he called her name; that was the best part of being able to cast a glamour. And, at least he *knew* her name; she'd worried at first that he didn't, but it turned out that he was one of those rare white guys who didn't stumble over it. She propped herself up against the wall, not sure what to do with her hands or feet when he didn't immediately sit down. The air, flat and stultifying in the cluttered office, met his skin with a static crackle.

He started the conversation in the middle. "Ever been to Alberta, Sujay?"

"That's one of those provinces you fly over on your way to BC, right?"

"Don't let Jonah hear you say that. He grew up in Manitoba." So, not in the mood for humour. Whatever was going on with the meetings and phone calls was serious. "But you're not missing anything. Except."

And that's how she found out that there was a new wellspring, and he wanted her to go see it. In person.

"Are we even *allowed*?"

"I've got Protected C clearance. Should do it. Besides, anyone else is going to be too scared shitless to get between us and that thing. You gots a passport, don't you?"

Sujay nodded. Flights had gone from ludicrously expensive to near-impossible in her lifetime—even her family's bi-annual trips to see her grandmother in Sri Lanka became pixelated video conferences. How Ian managed to justify the fare to the Budget Committee could be attributable to either low-level mind control or an extensive blackmail portfolio, and after six months of working for him, she was still afraid to ask which one it was. But her mother had always insisted she renew her passport, no matter how drastically the world was shrinking. You didn't know when they'd turn on you, when you'd have to run. Who they were was never specified: the Sinhalese, the old-stock Canadians, pinch-faced in their polite bigotry. Maybe humanity itself. Her mother had warned her, once the truth of her had reared from her fingertips and sparked across the carpeted floor of her teenage bedroom, had been confessed, shamefully, across the kitchen table. You always had to be ready to fly.

Called—to a hole in the ground, oozing magic into the soil—was a different story altogether.

She was familiar with this story. You followed the rabbit, stole your way through the wardrobe, opened the letter. Bit into the apple, even if it poisoned you, and barrelled headfirst into your goddamned destiny. She didn't need to see his face, pale even with the glamour, to know when a storm was coming. Of course she'd go, without hesitation. Of course she was scared. This was where her life as an MAI, as a charmer, began.

• • •

Shriekgrass grows in the places magic has touched, where no other life can gain a foothold. Pale and spindly, sharp fronds edge its drooping stems. It sways in the wind like the legs of a centipede or a human spine. It screams when cut, groans where it pushes through the dry earth and the cracks in the pavement.

A boy in school had once told Sujay that all plants feel pain, and the smell of freshly cut grass is actually chemical terror at the lawnmower blade. Plants, she understood—but didn't quite believe—were constantly communicating, but at a register humans couldn't perceive. Only the sentience of shriekgrass could be proven, a thin cicada death-rattle heard across the Prairies; only shriekgrass, it seemed, felt horror and pain not only in leaving the world but in entering it.

As their plane met the runway, she could see a sea of mauve

shriekgrass where wheat had once grown. It was rare in urban centres. She'd seen the odd patch on a neglected lot, but it was something she associated with remote, distant places, with countryside gone to wild, another signpost of nature's revenge.

She remembered that old song, *And the shriekgrass grew all around, all around, and the shriekgrass grew all around*, and waited for Ian to say something, anything, to break the earworm. Instead, he stared out at the grey of the tarmac, broken by the near-grey of the shriekgrass, fading into the even paler grey of the fog-choked sky, and to Sujay's tired eyes, seemed as drained and ethereal as the landscape when it rose up towards them.

The supersummer had hit the entire province with droughts and wildfires, but Fort McMurray was even worse than the smoking crater of hell that it apparently usually was in late September. Ian seemed unbothered until they'd cleared the sweltering tarmac, then launched into a torrent of semi-comprehensible *b'y da lards* and *by the fiddler's fuck stamps* apparently directed at whoever, amidst the dying hordes of his parents' generation, was responsible for fucking over the global weather systems to such a degree.

Their ride drove an old gas car. The driver was about Ian's age, and nearly as skinny, his skin sun-baked and hairline retreating into white-boy dreads. He clasped Ian in a giant bear hug, which Sujay didn't realize was a thing people were allowed to do without getting their hands bitten off.

"Damon," Ian said, half-greeting, half-warning. She shouldn't have been surprised that he had friends here. Ian had been everywhere, the rising oceans and the falling dollar eroding his roots just as swiftly as his own restlessness would have eventually done. The last scion of island men who couldn't stay put, who followed the harvests and the oil fields and the potash mines, clinging to their accents and their sentimental music and their wifi connections.

"It's been forever." Damon ushered them into the car. There was a pistol lying on the front seat next to him, which he moved so that Ian could take the passenger seat. He smirked at Sujay's obvious discomfort.

"Demons," he explained, which only made her more twitchy. She sat in the back, watching the two men—friends from the "bad old days," to hear Damon describe it—catch up. He rolled his sleeves up to his elbows to reveal scarred arms and, incongruously, a roughly rendered tattoo of a rabbit's silhouette with empty, almond-shaped eyes, as he started the car. It looked familiar. Was it from something?

Damon kept glancing at her through the rearview mirror. "That your new sidekick?"

"I don't have sidekicks," Ian said. "I get interns now."

"A wizard's gotta have sidekicks. Or apprentices, or what have you. You had that Native kid back in the day, used to follow you around—Jacob? Joseph?"

"Jonah. He works for me too."

Damon snorted. "Fuck. Seriously? I'd have pegged you for going the pensions-and-death route, but not him, not in a million years."

Sujay settled for staring out the plastic drop sheet duct-taped into place in a rusted metal frame as they bumped over the broken road. The air outside was dense and moist, and hissed into a thick layer of steam where it met the parched earth.

There were shadows in the mist, disappearing as quickly as they'd appeared, shapes that might have been trees, or telephone poles, or demons. The bipedal version of shriekgrass, the thing that men became when they drew too close to magic. "It was just gonna be some shitty suburb," Damon was saying. "Now that development company's gonna be rich when your lot buys them out."

"That's not the plan," Ian said.

"Oh, that's what you say *now*. With the SVAR sniffing around, your guys see the dollar signs, they'll change their tune *real* fast." To Sujay, he said, "You know this guy used to be a card-carrying anarchist?"

"I didn't know anarchists got cards."

"It's all mushrooms, you know? Magic is a fungus. You get infected by the spores, you're an MAI. You get bunch of people dosed and next you're seeing demons."

"Really?" Ian drawled.

Damon didn't stop talking. "You into that mind control mojo, Mallory? The SVAR, they got these new chips, basically juice them up with magic and then zap, they own you, you're basically a slave to the wizards now."

They came up to a dirt road that turned off the highway. Sujay yelped as they hit a pothole, and Damon grinned at her in the mirror. The road stretched out for a few feet before disappearing into fog. He pulled off to the side and scratched at his arm.

The tattoo was the Black Rabbit of Inlé. From *Watership Down*. The guy had the Grim Reaper of bunnies on his forearm, because that wasn't in any way weird or creepy.

"I'll be back, what, 4 pm? You want company?"

"We're good." Ian, shooting her an apologetic glance, stepped out. The soup of the air was so thick he seemed immediately less real, less present. Sujay followed him, lest he get lost in the mist and leave her without a guide.

The ambient magic churned out by the wellspring was enough to interfere with the illusion she'd cast on the trip up. There he was, stripped of artifice, as weedy and drought-starved as the blighted plains around them, as the shriekgrass, and she understood with painful clarity why he kept her around.

"This way," he said, syllables clipped and airless, and she followed.

She floated, more than walked, through the grey, her thin t-shirt clinging to her sides, stray curls of hair sticky on the back of her neck. Her hands clenched and unclenched, off-Pattern lest she accidentally trigger more magic than already surrounded them, but she could all but feel the air thick between her fingers.

"How do you know?"

His eyes were open but they might just as well have not been; he moved as if directed by a higher force, towards the source of the thing that animated every cell in his body. She tried to feel it too, even squeezed her eyes shut waiting for the wellspring to guide her, but all she felt was a white noise static, tingling in the tips of her fingers and the fine cilia of her lungs.

"What if there are—" she stopped. "You know. The people who..." She squint-ed into the fog. "Demons. Whatever. I mean, we don't have guns or anything."

Ian laughed. "You think guns would *help*? Damon keeps his for himself, if he actually gets up close an' personal." He stopped, then, as if he'd seen something that she couldn't. "The site's just up ahead. Quarantined, in case someone's an eedjit."

She tried to stop thinking about what the shapes in the mist had been. Tried, instead, to reach out, to feel some kind of kinship. The soft black hairs on her forearms were standing on end, her skin itchy, like she'd fallen asleep on the grass and awoken covered in ants.

"It's not gonna transform us, ducky. Might eats ya, but you gets to die human, or as human as you are now. We can start here."

"Start?"

"Wardin'." He had a notebook out, was scribbling the Pattern so hard that sparks flew from the tip of his pen.

"I don't—" God, she'd been so stupid, playing with emoji spells in her bedroom, casting glamours in the office like she was trying a new makeup technique, without even thinking about what she might call down. She didn't have the paltry excuse of having read None of the Right Books; she knew, like every genre-savvy nerd with the bulk of human myth and legend at her fingertips, that power had its price.

Ian had turned shriekgrass-grey, every bit of pigment leached from his body, because of what he'd done, what he'd been asked to do in the name of fixing the mess previous generations had left behind. He'd done more and more, every fraught negotiation and bitter compromise, until he was little more than an empty husk.

"That's why I brought you here. You wanna do somethin' useful with your life? There's a fly-in reserve in the blast radius of this thing, not to mention what happens if a moose or a bear wanders in, or some stund kid gone t' work the oil sands." He seized her hand, bent his fingers around hers, and sparked like a live wire.

The magic crashed over her, crushed her, ripped flesh from bone, took her apart atom by atom, until she was nothing, until she was the fog itself, settling heavy over wheat fields turned to sand.

What makes them demons, anyway? She heard herself ask it, a century ago, in another life.

Like it fuckin' matters, and she'd insisted no, it mattered, they'd been human before they'd haunted the wilderness by the wellsprings, before their names had been lost to madness, their very selves dissolved and reassembled into monsters. The humpbacked things in blurry cellphone footage, the creatures that moved as though each of their joints had been violently dislocated, as if filmed with a different frame rate, jerky and halting. She heard their voices in the blast-furnace wind, a cry like the shriekgrass' at the torture of existing in the world. They were things that lived just beyond the horizon, at the end of her own story, there but for fortune.

—and the shriekgrass grew all around, all around, and the shriekgrass grew all around—

Ian's nails clawed into her wrist. The loose cable of ward magic thrashed and jumped, looking for something to connect to.

I am Sujaya Krishnamurthy, I am twenty-two years old, I have a mother and a father and an older brother who aren't proud of me, I am a fucking wizard, *just like Ian, just like Vasai Singh,and I am* not *afraid—*

—grew all around all around and the shriekgrass grew all around—

"Sujay." Strands of magic cobwebbed in the thick air around him. She blinked rapidly, fought the weight of the fog on her eyelids that was willing them shut into sleep. Just beyond, she could feel the fog coalescing into Pattern, the Morse code she squeezed out into her stress balls, Ian's labyrinthian drawings, the photos she'd seen of Vasai Singh's resurrected Mumbai, gleaming white spires dripping with ocean water. Maybe that was what turned you into a demon, that moment where you became subsumed by magic's Pattern and forgot who you'd been before.

That couldn't matter. He'd brought her here to save lives.

—all around all around—

She caught the edge of the Pattern, breathed it in and released it. Magic pooled at her fingertips, burst from her half-opened mouth like vomit, her teeth burning white-hot against her lips. Her newly spun ward, a shade deeper and greener than Ian's, twined with his, coalescing into solidity and spreading through the mist. Shriekgrass wailed, and the ward trembled, but it was holding. Three strands would have made a braid, would have been stronger, but the spell, threadbare and wobbling encircled the woods where the wellspring hid.

The song said *green grass*, she recalled, not *shriekgrass*. Just a children's song, for a stupid TV show, written before shriekgrass even existed. How had she not remembered that?

Their hands were still locked together until she remembered that Ian was her boss, not her saviour, and broke away. She could see almost clearly in a ten centimetre radius, down to the white crescent-shaped indents his nails had left in her wrist. The fog was ebbing. Further on, something was moving through the skeletal ruins of the abandoned housing development.

The ward quivered. Ian's eyes flashed white. One of the strands snapped and sparked. "We needs to leave," he said. "Move."

"What about the spell?"

"It'll hold."

"We're not meeting Damon for hours."

"We're catchin' an earlier flight." He was already striding through the mist-draped plains. "Hope you brought good shoes."

She trailed after him, her short legs in a conspiracy with the barbed fronds of shriekgrass that stuck in her soles and the baking heat that pressed down on her, squashed her into the ground. Her lungs heaved in protest. She'd had nightmares like this, moving through a miasma that stood between her and her escape. "Ian!"

"I'm sorry." Ian's voice was gravel, and apology was such a rare sentiment from him that her head immediately jerked up. "I shoulda prepared you better. You needs to be ready to draw blood."

Near the edge of the fog, he pulled out his phone, shook it. Sujay squinted at her own, the screen milk-white and the bars greyed out. Ian nearly stumbled in his attempts to call and walk and murder the device with the sheer force of his hatred. He moved in and out of her field of vision, half-mist himself, and when he finally got a signal, she only caught snippets of the conversation.

"Yes, all ten blocks." Away from Ottawa, he hadn't had cause to shout at anyone for nearly 48 hours, and it was clearly getting to him. "Sweet buttery Christ. Do you know who I fuckin' *am*?"

"Did I do something wrong?" she whispered, but the dry, crackling air swallowed it. He barely even looked in her direction.

Damon's car was waiting, parked at a gas station an hour from the construction site. Ian flung open the passenger seat and barked, "Airport, now."

The car thumped over potholes and gaps in the road. A sliver of Damon's face, visible from the back seat, leered at her. His reflection, distorted in the plastic-sheeting window, became something monstrous, tentacular. Her hands, clutching the knees of her jeans, were cold and clammy, and there was nowhere safe to turn her eyes, not on Damon, reflected light rays becoming catfish whiskers drooping from his upper lip, not at Ian, sheathed within an illusion she struggled to maintain, lest his carefully constructed public persona crumble before her, his old friend, and the world.

• • •

Ian spent the ride back to the airport in pitched battle—with, as far as Sujay could tell from his end of the conversation, Toronto Police Services, Air Canada, and Eric Greenglass—snarling into the phone as Damon smirked and Sujay shrunk into the back seat. He all but dragged her up to the check in, claimed a new set of boarding passes, and collapsed into a pillar by the departure screen.

"What happened out there?" she asked. Something wrong with the spell, the cable-snap of the ward, but no, she could still feel it if she reached out. It must have been something else, something he saw.

"Tell ya when we get back." He went through the metal detector first, the X-rays of laptop bags and purses turning fuzzy as he passed by the carousel.

She moved to follow him, only to be pushed aside, roughly, into a separate, darker lineup.

"Hey," Ian called out, "that's my secretary," and the last she saw of him before she was shuffled away was one of the security agents trying to take his arm—politely, terrified, but decisive nonetheless—and him yanking it free, face twisted in fury. Even a pissed-off wizard wasn't a match for airport security.

Sujay was led into a room where three other women, two brown and one Black, sat stiffly in plastic chairs. One furtively nursed an infant. There was no chair for her, so she stood against the wall, shoulders sore but unwilling to put down either her purse or her backpack with her laptop and Panic Pete in it. No one spoke; no one asked what they were doing there. It was hardly the first time, though she'd been travelling under the assumption that Ian Mallory was a shield from the usual delays and harassment.

Idly, she wondered if she could have magicked herself invisible somehow. Default. White. But she'd thought Ian's presence—or, if nothing else, the extensive RCMP background check she'd had to undergo before she started working for him—did that for her.

The first woman was called in after half an hour. Sujay took her chair, still warm. Her neck ached. She stared steadily ahead, none of the women making eye contact with each other or the security guard who stood by the door.

She checked her cell. No signal; no word that Ian was coming to rescue her, if he wasn't sitting in a waiting room identical to hers. They weren't going to make the early flight. Checked her ticket; the squared-off blocks of numbers. She dug into her bag for the familiar talisman, dirt-smudged and worn on the dull surface of its head. It was a bad idea to attempt any glamour now—setting sparks off would no doubt mark her as a terrorist as much as her skin colour and her family's history in the LTTE—but she wanted something to do, something reassuring to hold. She kept her Pattern deliberate, steady. One of the other women chanced a puzzled look at her.

"Sorry," she said, and Pete's cherry red ears blew out the sides of his head. The woman quickly looked away.

After another forty minutes, the first woman passed by outside. She looked like she'd been crying.

"Miss Krishnamurthy?" One of the security guards, also female, small and trim in a neatly pressed uniform. She was blank-faced, efficient. Sujay had ceased to be a passenger to be moved from place to place and had become a set of variables and risk factors to be processed. They had two more guards waiting for her outside, and she was taken into a new, smaller room. One of the guards removed her purse, took her backpack.

"Stand over there, please. Hands against the wall."

She'd taken flights before; arguing with security was always a bad idea. Docile as a lamb, she placed her hands on the whitewashed cement wall, leaned forward with her palms supporting the weight of her body. The guard frisked her, small hands pawing at her breasts, her hips, the tops of her thighs.

One of the male guards emptied her backpack out onto the table—*"Why so many stress toys?" "Oh, she works for that wizard freak"*—her purse, wallet and keys and three different shades of lip gloss tumbling out onto the plastic surface, exposed to her interrogators.

"What's the password for your phone?"

"I don't remember." Cooperation was one thing; she'd be damned if he was going to read her blog, or, God forbid, her *Night Beats* fanfic. He shoved it in her face.

"Unlock it."

"I can't."

The woman showed no special suspicion of her. Her skin was a shade darker than Sujay's. There were layers upon layers of people who were just doing their jobs, and this was how atrocities happened, one compromise after another.

"Remove your clothes, please. No, not the bra, that's fine."

Maybe I have a shiv in my underwire. They were doing it just to fuck with her, Sujay decided. Because she wouldn't unlock her phone. She'd worn a loose-fitting cotton t-shirt and slacks for the flight—had even contemplated shorts and sandals, given that the heat seemed unlikely to let up any time soon, but decided at the last minute that it was too unprofessional for a trip with her boss—nothing that could conceal a weapon, unless she'd somehow squeezed a pistol up her ass. How long could they possibly hold her? She hesitated, heat rising to her cheeks. The woman *ahem'd.*

"Sorry, is this really—" The guard's face indicated that it was, and the prominent holsters on the ones standing by the far wall suggested it wasn't up for discussion. Sujay slid her shirt over her head and draped it over the chair beside her, then unbuttoned her pants. The air-conditioning was on full blast, and she shivered. She stood in front of the guard, hyperconscious of her two-day-old bra, the rolls of fat at her sides.

"Turn around," the guard said.

If you touch me, I'll punch you, Sujay thought, but of course she knew she wouldn't, that way lay tasers and forensic inquests. Where the fuck was Ian? She rotated, hands in the air, for the woman's perusal. She could feel the heat of the male guards' eyes on her, the residual magical energy that wanted to break through her skin to shock the woman's hands. She sucked it in like her stomach, her breathing shallow and tight.

They let her stand, in her socks, without speaking. Would they ask her to strip down further, hang out staring at her floppy tits and thick black pubic hair, every centimetre of her submitted for scrutiny, for risk assessment? But then one of the male guards nodded to the female one, and she was handed back her shirt and her slacks and commanded to dress.

"Shoes too," the woman said. "These floors are filthy."

"Yeah," Sujay said. "Thanks." She was escorted, without apology or explanation, down the hall to the waiting area.

Ian stood in the near-empty waiting area, scowling into his phone. The handful of passengers for the next flight were on their own phones, or staring at the flatscreen TVs mounted over the chairs. They seemed in a state of such shock that she had an uncomfortable moment where she wondered if she had, in fact, actually managed to put her clothes back on.

She tried to keep her voice bright. “They were total assholes,” she told him. “Maybe you should have found a white apprentice. We’d be almost home by—”

“Sujay,” Ian said, his voice softer than she’d ever heard it, and he pointed to his own photo, plastered across one of the television screens.

6

Gaby Abel, wife of the Prime Minister, MP for La Pointe-de-l'Île, and former Trade Minister, was God's gift to photographers.

According to Cynthia's sources on the Hill, Gaby was as well-liked by her colleagues as she was by the seventh grade students she'd taught before she'd entered politics. Which was to say she was perpetually awkward, flustered, and in over her head. The rumour was that she'd secured her cabinet position more through her marriage to Patrice than through any experience or competence in the portfolio, and with the former yanked out from under her and the latter on the rocks, she was courting oblivion.

All of that drama, personal, political, and otherwise, showed on her face. The long shadows of the afternoon wore deep grooves under her eyes, filled in the hollows beneath her cheekbones. Her English was slow and considered, no match for a press corps bent on giving her hell.

And Tobias was there to capture every pained grimace, every bead of sweat glistening in the summer's wake. He liked an interesting face as much as a beautiful one. *Portrait of a Lady in Extreme Discomfort.* It might not approach his masterpiece, the photo of Ian Mallory that had accompanied Cynthia's *Uncivil Servant* piece, with twin shadows from the cactus' arms arced behind his head like devil's horns, but it would do.

Around the bulk of the Nikon, he saw Cynthia rush towards the presser, microphone outstretched. She could have been on mat leave by now, but she wouldn't, as she put it, sit on the sidelines of history a second longer than she needed to. Admirable. Batshit, but admirable.

"Were your dealings with the Venezuelan government conducted with the full knowledge and approval of Cabinet?"

Gaby's head whiplashed in Cynthia's direction. She shouldn't frown like that, Tobias thought. It was bad for likability ratings. He hit the shutter release, just as glare slammed into the viewfinder. He swore under his breath and tried again, but the shot caught her just as her head turned down, her face entirely in shadow.

She plucked her words out of the tangled mess she'd made of the country's trade policy. "They were aware of preliminary talks, yes."

Cynthia got a followup. The one shred of grudging respect Tobias still held for the government came from Patrice Abel's insistence on freedom of the press, no matter how hostile the publication or how frequently it came back to bite him on the ass. "And you were aware of the sanctions placed by the Free States and the Eastern Coast at the time?"

Primly, her head held stiffly, Gaby said, "I hardly think anyone could be *un*aware of them."

Cynthia retreated back to his side to let the CBC's reporter take over that line of questioning. She was grinning.

"Get anything good?"

Tobias flicked through the shots. The *Post* was one of the few remaining publications to employ full-time photographers, rather than just betting on the quality of drone and cellphone footage, or trawling through Getty Images, and it was for good reason. You couldn't underestimate the impact of the right image at the right time. Cynthia could dutifully record Gaby's words, but it was Tobias' photo that would reveal whether or not she believed what she was spouting.

There was interference on about half of the photos. He scowled, shifting his angle. "I'll get something. Do you think Mallory knew what she was up to?"

Cynthia quirked a perfectly arched eyebrow in his direction. "You're not *that* new here," she said. "Nothing goes on up there that Mallory doesn't know about."

"It would have been a disaster," Tobias mused. "Not just hostilities with the East Coast rump state or the Free States, but our trade relationship with the SVAR."

Cynthia looked at him with what he could only describe as fond affection, the way you would encourage a child to puzzle out the answers to its question before you gave up in frustration and just explained it. "And he got Patrice to deal with it before it hit the press," she said. "She was the fall guy. Gaby gets the door open for a later deal, Parliament gets plausible deniability, and Patrice Abel gets about three days grace with some woman who isn't his wife. Meanwhile, Mallory looks like he's keeping party discipline."

No wonder Gaby Abel was so worn and drawn. He pushed down a rush of sympathy for her. "So Mallory was the one who threw her under the bus?"

"That's how it's always worked," Cynthia said. She smoothed her hair, readied her armour to go back into the fray. "Give it six months, she'll have a book out and everyone'll forget how much she reminds them of their mother-in-law."

"What about the inquiry?" someone shouted out to Gaby.

"Into MAI interference in government affairs." Cynthia, tilting her head up to whisper in Tobias' ear, filled him in. "Justice Nicholls. Hand-picked by Patrice Abel, it won't go anywhere." Then she pushed forward into the crowd again.

"The back-channel negotiations with registered Brazilian MAI—those were also approved by Cabinet?" CTV? Tobias didn't recognize the face.

Gaby was about to crack. Her heavy eyelids fluttered. "I'm sorry... I..."

"You conducted talks with known Brazilian MAI," said the *Globe* correspondent, whose series Tobias had also followed closely. "Without the knowledge of that country's government. Were you directed to engage in these negotiations by Mr. Mallory, or by the PMO under Mr. Mallory's advisement?"

Tobias could barely make out her quiet, "It was my own initiative."

"And when this became a political liability, you bore the consequences."

Cynthia, reenergized, burst through to the front, and Tobias moved to frame the disgraced minister's slump. "Madame Abel, are you afraid of Mr. Mallory?"

Gaby blinked. "That's an odd question."

"Please answer it."

"Ms Tan," she said, her voice a dry pile of sticks seconds from igniting. She made a face like she was giving birth to an entire litter of echidnas. "Anyone would be."

This time, he got the shot, just as the scream of an emergency alert tore through the crowd.

7

Sujay's mother called twelve times. Everyone was fine, of course, her family and friends weren't exactly regular Bay Street denizens, though her Facebook feed was a flood of Checked In Safes. Some of her readers on "Not Your Chosen One" had left comments—her spelling and references gave away that she was Canadian—but she'd get to those when they landed back in Ottawa. *Should* she go back to Ottawa? Ian wasn't a complete asshole. He'd let her go home if she asked, and she was feeling like a liability, all things considered.

She didn't ask. The government needed him, and he needed—

What the *fuck* did he need? The waiting area had been transformed into his personal office, with her casting a veil around the four facing seats they'd claimed before the press descended. While it shielded them from observation, it didn't stop her from being able to see and hear outside. The television screens, the moment of dramatic explosion, a blurry Tindr photo of one of the suspects, too pixellated to determine his ethnic heritage, not that it would stop people from speculating. People on their phones, people pacing, demanding to know flight information, people crying.

Finally, he ended whatever conversation he was having and slid the phone into his pocket.

"You okay?" he asked. "I shoulda— your folks, I mean."

"They're fine," Sujay said. "They're all the way in Scarborough. Just shaken, like everyone. Do you have anyone, er—"

"Everyone's fine," he said, with a certainty that the news lacked, and she knew immediately that he meant no one had died. He'd called it in, too late to save blocks of prime real estate, but in time to avoid bloodshed. He'd been so desperate to leave the wellspring, panicked in a way that she hadn't seen in all her time at the Broom Closet, in a way that no one who could see the future should ever have to be.

Everyone in the country was reaching out to someone, and he was ensuring that no one misspoke to the press, no one stood in the same frame as a billboard promising to "Blow Away Your Tastebuds," no one uttered the words, "terrorism" or "ISIS" or "Islam" until it had been vetted through a minimum of three layers of communications staffers.

"They confuse you for Muslim in there or something?" he asked. There were zero casualties, but property damage was bad for business, and unhappy businesspeople were bad for the government. It shouldn't have been enough to make his voice so unsteady.

"Something like that."

She could still feel their latex-gloved fingers, their suspicion crawling over her. She choked on the dry, recycled atmosphere of the airport, the claustrophobic press of frustrated, frantic passengers. She hugged herself, scratching at her skin until she could see long red streaks crisscrossing beneath her nails.

"Sujay," he said, voice low. She shook her head like she was trying to fix a recalcitrant hard drive. He put his hands over hers, and she stilled, looked up at him. "We'll be home soon."

"Do they know anything yet?"

"They know a little Tamil intern didn't do it from all the way in Bumfuck Nowhere, Alberta." He reached for a notepad in his jacket and had scrawled half a labyrinth, spreading out from the corner, before she realized what he was doing. She looked around, but her Somebody Else's Problem field appeared to be holding. No one noticed him tucking the notebook back, reaching out to take her hand again. No one saw the blue pulse under his fingertips that turned his skin to the grey it was beneath her glamour.

A weaker tug of the current she'd felt at the wellspring passed between them. The noises of the airport faded into irrelevance. She noticed how the rhythm of the ventilation system matched her own breathing, and her heart rate slowed. She closed her eyes, and the labyrinth stretched before her in thin threads of green and pink, that universal Pattern they'd found carved on stone in the Arctic, buried beneath the sands in the Tanami Desert, the rhythm she'd pressed into her stress toys until they'd disintegrated. It travelled through her bloodstream, webbed out from her lungs, and for a moment, the airport lobby had become her home, every corner of the earth was as much a home as her family's apartment in Scarborough.

Was this what they meant when they claimed Ian could alter consciousness? Was this—the welcoming brook of the great river that connected all of humanity, throughout country and history, to the earth—the reason why they were all so afraid of him?

"I needs you to get on a plane with me in five minutes," he whispered, "so's I can get home and convince Cabinet not to deport a few thousand innocent people or drone bomb a Middle Eastern city. I need to not be noticed for the whole flight unless they want to offer me those fancy mini-pretzels. Are you calm enough to do that?"

Sujay swallowed. Nodded. She was fine. Everything was fine, everything was under control.

"Good girl." He squeezed her hand, then let go. Her connection evaporated, became cobwebs and dust. Blood rushing to her head, she flung her arms around him. He staggered back with a startled, "Oof" and then his arms closed around her and they stood like that, at the Ground Zero of the spell she'd cast to keep out the world. "I wouldn't want another intern. You want me to sue the bastards?"

She forced something like a laugh. "Wouldn't do any good."

"It'd make me feel like a big man, though. What's the use of taking over the government if I can't throw my weight around a bit?"

Sujay grinned up at him. "Who said that chivalry's dead?" she asked, and took his arm.

• • •

Collective grief was a privilege afforded to other people.

Jamila spent the aftermath of each terrorist attack praying that the attacker wasn't Muslim this time. Sujay was much the same. The kinds of assholes who'd graffitied her dad's catering business after 9/11 weren't the kinds of assholes who'd notice that she was a Hindu agnostic.

Patrice Abel got to be publicly solemn, flanked by a cross-party contingent of Toronto MPs, and Gaby. With a magician's flair, he promised justice—once the facts wriggled their way loose to be examined and dissected. He performed gratitude for Ian Mallory. Bombed buildings could be rebuilt, but the evacuation had ensured no lives lost.

Gaby just needed to look good, momentarily displaced from her position as the most loathed person in the country.

Ian was running everyone off their feet, cognizant of too many variables that could go horribly wrong. Right-wing governments love a terrorist attack, he'd said, they made people scared and selfish and drove them to cling to authority. There would be fallout for the Party—the press, the Chamber of Commerce, their already pissed off American allies would all be at Patrice's throat.

"I hope you didn't say anything like that when Tan was interviewing you," Sujay said.

"Just get these photocopied and off my desk." He thrust a stack of papers in front of him like a shield, and was gone almost before she had time to snatch it away.

The *Post*, and the handful of media outlets still able to compete with it, were everywhere Ian was. Tan was waiting to ambush him with a microphone; Fletcher with his drone and camera. How much lead time had Ian given the authorities to evacuate? What was his response to the announcement that several of the affected firms were suing the federal government, claiming that he had the capacity to pre-empt the bombing altogether?

There was a certain kind of relief to being downhill as the shit rolled down, once you got used to the stench, anyway. For the next eight hours, Sujay was busy, too busy for shock or anger or delayed trauma, too busy to *process*. She was in motion from the instant she stepped off the plane. During a lull, long after she should have been getting overtime, she slipped out, took the bus home, and cried, quietly, in the shower.

Then she put on a fresh shirt, one without sweat stains or the memories of the guard's palms, new pants that hadn't draped over a chair as every inch of the body that had worn them was scrutinized and judged. No time to eat, not if she wanted to be useful. She checked the bus schedule. Winced. Fucking Ottawa.

• • •

Sujay found Ian in his office, the overhead lights out. Her glamour should have faded by now, but it still hung off him, concealing the shattered wreck she knew was underneath. The Broom Closet had hushed, down to essential personnel only.

"Good news is it's one guy," Ian said. "Bad news is Daesh claimed it. Which doesn't mean anything except what it means. Really, the good news is no one died."

It was out of their hands, then, at least for a few hours. Until Patrice finished the outrage circuit and needed a direction. If they were lucky. If they weren't, Cabinet would come up with ideas on their own.

"What happened out there?" she asked. "In Alberta?"

"Something unexpected." He spat the words out like a curse. A hand to his face, his fingertips ink-blue where they bit into his forehead. "Everyone else wants to know, and *won't* ask. Sometimes you need a controlled burn to stop a forest fire. You ever wonder why I don't play the lottery?"

She slid into the chair across the desk from him, the steadily multiplying stack of confidential folders well on its way to becoming the Border Wall.

"Oh, don't look at me like that, darlin'. I'm not *that* pure a socialist. I can see the future, I should be fuckin' rich. Maybe that way I'd have as much sway over Patrice as Suncor does."

"Why *don't* you?"

She couldn't tell, in the low light, whether he was smiling at her, or baring his teeth.

"You haven't been doin' your prognostication homework, have you?"

"I suck at it."

"You'd suck less if you practiced."

"Now you sound like my dad."

"There isn't *one future*. I'da put a bullet in my head years ago if that were the case." He pushed one of the crumpled bits of paper at her, a segment of labyrinth. "You go lookin' for lottery numbers, you're gonna see every possible combination, which is all of them. You go lookin' for terrorists, you see every daft kid dreamin' of his 72 virgins and every chinless loner prick with a case of blue balls that he blames on his ex-girlfriend. Every second of every day. This one was flagged in Wednesday's report—" He tugged at a file midway through the stack, threatening to Jenga the rest. Presumably he'd already seen the probable disaster, and gave up trying to pull it free. "Statistically equal to any other probability. But CSIS hadn't heard shit so it stayed low-level. No action taken. Two hours before he did it, the kid was sitting in his room, flipping a coin. Still shoulda seen it comin'."

She'd left one of her stress balls on his desk when she'd gone out earlier. Now he picked it up, rolled it between his fingers, then crushed it hard enough that the thin veil of still-active magic left scorch marks in the rubber. Little wisps of smoke pirouetted from the burns.

"You should bury your name," he said abruptly.

The airport might have been a lifetime ago; she was first startled that he remembered. "It's not going to change my skin colour."

Well. Maybe. She hadn't *really* tried. She'd changed *his* skin colour often enough.

"Not because of that. Names have power."

"No offence, Ian, but every brown person who's ever sent out a resume knows *that.* You're the walking nuclear bomb and *I'm* the one who gets pulled out for enhanced groping. Why do you think that is?"

"They've never done an exposé on my family," he replied, then, as if every option were equally catastrophic: "Or remote-geased me, or made my heart stop from halfway around the world. Why do you think *that* is? Why do you think no one knew who Jonah was when he showed up here? They got your name, they can do anything to you."

"No one knows who I am *now,*" she said. "Even people who work here get my name wrong."

"They'll know," Ian said. "Soon enough, they'll all know. You felt the thing out there, didn't you? This is where it *starts.*"

She tried, and failed, to contemplate a mentality where a terrorist attack in her home city was the least of her concerns. Instead, the weight of grief pressed her down, pain that no amount of magic could vanquish, and she couldn't afford to wallow, just keep moving, keep moving, as if she could outrun the vengeful earth's endless, all-consuming thirst.

• • •

After bone-deep terror came mind-numbing paperwork. Sujay never *intended* to eavesdrop. It was just that magic, at least in the institutional context of a prudent and transparent democratic government, really did consist of 10% channeling the primal forces of the universe and bending them to one's will and 90% justifying it to several committees using Excel spreadsheets and scatter projections. And legally, no one should have to work on a Friday after pulling an all-nighter.

Besides, Ian and Jonah having an epic blowout in the Broom Closet was at least as entertaining as trash TV.

"How is any of that my fault?"

"If I need to explain the legacy of settler-colonialism and the ways in which you continue to benefit from—"

"—by the fucking way this whole saga is also deeply offensive to *my* people."

"Newfies? Coke addicts?"

"Fuckin' charmers. *MAI.*"

"Oh, because 'no one likes me because I have superpowers' is exactly the same as land theft, residential schools, and mercury poisoning?"

"At least you're noble and spiritual and tied to the land, we get a ham handed allegory for why we can never integrate—"

Oh. That *was what they were talking about.*

Sujay couldn't take it anymore, and knocked on the door. She was met with a unison chorus of, "WHAT?"

That *absolutely* counted as permission to come in. Ian was behind his desk, bouncing one of her stress balls off the edge; Jonah was *on* the desk, perched on the corner, aggressively casual in faded blue jeans and a Metallica shirt—under a blazer, and it was Casual Friday, but *still*— with his boots on the visitor's chair. Any shyness she might have felt evaporated, any barrier of age and gender and status overcome by one, shining bridge of common ground.

"You guys watched last night's *Night Beats*. You guys...*watch Night Beats*."

"Everyone watches *Night Beats*, Sujay."

"I didn't," Jonah said. "Before. I was perfectly fine not watching *Night Beats*. My life was complete."

"You were estranged from your family and living in a tree. And you watch *Westerns*." Jonah had the patience not to look even more offended. "Look, people, you needs to understand the fuckin' zeitgeist in politics, and you gets a better read on what people's deepest fears about magic by hate-watching that flaming garbage fire than readin' Ipsos polls, okay?"

Jonah bent towards Sujay and stage-whispered, "He thinks Zombie!Brad is hot."

"You're fired."

She had to stifle a giggle. "Oh my God. Oh man. Welcome to the wonderful world of getting horribly disappointed by your favourite TV show. Anyway, it's like a rule that all sci-fi has to have the Cursed Indian Burial Ground Episode. That we had to wait seven seasons for it is a miraculous reprieve."

"Yeah, well," Jonah said. "*I'm* going to curse that shit if I ever get a chance. That had the trifecta. Mystical flutes, animal transformation, and Jordan— fucking *Jordan*— on a vision quest."

"It was the worst," Ian agreed. "Jordan should have stayed in Hell. Lilith has way better chemistry with Jane."

Sujay risked darting a glance at him. Did he read her blog? Worse...had he *read her fic*? Not that "Jordan needed to die after season 1" was exactly an unpopular opinion. And the chances of him being one of the approximately four non-Jamila people who followed her were vanishingly small.

Still.

"Also it's bullshit," Jonah said. "We live in the Age of Magic and if I have to put up with white people fuckery for my entire existence, I should at least get to turn into a bear."

"Really?" Ian drawled. "I think you're more of an otter."

Heat rose to her cheeks. She could only hope that neither of them noticed. "There's the Law of Conservation of Mass to consider," Sujay pointed out. "You'd end up being a very tiny bear."

Ian snorted. "Fucking hell. That's even better. Sujay, I'll gives ya $50 to glamour Joe into a very tiny bear. I mean it, it's essential for running the government effectively that I has at my side a very tiny angry bear. It's the only way this department will be taken seriously."

"Ian—" Jonah started.

"*Essential*, Sujay."

"Does the Law of Conservation of Mass apply to illusion magic?" Jonah asked. "If it's just a matter of manipulation of light particles I should get to be a regular-sized bear."

A knock on the door, and before Sujay could go over to answer it, Eric, comically balancing under a stack of file folders, pushed his way through.

"Bear," Ian hissed at Sujay. "Now."

She would ultimately spend the night working on her conjuring so that the glamour she would cast next time didn't have awkwardly front facing eyes, the texture of a Paddington teddy, and the grimace of a bad taxidermy job. So that, as long as she had the blessings of the universe to conjure at all, she could never summon up anything from that deep inside the uncanny valley. Jonah looked worse, in fact, than *Night Beats*'under-budget CGI and was, despite her best attempts at fierce and intimidating to the Very Important Men assembled in the room, utterly laughable.

"What the fuck?" Eric, to his credit, edged his way around the only-slightly-undersized Jonah-bear to deposit the files on Ian's desk before stopping, hands on hips, and blinking at the grotesque apparition in the bloody, beating heart of the government. "Why is there a bear in your office?"

"Why is there an obsequious lackey who barges into private conversations in your office?" Jonah said, his bear mouth moving just out-of-sync with his words.

Eric paled. "Oh God. Is that Jonah? Could he always turn into a bear? Because that's a thing the PM should know about."

"Grr," Jonah said, unconvincingly, and Sujay lost it.

"Sorry!" She covered her mouth with both hands, and Ian was laughing too, so it had to be okay, and she wasn't in trouble. Even if she couldn't focus enough to drop the glamour. "Look, Eric, um, do you watch *Night Beats*?"

"Seriously?" Whatever concern he had seemed to immediately dissipate, and he beamed. "I love that show. Did you see last night's? With the vision quest, and the flashback to Lilith's origin story, and Jordan being Chosen—"

A phantasmal bear claw swiped through his head. Eric gasped, but the paw was only a projection, extending out from Jonah's actual, and quite harmlessly distant, hand.

“Your opinions are shit,” said the bear. “You and the dead wife doppelgänger love-triangle plot line deserve each other.”

Ian propped an elbow on the bear’s haunch, around where Jonah’s shoulder was. “There you have it,” he said. “The great and wise mystical spirit of the Earth has pronounced his judgment. Now go forth and tell caucus I’ll have projections by noon.” He snatched up the files and flipped through the first folder, swearing under his breath.

Sujay grinned. She might get paid just over minimum wage, be subject to the worst bureaucratic scrutiny the capital had to offer, and apprenticed to a madman who could conceivably be a legitimate dark sorcerer with minimal regard for human life and property, but for a brief shining moment, she couldn’t think of anywhere she’d rather be.

8

In Eric's only slightly less-than-objective opinion, the Party *had* done well in the face of global jihadist terror. They had listened to all of the intelligence briefings, taken reasonable and sober precautions. They had pursued a sensible and balanced foreign policy to follow the minimum requirements of NATO membership without unduly antagonizing those who preferred their countries not be invaded. That Toronto had drawn the short straw this time was something that no amount of government oversight, magical or otherwise, could entirely avoid. In a city of six million and counting, there was bound to be a radicalized crazy or two.

The damage was no worse than a gas explosion might have caused, and the response, in the immediate aftermath, was swift, decisive, and professional. The suspect had been apprehended, alive, the one victim already out of the hospital, and blood donations briefly increased, more out of habit than anything else. Patrice gave a measured, sombre press conference, condemning the attack and declaring a fulsome investigation into what had gone wrong, all while wearing the right kind of nonpartisan tie. All in all, "Canada's 9/11"—as Fox was already helpfully calling it, interspersing the actual footage from a riot in Missouri—was mercifully free of clusterfucks.

At least, that's the perspective Eric would *have* had, if his heart rate hadn't gone beyond frightened rabbit levels in the past few hours, and if there weren't a half a dozen men in a variety of uniforms trying to convince Patrice to make an immediate show of strength.

As if they didn't have an actual magician on contract.

Everyone present—with the exception of Patrice, who shot a concerned glance in Eric's direction now and again—ignored his presence. He was invited because it was important to control the flow of information with the press, much of it hostile, swarming all over Parliament. And because it was a Cabinet meeting, and none of the illustrious elected representatives in charge of deciding the nation's fate wanted to be the guy who had to inform Ian Mallory of what they'd come up with. That was, in fact, what they paid Eric to do.

Eric's head ached. He lifted his hands to his temples and rubbed. He wanted time to sit with the fear, to let it settle in him, which was *only fair*— it's what anyone would want when their hometown was trending on Twitter for all the wrong reasons.

This is what you fought for. His mother's voice, and she was halfway right, even if she'd never been particularly supportive of that fight. The average age of the ministers and staffers around the table was the youngest in history, the very people who would, unlike previous governments, be around to face the long-term consequences of every policy they wrote. But it didn't change the fact that he wanted someone else to be the adult, for once, and take care of things while he got to have feelings about it.

The bomber, who'd been apprehended at his parents', was a 24-year-old engineering student. No criminal record, Facebook posts about dogs and weightlifting. Half Libyan, which was good enough for Fox, and, apparently, Daesh. Patrice's policy guys were already fighting with the RCMP about who had known what when.

It was in the heat of this argument that Ian Mallory chose to grace them all with his presence. Despite the volume in the room, Eric still heard him giving someone shit outside the door before bursting in, interjecting himself between two startled senior ministers. The room fell into immediate silence.

"Well," he said, cracking his knuckles, which sparked as if to remind everyone present that he could—if rumours were to be believed—strangle them all to death with their own tongues. Or something like that.

"As I was saying," the Mountie was saying, "There was *zero* evidence, that—"

"With all due respect," Ian said. "Shut the *fuck* up and let the grownups talk. What's our next step?"

"Who invited the fucking wizard?" someone—who apparently didn't have strong feelings about his skin remaining on the outside of his body—piped up. Ian shot him a withering glare.

"Whatever *he's* planning," Ian said. "Don't even consider it." He shoved back a curl of dark red hair from his eye and claimed the closest chair like a throne. "The Opposition's flailin' for a new leader but they'll wants to engage, and we don't. I've got my guys looking into DV shit. Profiling criminals is the cops' job, not ours."

As usual, he was operating on—well, Eric wouldn't say a *higher* level, as such—but carrying on an entirely different conversation, presumably with himself, or maybe with these mysterious *guys* he apparently had working for him, from everyone else in the room. "He's *hit a woman*," Ian explained, slowly, as if to a group of particularly dim-witted children. "I can guarantee you this. Normal twenty-four-year-old boys are getting laid, not making bombs, which means he had lady troubles. Either she called the cops and they let it go, or she didn't because she was scared of deportation, but in any case, it's a failure of law enforcement and not our immigration policies. Their fuckup, not the fuckup of whoever's not reading my security briefings, that's the message. Also, no one died, which you think someone'd be happy about. Done."

Patrice, at least, looked interested. He'd never publicly admit that Ian scared him, but it was obvious enough. For arcane reasons known only to whatever passed for a Deep State in the True North Strong and Free, Ian was the reason they'd won the election and probably the only thing between the fragile coalition and a non-confidence vote—and so he had the PM's ear. The Hon. Grant Hanson, Minister of Veterans Affairs, muttered, "Christ, what an asshole." As far as Eric was concerned, that was absolutely true—but that didn't change the fact that Ian, by definition, was always right.

"We averted tragedy," Ian concluded. "They can sue us all they want but it won't stick."

The murmurings of discontent weren't aimed at the unstoppable force that was Ian Mallory, unelected representative of nothing and no one and yet somehow the loudest voice in the room. Instead, they were aimed at Patrice Abel, the actual democratically elected leader of the nation, in hopes that he could somehow metamorphose his all-too-accommodating demeanour into an immovable object.

"I would like to take a look at all angles."

"You'll lose on immigration," Ian said. "You *can't* pick a middle ground when the Opposition's got a hard-on for a white ethnostate. You'll never be tougher than them, so don't fight tough. Fight dirty."

It was blatantly obvious that Ian had never won a fair fight in his life. He'd have been an adult, or close to, when the Cascade hit. He'd have grown up without magic, stringy and ginger and desperately poor. If Eric's own numerous childhood humiliations were anything to go on, Ian got the shit pounded out of him on a daily basis in grade school, and the way he carried himself now, as if he expected the world to bend under his will and thank him for the pleasure of doing so, spoke to a not inconsiderable bullheadedness.

"This isn't a *fight*," someone said. "This is a narrow escape. We got lucky."

"It's *all* a fight," Ian said. "If you ain't realized that yet, we got a problem." He stood up and swept himself out in a whirl of thin grey malice.

• • •

Brixton's wasn't overflowing during off-hours, and the wooden stools on either side of Eric were empty. He ordered a Mill St. Organic and darted another look at Lucy Fletcher, sitting at the other end of the bar.

He'd met her at some party, months ago. Not knowing who she was or that she was married, he'd flirted shamelessly until her husband had, in a smooth slide of his arm through hers, arrived to intervene. Tobias Fletcher worked with Eric's ex at the *Post*, making the whole exchange doubly awkward.

Now she was alone, framed by the deep red drapes, sipping a strawberry daiquiri. She posed decoratively on the edge of her stool as if in an ad for a much classier place. He warred a moment before moving closer to her, leaving a stool between them, a concession to the part of his brain that reminded him that a beautiful woman drinking alone in a bar is alone by choice.

She glanced at him through a curtain of black hair, and he gave a little half-wave in return. When she didn't immediately pretend not to recognize him, he cleared his throat, and his memory, as if by miracle, supplied, "Lucy Fletcher, right?"

"Guilty as charged."

"Eric—we met at the thing?"

Lucy's laugh must have cut a thousand boys down to size before she'd lowered her standards enough to marry Tobias Fletcher. "Of course," she said. "The *thing*."

"You sang," he said. "You were a revelation."

"A revelation." Was that how conservative women flirted, just repeating men's clumsy advances back at them until they fell at her feet? Heat rose to his cheeks, and he was grateful for the distraction the TV provided. He was a little unnerved to see how quickly the terrorist attack had fallen out of the news cycle before he realized that the bar was showing CNN. A typical mass shooting in the Southern Free States killed dozens on a semi-weekly basis; what was, for Patrice Abel's nefarious cabal, a career-shaking twenty-four hours, was for most of the world barely a ping on the radar.

In retrospect, it was only fair that she'd made more of an impression on him than the other way around. Lucy Fletcher sang like an angel and looked like a Greek goddess. Eric was the go-between for a mad sorcerer and a minority government with a tenuous grip on power. Only one of them was meant for the spotlight.

"Doesn't your crew hang out at the Met or something?"

"Too crowded," Lucy replied, which Eric doubted. As shaky as his own government's position was, every one of the traditional Big Three was in decline, dinosaurs unable to adapt to the new world of superseasons and wellsprings and demons. "If I wanted to hear about corporate tax breaks, I'd drink at home."

"I bet Fletcher's great at parties," Eric said.

"He has his moments." Even her speaking voice was heavenly. It whittled at him, hollowed him out, until there was nothing left of his faculties but a dizzy, half-formed desire for her. "But sometimes you have to escape from politics, you know?"

Eric did not know. And he certainly didn't know how anyone could be, with politics bearing down from the TV set, seeping into the scarlet walls and staining the rich mahogany of the bar, choking the very atmosphere of this stifling, stultifying city, a carcinogenic fog that no carbon trading bill could dissipate.

She didn't seem like the kind of girl impressed by acquiescence, so: "There is no escaping politics."

Her, rippling and silvery: "I make a point of it. Get away from journalists and MPs and wonks and their constant debating, and arguing, and *useless masculinity*, and focus on the things in life that are really important."

"Like strawberry daiquiris?"

"Like strawberry daiquiris." She clinked her glass against his, and grinned, her teeth straight and white.

"But that's no escape at all," Eric said, sliding millimetres closer. "The rum and sugar are shipped from Jamaica, and their pricing depends on the vagaries of international trade deals—which, incidentally, our government is neck-deep in renegotiating—and currency exchange, subject to the whims of the harvest, which are in turn affected by the pressures of climate change—which we are also working to address on a policy level. The price of the strawberries, is in turn, kept artificially low through the depressed wages of migrant farmworkers, made possible through the draconian immigration policies of the previous administration. And that—" concluding triumphantly, "is without taking into account the gender dynamics that made you order a quote-unquote-girly drink and not a beer like I did."

Another gust of musical laughter. "I've never been much of a beer drinker. So here we are together, trapped in this snare."

"Hapless victims of historical materialism."

"How terribly, awfully *tragic*."

"At least we have alcohol to console us. And good company."

"I'll drink to that," she said, and lowered her gaze beneath thick, fluttering lashes. "You must need an escape at times, don't you? I can't imagine that Ian Mallory is easy to work with."

Reaching the end of his beer, Eric snapped his fingers in the bartender's direction. "Not enough to cross party lines in my choice of watering holes." He glanced around, as always, where Ian was concerned, worried that the wrong ears might hear. More critical figures in the government than himself had seen their careers tarnished after finding out he'd been hiding inside a wall while they were talking shit about him. "Though he doesn't drink."

"Not at all?"

"Not where I've ever seen. I think there's some sort of sad backstory there."

"Seriously?"

"He's a workaholic tyrant who expects everyone else to be too. Draw your own conclusions"

"It sounds difficult."

"You have *no idea*." He bit back a torrent of—completely justified and well-founded, mind you—complaints. She'd come here to escape politics, and no one liked hearing someone else complain about their job. "So, are you, uh—" The truth was, he had no idea how to talk to her. The only thing they had in common was her asshole of a husband, who happened to have worked with his ex-fiancée in the production department of a newspaper devoted to attacking the government he worked for. "—Singing anywhere? You know, publicly?"

"I don't do that." She fiddled with the green plastic straw poking out above the rim of her glass. The bartender at last took notice and, blessedly, relieved some of the social pressure by offering them both refills.

"But you have an amazing voice. People still go to the opera."

"To see divas who *glow*. Literally. Singers who induce synaesthesia in the audience." She smoothed a wave of dark hair away from her face. "I was offered some minor roles. I'm not interested. I mostly teach these days. MAI singers still need teachers."

"Are there a lot of them?"

"Enough," Lucy said, the edge ebbing from her voice. She took another dainty sip to his swig. "It was a highly competitive scene before the Cascade."

"I guess I'm lucky that most of them don't want to be pencil-pushing bureaucrats."

"Just the one."

"Yeah, and he's a nightmare all on his own." He was trying, and failing, to keep it light. The conversation would always turn to this, a slow disaster two decades in the making, devastating to the creative world the way automation had been to manual labour. As hard as it was to conceive of Ian Mallory—the only MAI Eric had ever met—as some sort of next-level iteration of humanity, he'd never been able to shake the feeling that, no matter how many previous generations had considered themselves the last, he'd been born into the End Times. "Abel is terrified of him, you know."

"Oh?"

He was also probably, maybe, *definitely* tipsy. Which would have been pathetic after two beers if he hadn't been running on three hours of sleep and a coffee for lunch, also loosely attributed to Ian's iron-fisted discipline in a time of crisis.

"Yeah, I mean. Don't get me wrong. He's a necessary evil. We'd still be sitting on the fringes without him, at least until someone got an MAI on their side. But no one likes having. You know. *That* in charge."

"But Abel—"

"He's a bit too preoccupied covering up his affairs. Which is half of Ian's job lately. Can you even imagine? No one knows the full extent of what Ian's capable of, like maybe he can turn us all inside out, and he's busy keeping Patrice's scandals under wraps."

"Here's to honesty and transparency." She raised her glass. "And Mallory? His closet can't be skeleton-free."

"You have to actually have a life to have scandals. And all of Ian's life is public. Other than that, he lives in the office and eats insufficiently competent staffers." She looked legitimately interested, so he leaned in closer. "So. Wanna hear a secret?"

• • •

Leaving, he tried to kiss her. He couldn't be blamed. They were both wobbly on their feet, the afternoon creeping into a heavy dusk that settled over the near-deserted street. She hung off his elbow, and stepping onto the sidewalk, her foot twisted under her and one of her heels snapped. She picked up the shoe and regarded it with as much resentment as she did a singer who breathed rainbows with each exhale.

"Well, *fuck*," she said, pressing the spike back into place as though she could will the entropy of the universe to reverse.

"I can call you an Uber," Eric offered.

"I don't live far." Lucy slipped off her other shoe, looping the straps around her finger. "I can sober up on the way home."

"I can walk you."

She squeezed his arm. "You're fun," she said. "Don't get creepy."

Inebriation suited her, brought a light to her that he hadn't noticed missing when he'd found her drinking alone in the wrong bar. He leaned in, thought for an instant she had as well, his eyes open a fatal moment too long to not see her turn, swiftly, from his face.

"Sorry," he said, grudgingly relinquishing contact.

"Thanks," Lucy replied. "For the mostly non-political talk."

"Any time. Back to purgatory?"

"I love my husband. He just loses sight sometimes of what all of this," she waved, vaguely, in the direction of Parliament, "is for."

"What's it for?"

"People. Messy, complicated people who don't fit into neat, ideological boxes." She darted up on her toes to kiss his cheek. "Goodnight, Eric."

• • •

With the Broom Closet holding down the fort and the Opposition off to Vancouver to battle it out for the role of Head Pigfucker, Eric was released on shore leave for the weekend.

Having just missed the high holidays, he took a VIA Rail train back to Toronto and scanned through opinion polls on his tablet.

He forgot work only momentarily, as his mother swept him into her arms and his father, always hanging back, never knowing whether to embrace or shake hands, declared, "the prodigal returns" in his booming bass. He was herded through a 9 o'clock dinner and watched Abigail sigh to herself as she tried to spoon oatmeal into his brother Jakie's mouth, most of it ending up sloshed across his bib. His mother tried to defer political discussions until the following morning, and his father complained about the effect the government's spending priorities were having on his stock portfolio. The terror returned to him only later that night, as he lay staring at the ceiling of his childhood bedroom. His mother had insisted on keeping it as a shrine to the boy he'd been at 17, paperbacks and collectables arranged on the two shelves parallel to the oak captain's bed, posters—framed, of course; his mother would have never allowed thumbtacks—for 15-year-old superhero movies, the details of which he'd long forgotten, covering faded navy walls.

They could have converted it into a larger room for Abigail, or a guest bedroom, and hadn't. It wasn't quite the same as them telling him that they were proud of him, but it was something.

Ottawa might as well have been a million miles away, another time, the apocalypse a distant possibility in the anodyne *Scientific American* articles his younger self had poured over with increasing anxiety. He had to slap his own hand every time it crept towards the tablet. Numbers wouldn't budge over the break; no one would be polling until the new year.

When he slept, fitfully and briefly, he dreamt of Ottawa becoming the sparking labyrinth, an ouroboros turning in on itself, the windows of Parliament darkened and brimming with layers of long, sharp teeth. Of Lucy, in her red dress, singing into the storm that was swallowing the city.

Jakie was up before Eric or either of their parents, watching *Night Beats* reruns with Abigail in the living room. Every so often he let out a low Chewbacca moan, slamming his head against the back of the couch. Eric slid in beside him, cupped the back of his skull below the padding. Jakie leaned his face into Eric's shoulder. The sofa, like the rest of the living room, was a shining exemplar of form over function, too stiff and sleek to be actually comfortable. And white, which given Jakie's propensity for turning his immediate vicinity into a disaster zone, wasn't the best design decision of all time, though his brother and his aide aside, the living room could have been featured in a magazine spread. For now.

"Wanna play Mario Kart?" he asked as the credits rolled. Abigail raised an eyebrow. "What, video games are good for physio."

"Did you read that somewhere?"

"Google it." He fired up the console, patting Jakie's arm as he stood. His brother's head lolled on his neck, and Eric could convince himself that the contortion of his mouth was meant as a smile. Abigail placed her hands over Jakie's to manipulate the controller.

"How's Bronwyn?" Abigail looked contrite before she could get out the last syllable. Eric had, after all, come home tired and ringless. "And your minister?"

"Gaby." Abigail didn't follow politics, despite years of him urging her to do so. "Stewing on the back bench while the PM cheats on her." He wasn't going to dwell that deeply on the connections there, the months of failure and frustration. He'd been her assistant until the latest shuffle, and her fuckups became his fuckups, destined to follow him until someone else fucked up harder. He'd get his shit together after they swept the election. Maybe text Bronwyn while he was at it, see if she was still pissed. "But I'm the Broom Closet liaison now—you know, the magic people. Trying desperately to win the election with crystal balls and wands. It's a mess. You have no idea what it's like to work for a cosmic horror.

"Eric," Abigail said. "I work for your parents."

Eric let them have the first round. The light in his brother's eyes was worth it.

• • •

"We need to talk about contingency planning."

When his father spoke, Jakie and Abigail, and even his mother, polishing silverware in the kitchen, might not have even been in the room, for all the attention he bestowed on them. Abigail had two sons of her own, living with an aunt in Cameroon until the family sponsorship went through. Eric hoped his parents were at least paying her well.

"Do we?" Eric asked. "From what I understand, there won't be much of a future."

Dad frowned. He'd aged. Both of them had. Every time he visited—which was, contrary to his mother's claims, as often as he could manage to get away—they seemed to shrink a little more, folding inward, deflating like week-old balloons. It made him want to visit less, but he couldn't do that to Jakie.

"Assuming," Dad said, archly. "That your hippie friends happen to be wrong, and we're not dead within the next forty years, or is it 18 months now..."

Eric tried to imagine Ian's reaction to being called a hippie, then—not for the first time—wished very hard that if Ian had any sort of telepathic ability, it was limited by distance.

"What?"

"Nothing."

"You're smiling."

"No, I'm not."

"Your mother and I aren't getting any younger."

There it was. His parents were, at best, slightly less imperfect Jews than Eric himself, even going so far as to put up a Tastefully Non-Denominational Winter Tree in the window for the sake of their country club friends, but they at least had the guilt thing down pat. "We're not going to have the will talk, are we? It's morbid."

"About Jakie."

Oh. "I'm sharing a shoebox with a roommate right now, Dad. My entire apartment could fit in this room."

"That's my worry. When we're gone—well, it's best to start thinking about the transition before our hand is forced, don't you agree?"

Jakie and Abigail were on the floor, working through one of the puzzles he'd brought. Jakie cheered every time Abigail helped him slot a piece into place. "You guys need a hand over there?"

"Eric. If they keep squeezing me on taxes, what do you think is going to happen with your brother? Do you really want him in some kind of state home? Socialism's all well and good until it's your own family eating government cheese."

"Do you have to be so melodramatic, Dad? The Party is hardly going to start subsidizing the dairy industry."

"Be serious."

"I am being serious. And I get to see Jakie, what, four times a year?" Eric glanced, apologetically, towards his mother, then stood up, straightening his blazer, and squatted down on the (white as well; he wondered sometimes what his parents were thinking) carpet. Exchanged conspiratorial smiles with Abigail, and broad, guileless ones with Jakie— the only person who'd ever loved him unconditionally. "Hey kiddo."

Worse came to worse, he'd get a new apartment. What was the point of a family rich on previous generations' ill-got gains if their pinko scion couldn't ultimately use it for good?

Jakie, mercifully unaware of the debate surrounding his future care, of the rising oceans, of wild magic creeping in through the Earth's fraying places, burbled at him happily and slotted another puzzle piece into place.

9

Ottawa was on virtual lockdown, a taut, coiled creature waiting to strike. The Twitter cross-contamination didn't help, with Free States media reporting that the Communist Canadian government had thrown open its doors to terrorists and had reaped the rewards of its foolishness in blood.

Meanwhile, the bank and investment firm damaged in the blast had sent its lawyers after the feds, and the legal and economic tripwires that Ian Mallory had set off were cycling through CP24 in lieu of a properly photogenic body count.

Tobias' own job was over and done with quickly. He was allowed at the press conference before Parliament Hill became a shuttered fortress with him on the wrong side of it. Patrice stalled and deliberated and everyone else waited, expecting leadership. What was *with* him, why didn't he lash out, pass an emergency act, drop a bomb? Something, anything, to send a message of strength and reassurance. Tobias normally appreciated prudence in politicians, but he'd spent enough time embedded in the Middle East to recognize when an empty road was littered with IEDs.

In the absence of actual developments, Tobias waited in a bar, sipping ginger ale, and went home at 6.

Lucy was already home, seated on the edge of the piano bench, her fingers plucking out one long, sad note after another. She was a singer, not a pianist, but she'd learned to play as a child and she'd still accompany herself on occasion, her hands bone-white and hair a black ocean, like the curves of the baby grand itself, and he'd watch, silent and in awe.

She glanced up at the door, but otherwise ignored his intrusion. He'd always come second to music, and he was *fine* with that. He could hang back and listen, her song an insulating, timeless wall from the terror outside. God, she was so much better than he'd ever be.

The song ebbed out rather than ending all at once. Notes lingered in the ceiling beams as she stood, wordlessly, and picked her way over to him. She folded into him, still more music than substance, and he held her, felt the materiality of her, spine and shoulder blades, the prickling of her hair in his nostrils. For a few minutes, in the lobby of their house, the useless splendour of it, she was the only thing real, and he whispered again and again, *I love you, fuck I love you so much.*

"Everyone's fine," she said. She waved towards the laptop open on the kitchen table with its flood of Marked Safes. And he was home, the light dying though the living room windows, turning her cheek and forehead golden. Life would pick up just the same tomorrow.

Worse to think that, yes, of course it would. None of this personally affected him. He was just as likely to lose someone in a car crash, to cancer. He could wait it out, a frog in boiling water, and never know until the moment it tipped into the unbearable.

He was drowning in her, rescued by her, by her nails clawing for purchase in his scalp, her mouth by his ear. He lifted her and carried her to the bedroom, all the time promising that it would be all right, it would all be all right, it was right to lie, at a time like this, when lies were a thing they could shape hope out of. She clung to him, begging to lose herself in him as he did in her every time, and he thought he could survive all of this as long as she remained the centre of his world.

• • •

Izzy buzzed overhead as Tobias watched the press conference through his viewfinder. He frowned, adjusting the shutter speed for the distortion that Ian Mallory seemed to generate simply by existing. There was something wrong with his lens, wavering streaks across the frame that no amount of polishing would fix.

Cynthia Tan managed half a question that could be answered with a "person or persons responsible," before the chorus of questions grew too loud. Patrice, Tobias thought, bore it well. He was statesmanlike even, determined to not to quaver in the face of terror, but also not to panic, not to overreact. Utterly Canadian in his composure, his moderation. For a moment, Tobias allowed himself to find the sentiment comforting.

Tragedy had been averted, this time. And, as Patrice took great pains to point out, every time since the Party had assumed power. They had been elected to forestall future catastrophe, and they had kept that promise.

Tobias couldn't help but marvel at the Prime Minister's hubris.

He held his phone up to one ear. The Old Man's voice, thick and ponderous, was coming from a hotel suite blocks away, laptops set up in a semi-circle on his desk, each streaming a torrent of firsthand correspondence while Cynthia supplied a series of tweets.

"Cynthia's softballing," Tobias said.

Reid's lips would be taut, his eyes crinkling. "You want to be the guy that hits the PM with tough questions when his pet magician has just saved hundreds of lives?"

Tobias opened his mouth, ready to ask if that wasn't what the *Post* paid them to do, and then thought better of it. It wasn't a bad strategy, all things considered. The tabloid press could fire off Islamophobic insinuations, while Cynthia, young and pretty and appropriately diverse, looked restrained and waited for all the facts to come in. When the skin tone of the terrorists, their religion, their ethnic origin, inevitably came to light, the *Post* was free to hit back on refugee policy and a lackadaisical commitment to Canada's NATO obligations. Not to mention the folly of relying on a wizard where a national security apparatus should be.

Reid Curtis, in his official capacity as the owner of the *Post* network, had been at it longer than Tobias had been alive. He understood the weapons in his arsenal, knew when to deploy them. Patrice had himself a few hours of goodwill, while a city breathed a sigh of relief. Tobias knew that Mallory was somewhere behind the scenes, pulling the strings, putting his own people into place, but this was not the first government the Old Man—in his unofficial capacity, as horse whisperer to the rich and powerful—had helped topple.

"This is not my best work," he admitted. "I don't know what's wrong with the camera—how's Izzy's footage looking?"

"Fine. Focus, Toby. Mallory's got his fingers in a number of pies, and they're not all linked to his job description. You're my eyes and ears out there, so fly, my pretty, fly forth and pester."

• • •

"Sure it's beautiful, Toby, but it's not a vacation."

Tobias lifted his tablet and switched to the back camera, arcing it in a slow panorama of mountains and ocean, the fringe of trees, the orange sunset, motorboats streaking across the bay. The shining glass windows of the Vancouver Convention Centre with its space-age architecture and green roof. Back at the terrace, Mrs. Alycia Curtis and several of the other women were enjoying pina coladas and snapping pictures of the view with their phones. Tobias recognized a sitting MP from rural Saskatchewan, though most were aspiring candidates with a pundit or two in the mix. He propped the tablet back up on the table in front of him, point proved.

"I'm in a fancy hotel. On a patio. I'm even thinking of going to *Aida* on Wednesday. Which—I wish you could be there, though the *Sun* completely panned it, apparently you aren't missing much..."

Lucy rolled her eyes. “It doesn't count if it's work. Even if it's more fun than Ottawa and Ian Mallory.”

“It is,” he said. Then, impulsively: “Come out. I can switch my flight, take a few extra days. Make it an actual vacation.”

“Toby.”

“We can celebrate the fact that I didn't get turned into a toad on my last assignment and there's at least a 90% certainty that I won't on this one either.”

“I don't know, hon. I've heard the competition is pretty vicious.” She was halfway convinced. He could read it in her mouth, trying to hide a smile amid the checkerboard of pixels. “I have students.”

“Reschedule them. It's professional development. Apparently the soprano is a spectacular example of what not to do.” He shot a glance at the women on the next table. The Old Man's wife, dressed in sharp black and white herringbone, a wide-brimmed hat shielding her eyes from the glare, held court. She was around seventy and still managed an austere sort of beauty, her hair silvery white, her blue eyes piercing and intelligent. “Alycia adores you and would relish the chance for a politics-light afternoon or two.”

“And if I'm enjoying an afternoon or two of completely avoiding politics? And politicians?”

“Stay away from the leadership convention, then. But I have evenings free. Please?”

The last word sealed the deal. Lucy didn't care that magic would be the election issue, or that the man, or woman, with the right answer would be in a position to take down Patrice, and all he represented. But she'd have his back, no matter what.

• • •

“This way, my boy.” The Old Man maneuvered gracefully through the teeming masses. Tobias followed, his bulk a buffer between his increasingly frail boss and the various delegates, candidates, and hangers-on, Izzy humming happily above them to capture a sweeping crane shot of the crowd, bathed in blue and pink spotlights. The Opposition had seen an influx of new membership just as Patrice's polling numbers were faltering. Outside of its traditionally uneasy coalition of Bay Street professionals, small business owners, faith communities, and rural individualists, it had also courted people closer to Tobias' own views. If only it weren't for some of the complete wing nuts. They were, in his opinion, one degree removed from the crowds of anti-MAI protestors bearing broomsticks and making little partisan distinction between whose heads they were calling for at any given time. Politics hadn't been infused with gravitas since well before the US had split apart, but he could have sworn that the extremes on both sides of the spectrum got more and more buffoonish every day.

Still. There was something to be said for the perfect storm of an increasingly unpopular PM backed by MAI sorcery and the sense of foreboding that permeated every corner of contemporary existence. It had a way of bringing everyone together.

It was generally understood that the former leader of the Opposition, stepping down after an embattled three years, had lost the last election not solely due to the occult influences of Ian Mallory but to a complete deficit of personality. There were thirteen contenders to replace him, and Tobias judged at least six of them to be batshit insane. One, a homeschooled church girl from Halliburton, managed to slip anal sex and the slippery slope to eternal damnation into the most innocent discussion of tax policy; another, a libertarian gun nut, performed an approximation of scandalized outrage that he was not actually allowed to bring a firearm on stage with him. Most of the others were somewhere on the scale of opportunistic versus ideological, with the balance tilted towards the former, and would make fairly fine, if imperfect leaders.

The frontrunner, to the surprise and delight of the amateur bookies who'd sprung up in recent days, was Ansel Graves, an outspoken Bay St. quant who'd, quite publicly, seen the last downturn coming. Having been proven right, he'd quit investment banking for a career in politics, decrying corporate cronyism while advocating for balanced, technocratic approaches to the country's troubles. Young, photogenic, and just iconoclastic enough to set the Old Man's teeth on edge, he promised enough of a challenge to keep the fight interesting. Graves' most serious opponent was Quinn Atherton, a political insider from long before the Opposition had been the Opposition. He'd spent nearly a decade as a backbencher, patiently waiting his turn, managing to make more friends than enemies.

Tobias didn't have a dog in the race—he hadn't paid for a party membership since his third year of undergrad—but he thought with the social conservatives onside, Atherton had a better chance. He liked Graves enough, and several of their interviews had ended in marathon drinking sessions, but the younger man was just too flashy, too metrosexual Toronto, to win over the prairie delegates.

Reid was one of the ones who'd started a betting pool; he had fifty on Graves, mainly to mitigate his disapproval if the guy actually won. After some hesitation, Tobias had bet against both him and Cynthia to keep things interesting. He supposed a third party might still creep up from behind and take the lead, but he somehow doubted it.

He checked his phone; seven minutes to Cynthia's next interview, this one with the party president, followed by one with an entirely sensible Red Tory with no chance at commanding any more than a single digit percentage. Lucy's flight, if nothing went wrong, would touch down at some point late in the morning. He flagged a waiter for a cup of coffee. The Opposition had sprung for a catering company that served the kind of coffee he remembered from his youth, the stuff that was palatable enough to drink black. He planned to drink no small quantity. Between now and her arrival, it was going to be a very long night.

• • •

"If I had to guess," Tobias said. "Graves is the obvious one. But he's far *too* obvious."

"Besides," Lucy was jet lagged, but only Tobias would have been able to tell. Her eyes sparkled, her smoky eyeshadow bringing out the green of her irises. Even at her most exhausted, it would have taken a concerted effort for her to look anything less than dazzling. "If he were, he'd have never left Bay St. He'd be the richest man in the world."

"Money isn't everything, my dear."

Alycia Curtis, and not her husband, was the reason Tobias—and by extension, Lucy—knew that there was an MAI working for someone in the Opposition. She was far too discreet to have let that tidbit slip accidentally; it was a carefully honed weapon to be passed from one hand to the next. Alycia and Reid Curtis were a team, and she would never have given him anything that the Old Man didn't want him to have.

"And," Lucy added, "you can tell." She glanced at Tobias for confirmation.

The banquet hall was far too noisy a setting for prying ears, and the gentleman's agreement that kept the talk cordial over dinner meant that rival factions kept largely to themselves. Tobias *hmm'd* noncommittally and sliced his steak. "Not always."

"All of those sparks in your photos of Mallory," Alycia said. "Surely not Photoshop."

"Of course not," Tobias said. The steak was perfect, caramelized brown yielding to hedonistically rare at its core. "I just think he does it on purpose. For the drama." This earned him a raised eyebrow from Alycia, who knew *nothing whatsoever* about spectacle. "But Graves can't be one anyway. An MAI on the trading floor would crash every computer on Bay St., and probably the global economy."

"I don't think it's any of them," Lucy opined. "*If* what you heard is true, Alycia..." Ever conscious of discretion, she lowered her voice. "Anyone like that would want to operate in secret. To be the power behind the throne, not the face of it. Like—"

"You?" Alycia winked at her.

"Like Mallory."

"We're at least a generation away from MAI politicians, Surkov aside," Tobias said. "Assuming they can ever get to a point where magic doesn't turn feral and kill people. And it's none of the frontrunners." He cast a glance in Alycia's direction. The Old Man had said, more than once, that there were no secrets between them. Either she—and by extension the Old Man—knew exactly who the MAI was, or neither of them did. And he couldn't imagine the latter.

His thoughts were interrupted by the appearance of the man himself, frowning down at him like the judgment of God. "Honestly, Reid," Alycia said. "The man's been working himself to the bone for you. Will you let him finish dinner?"

"I'm afraid duty calls," his boss replied, kissing Alycia's perfumed cheek. "Atherton has a ten-minute window and the light is perfect."

Grumbling, half of his perfect steak abandoned on the plate, Tobias climbed out of his seat and followed him.

• • •

The sunset over the mountains cast ripples of red and purple over the turquoise water of the rooftop pool. Quinn Atherton, stretched out on a lounge chair with his tablet propped against the cupholder, watched his daughter Miriam swim laps in the pool, his attention shared between her and Tobias. The girl, a shimmering blue streak beneath the surface, swam as though she were born to water, an impression reinforced by the mer-maid scale pattern on her swimsuit. She burst upwards in a white froth of bubbles—"Daddy! Did you see me?"—before diving below. Tobias sent Izzy to catch her small arms waving at the edge of the pool. B-roll foot-age of the man being cute with his kid would endear him to viewers. He took up a position at an angle from Cynthia, focused on Atherton's face.

"Don't get me wrong," Atherton was saying. "I like Ansel. He's got energy, and new ideas, and give him a solid term or two as an MP and he's got leadership potential. But he lacks political experience."

"I've heard that's an asset these days. Less of a perception of corruption."

"Maybe in the former US," Atherton admitted. "But I like to believe that we're beyond that here. We're talking about running a nation in the face of the greatest crisis humanity has ever faced. He's not a politician, he's a gambler."

Up close, Atherton was much more animated than Tobias remembered; cynically, he wondered if he'd had coaching between elections. The establishment's preferred candidate wasn't much older than Tobias. *You know you're getting old when politicians start looking young.*

"What's your stance on the magic question?" There was never enough time to delve deep into policy matters in a short interview segment. It was a large part of why the foundations of democracy were so shaky these days. But Cynthia was too serious a journalist to avoid it altogether.

"You want that in a soundbite?" He closed in on Atherton. "We've dodged a lot of bullets, but it's only a matter of time before the inevitable catches up with us. Before some bad actor figures out a way to weaponize magic."

"Would you support a registry?" Cynthia asked. "Or the Iranian approach?" Tobias' life—and the country's politics—would be substantially less complicated if someone would just throw Ian Mallory in a very dark secret prison.

"It's not popular to admit it, especially given the laissez-faire streak that runs a mile wide here, but there's a time and a place for government regulation. And MAI activity is one of those cases. Maybe it works in China for their MAI to be integrated in the business sector, and we can't afford to fall behind the Chinese. But the current government is letting MAI set policy, and that's a step too far."

Miriam reached the side of the pool and boosted herself over the side. She towelled her dripping blond hair to damp, then wrapped the towel around her thin shoulders like a cape. Atherton's eyes followed her across the deck, until she found an empty lounge chair and flopped herself on it with a melodramatic huff.

"Cute kid," Tobias said.

Atherton beamed. "She takes after her mother. Regardless," he continued, "the choices before us are bigger than one politician, even one party. As a people, we are facing an existential threat the likes of which we have never seen before."

Cynthia nodded for him to continue.

"It's complex. If indeed the Cascade was a reaction to environmental damage, we need to make hard choices. We've created a disposable culture. If you don't like something, you throw it away, whether it's plastic junk from China, fast fashion from Bangladesh, a marriage. A pregnancy. And we've exported the worst blights of our culture to the developing world. Instead of embracing their native values, there's out of control population growth followed by migration, a frantic race towards some nebulous concept of progress that has brought us to the very edge of annihilation. Magic may very well be the Earth's immune system, curing it of its excesses."

"Us," Cynthia said.

"Unless we strike a balance. The Cascade has been part of our reality for a generation now, and you can't put the genie back in the bottle. You can't unscramble these eggs. Or unsoup soup. There's a million things you can't un." Tobias saw the moment at which Atherton realized he was rambling, and halted himself. A less experienced politician might have looked directly at Tobias' camera. Atherton had cultivated his unpolished edges, reminding everyone watching that there was a real person under the uniform of khakis and dress shirt.

"Most of your competition would like to at least try," Cynthia pointed out. Except Ansel Graves, who was far too interested in monetary policy and global competitiveness to even engage seriously with the Magic Question. *Better ours than theirs*, he'd quipped.

"We're a diverse and tolerant bunch," Atherton said. "Contrary to how our opponents would like to paint us."

"Well," Cynthia said. "The government's appointed itself the expert on diversity and tolerance, after all."

"Unless you believe that life begins at conception. Or you've worked for what you have." Atherton put on his patented concerned-statesman face. "We've seen the damage one MAI with an agenda can do. Imagine Ian Mallory's power in the hands of an ISIS terrorist, or North Korea, or a Mexican drug cartel."

"What's your proposed solution?" Cynthia asked.

"Don't you wonder if it couldn't all be better than this?" A politician's non-answer. Atherton watched his daughter, peering back at him through an oversized pair of heart-shaped sunglasses. "If not for us, then for them."

"In the past," Cynthia said, picking around the edges of journalistic objectivity like it was an unexploded bomb. "That particular line of questioning didn't lead anywhere good."

"This time it's different, though. The destruction is already upon us. But we get to decide what we do in the ruins."

• • •

"You don't like him."

Tobias paused, then rewound the footage. No flares. Atherton wasn't the Opposition's MAI, and the problem wasn't him or his camera. "I didn't say that."

"How long have we been married? You don't need to."

Lucy was on the balcony, a glass of wine in her hand. He'd been right to drag her out here, he thought, away from what responsibilities she'd managed to accumulate. She was barefoot, his shirt draped to mid-thigh on her, hair long and loose around her shoulders.

"I don't *not* like him. Why are we talking about Atherton again? I thought you wanted to get away from politics."

Lucy took a long sip of her rosé, slipped back into their room. "Alycia's been talking my ear off all day. The more excited she is about him, the less I think he's a good choice."

"I thought Alycia was your friend."

Her red lips pursed. “She is,” Lucy said. Too quickly, too lightly, for it to be entirely accurate. “She’s a lovely woman. But she does what’s right for Alycia, not the country.” The bed dipped where she perched beside him, folding her legs under herself like a cat and leaning her head into his shoulder. “He creeps me out.”

“Huh.” Lucy’s intuition was, as often as not, his secret weapon. He’d pegged Atherton as relatable, experienced, moderate enough to poll well with a wide swatch of demographics and ideologies. He had a sound platform and loyal delegates. But rare was the voter who chose on policies alone, and Lucy had always been better than Tobias at determining that other, elusive quality. This time, however, she couldn’t seem to put words to it. “An aura?” he joked.

But Lucy’s face remained serious. “Maybe,” she replied. “I suppose the Old Man’s endorsement is the only one that matters.”

“I just take the pictures,” Tobias said.

She finished her wine and placed the glass on the bedside table, freeing her hands to fold around his. “Atherton doesn’t want anything. I don’t mean that he doesn’t have ambition—of course he does, or he wouldn’t run. But he’s not worried about Graves, and anyone in their right mind should be.”

“He’s a long time operative. Maybe he’s genuinely okay with either outcome. He does have a young child.”

She shook her head. “He’s not ambivalent about it. He’s playing to win. But when you listen to him speak—his tone, not the words he’s saying—it’s like he knows that the race doesn’t matter. As if he already knows the outcome.”

“Maybe’s he’s the MAI after all.” He couldn’t be; it would have been against party rules, for one thing. “Or the MAI’s on his team.”

“Personally, I like Isaacson.” The old Red Tory, closing in on seventy and giving it one last go before retiring to his prize-winning zucchinis and his memoirs. Tobias liked him too, but he wouldn’t get past the first ballot.

“If you were Mallory,” Tobias said. “And you could. You’d rig the nomination.”

"Sure," Lucy agreed.

"Who would you rig it for? Isaacson?"

"Shelley Collins," Lucy said. "She terrifies the mushy middle, and Patrice Abel looks like the picture of competence next to her. She'd have no chance in a general election." She tucked a strand of hair behind her ear. "Graves is the only one with a good shot at beating Abel."

Tobias agreed; the Old Man's opinions, influential as they were, only went so far. This was, occult influences or not, still a democracy, and thank God for that.

He reached over and hit pause on the recording. Two days left, and he was determined to make the best of it. "Enough politics?" he asked Lucy.

She squeezed his hand, slid her other around his neck to draw him into a kiss. "For now," she whispered against his cheek.

• • •

Of course, Graves won. It wasn't even close enough to justify a recount. Between the carrot of lucrative magitech deals with the SVAR and the stick of magical terrorism, the party faithful voted for the one that sounded best for the GDP.

Standing on the stage in a line of disappointed hopefuls, Atherton was the first to shake his hand, wish him congratulations and good luck, thereby earning a place in his cabinet when and if their fortunes turned. There were still some corners of the world where politics were a gentleman's game.

Flush from the press of the crowd, his feet aching in his dress shoes, Tobias tried to catch the best angle on the winner. Graves dripped with a sheen of sweat, a triumphant grin stretched across his face. The Old Man—whose windfall mitigated whatever disappointment he might have felt—clapped him on the shoulder.

"The next Prime Minister, right here."

Graves shook his hand, then reached out to shake Tobias'. "We'll see soon enough," Graves said, before being swept away in a torrent of well-wishers.

"I need some air," Lucy said, and he followed her, out to the plaza where a group of the die-hard crazies had set up camp. They were an odd bunch, some with religious signs, others with Canadian flags, some equating various candidates, Graves and Atherton among them, with Patrice Abel in their unwillingness to confront the threat of Sharia Law. One or two wore flak jacks, or kneepads, and there were the ever-present brooms. About twice as many cops formed a barrier between them and anyone who might take issue with their presence. "Maybe not this particular air," she amended.

"Just ignore them," he said. "These things always come and go, but they go faster if you don't give them an audience." He looped his arm through hers, tried to steer her to the waterfront, but she stood a moment, wide-eyed, frowning at the minor spectacle. She shuddered, then acquiesced. The celebration was just getting started.

10

"So, you were right," Jonah said.

"That *is* what they pay me for, b'y."

It was significantly after hours, but if Ian wasn't going home, it was a good excuse for Jonah to not go home, where not a single picture hung on the patchy, builder-beige walls and where a lone mattress, with an unpacked box as a nightstand, passed for furniture. He had a TV, because he'd found it on the curb and it could be connected to his Xbox. It was about as far down the bleak abyss of pathetic masculinity as he'd ever fallen.

Sujay had gone home, because she was a normal person with a normal life, probably even a family that she put before the job and the appalling state of the nation. It was Thursday night, which meant an episode of *Night Beats*. Jonah had discovered, much to everyone's amusement, that Sujay had not missed a single episode in its seven-year run, no matter how ridiculous and convoluted its plot had become and no matter how bad the CGI was at disguising that while Lilith was an ageless vampire, her actress was very much mortal and perhaps getting overfond of Botox.

"There's a 911 call, but no arrests or charges." Jonah blew a kiss at his monitor. "Gotta love Big Data, right?"

Ian wheeled his office chair around to Jonah's side. "We got a soundbite?"

"We got a soundbite."

Ian flashed him a broad grin, and Jonah effectively shut down the little thrill of pride at that. Ian wasn't the same shining star he'd been when they'd first met, and Jonah wasn't the wide-eyed neophyte hick trailing his activist girlfriend into the hinterland, cowed into wonder by the fleetingest glimpse of blue sparks and shriekgrass. They weren't that, not anymore, and yet. They worked well together, like they always had—Ian performing witchcraft, and Jonah ensuring he didn't get burnt at the stake for it.

"How was Cabinet?"

"Complete shit." Ian stretched his legs out, hands folded behind his head. "The world's largest collection of walking Dunning-Kruger effects in full-on 'Now Panic and Freak Out' mode, like caving to the Opposition's fascism is going to win them some points with Joe Public. They're making the exact same mistakes every vaguely social democratic government's made since time immemorial. What the *fuck* are we doing here, Joe? Why'd we ever stop chaining ourselves to construction sites? We were really good at that."

"I'm pretty sure you could find a construction site *somewhere* to chain yourself to," Jonah said. "I was under the impression that you thought this was more effective."

"Yeah. Except. I can't fucking stand any of them."

"You couldn't have just stopped this guy before the rampant property damage?"

"Fifty-fifty he came up tails and lived a boring life. I'd rather have an insurance scandal than a civil liberties scandal. Besides, weren't we all for blowing up Bay Street back in the day?"

"Bold of you to assume I'm against it now."

Ian laughed, but with nearly everyone gone for the day, and Sujay's glamour waning, grey was overtaking the colour in his skin and hair in patches, stone beneath peeling paint.

"There was an accident at Blythe's work. She's okay—her co-worker isn't, apparently? She's supposed to be modelling CO2 levels, not playing chicken with Elder Gods in an experimental sub."

Ian immediately reached for a pen and a pad of paper; before Jonah even understood what he was doing, he was sketching the lines and spirals, detailed and precise, that formed a small segment of a bafflingly vast global puzzle. The pen strokes, as they multiplied over the page, crackled electric blue and lifted from the paper, shimmering half an inch above the surface. There was nothing more beautiful, or terrible, in all the world. "You wants me to, uh—"

Every line was a possibility, Jonah knew. Each a glimpse into a hidden world that Ian alone could unveil. A boy flips a coin and lights the country on fire, or doesn't. A future where Blythe still loved him, where he could be the husband and father she and Laura needed him to be. Or where she didn't, but where he could be at rest, and content.

"Don't bother," Jonah said. "She says she's fine. I'm supposed to believe her."

Ian kept drawing. Maybe he felt like he needed to; who the fuck knew what went on in his head? A strange, sick kind of power to have, to see every outcome and affect so few of them. "You ever try not fucking up with her?"

Jonah turned his attention to the documents from CEAA—an archive of maps and legal documents, some of them dating back to the 1800s—and wondered, once again, why he was really here.

"You get anywhere with that?"

Jonah pulled up his composite map on the ancient machine—Win95, bless Ian's blackened little MAI heart. At one layer, in soft pastels, the overlapping, organic forms of traditional territories. Above them, darker, treaties, current unresolved land title conflicts. Arcing across them, though the heart of fraught, contested ground, thin places, set to explode into shriekgrass, demons, the angry earth settling what humans couldn't.

Ian studied the map for a moment, then said, "Let's get the fuck out of here." He flicked Jonah's monitor off and stood, brooking no argument. Jonah followed, because fuck, what choice had he ever had? "Truck's parked up the street."

"Wait—" He struggled to keep pace with Ian's long strides. "Not the *same* truck?"

Grey and worn though Ian was, there was a glimpse of the kid he'd been, Baader-Meinhof lean and dangerous, in the gap between his teeth he'd never bothered to fix. And—stepping out into the sweltering night air—in the salt-rusted red Ford F-150. He'd driven it across the country, multiple times, and somehow kept it alive for twenty years, replacing it part by part until it was more the Ship of Theseus than Bessie, the hulking antithesis to politically correct environmentalism.

"I can't believe Patrice lets you drive this thing," Jonah said. "It's like a rollicking crime against humanity. Who even *drives* these days?"

"I do." Without a flicker of shame, Ian turned a key in the manual lock and then leaned across the front seats to open the door on the passenger side. "The government would fall in a day without me and hundreds of people would die. You think Patrice *lets* me do *anything*?"

Jonah ran a hand over the cracked leather armrest. He wouldn't admit that he'd missed the shambling, gas-guzzling environmental catastrophe. But it felt stable, reliable. Uprooted and cast to the wind, from one tiny apartment to the next, but at least Ian's hulking war machine remained intact. "You're a massive dick, you know? This is the vehicle of a massive dickhole. Who is overcompensating, and worse."

"I've spent the last twenty years saving the world, b'y," Ian revved the engine. "I'm allowed Bessie." The antediluvian radio, set to some nostalgic indie station, sprang to life, and he quickly hit play on the tape deck to flood the cabin with the scratchy strains of *The Very Best of Stan Rogers*, one of a handful of tapes that Jonah wanted desperately to believe had come with the truck despite knowing better. Jonah cracked the window open, a thin sheet of cool air slicing through the gap. "I'm not overcompensating for anything if you're wondering."

"I'll ask Senator Harrison," Jonah said sweetly, and Ian regarded him like something he'd scraped off the bottom of his shoe. Oh, he'd heard the rumours.

"You stay away from him," Ian growled. Jonah let it drop. Ian didn't have feelings, let alone catch them for a guilty neo-aristocrat with a receding hairline from Forest Hill who probably prefaced sex with a land acknowledgement.

Downtown, there were more bikes than cars on the road, especially this time of year, but north of the city, the traffic thinned to the odd car, most of them sleek and so streamlined as to be nearly invisible. Ian gunned the gas over the sloping hills, though the black cover of forest.

When they'd first met, there was no choice about driving if you wanted there to be food in the camp. With Bessie's cargo bed, Ian was usually in charge of the supply runs, and Jonah went with him, the choppy backroads the only way into town, tense and alert for signs of the cops or the RCMP moving in. After an hour, both of them would forget to be furtive. The crisp winter air was cold on his face and Ian drove like a man who'd never once in his life failed to talk his way out of a speeding ticket—magic, it had to be said, had its advantages.

Now, of course, no one was chasing him, and for once Ian Mallory wasn't the story. They could just be alone, with the burbling roar of the overpowered engine and the thin warble of the old tape filling in the silence, the howl from the open window ensuring no conversation could happen quieter than a shout. Jonah pressed his face into the window, a touch colder than the rest of the car with the wind rushing by. It had been years since he'd felt the rumble of the road, the pure speed of 3000 pounds of metal hurtling forward over concrete, and he could see why Ian had clung to it.

In the mauve dusk, Ian's pallor was less unnerving, the rest of the world as drained of colour as he had become. If they ran now, Jonah thought, if he left the arcane arts locked up in his office, would he be eventually restored to the man Jonah met two decades ago?

Not that he would. That was why he'd kept Bessie, clung to the old truck like he'd kept his old fiddle. Oh, Jonah didn't have to see it, he'd yet to be invited over to Ian's house, but he *knew* he still had it. Nothing else had stayed put since Ian spent the last of his savings on a plane ticket to Toronto to meet the famous Vasai Singh. He needed to pretend, as Jonah did, in the dark corners of bar washrooms and poorly lit parks, that he could escape if he ever really wanted to.

There was something like wilderness an hour northwest of the city. Ian parked the truck at the mouth of the hiking trail and sat at the steering wheel for a time, as if summoning the energy to move. Out here, he was completely grey, beyond the circle of Sujay's influence, thinner, and so much older. Was it the magic that had done it to him, Jonah wondered, or the toxicity of *Game of Thrones: Ottawa Edition*?

They walked, for a time, over a worn path dusty with parched earth, Ian incongruous with his shirtsleeves and collar sharp white in the darkness, Jonah no doubt just as out of place in his rumpled attempts at business casual. The night was blisteringly hot. Ian dropped into silence the moment there was no one stupid enough to shout at in his general vicinity.

"You think Patrice will be rational about the attack?" Jonah asked, so he'd have something to say.

"I think he'll do what I says. He's maybe only a third—40% at most—as stupid as he looks." Ian shrugged. "This is still the land of peace, order, and good government. The budget passes and there's some cash for Pharmacare, people'll forget we were shitting our pants six months ago." His hand, white and thin and luminous, trailed over the tall grasses. *Poison ivy*, Jonah wanted to protest, before he remembered that Ian had grown up in the middle of nowhere too, had the same sharp instincts for plants that might decide to fuck with him. "It must be so *fucking relaxing* to have a memory that only goes back a month," Ian said. "No wonder regular people are so well-adjusted."

The rest of it, Jonah thought, would happen very quickly. People would argue with their racist uncles on Facebook. Patrice would make some lip service to cracking down on terror. One or more of the corporate warlords governing the fractious shithole down south would attempt to turn it to his advantage, at which point Patrice would look the very picture of caution and reason by virtue of not actually having rabies. His priest back home always said it was easy to be a saint in Paradise, but Jonah'd thought that it was even easier to be one in Hell.

The thing was, civilizations tended towards stability and self-correction, right up until the point that everything went tumbling into chaos. Much like marriages.

"I mean," Ian said, and the little hairs on Jonah's arms prickled, suspicious as he was that the rumours of *actual fucking telepathy* might be true. "Did you try *not* cheating on her?"

"Most of the time we were out west, yeah. Didn't help." And wasn't any of Ian's business, besides, much as Ian claimed that Blythe was his friend and that she was at least a million times more than Jonah actually deserved. "Hey, Ian?"

The sliver of bone-pale, a jagged slash of high cheekbones and hollowed eyes, turned towards him. Fuck, this was *awkward*.

"Just, uh. Could you do it? Magic, I mean? Not that prognostication bullshit or anything. But I need to know that this—" The worst of it was that Ian knew what he meant: Ottawa and the oceans rising and the knowledge that no matter how many late nights and heated debates and lobbying and compromise, nothing they did mattered in the vast scheme of things, "—isn't everything there is. Not my future, I wouldn't want to know either, but—tell me there's still something *good* in the world."

He had the pen and paper out before Jonah had even finished talking. When it came down to it, that was what Jonah hated most about him. He'd have taken it back in a second. The very *last* thing Ian should be doing for funsies was freebasing the vast and terrible cosmic force that threatened to kill them all eventually—and Ian, specifically, much more rapidly. What even happened to someone once magic had drawn the colour from their flesh and blood, had shrivelled them into a skeleton kept animate through pure stubbornness? What would be left of Ian, after that?

Ian, conversely, never missed an opportunity to show off. His half-completed labyrinth, already hovering off the page, twisted and flickered above his hands. Jonah heard its low-frequency hum, the air currents warped and shivering in its wake. Ian brought it to float between them, like a child's Cat's Cradle, and Jonah's skin prickled into gooseflesh, just as it had the first time he'd seen what the Cascade had given to the world.

That fragile web, the pattern that connected the entire world, a colour that, when it had first shimmered into existence, every expert at Pantone had fought for the opportunity to name, one that all of human knowledge and progress had failed to register until the Cascade made it real, bent and twisted into smoke, forming, at long last, a giant, juvenilely rendered, cock and balls. Below it, two delicate strands wove into archaic cursive to spell out: *Ian Mallory is a massive dickhole.*

Okay, it worked, a little. Jonah laughed, and the labyrinth evaporated into the oppressive heat of the supersummer night.

"Well," Jonah said. "You're not wrong. What are you planning with the survey maps, Ian?"

"Go home," Ian replied. "Call your ex-wife and kid. And apologize, for fuck's sake." He waved away the last lingering atoms of the spell into blue sparks. "One of us should get to be happy."

Jonah squinted, but he actually *meant* it. The poor bastard genuinely thought that at some point in Jonah's sad, sordid attempt at a marriage, he'd actually been *happy*. He had—much as it pained him to acknowledge it—the sudden and absurd urge to fix his fucked-up life if only to make Ian's world make sense.

"I'll do what I can," he said, and Ian seemed mollified by it.

He didn't ask if, in any of the possible worlds Ian had seen, there was a future in which Blythe had stayed with him, in which they rekindled the love he could just barely remember feeling for her, in which Laura grew up happy and sane and well-adjusted, without the need to parcel her life into disconnected fragments, as Jonah had. He didn't ask if there was one where he stayed here, in the forest, until his bones were as yellow as the dry leaves beneath the trees, until they both crumbled to dust. And if there was, Ian didn't tell him.

11

Tobias bent over his laptop, dragging curves and levels in the hope that something was salvageable from the press conference photos. Did Patrice drag Mallory from his windowless office out in front of the cameras on purpose to confuse and befuddle the press gallery? Distortion lay like a heavy webbing around him and laced over the dry, brittle grounds in front of the Peace Tower. All of the photos were like that, and had either Izzy or the Nikon been a few years newer, he doubted either would have survived with their lenses intact. Gaby Abel, her appearance stiff and stage-managed, had an ice-blue streak that covered her face no matter how many angles he'd shot.

Cynthia texted: *PM's kid getting booked.*

It was enough to have him running for his bike, parked outside the office, texting back furiously as he looped the strap of his messenger bag over his shoulder. The Abels' three kids all attended public schools with minimal security. Anything more intrusive would have been unacceptable both to the Prime Minister's base and the disgruntled taxpayer.

Tobias met Cynthia at the police station. Going to the school itself would have shattered the boundaries of journalistic integrity. He was locking his bike to a post in time to see the kid being brought in through the back. It was the middle child, Martine, her slight shoulders hunched up to her ears, pink cornrows swinging in front of her face. She looked younger than fourteen, which wasn't helped by the large cop escorting her inside. It made for a dramatic composition.

He wouldn't be able to use any of the footage, but he sent Izzy closer to get a look. Martine had a black eye, and the cop's wrist bore a scratch that might have come from one of the girl's long fingernails.

Oh, it couldn't ever be a story, but it was interesting enough to stick around.

"*You.*"

Tobias recognized Gaby Abel's voice before Cynthia moved between the two of them. Her accent, somewhere between Haitian Creole and Quebecois, was as painstakingly contained as her ironed hair, and both were professionally tortured into submission. *See, I'm harmless, I'm just like you. Old stock, non-threatening, not some kind of Black Lives Matter radical who'd somehow slipped and fallen into power on accident.* Had she stopped to apply her makeup before running to rescue her daughter or did she just always looked like that?

Her eyes went immediately to his messenger bag. "Bring that thing back. Now."

Stern wasn't a convincing look on Gaby. She was a woman who'd been conditioned from childhood to smile too much, too wide, and this had been a problem reflected in her polling numbers, along with, it seemed, her parenting. The *SUN* cartoonists, in particular, loved her; a schoolteacher turned vaguely left-of-centre politician, and one prone to fumbling press conferences and verbal gaffes at that. She had more bad angles than good. It was easy to take a photo where her face was bent into an unflattering expression. Still, Tobias had a reputation to uphold, and Reid Curtis wouldn't let Cynthia stoop so low as to drag a frantic mother's name through the mud, no matter what backdoor deals that mother had allegedly made with unpopular foreign governments, no matter what devastation she planned to unleash on the economy in the name of a lower carbon footprint. He tapped the app on his cell to return Izzy to his side.

"It wasn't recording."

"Bullshit. I know exactly who you two are. And I am having a *very* bad day."

She pushed past Cynthia's apologies, and nearly knocked Tobias over despite being a head shorter than he was. He replaced Izzy in its case.

• • •

Tobias didn't *exactly* follow Gaby Abel and her daughter home. But only because Gaby didn't go home after retrieving Martine—released without charges—from the station. The same car that must have dropped her off circled back to pick both of them up. It went not to 24 Sussex but to a low-rise building on Carling. Hauling her protesting, teary-eyed daughter behind her, Gaby marched inside.

So she wasn't living with Patrice anymore. Not surprising, given the open secret of his affairs, but while Martine was a minor and thus untouchable, it must have taken considerable effort to keep a trial separation—if that was what this was—out of the press. Scandal aside, Patrice Abel's brand would take a beating if it turned out that he was maintaining an extra, unofficial residence on the taxpayer's dime.

That was a story, even if Martine Abel's juvenile delinquency couldn't be. Tobias liked to think that he wouldn't stoop to the level of sordid paparazzi, but at the very least, the Old Man would be keen to know the details. He ducked into the kebab house across the street—he was hungry anyway—leaving Izzy hovering in the dry hedge to alert him when she reemerged.

Gaby still managed to sneak up on him, despite her high-heeled shoes and his halfhearted attempt at surveillance.

"Do you not have anyone better to stalk? The Opposition's new leader? I'm sure he must be infinitely more interesting."

Mouth full of kebab, Tobias took in her crossed arms and her tight frown before he managed to swallow.

He wiped harissa sauce from the corner of his mouth. "Cynthia couldn't publish a story naming a minor even if she wanted to," he said. "You're lucky it was her who heard about it and not someone less scrupulous."

"I will let Martine know. After she is through with being grounded for the rest of her adolescence. Do you have children, Mr. Fletcher?"

He pushed down the image of Lucy, elbows to knees on the toilet seat, crying over a little plastic stick. "No," he said. "I can't even imagine."

"She was defending her father," Gaby said. Now that she'd come closer, he could tell that under the waterproof mascara and eyeliner— which held in place—her eyes were rimmed in red. "The things these children say to each other. They don't come by those opinions on their own."

"The last few months must have been hard on you, Mme. Abel."

"Months." She snorted. "Sure."

"I don't mean to pry—"

"Of course you mean to pry. It's what you do." She shook her head. "I wasn't born yesterday. I know what it is to be a politician. To be a politician's *wife*. Patrice has a good heart."

"But."

"He is easily led astray."

Somehow, he didn't think she was just talking about the affairs. He nodded for her to continue, but she didn't. "Look," Tobias said, "If you want to set the record straight..." He fumbled through his wallet before he found a card to hand to her.

"I know your game too, Mr. Fletcher," she said. "And where your allegiances lie."

"To the truth, Mme. Abel," he replied. "Only, and always, to the truth."

• • •

Reid Curtis sipped whisky on the rocks, and Tobias watched the wall-paper, eyes rolling over the whirls and flourishes of knock-off William

Morris. The pub was trying far too hard to be British and upper crust, though were it not for the flatscreen TVs on which the Senators were currently taking a humiliating pounding, it might have even been classy. Besides the sole waitress on shift, there was not a single woman present.

"You remind me of your father sometimes," Reid said. "He didn't back down from a fight either."

Tobias was in no mood to be buttered up. "I've already deleted the photos," he said.

"He was also as bad a liar as you." The Old Man's blue eyes twinkled. "Unfortunate, that good men are so often compelled to be honest."

The weight of experience was behind Reid. He'd seen governments come and go—some, to his liking, others much less so, admittedly, none like this one. The world in which he'd come of age had nothing like the Party, no one like Ian Mallory.

Mallory had sneered into Tobias' cameras, had taunted him, all to show just how effortlessly he could have a story buried, how little anyone cared. The attack in Toronto confirmed that an MAI in government was a useful thing to have around, and Mallory, once again, was on top.

"No one," the Old Man said, "actually cares about politics. Until it affects their lives. You and I, my boy, we're a breed apart. Ordinary people don't care about the truth, as long as they're less uncomfortable than the next guy."

"You'd think they'd start to, with a freak like that running the show." Why had he decided on lager? He tried to get the attention of the waitress, but she was absorbed in conversation with the bartender. "And the worst thing." The Old Man just smiled beatifically, motioned with a slim hand for Tobias to please go on, unburden his heart, purge himself of negativity so that he might ride forth, liberated, into battle. "The worst thing is that he didn't need magic to do it. He just needed a terrorist attack to drop a dead cat in the middle of the table."

His companion's attention fluttered briefly to the game, then back at Tobias, as if to reassure him that he, and his struggles, remained a priority.

"Well, two can play that game."

The Old Man finished his drink, and the waitress, as if by magic, floated to his side to replace it. "Let's talk about you. This is personal. Not just the government—we all hate them, everyone hates them, they hate themselves—but Mallory in particular. Why?"

This was not a story that could be told in words. It wasn't just Lucy—she was just the canary in the coal mine, the lone, beautiful voice that a capricious universe had stifled. She was an antique pocket watch that still kept perfect time, an artifact of a different time that served no purpose beyond its pure beauty. He'd have died for her when they met, and now, for a world that made sense. He was just one man, one vote in the ballot box, one lone voice in the wilderness, but he'd be damned if the churn of irrationality and the whims of sorcerers would rob him of self-determination, of freedom, of the possibility, however remote, to have his ordinary human life mean something.

And it wasn't Mallory's threat, either, if that had been genuine and not idle trolling. Mallory had meant to get under his skin, and Tobias wouldn't allow him that power.

"Thwarted ambition?"

"You're as full of shit as he is, young man," Reid said, his smile unflinching steel. "You're the most straightforwardly upright person I've ever met. That's why he's winning, for now. Because you play by the rules."

"That's why he's a monster," Tobias said. "And why we're not."

Reid contemplated his glass, the distortion of light that played across the amber liquid. "Monsters live in the shadows. And flinch from the light."

"Thanks." He almost said, "sir."

"Dig deeper," Reid said. "Shine a brighter light. That's your calling—that's your duty."

The thin crowd erupted in a half-hearted cheer; Tobias glanced up at the screen in time to see a puck slam into the back of the net. No one drinking at three in the afternoon cared that the world was falling apart, the delicate balance to maintain order and stability as the very oceans and earth roiled, as creatures like Ian Mallory slithered into the corridors of power. As long as it didn't affect them, as long as they could slide down the path of least resistance, claim that their contribution to the country was teaching their kids to be better people than they had been, as long as the game didn't get interrupted, they would accept anything at all.

Reid waited for the cheers to quiet enough to say, "Photographs don't topple governments."

The right one can. "Neither do secrets and lies." Though he couldn't envy the Old Man his wrinkles, the arthritic creak of his joints, he did envy him this much: the age before the Cascade, before parallel media streams, when a scandal still meant something. "Not anymore."

"I wouldn't be so sure."

"In that case," Tobias said. "I will take the ring though I do not know the way."

Reid responded with a blank-faced blink. Despite the irrefutable fact of the Cascade and nearly 80 years on the planet, he'd somehow managed to avoid reading anything that wasn't *Forbes* or a Churchill biography. Even as Tobias admired his single mindedness, he couldn't help but think that Reid was missing out on the more interesting parts of the human condition.

"Same as it always is," his boss said. "It's the SVAR, it's the backroom deals, it's the rift between the mushy left and the radicals and the realists. You want to restore sanity and truth to the world?" He raised his lips to his glass, visibly savouring its scent, rolling the liquid over his tongue. "Follow the fucking money, my boy."

• • •

The dark that fell over Parliament was unnatural. The lights were never fully out, any more than the Eternal Flame was ever extinguished. It was a rolling shroud over the buildings, rendering them bright one moment, black the next. Only the moon, and the flash of cars along

Wellington St., reliably lit Tobias' path. Armed with a roll of 3200 ISO film loaded into a just-short-of-antique Leica, Tobias set up the tripod at the bottom of the Hill.

There was nothing but black through the viewfinder. He relied on experience and instinct, bracketing each shot as he circled the Hill, camera first aimed inwards, then out towards the grounds. The camera led him, and he trusted it to get the shot.

He could feel the sizzle of magic over the short hairs on his bare arms. He saw nothing, but he was aware—just as he'd been aware of Mallory and his intern distorting his perception, of the wellspring and its treacherous siren song—of it webbing around him. The same force that had ruined half of his photos, enough to overwhelm even his old, reliable camera, leached across the grounds, coiling and spitting.

No, it hadn't been the camera. He'd realized it on the flight back from Vancouver. His Nikon was old enough that it should have functioned in the face of any wizardry Mallory could throw its way.

But the SD card inside—the same one he used for Izzy—was brand new.

The Leica, and its film, had been sitting in a cabinet since the last move. He had no idea if the film had expired, but nothing ventured, nothing gained.

Tobias pushed down his sense of unease, the stiff crackle of spider silk threads that brushed up against him and vanished when he tried to pluck them loose. The whole of the Hill was sticky with energy. So absorbed in what he was doing, he only noticed how many shots he'd taken when the film refused to advance. As he dug around in his bag for a new roll, something moved in the corner of his vision.

War zone instincts intact, he ducked behind the construction scaffolding draping the Nepean sandstone wall of the East Block. The torn corner of a tarpaulin flapped in his face. He edged forward, the camera braced between the bag, his body, and the wall to shield the film as he loaded the second roll.

He had almost convinced himself that the movement was nothing more than a shadow thrown by a passing car when he saw it move again, coalesce into a recognizable human figure walking out from the great Gothic Revival mass of the Centre Block.

Tobias would have recognized Ian Mallory by his loping gait even without the currents of magic lashing around him, bright icicle shards that burst from his hands and hung in the air for shimmering seconds before winking out. Tobias finished loading the film, moving by rote muscle memory awakened after years of inactivity, and raised the camera.

Surely Mallory would hear the clack of the shutter, the shift from one foot to another in the dry grass as Tobias angled for a better frame. But the man seemed absorbed in his work, weaving gossamer strands of energy between his fingers with the fury of a conductor bringing a symphony orchestra to its final crescendo.

What the fuck was Mallory making? A ward? A geas? A curse? If Tobias announced his presence, if he threw himself bodily between the sorcerer and the cradle of government, would he be interrupting a blessing of protection or an act of sabotage?

But no—his duty was not to interfere, not to be the story, simply to document and bear witness. So Tobias moved as quietly as he could between the towers of scaffolding, praying for the camera to speak to what he was seeing.

Just as Mallory reached the porte-cochère at the base of the Peace Tower, he abruptly stopped and lifted his head. Tobias' heart lurched—Mallory had a line of sight to where he crouched, skulking like a criminal.

Mallory was looking past him, distracted, and Tobias zoomed as much as the lens would allow. The viewfinder gave up little, but as he squinted, he could almost make out more detail.

What he had taken as a trick of the light, the night throwing the scene around him into shades of grey, was more than that. Mallory's face was ash, every bit the gaunt corpse that Tobias had briefly glimpsed in the Broom Closet. The red of his hair was dimmed to silver. Tobias' eyes had adjusted to the dark enough that he saw the contrast as Mallory moved in front of the brown stone of the tower.

Tobias, cursing himself for not bringing colour film, squeezed off his last three shots and pulled back into the shelter of the scaffold.

When he dared look out again, Mallory was gone.

• • •

It took Tobias an hour to clear clothes out of the walk-in closet and another eternity of swearing and stubbed toes before he found the developing tank and changing bag stuffed in behind litre bottles for chemicals.

Lucy had been reading when he'd barrelled through the door, but she'd sprung into action with the precision of a military wife, sorting equipment and changing the lightbulbs as he mixed solutions in the sink and agitated the tank. She hummed as he worked, the house cast in darkness except where the deep red of the bare lightbulb flooded over the surface of long-neglected counters and trays.

His pulse beat a rapid drum through his veins. He'd missed this, the splash of liquid and the smell of developer, the anticipation as he unspooled the strips of film from their reels and held them to the light. He clipped each one to a clothesline to dry above the sink.

"Did it work?" Lucy asked. She stood behind him, bending her head into his bicep.

Tobias squinted at the delicate lines that whorled and danced over the film. The negatives were too tiny to make out details. The lines, though, carried from one frame to the next, regardless of how he'd composed the shot, forming a pattern down the length of the film.

"I'll know soon enough," he said.

• • •

Developing prints was, if not strictly speaking magical, certainly akin to alchemy.

Tobias had worked through the night. Lucy had kept him company until around four, when she'd pled exhaustion and piled the duvet over her head. Morning light, the enemy of the art, threatened the cracks around the door hinges and the improperly sealed gaps. He shut off the enlarger's light and moved the sheet to the developer bath, tilting the tray gently back and forth as the chemicals breathed life into the image. The scene crept into being over slow seconds, the deepest shadows first, the tall black silhouette of the Centre Block. There was nothing to do with the print at this point beyond encouraging the movement of the liquid, trusting in his aged equipment and long dormant skills.

The lines where the spell danced across the paper, complex helixes and curlicues diving and weaving around the building and outwards over the grass resisted the developer altogether, as white and sharp as if he'd scratched them into the film with a razor. Even in black and white, it vibrated on the sheet, searing its bright lines into his retinas.

He fished the print out of the tray, into the stop and fixer, then clipped it to the clothesline. At the edge of the frame, Mallory's eyes, cold and resentful, wreathed in the spell that emanated from his hands, stared out at him. Frozen by Tobias' camera into a rawboned memento mori, he stood consumed by his own magic. This was the real Mallory, not the projection he'd seen, stripped of illusion and artifice to reveal the monster beneath.

Tobias pulled print after print from the negatives, each a puzzle piece that somehow joined the one before, no matter which order he developed them in. They didn't move, but the ends fit together even when he swapped the photos around. It didn't make sense, it couldn't make sense. Tobias, reminding himself that he was dealing with magic, pushed past the inherent illogic to contemplate what he was actually seeing.

Spellwork climbed, like ivy, over the walls of the stalwart architecture, choking the old bricks, clawing fingers at the stained glass windows. Parliament ensnared, it tentacled outwards across the grounds, into the streets. It was frayed in places, bunched in others, and where Mallory had passed through, brighter and more intricate than where he hadn't. Tobias had caught a spell in the process of maintenance. His old

Leica had captured the thing he'd sensed, the hidden tendrils that for all he knew could be poisoning the mind of every man, woman, and child in the country, its old mechanics tracing out the pattern that baffled his newer equipment.

Judging by how long it had been interfering with his photos and the effort to which Mallory had gone to hide it, the spell had been going on for some time. Whatever the fuck it was.

Lucy knocked on the door. He opened the closet to find her bleary-eyed in her nightgown, the sun glaring through the bedroom window.

"It definitely worked." She gave him a faint smile as she moved around him to absorb the array of prints strung from one end of the closet to the other.

"What are you going to do about it?"

"What else is there to do? Get these out into the world. Tell the truth."

Her hand searched for his and clasped tight.

"It's 5 am," she said. "Maybe let poor Cynthia get some sleep before you bombard her with the scoop."

He was already unlocking his phone, hitting the top name on his contacts. "She was never going to be my first call," he admitted, and waited for the Old Man to pick up.

Martine Abel wasn't the story. But this was.

12

Everyone else was working damage control. Sujay was watching Ian do a magic trick.

"Isn't that a bit. Er. Cliché?" Sujay watched Ian's hands as they shuffled the deck with the bored expertise of a poker dealer, an automatic reflex at a speed that, while slightly faster than was probable, was plausibly *possible*. He paused, letting the cards slide into one palm with a soft *thwick*, reached over the desk across from her, and snapped his fingers just beneath her chin.

"You wanna learn somethin' or not?"

"I'd just figured you were more the tarot type than Solitaire." She'd decided, after Fort McMurray and their charming little scene at the airport, that if he hadn't fired her over an utter lack of political viability, he wasn't going to do it over a touch of brattiness, if one could even fire an apprentice. Intern. Whatever. He probably even *liked* her, insofar as he liked anyone. At least he didn't yell at her nearly as much as he yelled at everyone else, which meant she either hadn't fucked up, or she'd fucked up too regularly for it to make a difference.

"You do *not* want me to read your tarot." She couldn't tell if he was joking. He could have already determined every one of her possible futures, had them mapped out like he had the consequences of a minor shift in budget allocation or an unexpected appearance of Patrice Abel in a church basement wearing jeans and serving up margarine soup to the unwashed masses. For all she knew, the ending of each possibility was a horrible death, and that was why he was, on the odd, past-normal-working-hours occasion, kind to her.

Ian was less desaturated than he'd been before the weekend, 1970s washed-out browns replacing gritty 1940s crime photos, the lines demarcating him from the drab office clutter crisper. Stray strands of his hair glinted a dull orange in the glow of the incandescent desk light. Next to the tobacco-stain yellow of the card faces, tracks of purple veins in crooked trees stemmed from his bony wrists. Not a healthy colour, but life nonetheless. The fingernails, though, those were still pale grey. Whatever life-force he'd retained had wormed its way through his bloodstream and then, presumably, given up the situation as hopeless right at the end. Maybe he'd gone a day or two without magic, enough to tug him back into the world of the living. Or maybe it was his own illusion field, weaker than the mantle she usually cast around him, whether because he was less of an illusionist than she was, or because he wanted her to think so.

When she'd come in for her interview, six months and a lifetime ago, he'd asked her for a demonstration. She'd complied, turning the office into a lush, shimmering jungle, crawling ivy up the wall and chairs, bright flame lilies exploding on his desk, the flashiest thing she knew how to do. He'd told her that from thereon, her primary task would be to conceal his deteriorating condition from the rubbernecking public, thereby demonstrating the First Rule of Magic: never actually tell anyone what you're capable of doing, lest some utter asshole force you to do it all the time.

"Cut the deck for me," he said, passing the block of cards for her. She did. Passed it back, and he shuffled it again. "Look up. Eye contact. Builds trust."

His eyes were as grey as the rest of him, pyrite-flecked, and it occurred to her that she might very well have no idea what he really looked like, if he was as powerful as they said. There were no photos of him from before the Cascade. He had no childhood, no past before he'd showed up in Toronto at Vasai Singh's side. For all she knew, no one alive had ever actually *seen* him. "How'm I supposed to see what you're doing with the cards if I'm looking at your eyes?"

"It's cute that you think this is about card tricks," Ian said. "You ask someone to do something for you, they'll buy into the illusion. You don't do favours, you asks *them* for favours. That's the buy-in."

"So they'll like you?"

A soft snort. "Oh no," he said. "They'll never *like* you." Sujay bristled, offended, before she realized he was talking about himself, too, that he took it as a badge of pride that he walked as uneasily as she did through the corridors of (minor, imperial-satellite) power. "D'you think the Neanderthals watched *Homo sapiens sapiens* sharpening their sticks and went, *Oh hey, I bet we'll be friends with those b'ys over there*? You make the bastards out there think you needs 'em, so they don't burn you at the stake. Take a card."

She slid the eight of clubs out, glanced at it, and put it back. He kept shuffling. "Now we see the illusion of free will. Important to give 'em that, too."

"I thought you were teaching me magic."

"What's more magical than thinkin' you got a choice in the outcome?" He pulled out a seven of diamonds. She shook her head.

Six of spades. "Nope. You kind of suck at this."

"Ah, fuck it, then." A final shuffle, and the deck burst into blue flame, settling to a pile of ash on his desk. Show-off. She looked around for the tell-tale drawing, but nothing; he must have done it earlier. That in itself was instructive; she hadn't tried to put any time between building up a focus and casting. "I don't know any card tricks."

He shrugged. "Put your hand through the desk."

"What?"

Ian scratched out another drawing, lightning-fast, and pushed his hand into the surface of the desk up to the wrist while the paper was still sending off sparks. There was nothing dramatic in it—his hand existed where the desk did not, and the desk existed where his hand did not, and any confusion about them occupying the same space was down to her imperfect understanding of quantum mechanics.

"I can't—" she started.

"Fuck can't," he replied.

She reached into the pocket of her blazer for Panic Pete. Squeezed—one-two, one-two—until she could feel the texture changing under her fingertips, a click, almost audible, locking her into the Great Cosmic Fuckery that they sometimes, stupidly, deluded themselves into thinking they could channel.

The Pattern caught her palm where it curled around the stress toy, the faint glow between them drawing a pale green line up the side of his jaw. She placed her hand on the desk beside his, and it vanished.

He slapped the hand, not hard enough to hurt but enough to reveal its location in space, the difference between the illusion she'd done and the violation of physics he'd committed. Caught, she looked away.

"Keep practicing," Ian said. "You'll be a half-decent charmer one day."

She liked charmer better than MAI. No wonder they'd had to give it some kind of official, sterile acronym, as if it could neutralize the wildness barely contained under their skin, erase all the words that humanity had named them over millennia. No wonder everyone—herself included—took refuge in stories about fictional monsters these days, vampires and werewolves and zombies, safely removed from the real demons that stalked the shriekgrass-clotted dead places. From the bone-deep knowledge that however much he taught her, the storm inside of her could overpower her whenever it chose. The *cacoethes* was just biding its time.

"Of course I will," Sujay said. "I learn from the best."

• • •

Sujay's official job description did say "other duties as assigned," but she wasn't sure that said other duties included stalking a former cabinet minister in the name of damage control. Her anxiety was through the roof. Ringing Gaby Abel's buzzer was a flashback of the awkward week she'd spent fundraising for Greenpeace in university.

Gaby made a habit of—in the way of all intersectionally fucked people who'd battered and clawed their way into a modicum of power—never letting the mask slip. Nevertheless, she had the familiar look of detritus left behind after a Category 5 Hurricane Mallory.

"You're one of *his*, aren't you?" she said, to Sujay's faint little wave.

"Is it that obvious?"

She motioned for Sujay to follow her inside. "No offence. But please tell me that you have at least graduated high school."

Sujay nodded. She kicked off her pumps, stopping to press the ball of one aching foot into the pile carpet as she padded into the small, drab living room. She wasn't sure if she should move the small heap of teenage spoor on the couch to sit down, while Gaby stood, or whether Gaby was just waiting for her to sit, or whether Gaby just wanted her to to state her business and get out.

"You on the policy wonk end, or the—" Gaby made a hand gesture that looked nothing like anyone doing magic, at least as far as Sujay had seen.

Sujay echoed it back. "Definitely that end."

The older woman turned from her—not a reaction Sujay was used to when she disclosed. But then, all of Gaby's piss-poor experiences with MAI were of the entirely mundane, workplace-drama variety. Gaby made her way through the little galley kitchen to the kettle. "Tea?"

"Okay."

"Word travels fast."

It was a relief that Ian wasn't there to get explosively offended. "He keeps a close eye on the *Post*. For each word they print about your daughter, he promised to remove something fun from his blackmail drawer."

She heard the clink of cups, the tension of the heat building in the kettle that was only barely a sound before the water bubbled into steam.

She moved a backpack aside to clear a space on the couch, placing it over a pair of pink track pants that flailed over the other half of the seat, and sat down, twisting her hands together for lack of anything else to do with them.

"It's nice that he cares," Gaby said from the kitchen. "About Patrice, anyway. Did he send you here to spy on me? Or does he want something?"

The backpack didn't zip fully, which Sujay hadn't noticed when she'd moved it, and some papers spilled out of the top. A math test, which the kid hadn't done well on, and a permission form, crumpled and overdue. Another paper was completely unrecognizable beneath angry black scribbles, some carved with enough force to punch through the page. Sujay hurried to stuff them back in before Gaby returned with a mug of tea in each hand.

"I'm here to put protective wards on your place," Sujay said. "In case Tan and Fletcher—or someone else—don't keep their word. But you have to consent."

"Wards."

"Like a magical shield." She took a long sip of tea. "Someone walking by will see your building, maybe even see you or your kids coming and going, but they'll find this information exceptionally boring and keep walking."

Gaby's laugh was short and bitter. "Where the hell were you seven months ago?"

"Would you really want to fall under the radar as a cabinet minister?"

"I might have gotten more accomplished."

Sujay struggled with the clasp on her purse, then rooted through the nest of receipts and lipsticks and the rats' nest of chargers for her phone. "For what it's worth," she said, "I think he's a bit sorry about how that all went down."

"Ian is never sorry," Gaby said. Her tone had gone flat. "That's the joy of never being wrong. It *would* have to be a white man with that particular ability."

Sujay swallowed, ducking the other woman's eyes. "He's not like that."

"Not to you," Gaby replied. "Not yet. But watch your back, Miss..."

"Krishnamurthy."

"Take it from me. None of those men will hesitate to throw a woman of colour under the bus. Ian Mallory is no exception. You'll see."

"Also." Sujay's face was swollen with heat. God, this was awkward. "He does want something. Obviously. I'm not supposed to talk about it. Just give you this."

She handed Gaby the letter and returned to her phone. There was a new Korean app to hyper-charge emoji spells; she tapped the ward sequence into it, and the summoning—to her relief—cannibalized most of her concentration. Wards were easier than phasing. A stray spark of green flicked off her phone and landed in the tea, fizzling for a split second before disappearing.

Sujay wasn't naive; they were all disposable, elected officials and civil servants alike, regardless of competence or good intentions. Their fortunes rose and fell with convenience and public opinion. And some of them were more disposable than others. If Gaby's treatment had seemed especially unfair, it was because the game had always been rigged against her. She wasn't elegant, and the tabloid press had been foaming at the mouth for her blood since she'd narrowly squeaked into office.

"Excuse me. I have to—" Sujay gestured weakly at the door with her phone, and Gaby nodded permission. The app *was* pretty awesome. One click to each corner of the door, and a glamour, backed by the force of thousands of users and half a dozen decade-old Linux servers stored in three different countries, descended like a shroud over the apartment building, shuttering it from the outside world.

The apartment had a fire escape in the back, and she moved to cover that, just in case someone got creative with a drone-mounted camera, which took her past the two bedrooms. The door to one was open, the room empty; from the other, she could hear a bass line, tinny through a set of headphones that must have been cranked to full blast. She hadn't thought that anyone else was home, but of course, the kid was suspended. The door was closed and the music had to have been deafening, but she heard movement behind her as she went past.

Sujay stopped. Turned.

"Hi."

The outlines of Martine Abel's fists were visible, balled up, in the front pocket of her grey hoodie, her pout defiant, her black eye sprouting into shades of yellow and green over her cheekbone. Her headphones dangled around her neck, still thumping music through the speakers.

Gaby snapped something at the girl that Sujay's ninth grade 67% in French didn't quite catch. Sujay backed away, the waves of anger radiating from Martine's slender shoulders palpable. Martine just rolled her eyes.

"I'm *not.*" Martine slouched deeper into her hoodie. "I just want to see the magic trick, okay?"

"Go back to your room." Gaby exhaled through gritted teeth. "My apologies, Miss Krishnamurthy. My other children understand how to comport themselves with dignity."

"She can watch," Sujay said. "It won't make a difference."

"You know what they wrote about my mother when she stepped down?" Martine trailed Sujay the rest of the way down the hallway. "'The public wanted Michelle Obama, but what they got was Winnie Mandela.' I think I'll write that in everyone's yearbook in June, what do you think?"

"I think a lot of people had to make tough decisions." Sujay glanced back at Gaby, then pointed the phone at each corner of the door. The air rippled, a vibration she felt more than saw, a ghost feather brushing over her arm. "Your mom included."

"You want to know what they say about my dad? The stuff they could print, anyway..."

"*Martine. Ça suffit!*"

The girl scowled, jammed her hands back into her pockets, and retreated back to her room. "You should put a selfie stick on that thing," Martine called, before slamming the door hard enough to shake the solitary wallhanging in the hallway. "Then it could be a magic wand."

Alone with Gaby, Sujay said, "Uh. It's done." Should she offer to glamour Martine, too? Gaby? It wouldn't last as long; an apartment was a fixed point, an apartment didn't fuck up an illusion field by breathing and speaking and moving. But it couldn't hurt, with so many eyes on them. At least until Patrice was in a more secure position. If Patrice was ever in a secure position. "They won't stalk you at home. If there's anywhere else you need to go, shoot me a text."

"That will not be necessary." Gaby guided Sujay back into the living room. Her cup of tea was sitting on the coffee table, abandoned and cooling. "He always has reasons," Gaby said. Quietly, although Martine's music was back on. "Anyone else, I'd say it's because he's a manipulative bastard trying to advance his position in the Party by kissing Patrice's ass, but. A manipulative bastard who can see the future? What was it that he saw? What does he want?"

Was anyone even supposed to know that much about Ian's powers? But Patrice must have some inkling, or Ian would never have gotten as entangled with the Party's fortunes as he did. And Patrice, three years ago, when the future had been a wide-open field of possibilities and not a snarled den of thorns, must have told Gaby. "I should go. I'm technically on the clock still."

"You seem like a nice girl," Gaby said. "You're walking right back into a nest of vipers."

"There's gonna be a Cabinet shuffle," Sujay blurted. It wasn't a secret, not really, and Sujay would want to know, if it were her, would want to be able to plan out her reaction. Ian would know she'd spill it.

"Oh?" Gaby drew out the syllable, voice tight.

"Ian wants you in Environment to replace Dina. Don't open the envelope until the offer's been made."

"There's an irony for you," Gaby said. The temperature in the living room dropped so fast that Sujay felt a pressure headache coming on. "Given that my husband wanted Dina to replace *me*. By no means."

"I thought you'd be happy?" Messengers got shot. Messengers got drop-kicked into giant wells. "It's back in."

"Not during a climate apocalypse. Tell Ian I've been patient. I've done what he's asked. He can find another scapegoat."

"You want me to tell him that?"

Her lips drawn in a thin line, Gaby said. "It won't make a difference. Thank you for the wards, Miss Krishnamurthy."

Book 2

The Devil's Waltz

Commission of Inquiry Concerning the Influence of Magic-Affected Individuals (MAI) On National Affairs

[Date Redacted]
To Her Excellency
The Governor General in Council

May it please your Excellency:

Pursuant to an Order in Council dated [redacted], I have inquired into and reported on allegations concerning the undue influence of Magic-Affected Individuals (MAI) on national policy. With this letter, I respectfully submit my Report and it would be appreciated if you would table it in the House this afternoon.

Respectfully yours,

Mr. Justice Tate Nicholls (Chairman)

The Allegations

My first order of business is to set out the allegations of wrongdoing on the part of the Government and its MAI contractors. At the commencement of this Inquiry, Commission counsel prepared and filed a book itemizing all of the various allegations made in the House of Commons and in the media...

//

JUSTICE NICHOLLS: Please state your name and position for the Commission.

GABY ABEL: My name is Gabrielle Abel, MP for La Pointe-de-l'Île. Min—former Minister of International Trade.

1. It is alleged that, as a contractor for the Canadian government, Mr. Mallory had undue influence over policy decisions...

//

JUSTICE NICHOLLS: Tell the Commission about Externality Assessments.

GABY ABEL: Before any new major energy project is approved, we conduct an assessment to determine every possible consequence of that project. It differs from an environmental impact assessment, as it looks outside the immediate area, at long-term impacts to the climate, the economic and health impacts on surrounding communities, that sort of thing. It's as if you could measure the tidal wave created by a butterfly flapping its wings in Japan.

JUSTICE NICHOLLS: And this is done through magic? Can you describe the process?

GABY ABEL: No. Because it's magic.

13

Jonah was in the office before dawn, roused by an emergency of the Signal, not general text, variety. *ABEL MTG W/ SVAR DEL GUARANTEE CLUSTERFUCK BRNG POPCORN :) :) :)*. His foot found the sharp edge of a laptop hiding on the floor among the dirty socks and underwear. He cursed Ian's particularly *unique* economy in texting vocabulary that allowed for "delegation"—he assumed, anyway—to be abbreviated while "clusterfuck" was spelled out in its full glory.

He flailed through the clothes piled on one of the two chairs he owned until he located a shirt that looked like it belonged in an adult's wardrobe. More crucially, it was the least wrinkled one he could find. Swallowing a cup of watery black coffee, he caught the bus past the Hill towards the Broom Closet, ignoring two messages from Ian demanding that he get there faster.

We don't all own broomsticks, he texted back. Ian responded with a middle finger emoji.

Riding past Parliament, Jonah caught a glimpse of the ceremonial teepee that protesters had erected by the Centennial Flame, as if he wasn't aware well in advance exactly what was at stake in the talks between Patrice's team and the delegation from the Silicon Valley Autonomous Region. A scraggly broomsticks-and-Red Ensign crowd was out as well, expressing their generalized discontent about socialism, immigration, and the audacity of magic to exist. Neither side seemed to know that the talks weren't happening at Parliament but in the basement of the Holiday Inn, in the expert negotiator's preferred habitat of boardrooms and no natural light. Jonah ignored the overwhelming sense that he should be inside the teepee and not inside the concrete fort of the Enemy, gradual-change-and-greater-influence rhetoric aside.

Ian met him at the door. "Shouldn't we be at the hotel?" Jonah asked.

Even his stalwart young intern Sujay had yet to make an appearance at her desk, though her glamour lingered. "Doesn't start for another hour or so," he said. "We needs to *strategize*."

Ian's desk was littered with papers, stacked into a cityscape of haphazard, safety-code-violating skyscrapers. His reports—collected descriptions of every way that any one of the government's latest policy initiatives was doomed to catastrophe—got printed out on reams of paper and handed off to Cabinet in thick envelopes, like he was sharing blackmail 8x10 prints in a Cold War spy drama.

Jonah sighed, and flipped through the papers, trying to make the masses of data into something like a plan before the SVAR delegation finished their morning kombucha.

• • •

A digression: when Jonah was a boy, the United States existed. As a *thing*. United, indivisible, out of many one and all that bullshit.

It existed in fractious, violent spasming, North versus South, red versus blue, coastal versus flyover, urban versus rural, and always, always, white versus anyone darker than a brown paper bag. It exerted its massive gravitational force and defined everything north of the 49th parallel by comparison. It was a clumsy, drunken policeman spreading

Coca Cola and puppet democracies throughout its half-assed, Made-In-China empire. Such a big thing, like a bank, like the oak tree in the ravine you played in as a child, doesn't change, let alone fall. And yet.

Empires fall, and the rapid change of the past two decades proved too much for the fragile fault-lines beneath them.

Patrice's team was made up of Chase Emory, the Minister for Science and Innovation, Gaby Abel, the new Minister of the Environment, Senator Calvin Harrison, the walking exemplar of smug white liberalism, and a jet-lagged gaggle of representatives from the Alberta Legislature and Silicon Valley North start-ups. Their mission was simple: Win over the SVAR, forestalling a Bay Street revolt in the wake of the bombing.

The Silicon Valley Autonomous Region, established after CalExit and spanning Oregon to California, was typically regarded as the sane little brother in the dysfunctional crime family to the south. It was fiscally minded, technologically precocious, and most of all socially liberal, with some of the world's most progressive policies towards immigrants, LGBTQ2 people, and MAI. Gigantic tech industry compounds, with headquarters, offices, residential and leisure complexes rolled into sprawling campuses, clung to coastlines and mountains beneath the shadows of wind turbines and solar farms. It almost made up for the unaffordable rental prices of coffin apartments, where the underpaid best and brightest collapsed into bunkbeds after 18-hour days. The homeless were violently purged from the spotless sidewalks, and the high modernist park furniture held retractable spikes. The SVAR collaborated with the medieval regime of the Free States for food and oil to fuel an economy that appeared to glide on touchscreens, hot yoga, and the occasional dip into well-funded but deniable coastal piracy. It held an uneasy position in what was less a nation than a tense free-trade zone. The left half of the US was held together by spit, duct tape, and commerce, culturally distinct and financially enmeshed. Jonah would have pitied them if they weren't, to a dudebro, utter pricks.

It was with this strange, contradictory entity that the Canadian government—a stolid beacon of responsibility, at least up until a magic-wielding lunatic had inserted himself into the nation's highest circles—had decided in its wisdom to open up negotiations.

• • •

"So what I'm getting from this," Jonah said. "Is that we are completely fucked no matter what we do."

Over the past month, between video calls to hereditary chiefs and lawyers, he'd watched Ian repeatedly lock himself in his office, *doing his thing*, as the civil service euphemistically called it. He'd emerge from whatever hypnotic trance he'd put himself in with a precise vision of the varied outcomes of whatever asinine idea some MP of Backwardslandia had suggested. He delivered his verdicts in colourful and indecipherable invective that might have been scathing if any of his victims spoke Newfie and was, at any rate, bowel-loosening for anyone on the receiving end whether they understood or not.

This time, though, he was just grim. Which, Jonah thought, wasn't a good look on anyone, but especially not on a clairvoyant.

"There is," Ian intoned, and Jonah was entirely willing to believe he'd been up the entire night to confirm the conclusion, "only one thing they wants from us."

The Silicon Valley Autonomous Region, for all its accumulated brilliance, for all its beautiful landscapes and intelligent architecture, had no wellsprings or known MAI of its own. Whether, as some had theorized, as Ian's mountains of paperwork and dozens of pre-Cascade urban fantasy novels implied, there was an inherent incompatibility between magic and technology or it was sheer dumb luck, the SVAR's closest trading partners were loathe to open negotiations. Its representatives had come, hat in hand, willing to trade magic for high-tech wizardry, and Patrice, though not politically unsavvy, was nothing if not as susceptible as a toddler to buzzwords and high-gloss toys.

"We don't needs them as much as they needs us," Ian said. "That's the good news. The only good news."

"And the bad?"

"We tell them no and it's embargo time. The SVAR is a bigger market for China than us. They'll cut us off if there's pressure. No more chips, no more rare earth metals from the Congo. Then you get the riots when no one gets their iOS upgrades and this is not, I'm told, what Patrice wants to be remembered for."

"Fuck." The SVAR, unlike the Free States, hadn't needed to fight a war for its own liberation from nanny state Washington. It had no standing army, just money and the DRM on everyone else's weapons guidance systems. They would win a trade dispute in the time it took for news of the next upgrade to hit the tech blogs.

"Fuck indeed," Ian agreed.

"And if we do the other thing?"

"Besides reneging on a key election promise so that we can all get the next Xbox? Or causing a wellspring spillover that turns the entire West Coast into Blunstone-wearin', turmeric-latte-sippin' demons?" He slammed a skinny fist on the stack of papers. "Both of which possibilities are in here, by the by, and then some, and none of it's pretty. Those b'ys over at the hotel, they don't know what the galloping fuck they're doin'."

Jonah had a brief, horrific thought of magic moving virally through software, turning binary code into non-Euclidian, Cthluloid monstrosities, of sentient DRM seizing pacemakers and self-driving AI in its tentacles, and shuddered. "Other options," Jonah said. "I'm listening."

"It can't look like us," Ian said. "Or the PM, obviously. We need to be benevolent. There're the protestors. We could be seen cavin' to First Nations extremism."

Jonah winced. That couldn't be what the surveys were for.

"Would that work?"

"Breathe, Joe. I'm not so corrupt that I'd throws 'em under the bus like that. Or you."

Jonah noticed that he hadn't answered the question. But he could count on Ian being relatively ethical, if he could, until he got desperate. And *grim*, while a bad indication, was distinct from *desperate*.

That left one major stakeholder, and it was clear Ian was unhappy with the idea. "So the entrepreneurs. Who fucking hate your pinko guts." He grabbed a file off the top of the stack. Ian's notes tended towards the incomprehensible, branching little trees of catastrophe in a cipher that probably made sense to about three people on the planet.

"There's Cal—Senator Harrison."

Jonah should have guessed it was going there. Normally Ian would have protested any kind of Senate involvement, both on high-minded democratic principle and bloody-minded pragmatism, but there went *Cal*, being a goddamn exception all over again. He hoped to fuck Ian wasn't thinking with his dick on this one.

"He speaks their language," Ian said, deliberately slow, as if puzzling out his own arguments, though he knew full well that Jonah knew there was a wobbling line amid the labyrinths that denoted Cal's role in the negotiations and whatever trade deal would come of them.

"TEDx is a language now?"

"And he'll do what I say. For a price."

"Like, a wide-stance price, or—"

Ian's glare did not fully belong to him. The ice-green was a trick of light twisted by his intern above the pallid grey evidence of his slow fade from the world. "A political price. He's not half as stupid—or thirsty—as you give him credit for."

Jonah had no doubt that somewhere, underneath the senator's bespoke hipster suits and his pretentiously exaggerated mid-Atlantic diction, there was a core of steel. Ian wouldn't have found him interesting, otherwise. But Jonah didn't have to pretend to like the guy.

"So he convinces our entrepreneurs that the SVAR pose a commercial threat. We pretend to be willing to bend on wellspring pipelines, the techbros threaten to riot, and we throw up our hands."

"Disruption's what they're good at." Ian frowned, tracing strands of the labyrinth. Jonah didn't need to have magic to follow the consequences—a tighter coalition between the SVAR and the Free States, or the Union, or China. A grudge, with resulting trade penalties, and little

Jimmy still doesn't get his iPhone at Christmas. "Conciliatory, Joe. I hired you to keep us all honest. But we needs to give 'em something."

Sujay chose that minute to arrive with three weak coffees and a box of Timbits. Ian must have texted her too.

"I got something," Ian said. "I'm gonna talk to Cal. Joe, make *this*—" He flapped the thick stack of papers on his desk. "—something that even the PM'll understand. Sujay, if anyone comes through that door who isn't me or Joe, stall 'em till I gets back."

He was already on his phone, presumably to Cal. Jonah took his coffee, cast a resigned glance at Sujay, and he returned to his work.

• • •

Blythe interrupted, with a phone call rather than a text, a rarity for her.

"There's a thing," she said, instead of *hello*.

The last time she'd called unscheduled, it was to tell him that she'd come face-to-face with motherfucking *Cthulhu* and almost died. She sounded more frantic now, but the tinny distance and her own rush to explain masked any fear that a normal person, a *civilian*, might feel. Funny how, through all their fights, through the broken crockery and promises, they slipped so easily into their old dynamic when the pressure was on, Blythe racing ahead of him, breathless, and Jonah never quite catching up.

"And there are blips. Several blips," Blythe added, quickly, translating from scientist-who'd-been-buried-in-this-for-months to regular person *sans* context. "But none recently. Until three days ago, when there was a temperature spike like the ones right before Y2K."

What she didn't say was, *the ones that started the Cascade*. Everyone, scientist or not, knew what a sudden temperature spike in the deep ocean heralded.

The world is ending. It wasn't, really. The world is never ending. What ends is the subjective, personal reality that one has carefully constructed over a lifetime, the plans and human ties and ideologies and the physical trappings of home and family that always seemed immutable, permanent. The Earth itself would, in all probability, march on, as it had through the Black Death, through the bloodthirsty colonization of Turtle Island, through both World Wars, through the Cascade and each one of its horrors and wonders—though whether at the end of this blip it would continue to be able to support human life remained to be seen—but it wouldn't end. It is only your own, personal, fragile world that is always in danger.

"The SVAR delegation is here," Jonah said. "I'm—I can get you a meeting, maybe in a day or two..."

"You know that bit in the disaster movie where the egghead in the lab coat is running down corridors, trying to convince the bigwigs that a volcano is about to explode?"

He drew in a breath. He doubted she'd worn a lab coat since first year university, but she'd made her point all the same. "That's where we are?"

"That's where we are. Except I'm not running down hallways because they were observing to see if I had a concussion and they haven't cleared me for frantic running."

He glanced at the clock on the monitor. 8:43 am. Technically, his work day was just starting. Gaby Abel, career reluctantly resuscitated to shovel shit like unexpected enviro-magical catastrophes, was at the Holiday Inn meeting. And Ian, the only person who had a genuine grip of the stakes, was in full-scale whirlwind mode, attempting, via black magic or seduction or bribery, to bend to his will the selfsame CEOs that as a young man, he'd declared guillotine-fodder.

"I'll do what I can," he told Blythe. He hung up with an apologetic look to the stack of papers, which after several hours of analysis, were barely closer to politically palatable. And there was the looming prospect of whatever it was Ian intended to trade in exchange for not tracking explosive pipelines through the Rockies.

He was calm. He was collected. Everything was still under control.

Sujay was at her desk, looking for all intents and purposes on top of things, which, he gathered, was the advantage of being an illusionist. "How well do you speak wizard?"

"Ehhh—" She made a so-so gesture, which he identified as unnecessary humility, given that she *was* a wizard. He herded her over to Ian's desk.

"Direct Ian-to-English translation: everything we do will fuck us. The SVAR delegation can't, under any circumstances, be allowed to leave with an agreement on wellspring access nor can they, equally important, be allowed to leave disappointed with our government. This slaughtered forest is an entirely unverifiable study of every potential outcome that led to this conclusion. Your first task, as Ian's *apprentice* rather than his *intern*, is to phrase that, and what I just told you, in government jargon so if it comes to a vote in Parliament, everyone knows what to do. The fate of the world depends upon it. Can you manage that?"

Not missing a beat, Sujay said, "Of course."

"I see why he likes you." He flashed her the grin that countless women had told him was irresistibly charming and roguish, and gathered what remained of his things. Let the girl keep thinking that the government ran on goodwill and ponies for as long as anyone could maintain that smokescreen. Poor thing; she'd probably gone into politics to make the world a better place, or something.

"Where're you going?"

"To help out an egghead scientist," Jonah said.

• • •

He cornered Gaby as she was leaving the women's washroom. "We need to talk."

"I'm sorry," she said. "Who the fuck are you?"

"Pretend I'm a six-foot-two Newfie with a piss-poor temper and I can kill you with my brain."

"I should have just resigned. This is not worth it."

"You need to take a look at these figures." He pulled up the document Blythe had sent him on his phone. All of the printers were down, of course, something wrong with the network *as fucking usual*, and the urgency with which Blythe had spoken suggested that getting IT on the line wasn't the most productive possible use of his time. "You're not going to tell anyone. They won't make much sense to you, so you're going to call up Blythe Augustine out of UVic and ask her exactly what to do, and then you're going to do it. She'll fly in to address Parliament if there needs to be a vote on something, but you're going to keep it all under wraps until the last possible moment."

"And why am I going to do that, Mr..."

"Also Augustine. Because what I think, based on what *she* thinks, we're looking at, is a statistically significant spike in ocean temperatures comparable to the first recorded event in the Cascade. As in, another *event*. It's happening again."

"Mr. Augustine. Do you have any idea of how many people I have calling up my riding office to tell me that there's a second Cascade?"

"The difference being that my wife—ex-wife, sorry—is right."

She rolled her eyes. "I'm sure she always is. She divorced you, after all."

He braced a hand on the wall by her head, not *technically* close enough to be breathing down her neck, but skirting the edge of her personal space bubble. Jonah had never been what anyone would call physically intimidating, but a sufficiently angry terrier could bite just as well as a Doberman. "Make. The fucking. Call."

It occurred to him that even if she did, even if Blythe was listened to—and he had no illusions about *that*—even if Gaby was, the government had approximately zero leverage. Granted, before the Cascade, there'd been no shortages of reputable climate scientists screaming that the sky was falling. They couldn't have known what would happen, that the feedback effect would turn Earth into Cloudy With a Chance of Hellfire, but they'd had catastrophic models nonetheless, rational charts and graphs and figures, and it hadn't mattered.

Because even if the government did the right thing—and even with Ian pulling the strings, Jonah had little confidence that it would—they were still one nation among many. He could no more expect India to follow Canada's lead than he could the Free States, let alone China or Russia, and he had no guarantee that the recommended course of action, pushing up carbon cap deadlines and the like, would make a difference so close to the threshold. Probably they were fucked regardless.

Still, he had to try. And if that meant being a bit of a devious bastard, well, wasn't that what Ian had hired him to do?

"C'mon, Gaby." His voice gone silky, he turned the borderline-sleazebag charm up to max. "You have a chance *to make a real difference*, here." That was always the vulnerability. Patrice's government ranged from neophyte staffers promoted to elected official well before they were ripe, to cynical long-term careerists, but they'd all had ideals once. Whatever Ian had said to get her to return to a dead-end ministerial portfolio after he'd thrown her under the bus, it must have been convincing.

"Send me that." She waved a tired hand at the screen. He did, and sent it on to Ian as well, in the faint hope that Ian was in a position to do something about it and that he wasn't, say, on his knees in Cal fucking Harrison's office. For reasons of fun, however Ian defined that, and not business, anyway.

"Thanks!" Jonah pulled back to a more respectful distance. "Ian said you'd make a great Environment Minister."

She swore at him in French, and for the purposes of diplomacy, he pretended not to understand.

• • •

He was just about to sit down for lunch when Ian appeared, as if from thin air, behind him.

"Time to go."

Jonah rubbed at his eyes, the screen blurring in front of him. "How's Cal?"

"In, for now. We got anything for Patrice?"

He flapped the report, hastily compiled by Sujay, in the air in front of Ian's nose. "Do not do the thing or we will be fucked." He blinked. "You want to take me to meet the SVAR delegation?"

"I want you to lurk outside and distract the *Post* people hanging around the Holiday Inn."

"Ian," Jonah said. "About that thing I sent. Can you—" It was always an awkward subject, made more so in the wan, energy-saving fluorescents that left him nearly as grey as he would have been without Sujay's illusion field. "If Blythe is right, and there's a second Cascade? That's a thing that's possible, right?"

He knew exactly how stupid and pointless a question it was. Ian saw every possibility, given equal weight, each vision equally vivid and real. He was a man who'd seen the Earth die in a thousand different ways in glorious Technicolour, seen meteor strikes and alien invasions and nuclear holocaust. (Not, it had to be said, nuclear *winter*, the subject of no shortage of Jonah's childhood night terrors. That was actually apparently impossible and based on improper modelling in the 1980s.) If a second Cascade *could* happen, no matter how small the likelihood, Ian had already seen it, and the havoc it would wreak.

"It's possible," Ian agreed. A sophisticated enough machine-learning system could spew out a list of everything that could possibly happen, but it was Ian's human experience, his control, limited though it was, over the blue branches of the labyrinth, that discerned which probabilities actually mattered and flagged them. And since he didn't immediately rush to assure Jonah that it was below their consideration, it was substantially more than *possible.*

"What does it do?"

Sujay's illusion field wasn't quite good enough to disguise the flash of white as Ian *saw.* He stood, frozen, surveying possibilities no one else would ever know, and Jonah pushed down his own violent rage, the urge to shake the ghosts possessing his friend loose from his eyes. He shouldn't have asked for this, not with so much riding on the SVAR meeting.

Ian's vision cleared, the white sizzling back into pale green. "Well," he said. "In one outcome, it makes me basically a god."

"Nice," Jonah said. "What happens in the *good* timeline?"

"Oh, that *is* the good timeline." Ian clapped him on the arm. "C'mon. Can't keep the SVAR waiting."

14

Sujay should have been used to the late hours by now. They came with the job, with this life that she'd fallen into. But there was a difference between late hours fulfilling some mundane but quantifiable task and late hours doomscrolling through endless feeds, broken by unpredictable flourishes of chaos where Ian would emerge, flustered beneath the glamour she'd cast, gesticulating wildly and swearing a blue streak. She couldn't focus on anything of substance. The moment she settled into a project, Ian had a stack of hand-scrawled notes in shorthand to be wrangled, with no shortage of effort, into something comprehensible. In between she squeezed Panic Pete, which was nearly worn out after the recent weeks of abuse, skirting the edge of the Pattern occurring behind a closed door only a few metres away. Neither the fall of the government, nor the end of the world, should have generated so much busywork.

The inside of the office was quiet. Maybe Ian had found some other exit out of the office and left her there. He wasn't trustworthy, was he? That was a defining quality of wizards; they lived in the liminal spaces between worlds, and lost track of this one, capricious and cruel without malicious intent, torn as they were between realities. Sujay wheeled her chair to one side of her desk and saw that the light was still on inside Ian's office, broken by occasional movement.

It shouldn't have been possible to be bored in the Age of Magic, especially not when you yourself were a magician. She should be learning to fly or building cities underwater or opening portals to parallel dimensions, not sitting at a desk, her lower back aching, while her boss attempted to work out a formula to stop what was left of the world from burning to ash.

What if Ian was wrong? What if the answers didn't lie in politics at all, and he'd clawed himself up to the top of a garbage pile merely to look over the edge and realize where, at long last, he was really standing?

There was a small envelope sitting on her desk, under a pile of papers that she must have dumped on top of it without looking. Inside, there was a sympathy card, with the *for your loss* scratched out under *Sorry* and replaced with *you got racially profiled*. Sujay snorted and opened it.

It was a scene from the latest episode of *Night Beats*, the moment where Lilith had leaned in close to Jane, her crimson lips parting, still dripping with the werewolf's blood. On the show, she'd been staked from behind before she could speak, but this was a different version, the lighting slightly different, and seconds before dissolving into ash, Lilith whispered, "I love you."

Sujay was jerked back to alertness by white-blue light, the burn of recognition that grabbed and shook each cell in her body, vibrating at a retina-obliterating wavelength. Sujay had never managed to disabuse herself of the notion that the lightshow ought to have been prolonged and graceful. Magic should have involved more wand-waving and less paperwork, should have been alchemical potions and dusty workshops and not spreadsheets and asbestos-laden offices. She'd never witnessed the work of Ian's mentor, the great Vasai Singh, but Ian's output tended to be awkward and sputtering, a current shared between two stripped-down wires and held together by duct tape and force of will. And he was among the most powerful magicians alive. Sujay's power was a wet match that sometimes, if she was lucky, generated a whiff of sulphur.

The rule, as unshakeable as any drafted in Parliament itself, was that Ian, once trapped in the maze of possible worlds, was never, under pain of death, to be interrupted. She had, like any human with a general interest in remaining fenestrated, obeyed it faithfully. But the light cut abruptly, and she heard the unmistakable sound of a fist hitting a desk, the silence following long enough that she gathered the courage to knock. When there was no response, she convinced herself that it was worth the inevitable verbal lashing she'd receive to enter unbidden.

She opened the door, not to a massacre, but a weary, de-oxygenated silence. Ian was a desiccated twig in his oversized leather armchair. Sujay's glamour was already fizzling out at the edges, clinging to the parts of him that she could remember the best, his irises, his mouth, the shock of red hair that curled over his forehead. The rest had faded to grey, his own magic devouring him from inside. There was only enough saturation left in him that the bruise-dark circles around his eyes were purple, not charcoal. If she glanced at him out of the corner of her vision, she could decipher the outlines of the man as he existed in his own mind. Looking at him directly, she saw a walking corpse.

She was holding him together, and he was holding the country together, and when their empire of spit and cobwebs collapsed, what then?

Paper blanketed the desk, the floor, avalanching over the rim of the waste bin, a crumpled landscape in white broken by the blue rivers of the inked labyrinth. Flickers of magic still turned the air to dry static. Her teeth ached.

"Thanks for the card," Sujay said.

"Thought you'd like it," he said. "They filmed it like that in three possible timelines but instead we got that bullshit episode. The fuck're you still doing here?" There was no accusation, no fire behind his words, just bone-grinding fatigue.

"I thought I could help." Halfway through the sentence, she tried to make it sound like a joke.

"*I* can't help," Ian snapped. "What makes you think *you'd* do any good?" He shook his head, ran bony hands over the paper dunes. "We lose this one," he said. "Every time. Every time*line*. We lost the night Patrice was elected, and every labyrinth looks like someone dumped a bowl of spaghetti on the table, except every time you find the end of the noodle, it's a fuckin' no-confidence vote. Or worse."

"That doesn't make sense."

"'Course it doesn't. I've seen everything, every possible thing but it's like there *were* pathways, there are places where there *should* be pathways, and there just...aren't. Since Alberta." His fingers spidered up to his temples, hung there. "Maybe you *should* give it a try. I can't see shit."

"Like I'm going to—" The sarcasm in her words dipped to sincere before she'd finished the sentence. He meant it. He flipped a memo from the PMO over to the blank side, a ballpoint pen on top of it. She shrugged. "Okay."

Sujay fired up the app, mumbling an explanation as she did. "And it even runs on an old phone," she finished. Hers was about one generation up from Ian's, and only occasionally fizzled out if she was overdoing it on the spell casting. She typed in the series of crystal ball and eyeball emojis.

"Try shutting down the Tar Sands completely. Fuel limits to non-essential industries, driving restrictions, flight taxes, beef taxes, the whole Green Agenda. Throw everything we can to get to zero emissions."

"Just us?" Her finger hovered over the flag emojis.

"It's all we can control."

"You're not seriously thinking about doing this. *Can* we even do this?"

"Call it an experiment." He glanced at her phone. "That app is stealing all of your data."

She focused on casting. Her hands picked up the rhythm as she entered the string of symbols with one, and squeezed on the stress ball—a new one this time, branded with the logo of a real estate office near her apartment—with the other. The Pattern crackled over the synapses in her brain, snaked vapour tendrils over her vision, each bearing the wisp of a possible future. She didn't see them clearly, not the way Ian did, but there were answers in the black smoke. Shadows on the walls of caves, all converging, in the flickering of the firelight, to the same end.

Even in her trance, never so deep nor as vivid as Ian's visions, she sensed his presence at her side, flickering in and out of the corners of her vision. He watched through her eyes as Patrice threw him to a public thirsting for oil and hungry for his blood, as the Opposition steamrollered the country forward into a smog-choked, boiling hellscape. The ground split, collapsing cities to bent origami, and from the core of the world arose the bleached-white spine of a titan that had waited millennia to burst forth.

The surface of the smoke rippled, breathed. The future was cloudy, but she was aware of her own existence in it, of Ian, knife-edge bright and brittle, and below both of their beings, another consciousness, a vast, alien sentience.

She strained to reach out to it. It wanted to enfold her, permeate the folded membrane of her mind, dissolve her. It wanted her to carry it forth into the world. It wanted to consume her. It wanted something beyond the capacity of human reason to comprehend, something deep and impenetrable, and just as it called out to her like the scream of a dying and distant star, the vision of yet-to-come burst into soap-bubble molecules and scattered.

She blinked away the film that had descended over her eyes. Every muscle in her body felt stretched to the thinness of an atom. She'd slid in the chair, bare arms stuck to the leather armrests; she dragged herself, her body leaden, back into the seat.

The remains of her glamour had dissipated. Not just Ian but the office itself had shrunken, shrugged on its framing, cracks erupting across its fading paint.

"You see what I means."

"I didn't see much *voting*." She took off her glasses and pinched the bridge of her nose. She recognized the seed of a migraine, a sharp spike of pressure just below her eyebrow. "Not after a few years, anyway."

"A few—" He shook his head. "What's the deal with the blog, Sujay?"

There was no point in feigning ignorance or pretending there were secrets in her life that she could keep from him. "It's personal."

"You're a charmer, ducky. You don't get *personal*. 'Not Your Chosen One.' Why not?"

A nervous giggle threatening to bubble from her lips, she said, "It was a joke. You know. When I was a kid, and figured out what I am. A wizard, like in all those lame-ass books I read, except I was. Well. The chosen one's always some thin white teenager."

"You're not a teenager?"

"I'm 22."

"Fuck me. Gotta fire you before I have to start paying you decent wages."

"Anyway. That's not me."

"Sure as fuck isn't." He stood up and patted her shoulder. "Go home. I really don't pays you enough to stay late."

If she stayed a little longer, would he tell her what it was that he had seen? Would it shift the probabilities towards a different outcome?

But that was how prognostication worked, wasn't it? Illusion, in so many ways, was straightforward by comparison. You concealed the present, replaced it with a better, brighter vision, a simple swap of outcomes instead of a gnarled rat king of possibilities. Her own magic like a glittering scarf sinking slowly into a murky swamp, she let herself out.

• • •

Jamila, coming off the late shift, was still up when Sujay logged into her laptop. Not for the first time, Sujay longed to be able to confide in her oldest friend, but the magically amped-up NDA pulsed menacingly in her head at her first thought of doing so.

Instead, she pretended to consider otherwise when Jamila asked her if she was coming back to Toronto for Thanksgiving. "Things are busy here," which was vague enough that the geas accepted it without protest.

"Just admit it," Jamila said. Hijab-less, her thick hair tied up in a messy bun at the top of her head, with no makeup and dressed in a red panda onesie, she was sprawled out on her bed, the wall of her bedroom still papered over with boy band posters that had begun cannibalizing it back when they were still middle school co-presidents of the Anime Club. "You think you're too good for Scarberia now."

She should get some posters too, Sujay decided. Maybe not band ones, which were ironic and cool when Jamila did it, but were hardly the mark of a serious politico. She was guessing that most of the junior civil servants decorated with lawn signs and maps, the way people in the riding association used to do. She hadn't actually been over to anyone's place since she'd moved to Ottawa. That couldn't be healthy, or normal.

"I have a *job*," Sujay snitted back. "Also no one calls it Scarberia except you."

Jamila laughed. "You're a whole mood. Seriously, though, your mom said she'll kill you, me, and the Prime Minister if you don't come visit soon."

"In that order?"

"Maybe..."

Sujay shifted the laptop's position in an attempt to make the webcam's pixellated version of her look less flabby and exhausted. It didn't work. "She's full of shit. As long as Anoj the Engineer comes home for dinner, she's happy. By the way, did you know my brother was an engineer?"

"I might have heard. Once or twice. But she does miss you."

"Despite her enduring shame?"

"Well, that *is* how it is." Her voice dropped into a remarkably good approximation of Sujay's mother's accent. "You are a doctor, an engineer, or a disappointment."

Sujay picked up the stuffed unicorn that lived on her nightstand and tossed it at the screen. "Being a professional wizard is just not enough for a brown mother."

"*I* miss you too, you giant weird mutant. I have no one to snark about *Night Beats* with. Did you love Jordan's resurrection?"

Sujay snorted. "As if the writers would have the balls to kill off the white male lead."

"And they did Lilith dirty *again*."

The unfilmed version of the scene was a geas violation too. Jamila would have loved it. "I don't remember the last time I had a normal conversation with someone that wasn't about magic. Or politics. Or the mess it makes when they get smashed together. Everyone in the game is a fucking nutjob." A little voice in the back of her head reminded her that this wasn't politically correct, but Jamila spent too much time trying to extract blood samples from the withered veins of non-compliant drug addicts to care about Sujay's lack of delicacy.

"At least they're better than the Ministry of Health." Jamila sighed, fiddled with the hood of her onesie. "They cut my shifts back at the hospital last week."

"I thought you were already understaffed."

"Exactly. Can't they do something on your end?"

She remembered the bones rising from the shattered earth. "You'd be surprised at the number of things we have zero power over up here. Maybe I should have gone into provincial politics."

"You think there are MAIs hiding in there too?"

"If there are," Sujay said, "they're definitely the Death Eater kind."

Jamila gave an exaggerated shudder, and quickly changed the subject—the completely *ludicrous* mid-season finale of the show they missed hate-watching together, friends from high school neither had managed to keep in touch with, romantic prospects or a pitiful lack thereof. When, half an hour later, Jamila logged off, Sujay found herself sifting for genuine comments among the spam on her long-neglected blog.

Some anon had written: *How do u live with being mai?*

She should delete it. Instead, she wrote: *It's who I am.*

Her laptop pinged again, this time a DM. *U can't do anything dangerous.*

Not unless you count being devastatingly hot as dangerous. Sujay paused before typing, *What can you do?*

Fix everything, her anon typed back. *Gov't's tracking us. We werent meant to have this kind of power.*

Not if I can help it. She paused, then added. *What do you mean, fix everything?*

It was long minutes before her anon replied.

The world isn't worth saving.

• • •

The red stare of the alarm clock slanted in a diagonal blur until she found her glasses. Four am. Fuck.

Ian picked up on the second ring. "What makes you think I was even awake?"

"There's a way out," Sujay said.

"Really." He dragged the word out, the patronizing tone of a father whose child has just handed him a banana and insisted that he answer a call on it.

"You saw it too. More clearly than I did. And it's something bad."

"Go back to sleep, Sujay. It's inappropriate to drunk-dial your boss."

"I'm not—look. It's something bad enough that you don't want anyone else to know. I've been covering up your real face for seven months, don't think I don't know when you're lying."

"I work for the government, Sujay," he said. "I'm *always* lying."

"I can help."

"Yeah." A creak of a chair as he shifted position, the crinkling of paper. Was he still at work? "I needs ya not to."

She reached for the closest stress ball before stopping herself. "Why?"

"Why the fuck do we do this?" His voice dropped to a whisper, though if they were being bugged, it wouldn't make a difference. "Vasai never gave a shit about politics, I don't think she could name her own MP, and she still managed to save millions of lives. I shoulda just adopted a bunch of stray cats, moved to an island somewhere, and sat out the apocalypse."

"You don't mean that."

"I like cats, okay? And they like me, much more than voters do. There was a timeline where that happened. I can't reach it now from any direction but I seen it back when I was a kid."

"How'd that work out?"

Ian laughed. "I died along with everyone else. But I gots to be happy first." The humour drained his voice as swiftly as the colour left his skin when she wasn't around. "Gonna be a lot of blood on a lot of people's hands before we're done diggin' ourselves outta this hole, and I don't want it to be yours."

She pushed back the objections that wanted to surge forward: She was in this game too, not some innocent child that needed to be protected from the consequences of her power. If the outcomes they both were seeing were really so dire, if it was really all Elder Gods and Ebola and catastrophic superstorms, it wasn't like she herself was going to be sheltered from it.

"I'm not just here to make you look pretty," she said. "Even if it *is* practically a full-time job."

"There's no timeline in which I tell you to trust me that you actually do, so I won't bother." She heard him move, envisioned him pacing. How did someone with such a restive temperament manage a desk job? He said, "Maybe you shouldn't do the whole prognostication thing. You think you sleep badly *now*."

"Ian."

"Only way to win," he said, "is to gives 'em exactly what they want. And God help us all."

15

Jonah only caught a glimpse of the SVAR delegation, stranded outside with their black-and-Bluetooth-clad security force. Wedged between two large slabs with froggy frowns, Jonah peeked between the wall and the edge of the door as it swung closed behind the last stragglers to enter. He saw a long conference table, men—mostly men, anyway, mostly white, youngish, some in grey college t-shirts beneath trim black jackets, others in sharp suits. He saw Cal, and Gaby, both doing their best to act like adults when their counterparts were complaining, loudly, that they couldn't find the wifi network.

And you think you want wellspring access.

He returned his attention to his phone. There was no word from Blythe, so he texted her: *Any word from Gaby?*

"I'm sorry sir, this is a closed meeting."

Jonah looked up to see Tobias Fletcher, camera in hand, his micro drone hovering over him like birds around the head of a cartoon character who'd met, unexpectedly, with a brick wall. Fletcher was a big guy, but the two SVAR security goons, each wearing the uniform of a different paramilitary company, dwarfed him. Where did they *find* these people? Were they grown in tanks in some SVAR bioengineering lab?

Lest he be accused of feeding into Tobias' massive ego, Jonah pretended to not have seen him. Blythe's side of the conversation produced a word bubble and the Ellipses of Doom. He watched Tobias out of the corner of his eye while he waited for her response.

She called. Mtg this week.

It'd have to be soon enough. At least something he had done right, if one could categorize Impending Apocalypse as something capable of going right.

"They don't want you in there either?" Tobias asked.

Jonah shrugged. "Insufficiently entrepreneurial and/or elected, I guess. And you? No photos allowed or—what. Just not invited?"

"What's going on in there? Wellspring rights? Sending our MAI to build wards for the SVAR? Arms deal?"

"I have full confidence that there will be a press conference," Jonah said, "when and if there's something to tell the press. In the meantime, I'm sure there are a half-dozen subjects out there prettier than Ian Mallory."

"Not as interesting to my readers, Mr.—"

"Jonah Augustine." He didn't reach out to shake the photographer's hand. "Carbon tax credits, intellectual property. Fucked if I know, but I'm sure it's intensely boring."

"Doesn't sound like much interesting is coming out of there."

"Joys of a minority government."

The quirk at the corner of Tobias' lips said: *Not for long, if I can help it.*

They stood, side by side, in stilted silence. He was aware—at first peripherally, and then, as the quiet stretched on, intensely—of the hum of the micro drone, the wheeze of the ageing and overtaxed central air. The gurgle of the coffee machine. It never failed to amuse him that Ian had replaced every Keurig at every meeting with an old-fashioned Mr. Coffee, owing to the effect his presence had on any Internet Of Things-enabled device. It had to be pissing off the SVAR reps. He measured about five centimetres of progress towards the door with each of the drone's rotations by Tobias' head.

"If you send that demented little toy anywhere near the inside of that conference room," Jonah said, bouncing on the balls of his feet, nowhere near eye-to-eye with his target. "I will shove it so far down your throat that you'll be shitting data feeds."

He expected a more dramatic response, but Tobias merely waved his fingers, indulgent and benevolent, like the Queen acknowledging her audience, and the drone obligingly retreated. Disarmed, Jonah played the one card remaining to him.

"It'll be hours before there's anything to report," he said. "No one will notice if we grab a quick drink."

Tobias actually laughed, probably because like most people, he looked at a guy Jonah's size and probable ethnicity and made assumptions about which of the two of them was likelier to get hammered enough to start spilling state secrets. At the very least, Jonah could keep him distracted—and the drone from eavesdropping—long enough to not interfere with the SVAR talks. It wasn't the out-and-out defeat that Ian probably wanted, but it would buy them all some time.

• • •

"So the Old Man literally has blackmail files on everyone."

Two beers in, and Jonah found himself legitimately *liking* Tobias, which was a bad sign. Had a solid bi-monthly paycheque transformed him into a member of the political elite already? In fairness, Tobias was too bland to dislike, really. He wasn't—or so he claimed—half as right-wing as Ian seemed to think. He'd waffled between parties, mainly voting Liberal in his youth, until the Cascade and its fallout made it such that the old categories no longer applied. He considered himself a centrist, and with a straight face claimed it was hardly his fault that Patrice Abel's populist movement had shifted that centre well into post-revolutionary Russia.

And he seemed to genuinely want to do the right thing. It was unfortunate that the right thing, in his eyes, involved dethroning Patrice and sidelining all MAI, Ian in particular, from any involvement in the political process. And also *sensible budgeting,* which in Jonah's experience, tended to lead to a shortage of affordable housing and a surplus of needlessly dead bodies.

"Most of his material's no good anymore." Tobias was probably three pints away, minimum, from slurring his words, but the beer had loosened his tongue substantially. That was the thing with these chattering class types—politics really *was* a game to them, and so you could sit down and debate the finer points of policy, as long as it stayed within a tidy Francis Fukuyama consensus, as though ideological differences were no more divisive than pineapple on pizza. Every so often, Jonah was rattled at the prospect that he might have been absorbed into the nebulous, pulsing entity that was *One Of Us*, Michif roots and eco-terrorist past be-damned. "Used to be, all you needed was blackmail."

"A live boy or a dead girl," Jonah agreed.

"The thing is," Tobias said, his pint glass landing hard on the coaster for emphasis, "the *real* thing is, is that the right are the real revolutionaries now. They're the ones who want change, ever since the 80s. The political right, the disruptors, the innovators—that's the only place for people with vision—"

"I can't tell," Jonah said, eying the difference between Tobias' glass and his own, and determining the gap was sufficient to take another sip. "Are you talking about the Republic of Gilead in the South or the Randroid SVAR CEOs currently trying to sell our government on shower heads that sell your biometric data to porno sites?"

"Dude, at least it's an ethos," Tobias quoted. Jonah snickered less at the reference than at how ill-fitting the words sat in Tobias' patrician mouth. "But the *left*, it's even more ideologically bankrupt, isn't it? It's fat trade unionists and your PM licking multinational boots in the hope of a few scraps from the table and a 10-cent hike in the UBI rates. Sharing articles on Facebook about how the next generation will vote in a socialist, hand-to-God, none of them willing to admit that they lost that fight well before the Berlin Wall fell."

"They *did* vote in a socialist, though. Didn't they?"

"A blip," Tobias said, and Jonah prickled. Just a word, not one he heard often, and now twice in one day. "Patrice is finished next election and we both know it. It'll be back to business as usual. If you can even call him a socialist—his party can't manage to purge its own anti-MAI faction, let alone build a gulag. Because all of them, every single one of his advisors, want a world that isn't ever coming back."

"Isn't that what you want?"

"The difference being," Tobias said. "I've got the balls to fight for it."

"But magic isn't all that different to automation, or globalization. We won't get those good, unionized jobs back, because robots and China, healthcare will have to be subject to market forces, There Is No Alternative, etc., but now *your* guys don't get unlimited growth or rational markets either because the planet has spoken, and because now you have Pandora City and why would someone mechanical-Turk for Amazon and live in a HubHaus when there's a fucking magical city in the sky that's abolished money?"

"Ah, yes. The old 'wizards will save us' routine. Vasai Singh's been dead for over a decade and in her place, what do we have? Your friend Mr. Mallory, harnessing the inexplicable forces of the universe to keep a frontman like Patrice Abel in 24 Sussex?" Tobias propped himself up with one elbow on the sticky bar. Jonah was being studied. He got that a lot, and from more interesting people than Tobias Fletcher. Categorized into one of his own buckets: megalomaniac, idiot, bootlicker, or star-crossed, sincere idealist.

Well, it's not gonna be the last one. Have fun with that.

"What's the deal with the SVAR negotiations?" Tobias asked.

Jonah tugged his phone free, typed, quickly, *Still stall?*, and glanced at the time. He imagined the conference room, the SVAR delegates, some ramrod-straight in their seats, girdled by generations of inherited wealth, others sprawled messily in defiance of their trust funds. Cal, composed and deceptively soft-spoken, two hours a day at the gym stuffed into a Steve Jobs turtleneck, and Ian, a rangy caged wolf restrained from pacing, or snarling, or chewing off anyone's face despite every instinct he had to the contrary. Tobias, amateur detective and broken clock that he was, had stumbled over something that resembled an insight. Jonah understood the necessity of Ian's ritual offerings at the twin altars of compromise and pragmatism, but surely the young anarchist he'd known was chafing inside his grey straitjacket.

"Give me something from the Old Man's blackmail drawer," Jonah parried back.

Tobias rolled his eyes and waved the bartender over. "Another round," he sighed.

• • •

An hour later, Ian finally texted back. *Tech-bros needed potty break. 2 much kombucha. Still w/TF?*

What can I give him?

His screen filled with a string of proposed items, partnerships and tariffs and transfer pricing.

Bore him to death?

Ian texted back a winking smiley face.

"The problem is," Tobias was saying, "the Party's entire grip on power is predicated on the belief that they can control the uncontrollable. You might as well be Venezuela in the 2000s, tossing handouts to the peasants like the price in oil is never going to fluctuate."

"Which is why the SVAR isn't getting what it wants." He rattled off some of the figures Ian had sent; he couldn't see the microdrone, but he had every confidence that he was on the record. "*Your* problem, Toby, is that you can't conceive of anything not being a commodity." He copied and pasted some of the more boring items Ian had sent. "Magic is maybe the one thing in the entire history of man's fucked up relationship with his fellow man that cannot be commodified. What's your email?"

Tobias told him. "You're leaking classified info on the trade deal?"

"Eh."

"Mallory is."

"Quid pro quo, Clarice."

"There's an MAI working for the opposition."

Jonah was proud of his poker face. He suspected it had, however, just failed him.

"I won't tell you who," Tobias said. "They're contract, like Mallory, but actually contract, unlike Mallory. The old guard hates it and the ambitious young wolves consider it a necessary evil. I'm telling you this because I think you can guess where I stand on the matter."

Jonah said, quietly, "Thank you."

"Yes, well." He straightened his tie, glancing down on his phone. "This isn't bad, you know."

"Fast reader."

"I keep up with politics."

A standoff. Jonah's mind helpfully supplied an Ennio Morricone score. They both reached for their wallets, business concluded.

"It's a pity you're in the wrong party," Tobias said.

"It's a pity you're on the wrong side of history," Jonah replied with a bright grin.

• • •

He found Ian again at 10, on a five-minute break from the negotiations, pale and tired and thin amongst the seemingly inexhaustible SVAR people, Sujay's illusion field around him spitting and crackling like a loose live wire. Still, he flashed a V sign with two bony fingers at Jonah's approach.

"It's gonna be days," he said. "And the policy wonks on both sides'll look at it, and the lawyers, and me, obviously. Hundreds of pages of this bullshit. But there's a baseline agreement."

"Cal charmed them?"

"Like I says." The man himself was partially visible through the open door, large hands gesturing at one of the SVAR negotiators. How a guy like that could come to side with the Party, with its half-assed attempts at internal discipline and its background noise of vestigial socialism, was beyond him, but it occasionally had its advantages. "He speaks their language." He snagged a passing staffer by the sleeve: "Get on Gaby," he snapped. "She drafts her bill by tomorrow. Go, *go*."

Jonah sagged into the wall, grateful.

"No idea who the fuck that was. But they're sufficiently scared shitless of me to find the right fucker." He watched the staffer disappear. "Blythe's Elder God blip. Not a complication we need. Especially now."

"Can you, uh—"

Ian's stare was hard, withering. "Sense it."

"Yeah. What's it feel like?"

For a time, Ian didn't answer. He watched, with some apparent interest, the movement in and out of the conference room. The government's and the SVAR's delegates were wary prey animals. Even as a permanent feature at Parliament Hill, eye contact from Ian was enough to send anyone in its blast radius flapping like a flock of startled pigeons.

"Y'know that voice?" Ian asked. "That whispery, constant little voice in the back of your head that tells you it's okay to kick that guy in the balls for talking too loud into his Bluetooth, or makes you want to ram your car into a crowd of pedestrians just to see what it'd be like to commit mass murder?"

Jonah nodded.

"Why the fuck do *you* have that voice? Never mind. Can't say I'm surprised, you'd be a spree killer if you weren't so easily distracted. So it's like that, right, but thousands of 'em. And they're not exactly whisperin' now." He tugged Jonah aside. "This arrangement is just a delay. The SVAR does what they wants, and they wants magic. We needs a controlled burn. Remember that weird skid-Marxist we stayed with at the G20—Damon? He's out by the wellspring spoutin' conspiracy theories. Send what I sent ya to him too."

"Why?"

"To keep an eye on what they do out there."

When a man who can see the future sounds uncertain, it's not because he's questioning the outcome. "Or," Jonah said, "You could just tell me what you're planning."

"For now," Ian replied, "a celebration of the cooperation between this great nation and the cloud of sentient vape smoke in there." He clapped a hand on Jonah's arm. "See you at the party."

• • •

He'd made a mistake by coming here. He was going to be *noticed.*

In his previous lives, whoever he'd been, he'd survived by adopting a certain measure of anonymity. He'd been one of an ever-changing roster of foster kids, another ski-masked face in the reclamation sites. He thought he could count on it here too, with Ian taking up as much space as he did, a klaxon howl of *pay attention to me*, casting a long shadow in which Jonah had always been comfortably invisible. But while he blended in just fine out west, everything about him was glaringly obvious in a room this pasty. It was worse than the anti-pipeline movement with its reversed hierarchy of cool, where his status as an *authentic equity-seeking person* bought him a very limited, very specific measure of infamy.

Here, though, Jonah was nothing but incongruous. Ian, for all his rough manners, still managed to dress impeccably these days and converse on the few policy details that Patrice wasn't trying to keep under wraps. For all that he was loudly working class and *MAI*, he was still white, and despite Patrice's efforts to the contrary, so was the vast majority of Canadian politics and media. Ian deliberately made himself into a spectacle, while Jonah was just trying to get through the evening, knowing that if he didn't at least remain passably sober, he'd have a hard time not upending a plate of cocktail shrimp in the face of the next person to gape at him.

He kept to the periphery as best he could, noting, with some amusement, the fool Eric was making of himself to Tobias Fletcher's pretty wife. She did have a set of pipes on her, and Jonah couldn't have been the first one to wonder what she was doing with a bore like Tobias.

"Hi," Sujay said, his labyrinth tattoo humming a warmth through his shoulder that alerted him to her presence seconds before she appeared. She had been casting some kind of below-the-radar mantle of which he was unreasonably envious, Without it, she'd be just as out of place as he was. She did clean up well, though. The just-short-enough black cocktail dress was much more flattering than the business casual she typically suffered through, and while he was pretty sure that her perfectly winged eyeliner had a touch of MAI glamour to it, he'd have done the same in her place.

He smiled at her. Scrappy political outsiders had to stick together, and for her part, she seemed relieved to have someone to talk to. "Weird party, huh?" she said.

"I think it's normal," Jonah replied. "I think we're the weird ones."

"Fletcher and his boss were totally talking about you." He was about to ask how she'd got close enough to the enemy to overhear, before he realized the immense espionage applications of her magic. God, Ian must *love* that girl. It made him wonder why he was even necessary to whatever elaborate schemes Ian was planning. "Senator Harrison was checking you out too. But it might be for different reasons."

He followed her line of sight to the far-too-cordial parting of the ways between Cal Harrison and Ian, suppressing a shudder of annoyance. The senator wasn't the enemy per se, and he was not *precisely* someone whose day Jonah was getting paid to fuck up. But the Party in its current incarnation was too new an entity to have any official representation in the Red Chamber—even if notable senior officials hadn't been outspoken about their desire to abolish it altogether, and Ian about his urge to put all of them up against the wall—so it wasn't like he was a friend either. Except, as rumour had it, of Ian's. The fucking hypocrite.

Well. And Jonah was bored. So.

Cal's smile, unlike Lucy Fletcher's, was as pleasant and noncommittal directed at Jonah as it had been at Ian, or anyone else. A consummate politician, that one. He'd been some kind of dot-com wunderkind before his knighting as a nonpartisan-but-basically-Liberal appointee, pure of intent and party affiliation, with an Old World affect that would have had him labelled, in the era he should have been born into, a *confirmed bachelor*.

Of course, he was also—if Ian could be believed, and Ian's impressions were seldom wrong—a double-dealer with the political maneuverings of a black mamba and his fingers in so many pies, both private- and public-sector, that he was banned from every bakery on the Hill. That had to be the only reason Ian had carried on a lengthy, and almost entirely discreet, on-and-off affair with him.

Which was to say that Jonah hated him on sight and, so long as whatever inevitable scandal didn't drag Ian down into the muck right alongside him, he awaited the end of Cal's career with some minor anticipation.

"You must be Jonah Augustine." He was aware of Cal giving him the once-over during the obligatory handshake. His grip was steel, but wrapped in a layer of soft skin that spoke of a luxury it felt almost unfair to mock. How had Ian ever managed to fuck him without tearing him to shreds? "I've heard a lot about you."

Jonah bristled. "Nice to meet you too. I think I read a profile of you in *Maclean's*, or maybe it was *The Beaverton* ..." Sujay raised an eyebrow, and he offered a grin of plausible deniability. "I hear you're our man on the inside."

By the bar, an extremely loud software developer, dressed in a loose-fitting graphic t-shirt that made Jonah's neck itch where his tie constrained it, was describing an ayahuasca trip he'd experienced on his last trip to Peru. He was irritating enough to pause their conversation, and Cal—clearly keen to establish that he wasn't that kind of culturally appropriating, nouveau-riche asshole—looked faintly amused before answering Jonah. "I've been a persona non grata in the 1% world for a long time." He turned to Sujay, who'd been trying to do her usual thing of sliding out of notice. "Miss Krishnamurthy. Lovely to see you again."

Enough with the pleasantries, Jonah decided. He was already sick of the fragile foundation of compromises and small talk on which the entire house of cards was built. "So what's this SVAR deal I've heard about, eh? We're letting them move in and set up shop here?"

There was the fire; Cal's eyes narrowed and he moved to block them both off from the rest of the party. "Not here," he hissed.

"Why Senator," Jonah said. "Surely the Opposition wouldn't use a nonpartisan event like this one to eavesdrop on us!"

Whatever else you could say about Cal, he wasn't stupid, and grasped the game immediately: spill top-secret knowledge to both the Opposition and the media, get Cal's old industry buddies stirred up, wait for the lawsuits and injunctions to be filed, delays and more delays, and all of it arm's length away from anyone directly associated with the Party or Ian. *See, I can play the game, even with the bad guys.*

"The tragedy is," Cal was saying, "I *have* seen their proposal, and it's a fascinating theory, it could revolutionize the way we do travel, transport, it could drastically cut down carbon emissions and resource depletion—" He snagged a mini-bruschetta from a passing waiter. "Have you tried these?"

The waiter was already gone, having brushed by both Jonah and Sujay.

"It's technology that *should* exist," Cal continued. "Magic for a better world. Isn't that why we're all here?"

Jonah could name half a dozen reasons why handing over even the smallest component of the armed nuclear warhead that was a wellspring to the SVAR was a terrible idea. The SVAR aimed to monetize anything that could be marketed, and wasn't likely to stay inside the lines of existing treaty arrangements. But there was only one reason that really mattered, and Cal knew it as well as he did.

"At the moment," he said in a low voice, "I'm here to prevent the government from appropriating Indigenous land, and the SVAR from accidentally making demon moose when they start fucking around with forces beyond their understanding. They won't stop at one lab."

"No." Cal had a split second of looking forlorn before noticing the huddle of disloyal opposition across the room, all of them enraptured by Lucy Fletcher's singing. "Look at that. Last of a dying breed, like a dodo married to a passenger pigeon. Something romantic about lost causes, wouldn't you say?"

"No," Jonah replied. "I wouldn't."

"If you'll excuse me." Cal gave a little nod to both of them, and swanned off into the crowd.

"What do you think?" Jonah saw Sujay frowning, worrying shreds of napkin between her fingers enough that they sparked blue. "Bets on whether he fucks up his part in all of this?"

"That's not how it goes," she whispered. "At least, that's not what I saw."

He mapped out the room, all the players, Tobias Fletcher and his drone, Cal, talking to a cluster of men whose fashion sense had never recovered from the death of the dot com bubble, the hapless human sacrifice who'd replaced Gaby Abel as Minister of Trade, set up to fail before he'd even scrambled for the lube to grease the wheels of industry. Pieces on a board for a vastly more complicated game. He could only hope that Ian, at least, knew what he was doing.

"I need a smoke." He was supposed to be keeping an eye on Cal, but Cal seemed more than capable of handling himself.

Sujay caught his sleeve. "Can I join you?"

Her teeth were perfect and whatever perfume she was wearing smelled like cookie dough. "You don't smoke."

"World's ending," she said. "It's probably time for me to acquire some vices."

"In that case." He looped his arm through hers. "Shall we?"

16

Tobias, ever the extrovert, couldn't begrudge Abel's administration a reception for the SVAR delegation.

Oh, sure, a minor terrorist attack had recently rocked the nation and the government got a daily grilling during Question Period about how a fanatic had nearly evaded Ian's prognostication, but the talks had been scheduled well before, and if you started cancelling the very symbols of hemispheric collaboration, the terrorists had already won.

There was nothing like a Hill party to loosen tongues and inhibitions, and Tobias was not the only media figure to happily accept the opportunity. It was one of those protracted cross-aisle parties, a crowd of undifferentiated quasi-urban sophisticates, juggling cocktail napkins burdened with cheese cubes and plastic cups between two hands suddenly rendered insufficient for the task. The SVAR delegation, running on fumes by this point, seemed amused by the old-fashioned nature of the gathering, debating whether or not the Canadians were being ironic. They were more accustomed to electronic music and designer drugs than the crudités and charcuterie of a government at least attempting the pretences of fiscal responsibility.

Reid Curtis rarely ventured out in public these days, but he'd wrangled himself an invite, along with his wife Alycia. She was ensconced in a cluster of fellow wealthy donors, murmuring approvingly at the chamber ensemble she funded. Their ethereal interpretations of Holst over the banquet had provided an impressive, though unsettling, beginning to the evening. Reid prowled the periphery, occasionally stroking his narrow chin or drawing closer to whisper a name, a snippet of information, in Tobias' ear. Tobias half-expected him to start making baseball signals, coded moves, as they coordinated their attack.

All of this fiddling while Rome burned. The AC in the bar was out, and Tobias, sweat-slicked, moved from group to group, all the while pretending that half of his shots weren't of Lucy.

The rules were as follows:

A SVAR representative has transcended the need for alcohol, and stares at the offered champagne as though a barbarian has offered him a horn of mead. Does everyone not have to be awake for yoga before sunrise tomorrow?

A senior minister (a few were in attendance, though he noticed prominent absences, including both of the Abels—Gaby supposedly occupied in meetings and Patrice on a mission to reassure the Chamber of Commerce that he had their best interests at heart during the delicate negotiations with their high-tech frenemies), was restricted to one glass of either wine or champagne. Any more risked the attention of the journalists present, perhaps an exposé about excessive alcohol consumption on the taxpayer's dime.

An established, respectable photojournalist was entitled to two plastic glasses brimming with heady, cheap lager, or a glass of white wine, but not both. The wife of said established, respectable photojournalist, dressed in a Carmen red, curve-hugging dress, slipping to expose one porcelain-pale shoulder, was entitled to drink as much as she damn well pleased. It disarmed her audience—two staffers, one of which he recognized as that irritating young man who followed her around like a puppy dog at bars—enough to laugh at her jokes. Tobias crinkled his empty cup between his fingers.

Tobias felt his age to the bone, the distance between them intensified by the mild buzz of the lager. The men framed her on either side, and if he angled the shot right, her red dress was dramatic against the grey of their suits. Just as well he didn't need to look at their faces. He refused to be jealous of Lucy's youth, of the way that the policy wonk—Eric Greenglass, that was the kid's name—hung off her every word, drinking her in with his ridiculously big brown eyes and crowding her personal space.

Now, a Newfie interloper whose formal title was utterly unrelated to his actual role in the administration, could, and in fact, was expected to, drink as much as anyone else present and then some. But Mallory stuck to orange juice. Tobias was surprised to see him at all. He was famously reclusive despite the column space he occupied, his constant running at the mouth meant to repel rather than attract, and his appearance suggested a distraction, an obligation, or both. He was dutifully circulating around the room—and, if propriety had permitted, Tobias would have loved to set Izzy loose to follow *him*—but always, Tobias noticed, not far from Jonah Augustine, twitchy in a suit that didn't quite fit properly.

Interesting. Jonah watched the room as intently as Tobias did—as closely as Izzy would have—and appeared to be just as conscious of the rules around who got to drink what. For his part, he had a beer, barely touched.

What *was* his deal? He worked for Mallory, but seemed to be outside his sphere of control, which from everything Tobias had heard about the Broom Closet, was an easy ticket to a pink slip and an inglorious exit from the bureaucratic ecosystem. Mallory didn't have friends, and—rumours about various senators and press personalities, some of whom were even present, aside—didn't invite his lovers out into the light.

And what was Mallory's *intern* doing at the party?

"Trouble in Paradise, eh?" Reid's voice was in his ear, glass of wine in hand. He'd broken off from the cluster of the media delegation to the hostile No Man's Land where Tobias found himself. He directed Tobias' attention to where Mallory stood, talking to Senator Calvin Harrison, a tall, austere presence who did not so much look as if he belonged in the room as much as it had been built around him, and to his exact specifications.

"Hmm?"

"You don't know about those two? They used to—" The Old Man's mouth pinched. "At any rate, they're much less friendly these days, but Abel needs the Senate's approval to pass the Climate Migrants bill. And so Mr. Abolish-the-Senate is friends with the ex, at least this evening."

Tobias laughed. "How do you even hear these things?"

"Forty years in the industry, my boy. This is tame; Abel's people will do anything to avoid an outright scandal, and Mallory keeps them all on a tight leash or tosses them on their asses in short order. I remember when it was all shouting matches and blow-jobs in the men's."

"Not you, I hope."

Reid responded with a non-committal "hmmph" and went as though to move on, but hesitated, eyes narrowing on Mallory. "Any progress there?"

"He's a tough nut to crack," Tobias admitted.

"He's good, but so is Cynthia. So are you." He took another sip of his wine, as if to drive his point home. "The floodgates aren't holding, Toby. It's the last days of the empire."

Before Tobias could point out that neither failing floodgates nor the end of empires generally boded well for anyone living through those times, the Old Man had drifted back into his protective cluster, and Tobias put his plastic cup—the *last* one, he promised himself—on someone's tray and moved on to where Lucy was definitely *not* flirting with Eric Greenglass. Just in case, though, he looped a protective arm around her slim waist, felt her lean her head into his shoulder.

"Lucy was just telling us about her opera training," Eric was saying. He had clearly had more than his allotted two glasses.

Lucy demurred. "I'm good enough to teach."

"She was brilliant," Tobias said, belatedly realizing that he should have said *is*, as if her devoted scales, half-heard arias in their living room, were somehow equivalent to her stolen career, and the corners of Lucy's red mouth frowned, just a little.

"Well," she said, "I can't make the air itself sing and vibrate with the Cosmic Pattern of the Universe—" Tobias could actually *hear* the capitalization, "—so what's the point?"

"You can sing for us," Eric said. "Where did those musicians go? They could back you up."

Tobias cringed, but he trusted her. She knew what she was doing. She giggled, "Oh *God*, not *here*."

"Lucy deserves a stage," Tobias said, squeezing her hip. "Backstage admirers, bouquets of flowers."

"I seriously love opera," Eric said, with the passionate conviction of someone who would have owned every one of the Tenors' CDs if he'd been alive in the 1990s. "I mean it."

Lucy laughed again, and moved, possessively, closer to Tobias. She cleared her throat. There was music, somewhere, but the chatter around them was louder. Her lips parted, and after a quick glance to gauge the distance between their cluster and rest of the party, she sang:

Thy hand, Belinda, darkness shades me,
On thy bosom let me rest...

She'd, naturally, played Dido too, the season after Carmen. A voice for tragedy, the brief article, buried in the *McGill Daily*, had said, a promising young virtuoso. Eric was enraptured. Tobias couldn't blame him. Lucy wasn't a wizard; she couldn't sing down the stars, she couldn't make her voice become waves of colour and light, she couldn't stop heartbeats with her vibrato, but she could *sing*.

"That was beautiful," Eric said, and Tobias rammed down the protective urge to *backpfeifen* his *gesicht*.

"Excuse us," Lucy said with a quick, embellished curtsey. Her hand slipped to Tobias', led him into the hallway, with its patterned carpeting that made his eyes swim.

"That man is in love with you," Tobias declared.

"Oh, Toby." She arched up on her toes to kiss him. "Our young Eric is a font of insider knowledge. At least after a few."

He couldn't disguise the relief. "You Jezebel!"

"You're not *jealous*?" Lucy grinned. "Even his own people can't stand him. He's some ambitious little shit, nothing more. But he hears stuff, and he likes me."

"What did he hear?"

"That new guy Mallory has working for him?"

"Jonah Augustine? I met him."

"Guess what he did before? The man was practically an eco-terrorist! And he's one of Mallory's hires—Eric had to go to BC to find him." Tobias was determined not to be petty. At least out loud. "So they know each other. Not from electoral politics."

"That's in itself a story." He kissed the top of her head. "Anything else?"

"Tons, but you have that look in your eyes."

"What look?"

"Like you smell blood."

"Maybe." He was distracted by a glimpse of a thin grey shadow stepping into the men's. "Tell me everything when I get back."

Curious, Tobias thought, how men dropped their guard the second the washroom door was closed. He unzipped two urinals down from Mallory.

"Keep that drone in your pants," Mallory said, not so much as turning to look. "We do piss, ya know. We're—biological organisms."

He'd almost said *human*. Tobias had to admit he'd wondered. "What's this I hear about you hiring a left-wing extremist?"

Mallory condescended to look nonplussed. "I've been called worse."

"You know what I mean. Jonah Augustine?"

Mallory side-eyed Tobias' briefcase on the floor, but Izzy had stayed nestled in its place all night. "Oh, *him*? Old buddy from back in the day.

Needed a job, we had a vacancy, consider it all part of the government's commitment to inclusive hiring practices." A toothy grin; an off-colour joke between two white men standing at urinals. He kept Tobias' gaze longer than he needed to, challenging him to react. "He speaks five languages, the Natives trust him, and with the exception of his lovely ex-wife, he's the smartest person I know. And he's got the one thing you and I are lacking." Mallory zipped up and wandered over to the sinks, scrubbing at his hands until they were red.

"What's that?"

Mallory patted his shoulder. "Faith in his convictions."

"So this isn't a sign that the government is pursuing a radical agenda? Or that you are?"

"No," Mallory said, the very picture of congeniality. "Don't forget to wash your hands."

Tobias stood for a few minutes longer over the sinks to avoid looking like a stalker, then reemerged. He expected to find Mallory already working the crowd, trailed by his usual entourage of friendlier media, podcasters and sycophants. It was the nature of the young to seek novelty, and a generation after the Cascade, someone like that still counted as such, at least in the glacial world of federal politics.

But Mallory was alone, barely visible as a lanky shadow in the anteroom, leaned up against the beige wall, scuffing a polished shoe into the patterned carpet. He gave no indication he'd seen Tobias' approach, but muttered, "Surely you must have someone more newsworthy to harass."

Tobias raised an eyebrow. "I thought we were being nonpartisan tonight."

"Just came out to listen to the music."

He allowed for a few minutes of quiet, the swell of a lone violin, imbued with the same mournful quality as Lucy's singing had possessed. She'd managed to find the musicians after all and convince them to come back for another set. "Purcell," Tobias said. "Wouldn't have thought that was your thing."

"You don't lives the first sixteen years of your life in Newfoundland without pickin' up some musical acumen." Mallory's eyelids fluttered closed at the last flourish of strings. "I plays the fiddle. Tan can put that in her next article if she wants."

"The headline writers would love that. The Devil Went Down to Ottawa."

"The Devil sells subscriptions."

Another thought occurred to him. "Do you—is it a magic thing? The music?"

"You think I'd be wasting my time in politics t'were the case?" He turned, peered into the room where Eric Greenglass was still desperately trying, and failing, to impress Lucy. "Take your wife."

"I'd rather you didn't."

"She has talent. It's not magic, but there. And there she is, the best years of her life slippin' away from her, regaling half-cut civil servants instead of being on stage where she belongs. I'll tells ya somethin', b'y." He wasn't much taller than Tobias, but nevertheless managed to loom over him, their heads nearly touching, conspiratorial. Tobias thought he glimpsed something, a ripple of a fish moving beneath the surface of a river, under his skin. "Wasn't the Cascade that did that to her. It's your beloved free market."

"Even if you're right—"

"I'm always right. It's my fuckin' *thing*, you see." If Tobias hadn't been watching him all night, if he wasn't close enough that if there were alcohol on his breath it would have been obvious, Tobias could have sworn he'd been drinking. He couldn't have been doing lines in the bathroom, not in such a public place as this, he wouldn't have made it into the inner circles of power if he'd ever been that reckless, but there was a wildness to him, a sense that he might come flying apart at a moment's notice. "You really believe that drivel your paper publishes, don't you?"

"If you consider the national desk of the most widely-read paper in the country to be drivel."

"That's the tragedy, isn't it?" Mallory clapped him on the shoulder, then leaned in close. "We just inked a tentative deal, lets the SVAR set up an observation lab near the wellspring in Alberta. They can't touch it, can't transport it anywhere else, can't bring it out of the country, they need to pay a fee to us, and a percentage of any profits coming out of their research has to be reinvested into the closest three reserves. They're working on some miracle bullshit, gonna save us all from climate catastrofucks with floating high-speed rail and reverse-engineering of Vasai Singh's impossible cities. Better hope there's not a spill, though I don't knows how you'd tell a VC from a demon if ya had to spend any amount of time with either."

"I thought you believed in keeping magic in the ground. Not letting the muggles learn how to use it." *And why are you telling me this?*

"Why'd you tell Jonah about the Opposition's pet MAI?"

Struck momentarily silent, Tobias could only move aside as Mallory adjusted his tie in the reflection of the fire extinguisher, straightened the shoulders of his tailored suit jacket, and prepared to head back into the maelstrom. "A man has to have principles," Tobias said finally. "Otherwise, what's the point?"

"All the worse for you. And me. If it were just politics as usual, you'd make a great fuckin' dance partner."

His phone buzzed against his thigh, just as a chorus of vibrations stridulated in an insectile cacophony above the music. Mallory already had his phone out.

Tobias didn't have Izzy out quickly enough to catch the millisecond of shock on Mallory's face. He'd seen it, though. He could swear that something had finally caught Ian Mallory by surprise.

It was his photo on every screen, Mallory in the centre of his spider-web, macilent and bone-pale beneath the fortress of Parliament, the evidence of magical fuckery plain and stark in black and white. Reid, true to form, had waited for the moment he'd deemed sufficiently dramatic to drop it.

Cynthia was somewhere in the crowd, but it was Tobias who got the soundbite on his drone.

"It's a protection spell," Mallory said, daring Tobias to call him a liar.

"Protection from what?" Tobias squeezed out, but the vultures were already descending. Jostled from all sides by the various journalists present, he was positive he was the only one who saw it.

Mallory met the eyes of his intern from across the room. She blinked behind her black-rimmed glasses and lifted a hand that crackled with green static.

Cynthia turned to talk to the man beside her, hands cradling her distended belly. Cellphones slid back into pockets. Several heads in the crowd shook in mild confusion, and the murmur of conversation rose again to fill the spaces social awkwardness had created.

Mallory turned, winked at him, and folded himself back into the crowd.

17

Laura emerged from the school stooped under a backpack, behind the initial flurry of loud, colourful dismissal. At eleven, she was now officially too old to be excited by anything, but she'd yet to don the permanent scorn of a teenager, and so she simply hung back from the noisy crowd, head bowed where she stood in a tight cluster of girls. She exchanged whispers—crushes? commiserations?—before waving goodbye and loping over to where Blythe stood.

One day soon, Blythe thought, if human civilization and the Vancouver Archipelago survived that long, she wouldn't be permitted to stand so close, to hug her daughter and ask her how her day was. Even now, she felt Laura hesitate, the girl's small face lean into her upper arm for a fraction of the time it might have once. Blythe wanted to hold her longer, but Laura was already in motion again, hiking up her schoolbag over one shoulder and fixing her long dark hair over the strap.

A network of bridges, some well-established, others planks of wood where flooding had rendered a regular throughway inconvenient, crisscrossed the patchwork of islands that formed their corner of the archipelago. Some were art installations, precariously employed makers and troublemakers trying to one-up each other with materials, stability, structure. Elegant bridges of curlicued wood pillaged from old furniture, organic sloping adobe bridges that housed potted flowers and gemstone inlays, punk rock bridges of milk crates and old bicycles. Others were functional, or slapdash, cutting across pathways that drew foot traffic like ancient ley lines. It seemed like every week there were more of them. There had been a semi-serious motion before City Council last year to give up on flood mitigation altogether and turn downtown Vancouver into the Venice of the North, navigated by gondolas and kayaks.

Blythe and Jonah had both agreed that it was a *badass* idea. That was the only thing they'd agreed about in six months.

"How was school?" Blythe tried.

"Boring." Laura walked faster. She'd end up with Blythe's height, but Jonah's restlessness.

It might have been a conversation-ender—for all of her own shitty experiences at school, Blythe would have never admitted to *boredom*—but Laura halted abruptly by one of the new bridges, this one purely utilitarian, just three wooden pallets lashed together with thick rope and staked into the mud. "What's the point about learning history if Dread Cthulhu's just gonna rise and devour us all?"

Blythe blinked. That combination of geekiness and fatalism came from both of them, the unfortunate but inevitable byproduct of growing up with activist parents, but how was she supposed to explain the End-of-Days-That-Wasn't to a child? She'd never quite come to grips with the vagaries of being the responsible one. She had a doctorate, for fuck's sake, a tenure-track position in the shrinking academic employment market, but the gritty details of motherhood eluded her. She knew, in a vague sort of way, that being a grown-up had something to do with putting food in the fridge and cleaning one's house to a standard that CAS didn't take one's kid away, making your rent payments regularly and, somewhere in one's apartment, owning a plastic bag stuffed to overflowing with other plastic bags, preserved for some obscure future necessity. But reassuringly explaining, in kid-friendly language, climate genocide and the rise of ancient, unfathomable forces, their alien brains indifferent to human suffering, that was something they didn't exactly cover in *What To Expect When You're Expecting.*

When the Cascade had rolled over them, nature and humans malleable and fragile in its wake, Blythe had never imagined living long enough herself to keep another person alive and sane.

"Where'd you hear that?" she asked.

"You," Laura said. "Edgar. Talking about tentacled horrors from the deep sea. You know our walls are made out of cardboard, right?"

Her brain jumped a track into Teachable Moment mode. "First off, Cthulhu has arms, not tentacles—you can tell by the suckers—and the thing I saw had bony structures that you wouldn't see in a cephalopod, and also Lovecraft is racist garbage anyway so I don't see why he gets to be considered an authority on anything."

Laura picked up the end of the rope and turned it over in her hand, picking at the frayed edges.

"But we are in trouble. Like, the whole world is in trouble."

"It's not because of the Elder Gods," Blythe said. "It's because of us. And if some people—" She gave Laura's shoulder a playful shove. "—had paid more attention in history class, maybe we wouldn't be in a situation where we had to deal with waking forces beyond our understanding."

Laura groaned and rolled her eyes. "You don't need to hide stuff from me," she said. "Or from anyone. I watch the news too. And they're saying it's probably Cascade 2.0. That's why the government keeps calling, isn't it?"

"Even if it is," Blythe picked her way around the words carefully, treading as lightly as she did over the questionable bridge. "It doesn't mean that everything is hopeless."

She wondered, sometimes, whether she had done the right thing in bringing Laura here, whether she'd done the right thing by any of them. Maybe she should have sent the girl back to Manitoba to spend time with her kookum, on the land, to gain some perspective. Jonah had been adamant that their daughter not grow up as disconnected from their heritage as he had been. They installed an app on her phone to help her learn Michif and Cree words, but she was still away from her people, caught up just as surely in the colonialist net, just as lost and fucked up as the rest of them with the world cracking and shifting under her feet.

And family aside, the land aside, Laura would be safer where it was landlocked. When the Earth bucked up to throw humanity off her back, what civilization remained would compress inward, take refuge on the high ground, huddle together on the plains.

Blythe resolved to have that conversation later.

Their normal afterschool routine was to go to the university so that Laura could work on her homework while Blythe and Edgar pretended to review the latest round of temperature readings, a thin veneer over their attempts to reconstruct an image of the creature from scratchy video and Blythe's half-dazed recollections. The bridges ended well before campus, the result of the Engineering and Environmental Faculties collaborating on a complicated flood mitigation system. The quad was soggier than usual, patches of yellow grass soaked in brown puddles, but the walkways were clear, and the basement archives were so far unbreached, despite being housed in a building more suited for the sunny California of the pre-Cascade era than for an island doomed to eventually sink into the ocean.

"Professor Augustine!"

There was a young woman running towards her, weaving between the scattered signs reminding students to stay on the paths and refrain from unauthorized gardening activities. She was one of the first-year kinesiology students who made up the bulk of Blythe's Intro to Environmental Science class. After a while, she'd learned how to spot them—tall, slim, honey-blonde, salt and sunburn wrapped up in pink Lululemon and possessing a level of enthusiasm that Blythe frankly found exhausting. Still, they were encouraged to fill out the Environmental Science classes to avoid it becoming dominated by arts majors who thought they were taking the easy way out with their mandatory science credit.

"Oh my *God*, is that your kid?" The girl—Cosette? Colleen? Something like that—stooped to be at eye-level with Laura. "Hey, what's your name?"

Laura told her, and Blythe was spared from the cringe moment of forgetting one of her 150 students' names. "I'm Colette." She kept talking, asking Laura the same flurry of inane questions adults always seemed to ask children, and Blythe normally would have tuned her out, allowed her outgoing daughter to take over the conversation—if her tattoo hadn't chosen that moment to prickle, as if the black lines delineating the labyrinth had each been poked in series by a fine needle, lightly, just enough to be there.

"You're an MAI," Blythe blurted. She immediately regretted it—it was entirely possible that Colette wanted to keep a low profile. That she might not even *know*.

Colette seemed unfazed, though. "That's what I wanted to ask you about, actually. I was thinking of switching my major. I want to look at environmental predeterminates for MAI and I'm wondering if your department might be into that. Or maybe Bio. Basically I just need some advice." Her voice dropped to just above a whisper. "I want to know what I am. *Why* I am."

Blythe had met two MAI in her life, which was more than most people, statistically speaking. Both were weirdos, but it didn't necessarily follow that *every* MAI was a weirdo. This one was *too* normal, even if she was making a valiant attempt at a regular person's life. Probably she secretly spent her weekends LARPing, or had a collection of mummified toes in her basement. Being an MAI made for unavoidable psychological damage, unless it was true that the younger generation was growing more tolerant. "I'll email you some papers," Blythe said. "There's a prof out of Delhi who's doing some interesting work." She struggled to remember what the girl's grades were like. Regardless, wading through K. Bharadwaj's jargon-laden studies would separate the committed from the drains on her time. She was definitely enthusiastic—Blythe remembered that much. Colette was the sort of kid who asked about dissection on the first day of Bio instead of trying to find an escape route. "But the nerds are always happy to poach students from the jocks."

"Awesome. Thank you *so* much." You would think Blythe had offered her a winning lottery ticket and a pony, not a low-key insult and a half-assed invitation to more work in a more rigorous program, but it was flattering to see a student excited about one's subject. "Sorry, you look like you're on your way somewhere. Nice meeting you, Laura!"

Blythe rubbed at her shoulder. Colette had run off before she could respond, her sneakers slapping a receding rhythm into the wet grass, the memento of her presence flickering in needle-bright sparks before fading to nothing.

• • •

Edgar hunched over the computer, switching windows when he saw Blythe at the door from the modelling charts to the data that the *Martha L. Black* had sent when it passed over the rift a few days ago.

The 3D rendering was still a work in progress. The conflicting measurements from Blythe's far too up close and personal encounter and the garbled readings from the bathyscaphe didn't help. In the days since, the readings had suggested that the chasm itself had shifted position, that it had widened, that it had ceased to exist altogether. Nothing suggested the presence of a living creature, or the corpse of one, immeasurably massive, and somehow possessed of the ability to induce brain damage by looking at it.

Which didn't mean it wasn't there. Video feeds didn't lie, and even if Blythe's eyewitness account wasn't satisfactory to the team, there was the issue of Dahlia, comatose after a month. Even if scientific curiosity didn't drive them towards understanding the thing, a desire to avenge their colleague would have.

So far, they had reconstructed an appendage. Unless it was a snake and the bit Blythe had seen was the spine, but the irregular readings from the ocean floor suggested there was more of it buried under the rock. Here, her own memories had proved more useful than the video footage, which somehow suggested multiple positions in space, despite her insistence that it hadn't moved.

Edgar rotated the map of the ocean floor's topography, the overlapping shapes where the chasm might have been. "This doesn't make sense. Even if it's alive—"

It is. Blythe knew it, but she and Edgar were both bound to the same evidentiary principles, as impotent and meaningless as they seemed. She couldn't throw assertions around. Not without proof—and that meant going back.

"—even if, that wouldn't change the *topography* of the ocean floor from one pass to the next. It's in the middle of a tectonic plate."

"Non-Euclidian topography!" Laura called out from behind Blythe's laptop.

Edgar raised an eyebrow.

"I don't know where she gets this shit either," Blythe muttered. "Probably her dad."

"Still, it's remarkable. For something so large and complex to have adapted to the crushing pressure of the deepest parts of the ocean..."

"Eh," Blythe said. "Same. It's not such a big accomplishment." Edgar snorted. She flipped the chair around and draped over it, one leg on either side, watching over his shoulder as he rotated the rendering on the screen. "So the creature—" Dammit, she wanted a better word, and she was under *no fucking circumstances* going to call it Dread Cthulhu. "—doesn't move, but the ground does. Cool."

"Well, we already knew it was a magic thing."

At least it was a diversion from the more urgent matter—the uptick in temperature readings around the area. The video conferences with Gaby and phone calls with Jonah had her up at strange hours, blurring the days and nights together until she had to set reminders for everything—drop offs and pick ups for Laura, lectures, department meetings. She ought to have been grateful for a government that, while flailing for purchase itself, was at least taking the threat seriously, but how could anything swim through the thick stew of bureaucracy that weighed down every decisive action? By the time they got around to *doing* anything, the world would be neck deep in melted ice caps and unblinking cosmic horror.

"It could be kaiju," Laura said, and Blythe had to wonder where, exactly, her parenting went wrong that her kid had come up with Lovecraft before Godzilla.

"She's got a point," Blythe said. "We've found abnormal levels of carbon-14 in amphipods in the hadal trenches. Thanks, US military industrial-complex!"

"Whatever it is, it manages to cause seaquakes and shift reality when it's dormant." Edgar closed the window, bringing back the temperature modelling graphs. "I'd hate to see what it does when it's awake."

"Hey," Blythe dug into her purse and retrieved a twenty and spun her chair backwards to where Laura was pretending to do homework. "Can you grab us some tea from the cafeteria? And get yourself something too."

Laura hesitated, but the thought of—presumably—a usually-forbidden chocolate bar proved to be too great a temptation. The moment she was out the door, Edgar looked at the charts. They were the culmination of last week's readings.

"Cthulhu, or Gezora, or whatever this is, might end up being the least of our concerns. How long?"

They were her own numbers, and she was as familiar with the trajectory of their lines as she was with the thin white network of scars on her palms, the goddamned labyrinth on her shoulder. "Six months," she said. "Maybe a year, if we're lucky." She tracked the trajectory with the cursor. "Gaby Abel's taking it to the UN in a few days. Hoping that the Cascade 2.0 is sexier than climate apocalypse is, I guess."

They'd gone through this before, Edgar, as endearingly apolitical as a scientist could be in this day and age, failing to understand how, when they had finally won a seat at the table, when Blythe's own ex-husband was a privileged advisor to the PM, when the government made all the right sympathetic noises, none of it ended up mattering. How they were just one country, not even a proper superpower, and despite the eroded shorelines, the baking supersummers, they had been insulated. They'd lived fat off the droughts throughout the former US, the high prices of wheat, they'd lost ice-wine but gained kiwis and bananas, while other places burned and scowled, wondering why they were the ones who needed to pay the price. How it didn't matter who sat on the *môniyâwak* throne in their palace built over blood and bone and ashes. They did not live in a democracy equipped to handle catastrophe.

He brought up a new window. "If you can get this to her..."

She hated that, for a split second, she thought he was going to offer some way out. Instead, it was just that document she'd seen circulating around the department. Most of her colleagues had put their mark on it at some point over the past few months, and she'd read a previous iteration aloud at Dahlia's bedside, because you were supposed to talk to comatose people, and that was what she'd had on her. It had a long, dry title, conspicuously avoiding her own research team's goofy acronym, that, like every climate change report, failed to capture the urgency. Maybe that's why they'd been ignored for so long. Her lab mates on the Research on Lakes and the SalinitY Ecosystem and Hydrography team, who should have never been allowed to name *anything*, were calling it the Blight Report.

Blythe supposed, in a sense, it *was* a way out. Just not a very palatable one. It was a last-ditch attempt to avoid the feedback loop that had triggered the first Cascade, that oozed out of the ground and reshaped the world, had turned forest to shriekgrass, men to demons and sorcerers, the dress rehearsal for the cataclysms to come.

There were other ways, of course. Longer ways. They could have transitioned to cleaner energy, stopped flying, contracted suburban sprawl into dense cities, stopped eating meat and using so much plastic, hell, they could have shut down a hundred companies and slowed the march to oblivion. They could have truly, genuinely decolonized. They could have taken the slow road, and rebuilt from the ruins of the old world. That was the future that she'd fought for, once, all the while knowing how unlikely it was to happen. Plan Zero was in the paper too—two roads out, one sustainable, one undeniably dystopian.

Her department was reluctantly proposing taking the same magitech hybrid that the SVAR was currently trying to harness for transport and turning it upwards, creating a net of shade to block out the sun. It was the kind of thing that got proposed every so often, and rejected, for good reason. It was a quick fix that everyone secretly hoped would be non-permanent and knew could never be.

"Great," Blythe said. "Yog Sothothery with a side-order of *The Matrix*. That's even assuming that Cascade 1.0 was caused by what we think did it, and that we're not seeing a radioactive kaiju that's just waiting for the cover of permanent night to attack."

"So it *is* radioactive kaiju." Laura had come up behind them so quietly that Blythe startled. She deposited a cup of tea in front of each of them. "Knew it."

"No one's saying that," Blythe said.

"I'm saying that. Five bucks says it is."

Edgar continued, not as if Blythe's 11-year-old daughter wasn't there, but as if she was one of them, privy to humanity's bleak choices. He claimed to be one of those no-future, no-kids types, though she suspected it was less because of a conscious choice and more because of a singleminded focus on his work that tended to prematurely end his relationships. "The Minister should know all the options. And don't think that the SVAR isn't working on something like this already."

What kind of mother *was* she? Talking casually with her team leader about blotting out the sun in front of her kid. Though if they did nothing, the lifetime of nightmares would be the least of Laura's concerns.

"The Opposition is making noises about a snap election," Blythe mused. She would have bet that five bucks that the political ramifications of Gaby Abel proposing either plan in front of the UN were not anything that had crossed Edgar's mind. "And something like this—no one's going to like it. We could end up with a much more hostile government."

"It's a window," he replied. "We won't get many more of them."

She nodded, pressing the heel of her palm into her forehead. She'd been getting migraines, on and off, ever since the dive.

"I could go down again," she said, far too quickly. "I think—I might have met someone who could replace Celene."

"Mom, *no*."

"We should understand what we're dealing with." There was no way anyone was getting back into the *Love Craft*, not with what had happened to Dahlia, not with everyone looking at her like she had an Old One nattering in the back of her skull, compelling her back into the ocean for motives far murkier than saving the planet or getting her name in some esteemed journal.

Even as she said it, she could see the future spread out before her, stark as a corpse waiting to be autopsied. They'd had a quarter century to adapt to the Earth's last-ditch warning system. They'd had longer—even if it wasn't *this* apocalypse, they'd known an apocalypse was coming. They'd held conferences, given tax incentives to green companies, fiddled even as their house was burning down around them.

"It's another report," Blythe said. "They've seen a lot of reports. What's changed?"

"You," Edgar said. "You've got the ear of the people around the table."

And the people around the table have a clairvoyant. Who would know exactly what following her team's advice would mean for their government. She was geased to secrecy, like anyone who'd had a window into Ian's process, so it wasn't like she could tell Edgar that Ian had likely already seen every possible outcome. Had no doubt watched her deliberation as she weighed which option to put her endorsement behind. She hadn't seen Ian in years, had only Jonah's rose-tinted assessment of where his loyalties might lie these days to go on.

"Honestly?" Blythe said. "I'd rather take my chances with Cthulhu." But there was Laura, spinning slow circles from a sugar high in her chair, a rim of half-eaten slave labour chocolate around her lips. Either way, her world would be unrecognizable from the world Blythe had known. Blythe nodded, slowly. “I’ll make sure it gets to them. I can’t be responsible for what they do with it.”

She could only hope that the ocean would have enough patience to wait.

18

Tobias followed Cynthia to Alberta for her piece on SVAR's project at the newly developed wellspring. The science desk had vanished during the last round of cutbacks, and besides, one couldn't separate business and politics from the grinding back-and-forth of human ingenuity and progress. She researched, and he watched the fallout from his photo unfold, far away from the action.

He had Mallory on the ropes. Well, the *Post* did, but his purpose and Reid Curtis' were one and the same. The chattering class generated thinkpieces about it so quickly that Tobias suspected they'd had the bare bones of it stashed away already, waiting for such an occasion. Everyone—everyone who wasn't Patrice Abel, and the out-of-his-depth Ansel Graves—was itching to make magic *the* issue of the snap election.

They just needed one more push. Like, for example, a semi-legal R&D adventure carried out under the government's nose.

Most of the specs Cynthia had received from the project were redacted, available only to the engineers and project managers under a detailed, though non-magical, NDA. They'd written a pre-approved press release and supplied some infographics that could, along with some firsthand interviews, probably be padded out into something resembling objective journalism. The SVAR people *did* have quite the inflated sense of their own intelligence. Still, if they pulled it off, maybe there'd be no need for the pre-flight guilt session reciting the plane's estimated carbon emissions.

The whole affair was tangled, and cheeky. The SVAR people were caught up in a regulatory nightmare of injunctions and delays, a veritable mummy of red tape and pending lawsuits that had Senator Cal Harrison's fingerprints all over it. And true to their ethos of disruption, they'd simply cut through the Gordian Knot and started to build the damned thing anyway, regulations and permits aside, while the vast apparatus of the federal bureaucracy lumbered after them like a drunken bear.

Well. That was what happened when your scientific research wasn't almost wholly dependent on government funding. If the project hadn't been infinitely more dangerous than ridesharing or short-term rentals, Tobias might have appreciated the nimble virtues of the private sector.

With time to kill and Cynthia occupied with interviews, Tobias sat outside of the airport, waiting for the bus out to the new suburb. Two elderly Native men were smoking. He'd quit years ago, but the smell remained alluring, his one caveat to youthful rebellion. It was also high-octane SVAR-repellant; the health nuts stood well upwind, and given that he was about to spend several days on site with them, he could use the reprieve.

The men watched in quiet amusement as the bare-armed SVAR engineers slapped at the midge swarm that had eagerly descended on them. For all their differences, there was still nothing funnier than a hapless American wobbling headfirst into the tail end of a Prairie supersummer.

Eventually, the one with the drooping moustache muttered something inaudible to the other, then glanced over at Tobias.

"You're not gonna get a quote."

Was it that obvious? "She's the reporter," Tobias said lightly. "I'm just enjoying the diesel fumes. You guys heading north?"

"Back to the rez." He jerked his head towards his companion, thin and drawn under a Harley Davidson bandana. Those deep lines in his face would read well on film. "Cancer treatment's done."

"Good news?" Tobias asked the other man.

"Done news." He took a long drag off his cigarette. The SVAR guys seemed impossibly young, their very vitality an act of cruelty. "You with those assholes?"

"I'm documenting the wellspring project." He had one business card, which he waved limply in front of them, not sure which man to give it to. Harley snatched it out from between his fingers.

"Hah. Glad I'm not gonna be around to see that shit when it goes up in smoke."

Tobias wasn't sure that pure magic was combustible, but he understood their heartfelt desire not to find out. "I thought part of the proceeds were supposed to go to your communities."

"Believe that when I see it," Moustache said. "You think this government's gonna keep its word?"

"When have they ever?" Harley chimed in. He was distracted, momentarily, by the torrent of swearing from the SVAR guys. "Leave it to whites to poke a goddamn stick at something they don't know shit about."

Tobias listened to them banter, wishing he could switch on Izzy for even a few choice comments, if only to put a tarnish on the thin veneer of community consultations and responsibility. Somehow, he didn't think the men would be particularly happy to be part of that story. Their conversation lapsed back into inside jokes cultivated over decades, into the kind of silence that spoke of long understandings and lifetimes spent somewhere small and isolated, buffered against the shifting tides of the last two decades.

He wished Harley luck as their bus pulled into the station.

• • •

Everyone is dying to see a wellspring, until they aren't.

"I'm going to puke," Cynthia said.

"I brought Gravol," Tobias offered, and she practically snatched it out of his hand.

"Don't know what I'd do without you, Fletcher." She dry swallowed the pills, smacking her palm against her mouth. "Think *they* came prepared?"

Watching the SVAR people, Tobias doubted it. They might have fancied themselves magitech innovators and disruptors, pioneers for a new age, but they underestimated human biology. And humanity, in the presence of magic, was at best uncomfortable and at worse, pitifully frail.

Tobias felt ill half a kilometre from the site. Gravol helped with the nausea—he'd heard that coca tea was more effective—but judging from the frequency with which some of them were running to the bus's sole bathroom, he was right that none of them had thought to bring any. By the time they pulled up to the camp, the smell was worse than the disorientation and the dizziness, nearly as bad as the tinnitus ringing in his ears.

The camp had cannibalized the construction site over a matter of weeks. An air-supported dome rose, a pale moon between the black stems of the tall pines. Closer to the road, the trailers where scientists and engineers lived and worked lined up at the edge of the site, large drums of drinking water barricading the tires. *Bad idea, if something goes wrong, they'll need to leave quickly.* It was a half-hour drive to the closest grocery store, but most of them lived off Soylent shakes and one or two were hard at work beta-testing a food replacement pill.

Wooden walkways crisscrossed the encampment, joining the trailers and the dome. He watched as figures in white hazmat suits awkwardly passed each other on the narrow beams in slow motion, like astronauts navigating a clumsy spacewalk. At first it made no sense—if anything, the prairies were bone-dry. Then he saw patches of pale lilac shriekgrass sprouting up through the parched earth, and realized that the susurrus wasn't inside his own head, but all around them. The moans and sighs were the plants as they grappled their way upwards from the soil. He worried Izzy free from its case and reactivating the Bluetooth, then yelped as the drone *stung* him.

One of the engineers—a woman, of which there were only four in a camp housing about 50 people—laughed at him. "Good luck with that. *Nothing* works properly here. They're using tape recorders and floppy disks."

Cynthia introduced them both as Tobias fumbled to retrieve his Leica.

"Emmeline Allaway," the woman said. "C'mon, I'll show you around."

• • •

Tobias' career began well before the commercial availability of micro drones—before, in fact, the pivot to video that had decimated journalism and necessitated the considerable-at-the-time investment in Izzy in the first place. He preferred the Leica anyway. It wouldn't do the sweeping overheads that Izzy got, but that was what happened when you sent your team into shriekgrass-plagued thin places amid an anthill of tech bros given a shiny new toy to play with.

Everyone in the camp was obviously extremely excited about whatever experiments they were running. None of them slept more than four hours a night. It was a point of pride to be able to hack one's circadian rhythms, which meant that Tobias and Cynthia, ordinary, non-bio-optimized humans, were constantly playing catch up in the midst of their technobabble.

At least he'd brought the Gravol. It made them both a number of friends. The camp was half a kilometre from the wellspring, the samples under the dome sourced from a trickle that had surfaced closer to the main road. But the site was close enough that the effects of magic, coupled with sleep deprivation, took their toll almost immediately. It manifested in different ways for everyone, but nausea was common, hallucinations only slightly less so, disorientation omnipresent. There was the paranoia that they were being watched, by the wellspring, by the trees themselves. It spoke to the determination, and consciousnesses frequently altered by more mundane means, of the team that none of it really slowed them down.

The experiments were confined to the dome, but they were permitted a ringside seat to a steampunk carnival. It was a dream job. Most of them were keen to tell Cynthia all about their various projects—what happened when you fuelled an internal combustion engine with magic? Applied it to the cathode of a Nixie tube?—the rare interview subjects who might actually talk too much. He was just as busy, documenting the team at work, the faces of the men and women inventing the future.

There was no safe way to work with magic. What he could see of it was silvery-blue, not unlike the sparks he'd seen Ian Mallory give off, a liquid that refused the usual rules of fluid dynamics, contained to the extent that was possible in iron-lined containers. They should have been more nervous, but what was caution compared to making history?

Five days, and one breakthrough, assuming the Leica could repeat its magic. And then the bus would return, and he would be on his way back to Lucy.

• • •

His fourth night at the camp was spent in what Emmeline dubbed the Party Trailer, a neon-lit haven of nerd paraphernalia that reeked of flavoured vape juice and marijuana. Cynthia had gone to bed, pleading pregnancy, leaving Tobias on his own to hopefully catch a miracle shot. He was offered several varieties of exotic chemicals as soon as he ducked through the low doorway into a raucous Ayn Rand utopia of loud-mouthed eggheads cordially one-upping each other.

"Don't mind them," Emmeline said. "That's their way of being friendly."

All drugs were legal in the SVAR; a libertine attitude to mind-altering substances had been one of their main points of contention during CalExit, but it still shocked him that serious professionals, the very people tasked with handling one of the most dangerous substances known to man, in proximity to a wellspring that had already proven itself eager to fuck with everyone's head, were spending their downtime microdosing LSD. Not to mention how they'd managed to get so many drugs into the country, but he supposed that was what the hazardous substance containers were for.

His was merely to report, not to judge. Tobias took a seat beside Emmeline, under a sign that warned, "Do not look at laser with remaining eye."

"Does it shock you?" she asked.

Tobias shrugged. "I went to university." A mechanical spider scuttled across the table, its body a serving platter holding a colourful assortment of pills. *Snap.* "Not Burning Man, admittedly. But I'm not as—"

"Uptight?"

"—straight laced as I look."

He spotted a few of SVAR's best and brightest that he'd met earlier in the day: Avery, who was working on the primary transport project, Fionn, who was on containment and fuel cells, Gavin, who was working on fuck knew what, but seemed to be supplying the camp with much of its hallucinogenic cocktail. He accepted a beer that came in a can, wary of so much as pouring it into a glass, and they sat on embroidered poufs, watching the spider move gracefully from one group to the next.

"What are *you* doing here?" he asked Emmeline.

"Same as everyone else." She took a drink of something that was in a wine glass, but was Midori-green with a wave of smoke coiling off the surface. "Solve the world's problems, and get rich on the way."

"Everyone talks like the Cascade is the beginning of the end," Fionn chimed in. "When what they're not seeing is the opportunity for innovation. A real paradigm shift, you know? Humanity 2.0."

Just when he'd been starting to like them, too.

"I was ten when Pandora City went up," Gavin said. Smoke curled around him, strawberry-scented wisps and eddies that blurred his features into an Impressionist painting. "Blew my fucking mind. All of those billions poured into contingency planning and one little Indian granny waves her hand and suddenly—bam. Problem solved."

"But people still died." Tobias took notes as he spoke, looking up every so often at faces outlined in pink and blue stripes of light. "Nothing Singh did fixed the crisis. We're still going to lose most coastal cities in the next few decades, and now she's not around to raise them anymore." *Including yours*, he didn't add. He was sure they had a plan for that; seasteading communities in the Pacific had laid the foundations for new floating cities, though the fragile new outgrowths had yet to work out a solution for the occasional tsunami or earthquake.

"People always die," Emmeline said. Far too casually. "Humanity endures."

Her pupils blown wide, laughing, drunk and high, she tried to kiss him on the walk back to his trailer. Gently, he put a hand on each of her shoulders, steered her away from him towards her own trailer. "I'm a married man."

"Do you know," she whispered. "I can see the future."

Tired enough to humour her, he said, "What do you see?"

"It changes. Everything changes. The ground shifts from under us, and only the tenacious adapt and survive. A gig economy for evolution. Bright and fierce and cruel."

"I don't think that's the kind of world I want to live in," Tobias said.

"Maybe you won't have to. 'Night, Toby." Her fingers twined with his for just a second before she danced away, into the fog-laced night.

• • •

He woke to cold, the tip of his nose frozen, a sensation that recalled early July camping trips, his boyhood before the Cascade had tipped the climate into its current death-spiral. It was late, or early—he glanced at a watch on the folding plastic table by his cot that had stopped at 4:02 am, unsure whether that was the actual time or not. The camp was silent, and at first he didn't realize the incongruity, didn't notice that the thing that was missing was the sound of human voices, of laughter, of footsteps. Only the wind-rush of shriekgrass, the distant screaming of life born and extinguished in pain, broke through the stillness.

Tobias dressed quickly, sliding on the uniform of jeans and polo shirt (he wouldn't resort to a t-shirt on the job, no matter how informal the culture of the camp), doused himself in bug spray, regretting that the supersummer had dragged on for so long that he hadn't so much as brought a jacket. Slinging his messenger bag over one shoulder, he stepped out of the trailer, into the clearing beneath a bruise-purple sky. Low-lying mist still shrouded the ground, dissolving the scaffolding into white.

Something was moving by the dome.

His senses went on high alert. This wasn't Syria; an IED wasn't going to rip apart the fabric of the universe, but he hadn't survived that to distrust the prickle of gooseflesh on his arms, the adrenaline spike in his veins. Passing Cynthia's tent, he slapped the fabric. "Get up. Something's happening."

She emerged, bleary-eyed. She must have slept in her clothes.

There was a rent in the side of the dome, the slump across the top indicating a slow collapse. Someone was inside. He knew they were focused on their work, but to risk suffocation? He switched gears and stepped out into what little light remained, pounding on the trailer doors as he passed them.

"Hey!" Tobias called. "Hey, get out of there!" He turned to Cynthia. "Get out to the road. Try and flag someone down."

"This is the *story*."

"You're pregnant and I have a camera. *Go*." He had the Leica out and was stalking towards the dome, praying that Cynthia had enough sense to run for help.

There was no wind, but the torn flap of the dome slapped back and forth, revealing, inside, a small huddle of figures in black, faces covered with balaclavas. One stood guard by the door, waving a box-cutter at Tobias as he approached; another was filming something inside with a cellphone.

Time stuttered. Coughed. Tobias was rooted to the ground, his legs iron, and afterwards, he'd wonder why, so close to Ground Zero, he had survived unscathed.

The three inside—who he'd later learn were members of an eco-terrorist cell determined to sabotage the wellspring project—were dissolved where they stood. The one guarding the door wasn't as lucky. As Tobias watched, the silver-blue consumed him, a cold flame burning inside of him, his tattoos—one was a bunny, and Tobias would never know why that small detail stood out—turned to black silhouettes on his hollowed-out arms. In the space between his black gloves and the bottom hem of his t-shirt sleeves, Tobias saw every vein as if his skin had turned to glass, the incandescent white of humerus, ulna, radius.

The dome, already wounded, collapsed around the glass man, and the paralysis at last released Tobias and he *ran.*

There was no time to even look properly as he sprinted, the breath tight in his chest, for the cover of the trailers. He saw Fionn, winnowed into spindly Giacometti proportions, Emmeline screaming as her elbows and knees cracked and bent backwards, neck twisted beneath a swollen, misshapen skull.

He stopped abruptly, the air thick in his lungs, leaning on the corner of a trailer. The demons weren't following him. They moved in slow, jerking contortions, twisting and turning limbs over each other, as if their new bodies were as startling to them as they were to him. Hands trembling, he pulled the camera to his face like a shield. Maybe he'd die here, but he'd die a fucking photojournalist.

He shot. And shot. The thing that had been Emmeline raised its head, craned its long neck and blinked at him, then loped, backwards legs tripping over each other, through the collapsed dome into the cover of the forest.

He heard, as if the damned sorcerer were standing beside him, whispering in his ear, Ian Mallory hiss, *what does magic want?*

To carry out its plans, Tobias thought, *bright and fierce and cruel.*

Tobias staggered past the line of trailers, ignoring the survivors, emerging stunned from sleep. He saw the road, the flash of headlights, of salvation, and then stars, and then, mercifully, nothing at all.

19

Sujay couldn't stop looking at the photos.

The Backwards Woman. The Thin Man. The Glass Man. Barnum and Bailey for the attention-deficit generation. Not humanity's image reflected in a funhouse mirror, gaping and hungry, but turned inside out, exposing the ugly mess at its heart. In this enlightened and cost-conscious age, rare was the newspaper that could afford to hire a professional photographer, and the *Post* had lucked out by having one on scene, with a camera that captured magic. She didn't generally think highly of Tobias Fletcher but in this case, she'd agree he deserved the Pulitzer he'd almost certainly get. On his ancient camera, he'd taken the clearest photos of demons ever taken, a veritable carnival of horrors.

Sujay had little time to comb the news, or even Twitter, for commentary, not with the lineup of civil servants and politicians who had decided—ill-advisedly, and with reckless disregard for their lives and future wellbeing—to pay a visit to the Broom Closet and express their opinions on Tobias' photographic revelations to Ian. He must have been feeling restrained, because only a few actually left in tears. She caught glimpses of the arguments through the crack beneath the door, black shadows sliding back and forth across the floor as his petitioners speculated, raged, pled.

She wanted answers too. Had he known? Had *she*? This wasn't the one-in-thirty-million chance of a terrorist attack on any given day, in any major city. This was a photographer for a print publication, for fuck's sake, catching him by surprise weaving a spell around the heart of the nation. This was magic's spindly hand reaching out to throttle the life from people that Ian had, maybe intentionally, trapped.

"Except," she heard Ian remark to the Minister of Trade. "I didn't have anything to do with it. We were all there when the trade deal was signed, and I bet you're even enough of a geek that you read the entire thing." At least, if he hadn't, the Honourable Arnold Van Hassel, P.C., would never have admitted it to a college dropout who had.

Eric Greenglass followed up the same line of inquiry. He hadn't been in the room, but he'd no doubt had input—perhaps more than Patrice Abel, who was, put euphemistically, more of a big-picture guy.

"And so you knows that there was enough red tape—agreed to, might I fuckin' add, by our good comrades in the Soviet Socialist Chamber of Commerce—to throttle capitalist innovation in its goddamned cradle. It's not the fault of this government if the SVAR decided to move fast and break things and catch tetanus from the things they break."

To his credit, Eric fell silent for a few seconds. Whatever his copious flaws, he wasn't entirely stupid, and he could read between the lines. He wasn't evaluating Ian's implication, he was evaluating the wisdom in saying it out loud. "But you knew they would."

Funny. Sujay had never pegged Eric as particularly brave.

"Don't needs to be a precog to knows a greedy bastard's gonna fuck around and find out."

Patrice Abel himself came towards the end of the day, wearier than she'd seen him in a long while, and if they spoke at all, the conversation was too quiet for her to hear through the door. It said enough that he came, not expecting Ian to make the five-minute walk to the PMO to visit him. He didn't leave looking happy.

Jonah arrived much later, well after the Hill had cleared but for a handful of steadfast bureaucrats and tourists capturing selfies in the golden hour against the Gothic Revival backdrop, or trying to recreate Tobias Fletcher's now-famous photo with flip phones and Polaroids.

"Damon was your friend too," Jonah said. He didn't even bother to close the door all the way, having spent enough time in the Broom Closet to know that Sujay would hear it anyway. Maybe he even wanted an audience.

He was talking about Damon Caldwell. The Glass Man. Ian's old friend, and Jonah's, apparently. He'd—on Jonah's whisper of suggestion— assembled a small crew of eco-terrorists to sabotage the SVAR wellspring project in the name of halting the exploitation of magical energy. Thanks to Tobias Fletcher's photos, a man she'd met once, and disliked, was practically a household name.

"I don't have friends," Ian said. "Present company excluded."

"You murdered him," Jonah said, and Ian half-rose from his chair, glowering, to shut the door between them. It did little to stifle their voices—either from her, or, she thought, from the listening devices that Ian was convinced riddled the office like termites. "You told me to leak information to him, knowing what he'd do. And you used me to do it."

"I'm not all-fuckin'-powerful. I couldn't make Rebel Without Applause do anything he wasn't already burnin' to do."

"You made me think it would be like our old ops. Get someone to sneak in, leak some photos to the press, show the public that the SVAR were breaking our terms. You knew I was sending him to his death."

"So would you, if you thought about it for five minutes." Ian laughed, if you could call it that. "You knew I was a monster well before you came to work here. You leavin' yet?"

Leaving? Time had been a blur in these past few months, but she'd expected Jonah to at least last longer than her intern predecessors.

There was a long silence. Someone opened a drawer. Someone coughed.

"You know me," Jonah said finally. "I'm ride or die. Even if you are a raging cunt."

To her ears, at least, he didn't sound convinced.

• • •

After Jonah left, she spent ten minutes or so pretending to work, and resisting looking at the demon pictures. Before she dared go into his office, Ian emerged from it, grey and bedraggled, his faded hair corkscrewed and unruly. Jittery, more so than usual. He was holding another deck of cards, which he dumped on the desk in front of her, some landing on the stacks of folders, others sliding to the ground, a few under the desk.

"I've been neglectin' yer education." His accent was about ten times thicker than usual. There should have been red around his eyes; the darker shade of grey was unnerving, the sclera shot through with dendrite lightning, bloodshot without the blood. She'd heard the coke rumours, everyone had, though she'd never actually been in a position to confirm or deny. He kept his vices ostensibly secret, away from the public where a thousand crabs scrambled over one another to drag him back to the bottom of the bucket. "Put those in order."

"What order?"

"Alphabetical." As she started working it out, he said, "The order that the Pattern suggests. It's not hard. Just listen. It never fucking shuts up."

"Jonah's right," she said. Two hours after her day officially ended; she'd earned a bit of snark. It wasn't like he could easily find another eager young MAI with compatible-enough politics if he fired her. "You are being a cunt."

Whatever anger he might have directed at her had been spent over the course of a day that had worn them both down to exposed nerves and exhaustion. "You're smarter than I was. Am. But it doesn't mean sweet merciful dick."

He was going to tell her what he was on about regardless. She sat back in her chair, picked up two of the fallen cards. Three of clubs, seven of hearts. Nothing in them suggested a pattern any different from the obvious.

"You needs to be powerful. Stop a man's heart with yer will. Crash cars with yer brain..."

"How do you—"

"Because everyone thinks about that."

Her fingernail found a flaw in the three of clubs, skirted the corner where the paper had started to separate. "That's not who I am."

"That's what ya becomes. A monster. Like me."

"Are the photos a problem?" She didn't bother specifying which—that his spell and the demons had made the news within days of each other meant that magic was once again trending, and not in a good way, and Patrice's already middling approval ratings were taking a plunge.

He didn't answer.

Every time she closed her eyes, she saw the fires, the earthquakes. Glass fingers, reaching towards her. She asked, "What's the point of any of this if it's not to build a world that doesn't need monsters?"

That was evidently enough to jolt him into a state that approached sobriety. He leaned an elbow on a stack of papers as if it might provide the scaffolding to keep him upright. "Tell me," he said, "when you seen that vision, all that destruction, the—" a wave of a long, pale hand, as if tracing along the arch of spine that she saw every time she closed her eyes. "Y'know. In all of that did you see me there?"

She hadn't cast around to see what her family was doing, as the earth retched forth abominations. She hadn't looked for Jamila, gloved hands stained with blood and ichor in the hospital's battle for one extra hour of life, one more soul condemned to watch the horrors unfold for a little longer.

But Ian was different; her friends and family were distant anxieties outside of the immediate blast radius. Her vision had been here, the ancient bricks turned to ash, the Rideau Canal, like a thick, glistening worm shot through with red veins, writhing free of its boundaries to snake over the shorelines. She'd been looking for a political solution, a way for Patrice's administration to stay afloat, and he'd been at the centre of it—until he wasn't.

"The SVAR project," he said abruptly. "It was a good plan. Wouldn't have worked but they couldn't have known that."

"Why didn't you tell Jonah that, then? Of all people, he'd get it."

"He's figured it out. Trust me. His problem is he's figured it out." He collected the cards without burning them this time. Sat across from her at the desk, as if he were one of the very supplicants that had barraged him all day. She was certain he was reaching to take her hand before he swerved, at the last minute, and picked up Panic Pete instead. "Sujay," he said, and there was a warmth in his voice that hadn't been there before, a kind of sadness. "If you're already stayin' late, I got one more thing to ask of you tonight."

20

"Sweet shittin' vinegar, Joe, this is a truly tragic fuckin' sight."

Jonah squinted up from the mattress, paused the TV as Klaus Kinski traded blows with Jean-Louis Trintignant's mute gunslinger in a saloon. Though there was no need to look up. He'd felt the prickle on his arm before the door opened. "What're you doing here?"

"Better question is why don't you lock your door?" Ian stepped over a pile of unfolded laundry to loom over him, peering at the screen. "This has gotta be a bit pathological. Like a Jew watching Riefenstahl for fun."

"Now you're a cultural theorist, too. I don't wanna talk to you right now."

"Yeah. The time for sulking in your desolate man-cave is after the crisis has been averted, not during it." He picked up the remote, dangled it a few inches from his face like he'd unexpectedly found himself holding a dried turd. Jonah stubbed his cigarette into the ashtray on the floor, vindictively, and tried not to be too pleased at Ian's cough.

"Your landlady lets you smoke in here?"

"I told her it was sacred tobacco."

Ian stared with the blank look of a white guy who's not sure if he's supposed to be amused or uncomfortable, then gave a short, barking laugh and Jonah momentarily forgot to be pissed off at him. Then he switched to CBC, which was covering Graves' latest pontifications on the Magic Question, and Jonah remembered that he hated anything to do with electoral politics.

"Behold our future overlord," Ian said. "Remember who the enemy is."

Jonah hadn't put money on the leadership race—no one in the government, let alone in the Broom Closet, was naive enough to bet against a man who could see the future. The outcome was never in question. In hindsight, he should have at least conned some of the junior staffers into betting against him.

"They couldn't get themselves an MAI candidate so they find a near-psychic banker. Just what the country needs."

"Could be worse," Jonah said. "Every time Atherton opened his mouth I heard every dog in the neighbourhood going fucking nuts. At least Graves isn't a sociopath. Any way Patrice beats him?"

Ian shrugged. "There're a few outlier timelines. But the budget doesn't pass. Don't tell Patrice."

Jonah shifted, the cheap mattress under him sunken nearly into the floor. Electoral politics might be bullshit, but interfering with them on occasion made him feel less than completely useless. "What's the play here? Force Patrice to step down?" Apparently they just weren't ever going to talk about what had happened at the wellspring, or the spell. What was a little proxy murder between friends, with the Party's future at stake? The mattress complained as Ian sat, as if the negligible weight of the other man was just a bridge too far for it.

Ian turned the remote over, fingernails picking at the gap where the battery cover started, then came to some kind of decision and switched back to the frozen DVD. "I think I've seen this one," he said. "Everyone dies at the end."

"Yeah. They had to shoot an alternate ending because it was too much of a downer for the Americans. What do we do about Graves? And the photos."

"Well." Ian hit the play button, and the saloon brawl sprung back to life. The amber wash of the old movie splashed over his face, a warmth that was nothing more than a play of light. "If you're still into your whole God shite you might wanna pray for him. It's not Patrice who mops up the shitstorm."

"So I *don't* need to go through his garbage?"

"Never said that." Ian squeezed his arm. "No rest for the lesser evil, Joe. I need to knows everything he's snorting, fucking, and planning before their champagne-and-orphan tears hangovers wear off. What his plan is for the wellsprings. And why Atherton wasn't pissed off at losing. Can you stop hatin' me for what happened to Damon long enough to find out?"

"Thought I was looking at land surveys." He ran a hand through his hair, tugging at the roots. "Did you predict how I'd react? Before you went ahead with it?"

"I never look into your future, b'y. Not yours."

"Why not?"

"You fuckin' know why not." He'd turned, already eyeing the door, so that Jonah couldn't see his face, couldn't ask him why he'd come here when he lived on the other end of the city and the same conversation could have been had over text, could have probably waited for the morning. He couldn't exactly vanish in a puff of smoke or a flash of blue light, but he was probably working on that next.

If Jonah was less angry, less of a coward, he could have asked Ian to stay, to put off driving back to an equally desolate apartment—or worse, to somewhere else—and watch a depressing Western with him.

He wasn't. He listened to the door slide shut, barely audible beneath the gunshots on the TV, and lit another cigarette.

• • •

"I'm fucking exhausted. Could you maybe get your wife to not drop any doom-and-gloom pronouncements until after the budget?"

"Ex-wife." Jonah shoved the heavy oak door shut with his shoulder, balancing two paper bags of sandwiches. One of them was already leaking, because it was that kind of a day and it was definitely going to be that kind of a meeting.

Jonah hadn't slept much either, and drawing the short straw on the lunch run hadn't helped his mood. At least Ian had a coke habit and an underpaid intern to get him through Silly Season. Jonah had Red Bull, detailed spreadsheets documenting Opposition malfeasance, and a schedule packed with Zoom conferences.

Jonah took his place between Ian and Sujay. The table was divided and arranged into factions. The Broom Closet people. The Party moderates, for whom Ian and his people were increasingly a liability. Patrice's loyalists. Gaby with her supporters flanking her, an impending divorce acted out in inter-party squabbles. The Budget and Finance Committee, nearly as grey as Ian himself these days. Cal Harrison, whose presence in the inner circle Jonah still wanted to protest. It was accompanied by a nagging voice in his head: *We need to be realistic, the Senate has to approve the budget, appearance of backroom dealings or not.*

Ian made a disgusted noise as Jonah unwrapped his sandwich beside him. "Seriously, Joe. Tuna? You appall me."

"Someone's in a pissy mood."

"I thought you were an environmentalist."

"Says the guy who drives...that thing."

Cal's face was pinched, drawn. They were on the outs again, Ian and Cal. He could see it in their posture, Cal shrugging off Ian's attempts to get into his space, Ian's bristling hostility towards the rest of the room. Jonah didn't like that he knew about it, didn't want to have to think about whether Ian's peevishness stemmed from the personal or the political. He didn't give a shit, at least insofar as it didn't affect the spending priorities. "Can you two gentleman stop bickering and attempt to focus? We have a budget to iron out."

"I did a lunch run as a favour," Jonah said, ignoring Cal completely.

"Not much of a favour if I can smells your fish breath."

"Don't people literally kiss fish where you're from?" Eric asked, because Eric apparently had a death wish, and really, why not? Watching Ian murder him would be a nice distraction from the budget talks for everyone.

"Why do you thinks I left?"

Sujay, timid, still learning to read a room: "We can switch seats, Ian."

"That's not the point," Jonah snapped. She flinched. Fuck, it was like kicking a puppy. No wonder she was the one person Ian was never an asshole to. It was practically physically impossible. "The point is Ian's being a douche and doesn't deserve sandwiches."

Ian sneered at him and unfolded, serpentine, from his chair, lunch already abandoned. He started up the PowerPoint. Draft versions had been bouncing between departments all week, shaping an election platform cunningly disguised as a final budget. The strategy started with someone in Communications re-branding the Blight Report to "Pathways Forward," and then somehow spinning it into a de-fanged Green Deal.

Jonah felt the twinge at the first slide. It wasn't clip art and animated transitions bad, but it was—unsettling. Windows 95 colour scheme and stray JPG artifacts kind of unsettling, the polar opposite of the glossy environmental platform that the Opposition was flashing around.

He leaned towards Sujay. "Nice font. Comic Sans was a little too fancy?"

"I can't help it," she hissed back. "The current version goes. Uh. Kerflooey. Around both of us."

It wasn't subtle. He could sense Ian's hand in the spell, the sharp blue of his pen, echoed in the lines he'd stabbed into Jonah's bicep twenty years ago. It didn't hurt, exactly, but it was more overt than usual, a glow of heat under his skin like a fever. But it wasn't just Ian, Ian's magic didn't shimmer like the air on a sweltering August day. There was a second layer to the spell, an alphabet in a language he could almost, but not quite, decipher.

Ian hadn't done this on his own.

Jonah glanced around the room to see if anyone else noticed, but they were nodding along, and that in itself was weird, when every meeting lately seemed on the verge of devolving into a brawl. It was the ward tattoo that signalled the presentation's true nature. There was nothing otherwise perceptible to someone who hadn't had magic circling the periphery of their lives.

"You guys made a cursed PowerPoint."

"I prefer the term enchanted?" She flexed her fingers. Her nail polish was chipped, strips of skin torn raw around the nail bed.

He opened his mouth once, closed it, tried again, then laughed, softly, under his breath. Now wasn't the time to conduct experiments, whether in magic or moral philosophy. But it also wasn't the time to point out that Ian was mindfucking everyone in the room except him.

Ian hadn't changed that much. He'd have thought this out, planned for every contingency, Jonah included. He had to know what he was doing, had to know that Jonah would see through any spell he was casting and side with him regardless. Wasn't that the whole point of keeping your conscience in another person? There were flaws in Ian's armour, but none that someone who hadn't known him the better part of two decades would have noticed.

Not for the first time in his life, he considered the precise number of eggs Ian was willing to break for their shining utopian brunch.

This said, he couldn't argue with the plan. It proposed six inalienable rights—food, clean water, healthcare, housing, education, and transit—and a plan to make each universal over the next four years.

Blythe would have preferred relationships to rights, and for good reason. One of Patrice's people was already arguing that the Opposition would hammer them on bringing up the idea of rights without a single mention of freedom, to which Gaby snapped that you couldn't exactly turn freedom into a costed line item to be included in a budget.

"You can when it's a stealth platform," Cal said. He couldn't have liked it—road to Damascus moment or not, he hadn't strayed so far from his aristo-VC roots that he'd embrace whatever socialism-with-a-human-face pipedream Ian was proposing. Not when they were in one of their off-again phases, at least.

It was only just marginally progressive by Jonah's standards, and he couldn't settle on whether it was radical enough to justify putting the whammy on their own side. It wasn't even that it was economically impossible. The slide on housing had several clunky infographics citing the TSpace and, of all institutes, the RAND Corporation studies showing the cost-benefit analysis of free housing. It was just politically impossible, and if Jonah wasn't the one to say so, no one else would, caught as they were in the Web 1.0 of Ian and Sujay's spell.

And why should he?

Wasn't that why they'd gotten involved in the Party? What was the point of chipping away at everything they'd believed in until they stood, not on a mountain, but a smoothed-out pebble near-identical to those strewn across the Canadian political landscape?

No one sat in a room like this without losing an ideal or two, but then, no one got into a room without holding those ideals in the first place. Back when they'd been young, they'd called that mythical future After the Revolution; now it was some nebulous beyond-four-years future in which socialism would somehow be realistic and palatable. They'd lived a long time in the land of Not Now, but One Day. The differences were never really the ideas themselves. The only fight was what people outside of the room would think of them.

Fuck it. Let Ian shake things up if he thought he could. It felt far too late, at the outset of humanity's long, bleak winter, but that had been the case all of Jonah's life. He had always been emptying the ocean with a teaspoon as the tide rose to his knees.

Through the cracks in the spell, Angela pointed out the infeasibility of instituting universal basic living standards for every Canadian within four years.

"The Opposition is promising clean green prosperity, b'y. Endless growth without devastation. When's the last time you seen an election platform that was realistic? It's about getting the ideas out, okay?"

They could do this, Jonah decided, already sorting announcements into micro-targeted social media ads while the conversation continued around him. The Opposition had its moments of temerity. Even Baby's First Scandal, with a first-time candidate revealed to have, in her possession, a real human skull of dubious provenance ordered off eBay, had been quickly swept under the table with a theatrical wave and all was forgiven. Why couldn't the government seize an outrage click or two?

Patrice straightened his tie, half-stood, broad hands braced against the edge of the table. "Will this win us the election?"

For the first time, Ian made eye contact with Jonah, and Jonah tilted his tablet towards him to show the stream of targets, his own, entirely non-magical labyrinth. The one that he might find his way out of, somehow.

"More often than not," Ian lied. Sujay's glamour gave nothing away. "Graves is polling somewhere between pink eye and the stomach flu. There's hope."

Angela was already fretting over the polling numbers. Ian had decided, for whatever reason, on a kamikaze strategy. The budget wouldn't pass.

If they were going to lose, they'd lose well.

• • •

He found Ian in the men's room, wrestling with the lid of a bottle of Advil that, in addition to being childproof, was apparently charmer-proof as well.

"Can't you just magic it open?"

Ian rolled his eyes and let Jonah twist it open. Jonah was rewarded for his effort by having to watch Ian dry-swallow a fistful of pills.

"What the fuck was that all about back there?"

"Proof of concept."

"I thought we wanted to win."

"Who said we wouldn't? There's a big picture here. We don't all have the luxury of fucking up our lives."

"Like you fucked up Damon's?"

"No one's hands are clean there, Joe."

He'd spent enough time hating himself; he didn't need Ian's encouragement. "Look, there's something I want you to see." He flipped windows on his tablet, from the hastily improvised media strategy to the data streams that had kept him up for several nights in a row. "Your labyrinth, right? It's a specific pattern. The same as Sujay's stress ball, or the little girl with the recorder that Blythe met. It's all part of the same thing."

"And?"

"So I scanned some of your drawings, and wrote a script to match the patterns to data sets. Everything I could think of—traffic, weather, the stock market, consumer spending patterns—and it was all just random. Every so often I'd get a hit, but it would be, like, three points of correlation."

"In English, b'y."

"Human activity is random. Magic only appears to be."

Ian leaned in, air of cool disinterest rapidly evaporating.

"Donations from several shell corporations. They're—practically non-existent by corporate donor standards. At first I thought it was some sort of Kiva microlending scheme with multiple charities, but the numbers mapped with the capital-P Pattern. Not just bits of correlation but almost a complete overlap."

Ian, in a sudden bout of improvised technological literacy, said, "You made an algorithm that detects magic use."

"Kind of? After the fact. It wouldn't work for magic itself, but in this case, the MAI left a paper trail. Like your labyrinth sketches. Inert, so they don't conflict with the script."

"The MAI."

"Tobias Fletcher said the Opposition had one working for them. And I think he's right. The guy's a flaming douchebag but he's consistent, and he hates magic more than he hates socialism. All of the companies trace back to a think tank, the Walsingham Institute. We get a list of employees and a list of Opposition supporters and I will bet you we'll find someone casting a massive fucking spell."

Ian's hand clapped his bicep. His fingers, through the thin cotton of his dress shirt, were cold steel. "I could kiss ya right now."

Jonah smirked. "Not if you don't like tuna."

"Any idea what he's up to?"

That was a harder proposition. "A lot of it does actually look like charity. Youth organizations, after school music programs for kids, university grants. Feel-good rich white people stuff. And then there's the weird shit, like a grant to a music video production start-up in the Lower East Side. A conservation NGO run by an ex-anarchist. It might be that the recipient doesn't matter, just the pattern of the numbers."

Ian didn't look convinced. "Someone with resources like that, Opposition backing, and magic? It'll be more'n numbers. Two birds, one stone."

There were still too many loose ends, especially with progressive causes mingled in with the politically neutral and downright reactionary ones. The why was obvious, and Jonah might be closing in on the who (but anyone with that level of juice and resources could keep themselves hidden?), but the what-the-fuck was a different story. What would he do, in that position? Uncover dirt on the Party's candidates? Turn Graves from a placeholder to an actual charismatic leader? Interfere with Ian's visions? Rejig the poll numbers? All of the above? All they really knew was that there was an enemy, somewhere, with serious firepower, and nothing about the campaign could be trusted.

And the fucking photo, the web around Parliament. Ian should have seen Tobias Fletcher coming. His failure mode wasn't missing an enemy's attack, it was too much potentially correct information. The Opposition's MAI cast doubt on everything, including Ian's strategy.

He had to know what Tobias knew.

Ian would hate it. Tobias was a one-man crusade hellbent on purging MAI influence from the political landscape. Jonah was reliably certain that Ian would have Tobias quietly murdered if he could. The one consolation was that roping Tobias into an investigation of his own team was guaranteed to also make Tobias incredibly miserable.

Ian couldn't be trusted. So Ian couldn't know. Not yet, not until they knew more.

Well. Hiding from the All-Knowing, All-Seeing Eye was a difficult proposition, but not an impossible one these days. Ian was preoccupied, but worse, as bitchy as he was being, Ian still trusted him.

"I'll keep looking into it," he promised.

He waited until he was outside to text Blythe. He didn't like that prospect either, but she was as much a walking magic detector as he was, and Graves was hitting Victoria in two days.

Hey. How'd you like to go to a really bad rally?

21

"Fuck this," Laura said, pricking herself with her needle for what had to be the hundredth time.

"Language!"

The girl scowled. "*Maudit seigneur.*" She must have gotten that one from her kookum, who, at least in Blythe's experience, was loathe to censor herself in front of children, but at least seldom provided much in the way of a detailed translation.

Laughter only encouraged the sort of behaviour that a good mother should discourage lest CAS get overly interested in her family. Blythe stifled it and told herself to be grateful for the temporary reprieve of watching her daughter struggle over her beadwork, rosebud lips pursed in concentration. She had a talent for it, the bandaids layering her fingers aside. Her stitches were small and neat and even, and she was getting faster, the mouse tracks snaking white over the dark denim of the patch she was working on. Better than Blythe had been, anyway, back when her mother had tried to teach her. Blythe had always been a child of numbers, of wriggling worms hidden beneath old bricks, the pinch of a crawfish claw in her tiny hand. There was beauty, of a kind, in taking the world apart to see its inner workings, but a part of her was grateful that her daughter was more receptive to her grandmother's lessons than she had been.

It was better than watching the election coverage on TV. Blythe put no small amount of faith in Ian Mallory, despite all he was and all he'd done, but it was hard to imagine the outcome changing much.

And Jonah. Fucking Jonah. Who wanted her to just wade right into this particular fetid sewer and splash around, as if she had nothing better to do with her time. She'd rather facefuck Cthulhu but she was going to end up doing what he'd asked anyway, because as far as she knew, there were only two people in the world with reliable magic detectors, and the other one was busy selling out to the *môniyâwak* electoral system on the opposite side of the continent. She could resent him right up until she had to consider what Graves' half-assed environmental policy would mean for the oceans and wellsprings, and then she, too, would give in to grim realism.

The small muscles in her jaw clenched, twitched. There was so much to fear in the world and while the Earth burned and choked, there were grown men afraid of MAI, of brown folks, of women. She itched to scream at them, to flail out gracelessly with fists and knees that had never been coordinated enough to dance but might, given enough anger, transform her into a living weapon.

Laura, crosslegged on her bed, dutifully tugged at a loose thread and caught the freed beads between the creases in her fingers. Warmth blossomed under Blythe's ribs. For a time, maybe she could pretend that they weren't all absolutely doomed.

Fuck it, she texted back to Jonah. *I'll do it.*

• • •

She ended up dragging Dani with her. Dahlia would have been more fun to bring along and snark with, but Dahlia's current level of consciousness, bordering 9 on the Glasgow Coma Scale, approximated that of the crowd. Blythe dutifully took pictures with her phone. She wasn't tall enough for a good overhead view, but it was enough to get a sense of the kind of people who showed up at the Innovation Island Building to hear Anson Graves babble on about start-up tax incentives. She'd expected a mass of retirees, and they did make up the majority of the assembled, but there were also younger faces, not all of them white. Blythe pulled the brim of her cowboy hat lower over her face, hoping against hope not to be caught on camera even though there was nearly as much press as audience.

She watched the local candidate—a shabby, aging farm manager at odds with the Pottery Barn chic of the campaign—warm up the crowd. Checked her phone. There was no sign of Graves yet. Someone offered them wine. Dani hesitated; Blythe gratefully accepted.

"Aren't you on duty?"

"This is purely volunteer. You wanna bet whatever this crowd drinks is better than we could afford?"

Dani shrugged and they clinked glasses. "I guess it'll make the speeches more bearable."

The farmer was going on about property rights and temporary labour law reform. Blythe doubted anything could have made listening to him bearable. *They're really pushing this guy*, she texted Jonah, accompanied by a photo of the cameras and drones that circled the well-dressed, multicultural crowd behind the podium. It wasn't like she'd been to a ton of campaign rallies, but there was something about the tight focus of the cameras that suggested they were cropping, trying to make the crowd look bigger, more engaged. You'd think that the press would prefer someone like Patrice in power, with a well-funded CBC and the fractious Party always giving them something to write about, over a technocratic automaton like Graves, but Blythe hadn't been out of politics so long that she didn't remember how dark money worked.

"Are you seriously texting your ex?"

"Coming here was his idea." She could only imagine Past Blythe, of the crowbars and lock-ons, agreeing to waltz right into the den of the enemy. "We used to talk about firebombing these assholes."

"He sounds not entirely free of assholery himself."

"Yeah." Blythe could really, really use a cigarette right now. She'd been out on the ocean too long, spent too much time around scientists who wore graphic t-shirts with awful puns on them, to be seduced and wooed by the sheer practicality of Graves' fiscal policy. She doubted she even passed as a serious voter. She was probably too scruffy, had missed some marker of class or status. Were they searching her face, beneath the shadow of her hat's brim, for the epicanthic folds of her eyes? She had the sudden paranoia that she'd left buttons on the strap of her purse, but a quick glance downwards suggested nothing overtly political. A fresh-faced volunteer offered her a sign, and she politely demurred, thrusting her hands into her pockets. She huddled into her windbreaker, turning inwards, turning invisible. "There's a reason we're divorced. Reasons, plural."

"I'm sorry."

Jonah was the least of her problems, all things considered. "He's—well. He wasn't a good husband. Or father. He tried, in his way. There was a lot of fucked up shit that went on when he was a kid. He grew up in care, and you don't shake that, not really ever, and his foster family was—he doesn't talk about it. We don't all get to live our ideals how we might want. Sometimes you just break yourself into different people and fail at being all of them instead."

Dani looked skeptical, and Blythe remembered that defending Jonah's poor life choices and myriad personality defects wasn't her job anymore, if it ever had been. Before she could dig herself deeper, a phalanx of RCMP and a cheer announced Graves' arrival.

Graves was much shorter in person than he looked on TV, and the beefy security detail didn't exactly help. At first glance, he was indistinguishable from the carefully considered casual of the entrepreneurs his campaign had surrounded him with, childless, serious young men who kept foosball tables in their penthouse condos and roofies in the medicine chest.

He also didn't give off a whiff of magic. She could feel a low background thrum of *something*, but it might have been anyone, could have been something they were working on inside the building, or an audience member with latent ability. The spell Jonah was after was something bigger. Graves might be a liar, woven through his core with the mendacity of any politician, but beneath it all he was an ordinary human being.

Okay, so, that was a bit of a disappointment. When it came down to it, she didn't put much stake in Patrice Abel's Party being substantially different than Anson Graves' where it mattered, but catching out the leader of the Opposition as a hypocritical MAI would have made for an entertaining news cycle in the face of apocalypse. She took Dani's arm and slid through the crowd.

"C'mon," she said. "We've got wizards to hunt."

• • •

You could tell the indie journalist because Graves' own detail kept trying to box him, refusing him a long shot of the crowd. He'd done his best, even donning a sweater vest for the occasion, though he must have only owned one pair of glasses because the horn-rimmed hipster look was a dead giveaway. Blythe was legitimately surprised that they'd even let him in. He made a beeline for Blythe and Dani, shotgun mic thrust forward.

"Can I ask you about—"

Dani started to shake her head. Blythe said, "We're just here for the free hotdogs."

"I'm looking to interview undecided voters."

Blythe adjusted her hat. "That's not me."

He started to move on when they all heard it, like the distant rumbling of thunder. Blythe felt it before the orchestral score, a tinny blast through a rental sound system, drew the crowd's attention, a small shockwave centring on her tattoo. She regained her step and spun to see a small cluster of people across the street, some wearing the candidate's oversized t-shirts, some waving the Canadian flag or the Red Ensign, others holding slick signs denouncing the Party, Patrice, MAI. Most were young, maybe in their teens or early 20s. They were singing the anthem—badly—holding out selfie-stick mounted cameras at themselves and the rally.

The reporter groaned.

"Who're they?" Blythe asked. *Besides brimming with magic*, she thought, but of course no one else would have felt it. It wasn't the sharp specificity of an MAI. No, they were the recipients of the spell; it hung over them like a shroud.

Given their signs, they had no idea.

"They call themselves the Dominion Society," he said. "Anti-immigrant, anti-commie, and most of all anti-magic. Graves is smart enough to not want anything to do with them. Officially."

"And unofficially?"

He looked pained. "You see those signs? They're not basement-dwellers." He lifted his DSLR and snapped some pictures. Blythe did the same with her cell, then sent the least glitchy one to Jonah. "Uh oh. Here comes trouble."

The ache in her shoulder intensified as another group, this one scraggly and masked, announced its presence with shouts of "Fascists out!" Their signs and banners were clearly homemade, though devoid of the symbols and slogans she recalled from her not-entirely misspent youth.

Graves' security detail whisked him into a waiting car, while several of the RCMP officers moved between the local guy and the two groups. Her new friend, meanwhile, was fiddling with the camera settings. "You should probably get out of here," he said. "It's gonna get ugly."

"Don't say that to her," Dani said. "It'll make her run in the wrong direction." She tugged at Blythe's arm as the reporter moved closer, angling for a better shot.

A notification from Jonah popped up. *WTF is going on over there?*

She ignored him and set the camera to video just as the first Black Bloccer landed a punch, tried to push down the thrill of adrenaline that threatened to burst out from her skin. The cops moved in faster than she could. Someone was shoving into her, clawing at her face, nearly knocking the phone out of her hand. She saw the reporter go down under a stray elbow, blood dripping from his temple.

Dani hauled her up the street, away from the fracas. "You really are a danger-magnet. Some of us need to be up at 6 am tomorrow and not in jail."

"Yeah." She shook her head, catching out of the corner of her eye graffiti, freshly spray painted at the corner where the masked kids had marched from. *NOTA.* The fuck was that supposed to mean? She hadn't strayed so far from her shit-disturbing roots that a new activist movement wouldn't have pinged her radar. She snapped a picture of it and texted it to Jonah. *Graves isn't MAI but the Dominion Society and whoever these guys are reek of it.*

They're MAI? All of them?

She picked up the phone. "No, I don't think—there aren't that many MAI in the whole country. More like someone *did* something to them. And what's NOTA?"

"No clue." Jonah's voice was gravel-thick, tired. What was it, 11 pm there? From the voices in the background, he was still at work. She could hear him typing. "None Of The Above. It's a meme. Maybe we should be asking Laura."

She glanced behind her. They weren't being followed; their Respectable Citizens attire melted them into the still-bustling street, where the commotion of the rally already felt distant, a 30-second CTV spot and a crawler reminder long after bail had been posted and jail cells emptied.

"Ah," Jonah said. "Here it is. None of the above represent your interests. None of the above will keep their election promises. None of the above tells the truth. Vote for none of the above. Hashtag NOTA." He was quiet for a second. "They're not wrong. I'll talk to you later, okay?"

"Jonah—"

"Give Laura a kiss from me."

"What aren't you telling me?"

The silence on the other end reminded her that the answer to that question was more than she could ever guess at. "Thanks, Blythe," he said, and disconnected.

"Yeah," Dani said beside her. "You really dodged a bullet there."

"If you can call a decade of marriage and a kid together dodging a bullet," Blythe said. "Sure."

She breathed in deep, smelling ozone. Frost-white winter had yet to curl its fingers around the Archipelago. Magic clung like static to the power lines and street lights, seeped into the drought-parched sidewalk. In the approaching dusk, she felt small, dwarfed beside forces that she could only sense the shapes of, shadows flickering on cave walls.

Blythe knew enough of magic to understand that it cared nothing for human morals, let alone politics. There had been nothing malicious in the brawl, no more than a child slamming two action figures together. The same force, acting with two different hands, with no intent behind it beyond raw, unadulterated power.

By now, it almost felt familiar.

22

Being tossed headfirst into the perpetual motion machine of election strategizing might have been the best possible distraction from an impending eco-catastrophe. Eric was one of the few who'd read the Blight Report cover to cover, and one of the fewer still who'd understood it (minor in Environmental Science, thankyouverymuch). That meant that as much as Gaby Abel was in a high octane freakout, the mood on the Hill remained eerily calm in the face of what, decoded, suggested nothing less than impending catastrofuck.

Or perhaps it was just that everyone was more consumed with the by-election in Battlefords—Lloydminster, where Ansel Graves was putting on a show for a sleepy electorate willing to check off an X for anyone who promised to lower their taxes, heat death of all life on earth be damned.

"We need to get Patrice in a debate with him."

That was Angela Kim, Patrice's Chief of Staff, who was definitely on team Not Panicked Nearly Enough and who was, instead, deeply excited by Graves' win. She'd sprung for Timbits for the entire team on the bleary Tuesday after the leadership convention, with extra of the chocolate ones, no less. As far as she was concerned, he was capable of alienating the entire base. Too socially liberal—or at least socially apathetic—for the fetuses and firearms crowd out west, too fiscally unpredictable for his former Bay St. Colleagues, too techno-utopian for anyone with half a brain and an ounce of self-preservation. He was the weaker choice, and in Angela's eyes, the path to a majority government, if only Patrice could keep out of trouble and Ian out of the spotlight.

If, if, if. Eric wasn't so sure. It wasn't just Patrice's numerous affairs, poorly buried landmines that might go off at a moment's notice. Or the Blight Report and the fear that the election might end up being the least of everyone's concerns.

It was the elephant in the room. The public might tolerate an MAI who stopped terrorist attacks, but not one who cast mysterious spells around the heart of government. Nor one whose role in the worst magical disaster in a generation was still unclear.

Eric wanted to share Angela's optimism. She'd worked for some of these politicians before they'd coalesced into the Party, had shrugged off everyone's suggestions to run for office in favour of thankless backroom drudgery. Even Ian seemed to respect her, to the extent that he respected anyone who didn't directly answer to him. There was more grey than black in her hair these days, with each successive scandal, and it was good to see her in a chocolate-glazed-level cheerful mood for once.

"The last thing we wants is to get 'em in a room together," Ian said. He was drawing again, which Eric had once taken as him not paying attention, but apparently that was what he used to channel magical energy or whatever it was that he did. His intern and his—whatever the fuck Jonah was to him—seemed no less restless.

"Patrice is smarter," Angela countered. A sentence rarely uttered by anyone, ever, and in Graves' case, damning with faint praise, but she wasn't wrong. Gaby made a good show of not reacting. "He polls better. He's more likeable. Graves had the advantage on the economic front if the public's feeling insecure about the deficit, but he overthinks, and he doesn't have much of a plan for anything else. Just imagine having a beer with him."

That explained Angela's glee, anyway.

"We should have Patrice hit community events." Eric didn't want to agree with Ian. Or rather, he didn't want to be seen as sucking up to Ian, which was how certain other parliamentary assistants had met with swift demotions. "It's almost Thanksgiving; he could show up at soup kitchens. That's always a good segue into what we're doing to reduce income inequality."

"By reminding everyone that there are still soup kitchens in the Party's social democrat utopia?" How Jonah had finagled his way into these meetings, Eric had no idea. But his analysis tended to be as accurate as Ian's, though that stemmed less from periodic glimpses into the future and more from his trips spelunking in the Worst Places On the Internet. And, if the rumours were true, the occasional Rockcliffe Park dumpster. "That's a nice visual."

Patrice himself was in Paris for the G8, dodging teargas, eggs, and the neoliberal consensus of the other leaders of the developed world. He stuck out like a sore thumb there, and the irony wasn't lost on anyone. In the run-up to the summit, *Charlie Hebdo* had published a cartoon of him as a street beggar pleading with France for reparations for Haiti.

(That much, Patrice had taken the high road on, winning him half a percentage in the latest phone survey as a reward for good behaviour. And there was no proof that the anonymous, badly translated comments suggesting that the Kouachi brothers hadn't shot enough cartoonists came from a Laurier Ave. West IP address, given that they'd been routed through a proxy server.)

"Graves can't manage a sentence that doesn't sound like it was written by a committee," Angela said. "We position Patrice as a man of the people—" Eric could *feel* all three of the Broom Closet crew wince. "The Opposition has been leaning hard on populism but they couldn't have chosen a better representative of the elite if they'd grown him in a lab. This is a *gift*, people."

Jonah was drawing too, without even the excuse of being an MAI or channeling any sort of Mysterious Cosmic Energy. Or maybe he was writing something. He passed it to Ian, who snickered, and he saw Sujay lean over in an attempt to read it before Ian snatched it away. They weren't just old friends; they were a well-oiled machine, a brutal, efficient coup d'état waiting to unfold. Granted, a coup d'état with the sensibility of two twelve-year-old boys who'd broken into their mother's liquor cabinet and found dad's cache of porn on his laptop.

"They elected a geek with all the charm of Bell's automated phone support," Ian said. "That's good for us. Let him dig his own grave for a bit before we go after him directly." He went back to drawing, pausing only to snatch a Timbit from the box. Every so often, the drawing sparked. Everyone, in quiet conspiracy, acted like they didn't notice.

"Sure, get Patrice out there talking to people," Angela said, "but let's hit Graves where he's weak before he starts filling in the details. Social policy. Magic strategy. Climate change. None of which he cares passionately about."

"Maybe keep the climate catastrophe talk to a minimum when people are flying home to visit their families and eat turkey," one of the staffers suggested. Jonah stared daggers at him, which probably meant that Eric was never going to see that particular staffer again. There were good reasons why he didn't generally bother learning anyone's name.

Ian stopped drawing, and drum rolled on the desk. "Eric's right."

So unused to hearing that combination of words, particularly from Ian, Eric said, "Sorry?"

"I hate it as much as you do." Ian directed his words towards Angela. "A debate takes him two points down, the National Kissing Hands and Shaking Babies Tour takes him one point up."

"That makes no sense," Angela shot back.

"And if it gets out that he's fucked some staffer—*again*—that's three down. So someone work on paying the latest one off before it blows up in all of our faces. *Quietly*."

"Why?"

"Why doesn't Patrice keep it in his pants? I don't know, Angela, maybe you should ask him when he gets back from Paris."

Gaby sucked her teeth. Eric threw her a look that he prayed came off as sympathetic and not pitying. The sinew and veins bulged in her lean arms, braced against the table.

"Why," she asked, "is it so important to keep him out of a debate with Graves?"

Eric glanced at Ian, who was up from his seat, scanning at the latest polling numbers that Sandra had posted. No one was going to say it. No one wanted to say it.

"Graves is going to alienate his base," Eric said. He sounded tentative even to his own ears. "But he's also going to scoop up the liberal mushy middle, and it's not like the hard right was ever going to vote for Patrice anyway. It's just going to highlight the one *other* advantage that Graves has."

"You're not supposed to say it out loud," Ian said. "Congratulations on having the dimmest view of Canadian voters of anyone in this room, though."

"Second dimmest," Sujay muttered.

"I'm not saying I agree with them." Eric raised both of his hands, palms outwards. *Don't shoot the fucking messenger*, even though Ian must have by now have amassed a skull pile of dead messengers worthy of Khorne. "I'm just saying if you think the *Charlie Hebdo* thing was bad ..." If the PM were in the room, he'd have settled the discussion quickly. Patrice had a soft spot for the MAI who'd won an election for him, much to the resentment of policy analysts who'd racked up considerable student debt to do the kinds of predictions that Ian managed by doodling on napkins. But with Patrice absent, egos came out to play, and Eric would be lying if he claimed to be unaware of at least a half-dozen ministers and staff who were of the opinion that the Party's re-election chances would be improved without Patrice, without Ian, or without both.

The thing no one on the strategy side wanted to admit to Ian was that he'd won them the first term, but magic was set to hamper them for the second. The plan was to get his advice and then cut him loose before he became as much a liability as Patrice's dick.

"We need to talk about net zero," Gaby said, wearily. She and Angela had been at each other's throats in an eco-socialist reenactment of *Mean Girls*, and while normally that would amuse the hell out of Eric, he wished they'd put it to rest, at least until Patrice had a comfortable 10 percent lead. Angela was a Patrice loyalist, and Gaby was still pissed off that she'd been thrown under the bus to keep him afloat. "It's going to be our legacy."

"Can we not talk about legacies when there's still an election to win?" Eric said.

"Voters are willing to accept all kinds of austerity talk when the economy's bad," Gaby was saying. "Even if they're poor, even if they're going to suffer more. Frame it like that. We all make sacrifices, blah blah."

"The economy is quite steady," Angela said. "If you look at the employment figures–"

"We call it a war, then," Jonah said. "Voters like a war."

"We make the Blight Report public."

Eric heard himself say the words, but didn't realize they'd come out of his own mouth until every head in the room turned to look at him.

"Oh, that's just great," Sandra, the consummate pollster, said. "He's Black, he's a second-generation immigrant, he's *Haitian*, he's got a scary wizard running the show—no offence, Ian—and now he's some kind of super villain who wants to blot out the sun."

"It doesn't need to come from us." That was Jonah, who, as far as Eric knew, was the very reason they had the report before the public did, the only reason it hadn't sunk into a bureaucratic Swamp of Sadness along with a million other well-intentioned but unparseable dire warnings. The whole idea had been to spin it in a way that might be more easily swallowed by a frightened electorate, feed it to the friendlier elements of the press—few and far between, with Reid Curtis' media empire gobbling up small town outlets. To turn it into a fairy tale of sustainable development and contingency planning. Meanwhile, anyone who'd actually read it knew that humanity was about to be perma-fucked. "Leak it, let Graves flounder for a bit—you just know he'd like the solar shade thing, it's right up his techno-masturbatory alley—and the hard path starts to look good by comparison."

"That's not complete shit," Angela said. "It'll distract him from the *Post* investigation." She stopped abruptly, glanced nervously at Ian, then at Eric.

"The fuck are you talkin' about?" Ian turned from Sandra's Polling Wall of Crazy to loom over the table.

Eric had once been witness to what happened when Ian got genuinely angry, over and above his baseline rage-against-everything mode. He'd been escorting Gaby to cabinet, past the gaggle of Alt Reich fuckboys who were an increasingly regular presence on the Hill, and one of them had let loose a racial slur. Gaby was used to it, and Eric thought that Ian must have been too, except that this was well in the middle of Gaby's Venezuelan-flavoured downward spiral and he apparently didn't feel like letting it slide by this time.

Ian had thrown a brown note at them. Just casually drawn a series of lines, which hovered, warbling, above the paper, and tossed it in the general direction of the protestors. Eric felt more than heard its low groan, churning in his bowels, a sick and uneasy gravel that resonated in the thick, soupy air. He'd felt ill, and then he could smell it, the sound dissipating under the cries of the fifty underprepared fascists, the police in their dark blue uniforms all losing bladder control simultaneously. It was a meme before the afternoon with half a dozen autotune remixes ("The alt-right is full of shit!") The Party scurried to avoid and deny, and no one was 100% sure it was him and not the KFC they'd grabbed before heading to the demo.

"Be happy I never do that in Parliament," he'd said, more to Gaby than to Eric, and kept walking.

Ian looked approximately that mad now, and Eric felt the tea he'd had in the morning slosh uncomfortably.

"The photo has more legs than we thought," Eric said, and eyes that could immolate entire solar systems swung to glare at him. He should have just let Angela deal with it. Ian liked her better.

Yesterday afternoon, while Ian had ironed out the statistical probabilities of each of the Blight Report recommendations actually succeeding, Eric and Angela had met, briefly, to discuss how to break the news.

"You must have seen that coming," Angela said. "It'll be an election issue..."

A frowning flicker crossed Ian's face that might have been one (1) actual emotion. It looked suspiciously like concern, if Ian was capable of concern, or any emotions beyond irritability towards humanity in general. "Find a way to put a cork in it."

"Ian," Gaby tried for placating. As if you could placate a thunderstorm. "Be reasonable. We have to give the public something."

Ian snapped, "I'm so glad you're back. At least your bad ideas are sometimes funny." Ian then turned his wrath back on Angela, and Eric breathed a sigh of relief. "Make this go away." He mimed waving a wand. "See? Magic."

The conversation drifted on from there, a discussion of foreign policy positions, their NATO obligations, and Eric excused himself to the bathroom.

Jonah was waiting for him as he left the stall. Jesus, did Ian hire specifically for the ability to be sneaky and weird?

"Someone's hoping to get noticed." Eric, who'd lasted months as Broom Closet liaison, was well used to being menaced. Jonah was a clenched fist in search of a target. Disheveled, long black hair falling into his eyes, he looked like he'd slept in his clothes, if he'd slept at all.

"Ian's decided I need a sitter now?"

"Don't you?"

Eric straightened his collar. "Ian needs to go. Even Patrice sees it."

"Patrice isn't your problem. The Party is your problem."

"And Ian is the Party?" He meant it as sarcasm, but Jonah nodded, wide-eyed and earnest.

"Don't forget it, either."

23

An unseasonal cold struck mid-October. Tobias should have been celebrating the budget's defeat and the non-confidence vote that guaranteed a snap election. But the grass was frost-brittle under his shoes when a year ago, it had been sweltering. The land was sick, wasting away as it awaited its new king.

Lucy would be waiting with champagne at home, but that was hours and a river away. Now, he sat between two Corinthian pillars, the stone slab cold under his ass. He checked his phone—had he gotten the time wrong, the place? A coffee shop, if less theatrical, might have been a better choice.

"If it's any consolation—" Jonah Augustine stepped out from behind a pine, all scuffed leather and flannel and rumpled swagger. Frost or not, Tobias hadn't heard him coming. "I don't want to be here either."

Not tall to begin with, Jonah was dwarfed by the trees and the Abbey Ruins, fingers twined through shrivelled tendrils of dead ivy, kicking at the ancient brick with his heel. Hell of a place for a clandestine meeting, but Gatineau was far enough off the beaten track that they weren't likely to run into anyone at this hour. Even with the unseasonal chill, Tobias admitted a certain poetry to the grounds.

"You called me." Seeing Jonah make no move, Tobias crossed over to him.

Jonah craned his head towards the archway above him. "Say what you want about colonizers, your people knew how to make some pretty buildings back in the day. How's Graves? As boring as he looks on TV?"

"You didn't drive all the way to Gatineau to ask me about Graves."

"Yeah. He's not the secret MAI. You know who is?"

"I genuinely do not."

Jonah, his breath already a diffuse white eddy in the cold air, lit a hand-rolled cigarette. "Too bad. I was hoping you weren't as clueless as you look." He swung his backpack off one shoulder and unzipped it, tugging a file folder free. "Sorry for the low-tech. It's got its utility. Such as not leaving data in your enemies' hands."

"What makes you so sure I'm your enemy?"

His shoulders dropped, if only slightly, and he leaned against the brick, one leg bent to rest the folder on his knee. "Well," Jonah said, around the cigarette. "I'm kinda hoping this time that you're not."

Tobias blinked. He crossed his arms. Uncrossed them. Searched for something to do with his hands while Jonah smoked. "Mallory doesn't know you're here."

"My hours outside of work, limited as they are, are my own."

"I was under the impression nothing went on in that office that he didn't know about."

Jonah took a long draw of smoke. Exhaled rings into the darkness. "This election should be a cakewalk," he said. "Sure, Patrice has scandals, but none of them are as bad as what your Etobicoke North candidate did with the hockey stick to that kid when he was at St. Mike's." At Tobias' raised eyebrow, Jonah shot him a taut, bitter grin. "Check your Twitter in an hour. Also, eww. Look, I don't think we're moving fast enough, but no one in this country likes fast. It's still better than backwards. And Graves doesn't know how to talk about magic."

"He's squeaky clean."

"So's bleach, but you don't see the voting public swallowing it."

"Let me get this clear," Tobias said. "You're alleging election interference."

"It's the Opposition's way. If you can't win, you cheat. Except our side has a guy who can see it coming. Unless."

Jonah Augustine's brain might have been a rat's nest of loose electrical wires and crumpled half-written manifestos but Tobias could follow his logic this time. "Unless it's interference of the magical kind."

Jonah nodded. He opened the folder, showed Tobias the telltale number trail, the tangled detritus that the spell had left in its wake. "Except I didn't know what it was supposed to do. Not until that shit went down in Victoria between the Dominion guys and NOTA. You can't sway people's opinions, not by much, and the Party's policies are popular. But you can convince people that it doesn't matter, that we're all fucking doomed anyway. The Right will vote regardless; you could run a can of creamed corn against Patrice and it'd have a fighting chance as long as it was pale enough."

"That's not fair—"

"I know, right? The Party got in because the tide turned, because the 18-49 demographic were all suddenly more terrified of climate change than tax hikes on money that they weren't making or spending."

"And because you had Ian Mallory on your side."

"And that. But say all those young people stayed home instead. The Party still looks great in the polls, the strategists are happy, but E-Day is a different story. I couldn't figure out why our MAI friend was funding the Left along with the Right, until I realized that it was the faction of the Left that's abandoned electoral politics altogether."

"None Of The Above."

"No lords but the meme lords." He stubbed the cigarette into the venerable brick wall. "The best lack all conviction and the worst are full of passionate intensity. Etcetera."

"I wouldn't have pegged you for a Yeats aficionado."

"Yes, I too passed Grade 12 English. Bigot." Jonah huffed at him. "It might be enough to swing the election. But it's also a big fucking spell, and I don't think even you are naive enough to believe that it ends with Graves in 24 Sussex and a plan to lower the deficit."

Tobias ran his finger down the colour-coded columns of numbers, Jonah's small, neat handwriting annotating the connections between them. He had the receipts. He might have made a decent investigative journalist. At the very least, he excelled at pattern-recognition. "Do you have a name?"

"That's what I need you for."

"Why me?"

"Because your politics are full of shit, but you're honest about what you're against, and I don't think you could sleep at night knowing that your guy won because he had some dark wizard fuckery backing him up. And because they're your people." Jonah shoved the folder in Tobias' direction. "Do your thing."

Tobias duly photographed each page, feeling more like a Cold War spy with each shot. His fingers were stiff, unmoving. He'd never frozen, not like this, not on the battlefield, not when it had mattered.

"I bet you're looking at those shell companies right now and short-listing suspects," Jonah said.

"Yeah."

"I hope to fuck you're half the nosy shithead you claim to be. Call me when you come up with some names."

"I can think of a few."

Jonah waited for him to finish, then zipped the folder into the backpack. Tobias watched his dark speck fading into deeper black. Whatever he'd said, he was still the enemy, and Tobias had no obligation to tell him the truth.

The truth was he didn't have a shortlist, or even a few names.

He had one.

• • •

Lucy's arm draped like a silk scarf over the couch, one pale bare foot tucked under herself. She'd barely made a dent in her wine.

Tobias, pacing, was on his third glass.

"Alycia," she said again. "Alycia Curtis. Who's had us over for dinner more times than I can count. Your boss' wife."

"Yes," Tobias said. The last time she'd asked, seven minutes ago, before he'd gone over the pattern of transactions and donations, he'd managed an "I think so." The buzz had stripped him of pretence, and now he couldn't even summon that caveat.

Her lips mimed the shapes of words, "but" and "why" and "how," but none of them fit in the absence Tobias' pronouncement had left. Alycia Curtis was a loose ball bearing, rolling over the inside of his skull, searching for something to bump up against. Alycia, the heart and conscience of her husband's media empire, the poised and elegant face of compassionate conservatism. Alycia, with her careful, handwritten ledgers detailing her charitable donations, all the time using them to weave a shining web around Parliament Hill no less pernicious than Ian Mallory's.

"Does Reid know?" Lucy finally managed.

Tobias put his wine down on the glass coffee table and sunk into the couch beside her, tracing the outline of her foot with a finger. "I can't imagine that he doesn't. How do you hide something like that? From someone like *him*?"

She shifted, stretching out her legs so that both of her feet were in his lap, small and smooth and oddly heavy, little porcelain sculptures. "Reid backed Quinn Atherton, not Graves, remember? If Alycia were really an MAI, interfering with election results, wouldn't Atherton have won the leadership?"

"Atherton's hardline anti-magic," Tobias muttered. He was already dredging up possibilities: Reid and Alycia quietly disagreed, Alycia's powers had developed, somehow, in the last few months, Alycia had no interest in the leadership, she really possessed the moral centre that he'd believed she had and had held back, except for now, when it counted.

But none of that mattered. Jonah's evidence wasn't ironclad proof, but it was enough. Alycia Curtis, whose husband's career was built on decrying the influence of MAI in politics, was herself an MAI, and she was using her powers *now*.

"She must have her reasons," Lucy said, softly. "She might think—I guess it's the lesser evil, from her perspective?"

"Of course she thinks so." Part of him wanted to laugh, dissolve into champagne bubbles of hysteria, at the absurdity of it all. "So does Ian Mallory."

He could see now why Jonah smoked. He reached for the wine glass, leaning across Lucy's feet, and pulled himself back. His limbs were mechanical, his body moving without him, as it had during those long, quiet moments in Syria, knowing the bombs might fall at any moment, thinking that if they did, it might feel like relief after all the waiting.

Lucy's eyes glittered in the darkness, sharp and bright as knives. He must have been quiet for too long.

"It can't come as a shock that politics is rife with hypocrisy," she said. "Toby, you're the most ethical man I've ever met, but you're not stupid. I know you have convictions—it's why I fell in love with you—but it might be a matter of which evil you're more likely to be able to influence."

"I've seen what magic can do. There aren't good wizards or bad wizards. It corrupts everything it touches. It wasn't meant to be used by humans."

She reached for his hand, her thin fingers twining between his, her other hand rising to cup his face and tilt it towards hers. "What are you going to do about it?"

Lucy had been raised to never speak directly, to whisper demure suggestions for another to enact. He heard it between her words. Stop fighting with one hand behind his back. What good was the noble route, if it led only to ignoble ends? Fight Ian Mallory with the only means he had at his disposal: the man's own words, and an editing suite.

He shook his head. Each word died before it reached his mouth. He buried his face in her long black hair, breathed in the rose bloom of her shampoo, and held her close.

• • •

"Scotch?" the Old Man asked, as if this were one of their normal after-work chat sessions, as if Tobias had not just dropped the bomb that he knew what Alycia was.

He'd asked to meet in that terrible pub that Reid so loved, both in hopes that it would make him drop his guard and feel less like an accusation, but also because it was his own private domain, away from the company of women. Away from Alycia.

"If you're having it." As if that was even a question. Were he not distracted by weightier matters, he might have had it in him to be concerned about just how much Reid was drinking lately.

Reid signalled to the waiter and picked up the thread of the conversation, barely missing a beat. "Of course I know," he said. "Could Lucy hide something like that from you?"

Probably.

"I'd have expected you to connect the dots sooner. But I suppose you were distracted chasing after Mallory."

"How are we even having this conversation? Part of me still thinks I'm going to wake up, and—"

"Everything will be like it was?" The Old Man glanced behind him, muttered, "Where is he, with the drinks? Tobias. My boy. Nothing was ever like it was."

"Does Graves know?"

The Old Man snorted. "Don't be ridiculous. You've seen the man—he's a robot. He wouldn't care, but you can't have a conspiracy with that many moving parts. He'd blurt it out the moment it felt politically advantageous."

Was this the part where the villain monologues? Tobias didn't *feel* particularly caught in a Rube Goldberg deathtrap, and Reid was his usual calm, pleasant self, as if the waves of anxiety roiling from every fibre of Tobias' being were below his radar.

Reid expected Tobias to agree with whatever fucked-up plan he and Alycia had concocted between them. Shrug, let the rotten foundation of the country's government shift another inch or two. What was another sin, piled up against the weight of all of Patrice Abel's?

"That's part of what I don't understand," Tobias said. "Polls aside, you don't need magic to create voter apathy. My source—" He'd almost said Jonah, but this was rapidly becoming a game of who knew what, and Jonah was a card he'd rather keep flipped over until he knew what the Old Man's game was. "—seemed to think that the spell she'd created was a very big spell."

"Naturally," Reid said. "The election is just the beginning."

"So you are interfering."

"Tell me. How would you stop someone like Mallory? What was your plan there?"

The waiter chose that moment to interrupt with the drinks. Reid looked almost amused.

"Shine a light on him. Wasn't that always the plan?"

"And then?"

Tobias took a sip instead of answering. He wasn't much of a Scotch man, but he had to admit that the Old Man had good taste. Peaty but smooth, a stinging nostalgia that burned and comforted in equal measure.

"When the public shrugs and decides it doesn't care, because Mallory might have cast a spell over their little brains but Abel is giving the masses handouts? He's racking up debts for a future that hardly any of us will live to see, and if it takes dark magic to get us there, so be it? What then? This isn't a Hollywood movie with fifteen minutes left to wrap up the plot, Tobias. You need *follow-through*."

"Fuck the public, is that it?"

"Beat them at their own game. Because it's the only way they will be beaten. Go back over your interview footage. He's given you enough rope to hang him. Have you noticed yet that you're the one person he never sees coming?"

Tobias shivered. Every decision that the government had made, every policy twist and turn was with the assumption that Mallory was as close to infallible as a human being could get. But Tobias' photo had caught him unawares. How long had Alycia been working her spell? Had Patrice himself been part of some greater plan?

The questions all tumbled over one another. Why the barely electable Graves over Atherton? Why send Tobias to push an anti-MAI agenda, knowing it would eventually ensnare Alycia? Why the conspiracy, when he claimed he trusted Tobias? How powerful was Alycia? What could she do? How much control did she wield over the spell she was casting?

What did magic want?

He didn't feel like a warrior of Gondor charging forth into battle. He was a Hobbit stumbling past the Brandywine into the Old Forest. And the Old Man, his patron for so many years, his friend, was looking a hell of a lot like a Nazgûl waiting in the shadows.

"You're asking me to doctor the interview footage."

"I'm asking you to put together the puzzle pieces Mallory gave you," Reid Curtis said. "Clearing a path for democracy is only the beginning. The project we're embarking on—it will be truly unprecedented. And I want you to be a part of it." He reached across the old oak table and clapped Tobias's forearm. Tobias noticed the wrinkles, the liver spots. "Look, son, I know you have principles. I respect that. But I need you to see the bigger picture."

He kept talking, visions grandiose and vague, and all Tobias heard was: *Think of your career. Think of Lucy.*

Lucy had all but told him to be pragmatic.

Reid said, "It's the very lightest of cuts. He's already said all he needs to. You look disgusted, boy. Have another drink."

"I'm fine," Tobias said.

"Then have some fucking balls. To do not what is right, but what's necessary. I know you have it in you."

Tobias nodded. The worst thing was, he did. No matter how much it rankled, no matter how much trust Jonah Augustine had, in a fit of desperation, laid at his feet.

When he'd been in Syria, his unit had briefly worked with Kurdish separatists, communists with their own agenda and a view of the West only slightly less unfavourable than their view of Daesh. In the end they'd retreated, leaving their allies to fend for themselves in the unforgiving desert, because the greater objective mattered.

He could tell himself that stakes were lower, this time.

He could live with it.

He could.

• • •

Lucy was already asleep, the bedroom door ajar, her hair fanned out across the white pillowcases like an ink spill. He slid his shoes off, padded near-silently into the dining room.

There, he set Izzy to upload to his private cloud server. The little drone whirred, pleased to have been let out of its confines in the pocket of his blazer.

He heard her stir, murmur, "Come to bed."

"Soon," Tobias promised.

• • •

Cynthia Tan followed the campaign trail, not the numbers, and Tobias shadowed her. Poll-tracking was automated and real time. An earthquake in the Northwest Territories, injuring three workers and seeding several square kilometres with shriekgrass, rendering the area uninhabitable and unusable, was good news for the Opposition. Natural disasters made people frightened, supernatural disasters doubly so, and scared people swing to the right. One point up. The news, trumpeted loudly by government sources, that the earthquake might have been related to unauthorized fracking in a region under a legal dispute between ConocoPhillips, the government, and the neighbouring Dene—the latter two having expressed opposition to the fracking project—shifted the point back in the Party's favour.

The government's threats to nationalize ConocoPhillips and any other company that attempted something similar in the future, disregarding polling numbers entirely—well, that was risky business, and had a ring of familiarity about it. It could only have come from one tiny, windowless office, only from one person. Who, despite the increased scrutiny on him, was apparently throwing caution to the wind.

Meanwhile, the campaign bus, emblazoned with Ansel Graves' beaming face, was an electric-vegetable oil hybrid, and left Tobias' clothes smelling of French fries. He shot pressers in small towns, dilapidated farms and factories and oil rigs. He attended fundraising galas and kitchen parties. He lived for the small but increasingly enthusiastic crowds, the work-callused hands and flint-bright eyes. He acquired a favourite flavour of granola bar. Caught up in the whirlwind of the early days of the campaign, he had little idea of what was going on outside of the team's bubble, beyond tweets from the Ottawa desk. It was a strange, heady, upside-down way of doing politics.

"The future may very well be green," Graves was saying. Someone had been at his hair, taming it into submission to make it less of a punchline. Tobias saw Alycia's hand in that, despite protestations from both of the Curtises that they had no skin in this particular game. He'd lost a few buttons on his collar too, and the tie, though he'd kept the blazer for most appearances, no doubt thankful that they had, at long last, left the supersummer behind. Good choice; Patrice might have exuded more personal warmth, but he couldn't afford to look any more casual than he already did. Graves could take it down a notch or two and triumph on the backyard barbecue circuit. Or, in this case, a logging trade show, where his open-for-business message had met a warm response, and a hulking harvester with three massive hardwood trunks on the conference hall floor provided a rustic background and excused a slip into blue and black flannel. "But in the meantime, we need to look after our own."

He'd been coached too, and his campaign team seemed pleased with the job they'd done. Graves had folded some of Atherton's populist schtick into his own platform, both politically and in his manner. More importantly, he'd picked up some of Atherton's anti-magic rhetoric. Tobias knew him well enough to know that his heart wasn't in it, but that ambivalence didn't translate on camera. Patrice Abel steadfastly avoided anything that resembled a formal debate, some nasty surprise no doubt hidden up his sleeve.

"We're poised to become a global superpower," Graves continued. "We've been spared the worst of climate change and blessed with an abundant supply of resources. Our power comes not out of the barrel of a gun but out of the earth and the lakes and the forest."

As Izzy adjusted the angle, then swerved to collect B-roll footage of the crowds, a John Deere sales rep demonstrating a loading claw to a photogenically grizzled lumberjack, Tobias wondered if Graves had come up with that line spontaneously or whether it had been workshopped, carefully, by a focus group.

"But we need to protect the livelihood of hardworking Canadian taxpayers and their families, and like it or not, many of the jobs driving our economy are in extractive industries. If we are going to transition to green energy, we need to be sensible, and have a plan in place."

Cynthia asked, "Some have attacked your magic policy—including some from your own party—as failing to deal with the mounting threat of bad actors."

"It's all there in the platform..." Graves' team had already supplied Tobias with the visual, a friendly infographic outlining the planks of his approach in shades of blue and green, and a supplementary novella-length glossy brochure. The problem with digital, Tobias thought, was that it moved the art and the inquiry to the editing suite.

"What's really exciting is the potential for magic to provide us with solutions that twenty, thirty years ago might have been unthinkable. The present government's approach has been cautious—and while that caution isn't unwarranted, given the tragic incident in Alberta—" A pause. Tobias could feel Graves assessing the crowd's reaction, recalibrating. "MAI set the agenda but fail to act in the national interest. I believe we can do better than that. We can have growth, prosperity, an economic system that rewards innovation and hard work."

Tobias nodded, waved two fingers, and Izzy returned to his palm. Graves visibly relaxed.

"You'll have to get more comfortable with the camera if you plan on being PM," Tobias said, after the presser.

"Cameras, sure. Portable spy devices?"

"Tools of the trade, unfortunately."

The Old Man had given Cynthia more critical leeway than he had on the last campaign. Either he was secure in Graves' inevitable victory—given the heart-attack ECG stutter of the polling numbers, it would have meant that he knew something the rest of them didn't—or he disliked Graves enough to not care about the outcome. Tobias couldn't see how the latter would be the case. Graves was merely the face of a collective intelligence, and Reid Curtis was one of the brains behind the Opposition. Their every policy was carefully reviewed and vetted through him. His boss—and his MAI wife—had something up their sleeves, and he needed to know what.

Someone's phone alarm chirped. Graves cast a last look at the trade show floor, and then adjusted the lapels of his flannel coat. "Back to the bus. I—"

The bang came out of nowhere. Tobias' body moved before his brain registered the sound, throwing an arm over Graves and knocking them both onto the floor, the chemical reek of industrial lemon polish sharpening his senses, a narrow corridor of clean air below a dull purple smoke bomb. Graves scrambled to his hands and knees, and Tobias saw, from within the billowing clouds, a cluster of hazy grey figures emerge. He snapped open Izzy's case, sent the microdrone flying up to catch a slow tilt shot of the intruders.

The two in the middle parted from each other, unfurling a banner between them.

MAI REGISTRY NOW.

Security—and more than a few burly forestry workers—were on them in an instant; Tobias climbed to his feet, offering Graves a hand up as the smoke cleared. He hoped Izzy had been fast enough to catch the smoke bomb.

"Just crazies," Graves muttered. He waved away one of the members of his own detail.

"There's a lot of that going around." Tobias watched one of the guards fold up the trampled banner as they headed for the door. His heart was pounding, unconvinced as ever that he'd left Syria, that he wasn't back in the Alberta Badlands watching a man turn to glass. "But hey, you have a free platform point."

"I'll keep it in mind," Graves said dryly, and loped outside to the waiting bus.

24

"*The* Post *investigation points to a government ruled by magic. We cannot trust that any vote cast is uncorrupted, that the electorate's opinions are even their own. We owe it to our children to take our democracy back.*"

"I'll say this for Atherton." Jonah rolled the paper, torn into strips, into tiny missiles, and launched them at the TV. Most didn't make it. "He has the balls to say the quiet part out loud."

"That's why Graves keeps him around," Sujay offered. "As an anti-magic attack dog."

The Broom Closet was a conspiracy theorist's basement horde of pushpins and coffee-stained printouts. Jonah's maps. Tobias Fletcher's photos. Spreadsheets, detailing the spell cast by the Opposition's MAI. Sujay flipped the fidget spinner over between her fingers.

Eric said, "He's right, though."

Jonah's head snapped up from the maps on Sujay's desk, and she tightened her grip on the fidget spinner, stilling its parts.

"Not about what Ian can do," Eric continued. "If he could control people's brains, we'd be higher in the polls. And obviously not about immigration, or the economy, or—but. He's right about how addicted this government is to magic." *To Ian*, but he didn't need to say it. "Like fucking *junkies*. Come on, you both see it."

"Why are you even here?" Now Jonah was building a miniature catapult out of office supplies to launch his little paper missiles at the television. "Anyway, fuck the polls. Everyone lies. You might as well predict the election on *Night Beats* ratings."

"What does—" Sujay started.

"Only old people with landlines count," Eric snapped. "The photo might not fuck us on its own. The SVAR incident on its own might not fuck us. The photo plus the SVAR incident and the Blight Report—that's a fuckup that's going to lose us the election, and all this for a guy who famously doesn't fuck up."

There was at least 50% more testosterone in the room than Sujay could tolerate. They might be carrying on in what was nominally her section of the office, but if actual dicks were whipped out and started swinging, she was leaving.

"The problem," Eric was saying, "is Ian is too invested in his magic and his games to give two shits about what happens to the Party. Or he wouldn't be waving spells around where the *Post* can catch him in the act, or bringing in an outside agent with no Party loyalty—no offence, Jonah—to conduct land use surveys that the voting public doesn't care about—also, no offence, Jonah, and what are *these* even *for*?"

"Honouring the government's commitments to reconciliation," Jonah replied silkily, sliding the maps under a folder.

"Ansel Graves might buy that line," Eric said, and Sujay followed his gaze back to the TV, where the Opposition's presser was wrapping up. "I can guarantee you that Quinn Atherton wouldn't. You're not stupid, so why let him lie to you?"

Sujay didn't need to listen to the two of them perform their best impression of Jordan vs. Mirrorverse Jordan. Instead, she let the fidget spinner snap into the Pattern, magic splooshing from her fingers onto the survey reports, veins of light branching over the map, the capital at its heart, echoing the lines of spell in the photo.

Oh. *Oh.* It wasn't a ward that Ian had set around Parliament. It was a lightning rod.

Did Jonah see it too? He had to, at least the vague shape of it; he wasn't an MAI but he understood magic, what it could do. Otherwise, he'd have never caught wind of the Opposition's MAI. Ian might have tried to keep Sujay above the fray, but he'd never had the same caution about Jonah.

Jonah just seemed irritated. He'd been pissed enough about Damon. When the world cracked open, when he finally saw his own part in it, there'd be hell to pay.

But before that, there was still an election to win.

• • •

Sujay hiked her umbrella against one shoulder, adjusted her grip on her bundle of door hangers, and rapped on the frosted glass.

The light inside was warm yellow, illuminating a modern living room, sleek couches framing a flatscreen TV, a reclaimed wood kitchen island visible past the archway that split the ground floor in half—tasteful, inviting, and best of all, dry. A shadow moved past the dividing wall. Maybe there was a person in the kitchen or a pet moving across the floor below her line of vision.

Come on, I know you're home. The doorbell had a ring of LED lights around it and played "Ride of the Valkyries" when Sujay rang it.

Sujay counted to five as she worked to separate out the top door hanger from under the elastic. Everyone pretended to be out on election night, but these people were doing an insultingly bad job of it.

Her thighs burned as she climbed down the stairs. How did these people haul groceries up and down those steps? Then again, they had a customizable LED doorbell; they probably also had staff to do it for them. No wonder most politicians ended up hating the public so much. The public was stupid and awful and deserved everything they voted for.

Her canvas partner was a retired librarian named Amy with lank grey hair and rows of pins from campaigns past dotting her extremely practical windbreaker. She'd started out the evening in a good mood, before the pressure shift had kicked her arthritis into high gear and the handful of people answering the doors assured them both that they'd vote when the rain slowed down a little. The riding association's equivalent of a grizzled war veteran, Amy knew a losing night when she saw one. 338 had their candidate squeaking out a narrow victory, but that was before the ice pellets had started falling.

"People answer polls with their hopes," Amy said. "And mark ballots with their fears. Just to the end of the street, and we'll call it a night."

Sujay yawned and checked the time. Half an hour until she had to head back to the polling station to scrutineer. The rest of the block wouldn't take that long, not if people kept refusing to come to the door.

Anoj had emailed earlier, worried about her long gaps of silence, assuring her that he'd voted in the advance polls last week. Jamila had texted a long winded story about canvassing in Scarborough-Rouge, its long stretches of desolate suburbs with no pedestrian traffic, darkened houses dripping with Halloween decorations. This is how white people die in horror movies. An hour later, she'd texted Sujay a video of a pine marten eating an ice cream cone.

Sujay held the phone in both frigid hands, a promise of respite to come. She would answer it all later on, during what was still being called the victory party. She'd have a drink or three of shitty lager and pretend she had something in common outside of politics to talk to the nice riding association volunteers with.

It was just an election, and the Party had a history of varying degrees of a bad showing in all of them, right up until the last one, when they'd been as startled at their win as everyone else. Everyone but the very youngest volunteers had coped with disappointment—Amy, even Ian. A critical part of the democratic process. When you started wanting one party in charge, forever, even your own, you became a person who shouldn't be permitted within the same postal code as power.

She glamoured her wet hair into an improvement over the tangled, dripping mess it was on the material plane. If she still had a job come the morning, she'd ask Ian if he knew a way to actually glamour herself dry.

"How do you keep doing this?" she blurted out to Amy before she could stop herself. She rubbed at her hip, scowling.

The older woman patted her arm. "Get yourself sensible shoes," she said. "There's way too much walking involved in building a better world to wear heels like yours."

• • •

She should have just gone back to the office.

The bus at this hour would take forever, and the walk to her apartment was even longer. Still, it would have been quieter than the bar by an order of magnitude. And while Ian tended to frown upon drinking at work, someone else with the questionable privilege of having to deal with him on a daily basis would have stashed away a better quality of alcohol than what was available on tap.

Jonah was around somewhere, darting in and out of the bar to smoke, then dry off, then smoke again. She didn't know anyone else well enough to strike up a conversation. Jamila complained all the time that once you were out of university and working, it was impossible to meet anyone, but at least Jamila's workplace wasn't a nest of maladjusted sociopaths.

By the time the Quebec polls were in, the extent of the damage was already evident; they had a smattering of seats in the Maritimes, but almost all of Quebec belonged to the sovereigntists and Ontario belonged to the Opposition. Both Abels clung on, barely. Sujay's head throbbed. She never wanted to hear the Tragically Hip again.

Jonah side-eyed her third beer. She gave him the finger.

Six seats became seven. The booming retro techno was an onslaught, the stench of off-gassing balloons an assault on her lungs. If she went into the bathroom again, it would look like she was crying in there.

Freezing rain thudded against the bar windows, sliding down glass and turning to slush on the ground.

"You're drunk," Jonah said.

"You're not my real dad," Sujay snitted.

"Fuck it." Jonah tugged at hair that had gotten only more unruly in the last few weeks before the election. "I'm calling Ian to drive you home."

• • •

Bessie pulled up seventeen minutes later, just as the Party was shut out of the Prairies. Nunavut had returned one candidate, and there was still some hope that BC would come through for them, but the greatest bulk of seats were gone, collapsed into chattering commentary about the prospect of the Party losing its status altogether.

Ian leaned across the front seats of the truck and pushed the passenger door open. Height and inebriation conspired to shift her centre of gravity and turn her stumpy little legs into useless weight. Jonah squeezed into the bench seat, helping Sujay up after him.

"We can talk about anything you want," Ian said. "As long as it's not fucking politics or magic."

She'd been worried he'd be mad at her. "What's your favourite episode of *Night Beats*?"

He didn't even hesitate. "Obviously the Halloween one. Not the latest one, last year's. Where Lilith has the fake vampire teeth and the bloody face paint and the bad guy of the week is just fucking with everyone's dreams to commit tax evasion."

"You would like that."

"It's realistic."

"You didn't find Jane's dog ears a bit problematic?"

"I tolds ya not to get political on me, Krishnamurthy." His fingers tightened on the wheel. "It's the only episode where no one actually dies. Joe?"

"I don't watch that shit," Jonah said. Before Ian could point out the lie, he said, "The one where they go to the Shadowrealm for the first time and the Middle Realm just...peels back and falls away like dead leaves, and you see the magic underneath."

Sujay mumbled, "Shitty CGI."

"You don't get drunk very often, do you?" Ian was silent for a while. "You gots a cat? A dog?"

"My landlord doesn't allow pets."

"That's illegal."

"I know." She shifted, her throbbing forehead pressed to the cold glass of the window. "I can't even keep plants alive. I had a hamster when I was six. I really wanted a dog, so I guess it was a compromise? Anyway, turned out that she was pregnant when I got her. Apparently hamsters don't exactly view motherhood the way we do." She laughed. "Sorry. We're supposed to be cheering each other up."

"You don't think that's funny?" He pulled up beside the curb in front of her apartment. "Sleep it off. The results won't change if you stay up and watch now or wait for the morning."

"I think I'm gonna puke."

She heard an irritated huff, and then Jonah was smoothing back her hair, pulling it into a ponytail out of her face with one hand while opening the door with the other. She retched once, throat burning, onto the grass.

"Sorry."

"It's practice for when Laura's a teenager," Jonah said.

Ian paused for too long before saying, "Guess it will be."

She stumbled out of the truck, hacking.

"How did we get everything so wrong?" she blurted. "Not just you, but...the polls. The analysis. The strategists. The whole thing?"

"Who says I got it wrong?" Ian leaned out from behind Jonah, pushed hair that had grown slightly too long for respectability from his face. "Sometimes victory is just reducing the margin of defeat."

She picked her way across the icy ground to her apartment, praying the whole time that she wouldn't stumble before Ian drove away.

25

Jonah heard the fiddle from outside the door. Hummingbird-fury ebbed into dove-melancholy, and though the fiddler had been born on an island outside of regular time, had first bled fingers over each pizzicato and arpeggio half a continent away, the rhythmic attack of the bow across cross-tuned strings was something he'd picked up out west, and the music would never not sound like home. Jonah slid against the wall, the edge of the hallway's yellowing wainscoting biting into his spine. The wallpaper above it was brown, cut through with black mold, and peeling from the walls. There was no reason, even in a housing bubble, for anyone who made Ian's salary living in a building like this beyond sheer indifference to his surroundings.

He closed his eyes. The Devil's Waltz washed over him, seeped into the piss-dank carpeted corners, sunk into his bones and bloodstream. Jonah waited for the music to pause before letting himself inside.

If he'd known then that it was the last time he'd ever hear Ian play, he might have waited outside a little longer.

Even at the very minor B&E, Ian didn't turn, a smear of grey ash pushed to one side of the window, glamour shed like dry, crumbling snakeskin. The interior of the apartment was white, blindingly so, its Apple Store minimalism a stark contrast to the 70s horror movie of the hallway. Beyond the lonely aloe vera on the windowsill, Jonah was left with the distinct impression that nothing lived there.

"Joe."

"Don't tell me you didn't see me coming."

"Don't tell me ya thinks you're the first person to pull that line." He lowered the instrument to rest it against the back of a bare wooden chair. Took two steps towards Jonah and stopped there, the distance unbridgeable. "Little priest," he growled. "Come to save my soul from eternal damnation?"

Jonah halted his hand before it could reach for the wooden crucifix around his neck and hooked his thumb through a belt loop instead. "Is that still a possibility?"

Ian shrugged. "Bold of you to assume I still gots one."

Oh, but that was the problem, wasn't it? Ian wanted the world to believe he was a hard man, but Jonah couldn't fault a shark for acting in its nature. Only humans could sin. "What are the maps for, Ian?"

"You already know."

"And the spell? You lied about it."

"That's what I do, Joe. I see things. And then I lie about them." He shuddered, the movement of every sharp bone visible under the thin fabric of a t-shirt—grey as well, as if he'd designed his entire wardrobe around minimizing the contrast between the wreck that magic had left him and the rest of the fading world.

"Not to me."

"You'da never have gone along with me."

"You used to have a conscience."

"I have calculations, Joe. Same as I always did." He braced against the counter between the living room and the little galley kitchen, fingers like dying spiders pressing into the wood veneer.

"What did you do?"

Ian slid a neglected salt shaker over the counter and circled it in blue fire that arced across the laminate. "Blythe's right. Nothing stops the Blight. Worldwide death toll's in the millions, and that's not countin' the ones who go mad, or go demon. There's a lot of places that'll be uninhabitable when the dust settles. We can evacuate the thin places, but those people don't get to go home after."

Beneath the magic, a ghost image of the map he'd laboured over, the tiny dots of reservations and the larger shapes of traditional territory in dispute, thin places in shadowed webs across them, with no concern for settler or Native, wilderness or city.

"And the spell?"

With a flick of one finger, the direction of the lines changed, twisted away from major cities, from the reserves, to oil sands and suburbs and the devastation the Anthropocene had visited on the land. "A lightning rod," Ian said softly. "I can't change what happens. Just who pays the toll."

"Decolonization by magic."

"Somethin' like that, yeah."

"People will die."

"They were always gonna die, b'y." He moved almost too fast for the human eye to perceive, the air parting around him to close in on Jonah. "Tell me you'd choose different."

"I wouldn't have that right. You made them think you'd *protect* them."

"And I said I'd protect Patrice and the Party and that I'd protect this two-bit slimy prick whore of a world, but I can't save it all, eh? Not with humans shitting up everything they touch."

You're human, Jonah almost said to his desaturated face. If he repeated it often enough, it might even become true. "There had to be another way. Out of all the futures—"

Ian shook his head. There wasn't a future with a happy ending. But if Ian was still concerned with where the Blight landed, there had to be something past the next few months beyond fire and void.

"You can't wave a wand and make people better."

"I never asked for this," Jonah said. "I don't want any part of it."

"You always were." Ian snapped his fingers, and the spell evaporated. "You goin' back to sitting in trees? Into the bosom of the Holy Mother Church? Which Jonah Augustine are you gonna to be next?"

"Maybe the one that's not named that."

"Names have power, you stupid little shit. People know who you are now. You tell them your name, they—"

"Fuck." He drew his fingers through his hair. He wasn't stupid; he knew Ian's obsession with names wasn't metaphorical. Knew he was on someone's radar, that he couldn't just slip back into anonymity. "I'm going back out west."

"There isn't one single reality where Blythe takes ya back."

He searched the room for anywhere his eyes could rest, but the glaring white offered no respite. "I can be less of a fuck-up for Laura."

"Nah. You can't. They don't needs you, I do."

"You don't need me," Jonah said. "You want a smokescreen. You can't make this about justice, not when you're just another white man, trampling over other people's autonomy, thinking he gets to make decisions for everyone else."

Ian didn't protest this, only said, "Is that what you think I am?"

"You ever wonder why no one sticks around long enough for you to fuck up their lives, Ian? Everything you touch dies."

"Joe," he replied. "I sees the future. Everything's already dead."

Ian took a step backwards, head tilted downwards as though Jonah in his red plaid jacket and blue jeans was too much colour to take in all at once, as though he hated himself more than Jonah could possibly hate him. Jonah almost wanted to hug him. It wasn't the time—the rage was still so fresh it burned—but he could imagine a time when it wouldn't be. They'd lost touch and found each other so often over the decades.

There would come the right time, one day.

Ian spat, "Back to your moral high ground and the ex-missus. See how she takes it."

Jonah reflected, briefly and regretfully, on how much simpler his life might have been, had Ian Mallory not been so fucking beautiful.

"Go fuck yourself," Jonah said, the way another man might bid a heartfelt goodbye.

26

Eric spent the day shielding Patrice from the press ("Do *not* talk to them, do not let Gaby talk to them, and for the love of all holy fuck do not let Cynthia Tan in particular near him until we have a narrative") and listening to him split a muttering monologue into a dialogue about whether or not he should step down as the Party's leader. Three years ago, he'd led them to an historic win. Now they were on life support.

Surely, Eric thought, if Patrice were to be condemned for their defeat—at the hands of a placeholder like Graves, no less!—he deserved some credit for their victory as well. Eric wasn't so naive as to believe politics worked like that. Otherwise, it'd be level-headed Gaby, with her multiple degrees and the conflict resolution skills of a Grade 7 teacher, running the whole show, instead of being so toxic that she couldn't even stand next to her husband during his concession speech.

He hoped whoever'd been appointed her minder was having an easier job keeping an eye on her than he was with the soon-to-be-former PM.

"Did he lie?" Patrice was asking him. "Or was he wrong? I don't know what's worse."

"You didn't actually think that spell was to keep us in power." Ian had been almost as scarce on the ground as Gaby had been since the disastrous results had begun trickling in, citing a need to analyze the inconsistencies between the polling data and the actual votes. "Either way," he said. "It's not a good look."

"We need to regroup," Patrice said. "Appoint an interim leader to keep the boat steady until..."

Eric didn't ask, "Until what?" Instead, he pointed out, "Three election cycles ago, we didn't even *have* a Party. It's looked grim before."

But not during an impending global magic-environmental catastrophe. Neither of them needed to say that either. This wasn't a polite gentleman's disagreement. It was a terrifying life or death struggle over which they, at best, exerted a modicum of control.

"And Graves will fuck up eventually. He's got no experience, the Opposition—" He'd have to stop calling them that. They were the Government now, one with a plurality, and the country was all the more screwed for it. "—they all hate each other, the social conservatives and the fiscal conservatives and the centrists and the libertarians will all be at each other's throat before the first year is up."

Patrice's big hand clapped his shoulder. "That's why I like having young people around," he said. "So optimistic."

• • •

Patrice was careful, patient. A man in his position had to be. He was simply too big, too much of a presence, too much of an inherent threat to the status quo to be anything but soft-spoken and accommodating to compensate. For the first week, he emerged only for a concession speech and a delicately worded congratulations to Graves that could only be read as snide if one were determined to be uncharitable.

Eric had worked hard on that one. With the Party shedding support in the wake of the circular firing squad, Eric was, apparently, one of the few people Patrice trusted to write his speeches.

Eight days after losing the election, Patrice announced that he was staying on as Party leader, pending review at the convention in the spring. He did so while Gaby made the rounds at the children's Parent-Teacher interviews, managing to embarrass the handful of reporters shameless enough to try to get a comment from her.

It was the best Eric could have hoped for, and his relief lasted a whole 48 hours, until Cynthia Tan, Tobias Fletcher at her side, ambushed Patrice as he was leaving Stornoway.

"I just have a few questions," Tan said, and Eric mouthed, "No." Patrice ignored him.

"Watch the hedges," Patrice said, as Fletcher's little microdrone shook loose a cloud of powdery snow.

"What did Ian Mallory tell you that the Parliament spell was for?"

Patrice was careful and patient, but he was also stubbornly committed to freedom of the press. It was only one of many fatal missteps he'd taken over the past three years, and afterwards, Eric would find himself wondering which mistake had knocked over the first domino, had ensnared them all such that even Ian, with the branching tree of possibilities laid out before him to see, couldn't find them a pathway out.

"I never asked," Patrice replied.

Maybe it was never in their control. Maybe there had never been a good option. Eric didn't want to think that all of their fates were so predetermined, but as that last, deadly winter closed in, he supposed it was all academic anyway.

27

The bus was always late these days, between the snow and municipal budgetary cutbacks. Compounding the insult, two SUVs had disregarded the weather and taken the corner at top speed, splashing mud across the bottom of Sujay's winter coat. She clambered heavily up the steps, stood in the packed compartment of cold, tired commuters, her face wedged in someone's armpit and someone else's shopping bags nudging up against her boot.

Not that anyone cared if Sujay was late to work. She'd eked out the last two weeks, nominally to tie up loose ends and pack up the office. Before documents could be dumped in the shredder, or files deleted, she had to bury each one, sink it below collective conscious memory, erase it from the past and future. The process left her drained, and she caught herself looking at the tops of her hands, nail polish chipped and cuticles raw, to check if there was still pigment in her skin.

Though the Broom Closet operated on a shoestring budget it had no chance of renewing its contract with the new government, even if Ian were willing to sacrifice his last two morals for the noble cause of paying rent. The Party, now stripped down to its barest bones, likely couldn't afford a full staff, even an intern as underpaid as Sujay was.

Her glasses fogged, panting for breath, her boots skidding over papers carelessly tossed on the ground, she spluttered out apologies even as she was tugging off her coat and scarf. The door to Ian's office was open, a rarity even when, as now, he'd been the only person in the office.

"Sorry—"

"Shag it. C'mon in."

He waved a hand from behind his desk, gestured for her to come closer. She edged her way around the laminate fortress to stare at the CRT monitor. It was Cynthia Tan's latest interview with Patrice.

"At least he's still saying nice things about you," Sujay said. "You thought he might throw you under the bus."

"He did." Ian's voice was flat, the lilt battered out of it. "I thought he might have been smart enough to do it on purpose and get something out of it."

The cut might have just been that of a razorblade. Century old footage, lying on a memory card somewhere, a trap waiting to be spring by an unsuspecting, well-meaning PM.

"What you're doing," Tobias Fletcher said, *"It's the death of democracy, of individual freedom and choice."*

Ian: *"What concerns you more? That I can somehow control the minds of 34.58% of the country's population—including hers—or that all this might have been what they wanted all along?"*

Then Patrice, fatally: *"I never asked."*

"It won't stick," Ian said. "I'll beat the rap, but not the ride." He was wearing a watch. It would have been an anachronistic affectation if cellphones kept proper time after an hour or two in his pocket. "We don't have much longer."

"This is bullshit—"

"The spell wasn't about the election."

"Why lie, then?"

"I'm not a miracle worker. Morale dips, we lose our twelve seats and have nothing to rebuild from, assuming we still gots a world in the next four years. A lie gets us to the least worst outcome."

Inevitability settled around her like a cloak, its weight familiar enough to be almost a comfort. She'd conjured enough shadows of the future to know. She had never expected a happy ending. She'd lied to herself that if she worked her ass off, they'd have four more years of the same.

And the other things, the worst things, the visions so strong they broke through all of her inexperience, her own mind's resistance to seeing. The fury of the earth clawing through its living prison of soil and stone, bursting cities apart, burying entire ecosystems in its wake. The future was a wall that even Ian couldn't see around anymore.

Outside, boots tramped up the stairs to the third floor. The staircase was always so echoey; she couldn't tell how many of them there were. More than was necessary to arrest a middle-aged bureaucrat for a white collar crime.

"Ian..." she started, as the door crashed open.

Sujay had never been brave. Oh, she came out as bi to her parents when she was fourteen, she made phone calls to complete strangers even though she hated doing it, she posted un-beta'd fanfiction for the whole world to see. She'd walked into the office of a scary sorcerer and applied for a job as his apprentice, making it clear that no matter how much he yelled and insulted her, she wasn't going to be cowed like all the good, obedient girls who had come before her. But she wasn't the kind of brave that stood in front of three armed RCMP officers and told them to leave her boss alone, no matter what Ian said she'd have to become in the wake of the Earth's shattering.

"Don't you dare," she said, placing herself between Ian and the men who'd come to arrest him. Her breath caught high in her throat, stuck to the roof of her mouth. She squeezed her stress ball in rhythm—there had to be something she could do, she could make them disappear, make them look like two other, completely innocent people, *think, Sujay, just fucking think.*

Ian growled, “I knows you're not some stund, girl,” grabbed her wrist, and dragged her into the wall.

• • •

Sujay forgot how to breathe.

She should have had a lungful of drywall and asbestos, a wooden stud impaling the length of her body, but they were inside the wall while avoiding the matter of the wall, their own molecules existing where the wall’s were not.

Relax, she thought, giddy. *It’s just magic. And Heisenberg’s uncertainty principle.*

At least now she knew why he wasn’t afraid of prison.

Ian’s grip faltered in hers. His half-assed glamour in tatters, he reeled on his feet. Blood dripped from his nose, the corners of his mouth and eyes, the colour of slate. Without thinking, she reached out to steady him, and stooped, he leaned his forehead into hers and took in a choked, shuddering breath.

“I thought we were in trouble there for a minute,” Sujay whispered.

“You have no idea.” He took her other hand and pressed a set of keys into them. “When the time comes—and you’ll knows it, when the time comes—take Bessie and drive. Fast as you can, anywhere you can get to.”

“Where will you be?”

“Oh.” He laughed. “I’m goin' with them b’ys out there. I’ve been running away my whole life and I’m tired. You, though. You’ll be a badass charmer. You are now. You remember how to do a brown note?”

“Gross,” Sujay said. “But. Yeah.”

“You’re gonna throw one at ‘em when we come back out. Give you enough time to get away.”

“Won’t that hit you too?”

He wiped the blood running down his cheek into a smear. “I haven’t eaten in three days,” he said. “I’ll be fine.”

"I'll call a lawyer. Um, you must know some lawyers, right? Never mind, I'll look it up—"

"Sujay."

She put the keys away. "It's not like you murdered someone." *No more than bureaucrats have been murdering people with a signature since some ancient king realized that the worst part of his job was governing and handed it off to an advisor in order to get more feasting and wenching in.*

"Someone out there's doin' much more than scribbling labyrinths on scraps of paper, ducky. And they're up to somethin' nasty." He found a stray strand of her hair and tucked it behind her ear. "You're the best intern I ever had."

"Didn't you drive all your other interns to nervous breakdowns?"

"See? The best one." He squeezed her hand where it still gripped the ball. "There was so much more I wanted to show you. But you needs to run, and keep on running. No one's comin' to save you now. You ready?"

The light was blinding as they stumbled out of the wall, and she nearly fell before she remembered what she was supposed to do. The power surged from her hand, through her wrist, lit up her veins, before bursting out of her in a vibration below the range of human hearing. Her magic, deployed before now only as a shield, became a bloodied, filthy sword.

The coppery sting of Ian's blood was drowned out by the squelching stench of voided bowels, the cries of startled cops not briefed in any detail about who they'd come to arrest. He shoved her away from him, towards the door. She buried her mouth and nose in the crook of her elbow and collapsed into the door frame, her entire body shaking, bile rising in her throat.

And, like an idiot who'd read all the right books but never quite internalized what they'd been trying to warn her about, she looked back.

Two of the cops—dark patches on their trousers, so hey, she was gaining some skills after all—had Ian pinned by his desk, arms twisted behind his back. The third advanced, baton in hand. He was on his knees in a pool of someone else's piss, and she could tell herself that the blood was there from before, the consequence of overextending his already strained powers. Too much magic. Too much coke.

Not violence, not a grotesque harbinger of the fate that awaited them all. Not a cracked mirror revealing Sujay's own future.

Convinced her legs wouldn't carry her, her palms catching splinters as she clawed the wall, trying to hold herself upright, she staggered down the stairs to fall to her knees on the sidewalk, vomiting into the snow, then stood, shaking. She ran, until she realized no one was chasing her, until she nearly forgot what it was she was running from.

28

Eric's desk was the aftermath of a hurricane. Sujay had swept away anything vaguely magic-related in her Great Purge of incriminating evidence. But that hadn't reduced the pile of Blight response strategies, focus group reports, polling stats, and rather charmingly, more holiday cards than he'd expected. Patrice had remembered to source a Hanukkah one. Angela's was a pleasantly non-religious scene of penguins with a note on the back that said, "Social media strategy due as soon as you get back. Don't be late this time." As if he hadn't forgone sleep for the last three nights in an attempt to weave some kind of narrative that didn't have the Party on its back foot, flailing madly against the impossible.

Even in his exhaustion, there was something comforting about sorting it all into order, as if he could prioritize problems that, in his own mind, jumbled together with indistinguishable klaxon howls. The Party's defeat. Patrice, failing Ian and falling on his own sword in the process. Convincing his parents to keep Jakie at home. The end of the fucking world, large and looming and yet no easier to conceptualize than if he stared at the wall in front of him and tried to fit the whole city in his field of vision.

He couldn't do anything about his headache, but he could at least stack folders from least apocalyptic to most, and feel as though he were in control of this one, small corner of his life.

Amid the chaos was a single ice-blue folder. Sujay must have missed it in her rampage. He sat behind the desk, cleaned off his smudged glasses, and opened the file. It was a plan that had gone back and forth, mapping out the probable areas that would be uninhabitable in the next few years, between environmental and magical catastrophe and the perfect storm where the two met. It must have been sent months ago, before the election, and had somehow gotten lost in the shuffle.

There was something caught in his eye. His vision, irritated, blurred. Overlaid on the drab office was the rich wood of Brixton's. One blink and he was staring at thumbtack-pricked beige, the next at a beautiful woman drinking alone, laughing at something he'd never said.

"Come look out the window," Lucy Fletcher said. "The sky is red."

He moved around the desk that was also the bar to stand beside her at the wall that was also the window, and there the atmosphere steamed and curdled, smoke rising from the burning cars stopped in the middle of the pavement, patio umbrellas turned to skeletal bat wings, the GoodLife Fitness sign melting onto its cladding.

Eric had been born into an age of horrors and wonder. He'd read the Blight Report. He'd seen enough demon footage. The camera distortion in those photos had been a mercy.

Lucy turned back towards him, hundreds of thrashing mandibles beneath her black hair. Her shoulders dislocated with the grind of crumpled metal, new, cartilaginous joints breaking through the skin.

His own cry broke the spell but the vision lay heavy over him, like mucus on his lungs. He flipped over the page and there was the telltale labyrinth, scrawled on the back of the report.

Beneath it, a date, three days from now, and the words: CSC Joyceville Institution.

• • •

"I wouldn't have come in this weekend if you were just going to nag me about moving back here." Eric knew that he sounded like a petulant child. Abigail's eyebrow raise would have normally shamed him into a retreat. Not this time. He was braced for a fight. The tension he'd been holding in for a month now jittered to spill free over his mother's lemon-polished dining table.

"What's left for you there?"

His mother, ever the peacemaker. Her blush pink blazer was untouched by the blast radius of the oatmeal Jakie was flinging around. She was the only woman Eric had ever known who wore makeup to breakfast.

"My job, for one."

His father waved away the imaginary onslaught of Eric's arguments. Eric had been among the handful of staffers Patrice had retained. Another set of parents might be proud of their son's accomplishments, his tenacity.

"How effective can you really be?" his father pointed out. "One of your bosses is in jail, and there are knives out for the other one—"

"—Ian's not my—"

"You and I don't see eye-to-eye on politics, and your mother and I accept it. You've accomplished what you can, but there's no point in going down with the ship."

"Patrice is still the leader of a major party." Third party now, with the sovereigntists holding the official Opposition and the ear of the new government. But parties had bounced back from worse, their predecessors included. "Someone needs to stand up to Graves."

"Oh yes," his father said. "Such a terrible thing, a balanced budget."

"Have you ever thought of how they're going to balance it?" Abigail was doing her best to hide a cringe. She hated it when Eric fought with his parents, and he hated putting her through this every time he visited. "They hired KPMG contractors to evaluate the medicare costs for people not working or in full-time school. Apparently disabled people are sucking up too many taxpayer dollars that might otherwise subsidize billionaires." There were times when he was glad Jakie didn't understand a word of the political discussions they had around the dinner table. Eric pushed down the lurching worry of what if he does, what if he understands everything and he's just trapped—

"Jakie will be fine," his mother said. "We have private care."

"Other people won't be so lucky."

"Other people," she replied, "aren't our responsibility."

His father interjected. "The Walsingham Institute is hiring. I know Tony pretty well. He could get you in, competitive salary, benefits..."

"You want me to go work for a think tank?"

"They give away more to charity than your party takes in annually. You'll do far more good, if it's guilt you're concerned about."

"I have a job, Dad."

"I'm not talking about a job. I'm talking about your future."

"We're not having this conversation."

His mother shook her head. "You'll see," she said, Stepford-smiling. "This is all for the best."

• • •

Eric stopped by Joyceville on the drive back to Ottawa. The new government, in one of its first acts, had eased up on fuel taxes, making his parents' old hybrid viable again. He'd missed driving. The 401 stretched before him like a promise, cutting through great slabs of Ordovician limestone, the sky wide and cloudless.

According to Sujay, Ian was refusing to see anyone except his lawyer. Not even her. The poor girl, infatuated as she was with him, had been devastated—and, as far as Eric could tell, needlessly so. Ian was in minimum security. Patrice, and his law degree, didn't think the charges would stick. At best, it was a creative reading of Section 365, at worst, a fundamental misunderstanding of how magic worked. If nothing else, it would give Ian a bad boy edge when he had to inevitably produce a tell-all memoir along with the requisite mea culpas. There was no need for drama, except, well. This was Ian, so he was obviously being dramatic.

Eric's list of job duties as liaison for Patrice's government had never included being subjected to a drug sniffer dog or a strip search or—it had to be said—walking into a correctional facility of any kind. The white fortress stood stark and grim against the snow, a hulking, hooked barbed-wire fence separating it from the civilized world. Eric yawned through a 2000s-era video about keeping drugs out of prison before being led to the visiting area. He'd expected a telephone and plexiglass, like on TV, but the whole room was open and making what was clearly, in the mind of someone completely psychotic, an attempt to be welcoming. To Eric, it looked like a high school cafeteria, with round chairs attached by steel poles to the tables. In the corner, two toddlers played with a sad clump of plastic toys, their parents bunched together and whispering at a nearby table.

He sat down, rubbing at his arms. A gust of cold air whistled through the dusty vents. Did they have the AC cranked up in here? He scanned the room, and seeing no sign of Ian, or anyone beyond the handful of dejected inmates and their clearly exhausted families, settled into a chair by the exit.

Fifteen long minutes—without his cellphone, which he'd had to turn in at the front desk—they brought Ian in. Immediately, Eric saw why he hadn't wanted Sujay to visit. He'd aged, visibly, inexplicably, over the past month, his hair gone mostly grey, the stubble that lined his jaw entirely so. He was shuffling, feet dragging, shoulders slouched. They'd cuffed his skinny wrists together. None of the other inmates were restrained, but then, none of the other inmates could walk through walls. That was also the justification the court had given for denying him bail.

Eric had never thought about Ian being old, per se. Certainly he was old enough to command a certain authority, but it wasn't a requirement; anyone who could make someone shit themselves with a snap had, by default, authority. But he had, despite archival video evidence to the contrary, a set image of Ian having always been the same vague middle-age, exempt from the normal human processes of entropy and decay.

Even so, it'd been a month. What were they doing to him in there?

"Stop playing with that." He followed Ian's glare to where his fingers toyed with the cylinder in the middle of the table. Oh. A microphone. Of course they were being recorded. Flushing, already off his stride, Eric yanked his hands off the table.

Ian maneuvered, frowning, onto the seat across from him, the awkward H-shape of the poles forcing him into a contortion to accommodate his long legs. Diminished as he was, he still took up too much space for any institution to handle.

"How're you holding up?" As if Ian was just enduring an extra-long work week, or mourning a distant aunt, instead of killing time in a federal penitentiary.

"Best kind, b'y. Gots three new tattoos and a prison wife."

There was nothing to be gained by engaging. "Everyone's asking about you," Eric said instead.

"No they're not."

He should have known better than to assume Ian would be grateful for the company, or indeed, had agreed to meet with him for any reason beyond wanting someone to shout at. "Well, Sujay is, anyway. She misses you. Why don't you—" Another sharp glare stopped the sentence in its tracks. "Well, is there, uh. Anything you need?"

"I needs ya to tell Patrice to keep movin'. He's down but not out, unless he keeps up this humble bullshit. Send him out to get the pulse of the nation or some shit."

"Patrice isn't going to be interested in what you have to say. Given. Y'know. Everything."

"Why do ya thinks I called you here and not him? Convince him. You can both thank me later."

Ian started to get up, a difficult proposition with his hands cuffed.

"Ian—"

He slid back down, grinned, as if it had been his decision to stay put. "How's that Tory girl of yours? Fletcher's little wife."

"Lucy? She's—" A flash of crimson, a chitinous swelling of the jaw. He hadn't seen her in two months and eleven days, and then, it had only been in passing, at some fundraiser, and she'd smiled at him, catching his gaze, and she'd said nothing. "Anyway, like you said. Fletcher's wife."

"You've been lookin' at her like the CIA after Cuba. Everyone's noticed. Day's gettin' late, b'y, do that at the once."

"You don't actually want to talk about my love life, do you? Or lack thereof?" Not that he should assume that. Someone like Ian, checkered past or not, must be bored to tears in prison.

"Fletcher won't listen to you, or me, but he'll listen to the wifey. Maybe. Desperate times."

Eric tensed, fingers, banned from the tabletop, clenching the fabric of his trousers. "When's it gonna happen?"

"You think I'd let it happen if I knew for sure? Someone sneezes the wrong way, boom."

"You'll be out soon, though. The court date's, what, a few weeks away? The charges won't hold up in front of a judge."

Ian fidgeted with his cuffs, as if they, and not a complex ecosystem of elites determined to keep the threat to their power out of the picture, were the thing keeping him here. His wrists looked thin enough that he could slip out of them with the barest modicum of effort, even if he and the laws of physics hadn't had a certain understanding. His hair had gotten longer too, enough that it fell in his eyes. Eric's stomach roiled. If Ian wasn't concerned with a probable release date a few weeks from now, that pushed the timeline of whatever catastrophe awaited them far closer than even the worst projections in the Blight Report.

"Does Sujay know that it's all about to..." Funny, everyone talked about the apocalypse like it was an imminent fact, as if it was one monolith. But the Cascade hadn't been like that, so why should the Blight?

"There's a hundred ways it can happen. Maybe here, maybe halfway around the world. But it's gonna happen."

Weakly, as if it mattered, Eric said, "I have a family."

"We all have family."

"What am I supposed to do?"

"Enact Plan B."

"There's a Plan B?"

"D'ya thinks I'm a total idjit?" He waved his hand over the microphone; fingers crackling static in the millimetres of air above it. "Four people know the full contingency plan: Patrice, Gaby, Jonah, and the poor fucker who had to write it. Everyone else has bits and pieces. Patrice has been siphoning money from the budget for the last three years to build up storehouses and long-term shelters. There are maps of thin places close to populated areas—you'll have to evacuate those first, of course. Make sure they're made public or Graves will use it to fuck people over. Patrice was sitting on this but it's time to pull the trigger."

Eric exhaled. "You could have led with that instead of giving me a panic attack."

"Don't get cocky. Most of the time Graves decides too late, or fucks it up somehow. He'll need the Opposition at least, and it's still not enough, but Graves will listen to Fletcher, and Fletcher will listen to his wife."

"She barely knows who I am."

Ian laughed, though there was no joy in it. "I said it was Plan B. Get Patrice to draft an emergency bill ahead of it, he'll look like a hero, and when he's right, Graves and his Shitler Youth won't lose face if they back him. One thing Patrice is good at's crisis management."

"We never really had a chance of stopping it. Even if we'd done everything right."

"We're one shitty middle power. I kept magic out of the SVAR's hands but—no. We were always gonna be fucked."

Over Ian's shoulder, one of the toddlers planted his ass solidly on the linoleum floor and began to loudly wail. His mother got up to comfort him, the father, face bewildered, seemingly paralyzed at the table in his ill-fitting prison uniform.

The kid was right to cry. How many people had no concept of what was about to happen to them?

Eric asked, softly, "Why me?"

Ian rose to loom over the table. Below the sleeves of his uniform, Eric could see the corded sinew of his arms, the blue of his veins almost grey.

"Because you failed me, you little shit, you and Patrice both. You're going to spend the rest of your very short life feeling guilty about doing it, so you might as well repent now."

• • •

On the radio, driving home, they were talking about a record tsunami in Japan, triggered by volcanic activity in Indonesia. Another outbreak of Ebola in Zimbabwe, this one resistant to the treatment they'd developed during the last epidemic. Each soundbite was its own small apocalypse, had ended someone else's entire world. Each devastated with its enormity, and were somehow too small, too distant, to be the one that mattered.

The snow lashed across his windshield, turning his view into a *Millennium Falcon* star field.

Eric shut the radio off, switched to a playlist on his phone, and drove into the storm.

29

Blythe stood at the docks, shivering in her parka, Laura's hand cold and heavy in her own. The first flecks of snow caught in the wind, dancing over grey sky, mottled sea.

It was just like Jonah to be late, even if a ferry delay in bad weather wasn't, technically speaking, his fault. She felt foolish waiting, like a pining Gothic heroine.

"Oh, when will my husband return from the war?" she muttered. Laura—barely shorter than her after her latest growth spurt, glanced up with a raised eyebrow. "Nothing," Blythe said. "Never mind."

"You sure he's on this one?"

She wasn't, and had to check her phone again just to be sure. She pushed down the surge of shame that threatened to rise in her esophagus. For years, she'd prayed to anyone who'd listen to freeze the love of him out of her heart. She'd moved on, of course she had. There had been friends, even other lovers. Above all else, there had been the ocean, fierce and fragile, that called to her as no mortal man ever could.

But still, as the ferry docked and he emerged from its grimy white deck, his hair long enough to be tied into a real ponytail now, a duffle bag containing all his possessions slung over one shoulder, she wouldn't deny the skip in her breath. It would be treacherous, to the girl she'd once been.

• • •

Blythe had decided to marry Jonah when she was eight years old.

Her mother spread open the photocopied pages of her elementary-school yearbook on the coffee table, stubbed out her cigarette into the ashtray and asked her which boys in her class she liked. The twenty-first century, if it had penetrated Taché at all, did so grudgingly. Blythe didn't have a ready answer, so she pointed to Jonah, who was always kind to her, and sat a row behind her in class, a boy with a quick, easy smile and jet black hair that his foster family insisted on wrestling into a buzzcut. She knew next to nothing about him. The handful of other Indigenous kids said he was an apple, raised by white Catholics who'd taken him in after CAS forced his birth mother to sign something in the hospital. Hundreds of years of history, of family roots torn up with a signature, but he was Métis, like her, both of them adrift in a world that had reared up in pain and struck anything in range.

The next day, bursting out into the bright June sunlight from their sweltering, air-conditioning-deprived classroom, she asked him to be her boyfriend, and he said yes, and, haltingly, put his broad, sweaty little palm into hers.

He would not be the last boy she loved, though she would be the only girl for him. They fell together naturally, bucking for top place on the honour roll, for the athletic scholarships, for the citizenship awards. Blythe, running ahead with her long, skinny legs, the first to reach out her hand, and Jonah, almost catching up. Blythe, rewarded by her teachers and peers for her obedience, her studiousness, for the watchbands she wore painfully tight around her wrist and peeled off in September to demonstrate the lightness of her skin. Jonah, described euphemistically as "lively," who punched boys twice his size for calling him a half-breed, succeeding in-spite-of rather than because-of, born to be holy but sneaking cigarettes behind the dumpsters in the parking lot.

Blythe had decided they needed to get the fuck out of Taché when they were seventeen. That was the year that the Cascade hit, and they were both so beautiful, with eyes and hearts open to a world that dissolved and reformed around them. They stayed awake into the night, watching videos of men who could melt nails with their eyes and Vasai Singh raising Pandora City from the sea above drowned Mumbai, the future's gleaming spires spinning together from salt and prayer, from pain. They lay propped up by elbows on Blythe's faded pink duvet and asked each other what it meant. Knew that it meant they could no longer stay in Taché, for Blythe to stagnate, for Jonah to study the Bible after school at the church.

So they applied for university together. Blythe joined the International Socialists and Jonah mocked her for it, at first. He quickly became their shining star, a real live colonized subject, a sideshow spectacle for the progressive set. Blythe left first, too, and Jonah followed her, from organization to organization, and then finally, fatefully, north, to the pipeline camp etched out across the barren, austere landscape of the Canadian Shield. She let her red hair grow long, and dread, and stopped shaving, and he told her, with each and every subsequent iteration of her transformation, molten and open-eyed and honest, that she was beautiful.

It was there, in the pipeline encampment, that he met Ian Mallory, there he disappeared for long stretches into the snow to think, a tiny receding figure beneath the arc of sky and the splay of the Northern Lights. There she learned to go limp and make her body heavy, bond herself to the earth, that it might absorb the blows of the baton. There, where they fucked, furtively in the tent, and conceived the first of the three children they were to lose.

She knew, even then, that one day she would lose him too, that he would ebb from her as the world advanced on them. She knew, but she strove, nonetheless, for love and meaning in all that chaos. And when it was done, when the tents were toppled and the placards confiscated, and the good middle-class uni kids had gone home, she'd once again taken his hand.

Blythe finally asked Jonah to marry her, for real this time, when they were both twenty, and they'd broken up and gotten back together again half a dozen times, and he'd sat on the battered futon mattress they shared, shaggy head in hands, sobbing that he'd made a terrible mistake by leaving. She was pregnant the second time, and she hadn't told him, and when she did, he'd weakly nodded, yes, yes.

Blythe could all but identify the moment his love for her had receded. They were having coffee in the breakfast nook of their apartment. She'd lifted one bare, sun-warmed foot to touch his ankle, and he'd pulled back; absorbed as he was in reading the news on his tablet, she thought he probably didn't notice, but she'd known.

She lost him little by little. To his work, to hers, but mostly to bars, and the nights he came home, booze-drenched and a faint latex smell on him, nights she'd roll over to touch him and he'd roll away from her.

Blythe decided to leave Jonah when she was twenty-six years old, but it didn't take all at once, not like love had done. There was the fourth and last pregnancy test, for starters, the one that stuck, the resurgence of romance that came with an optimistic prognosis, the shared project of Laura. They'd always connected best when they had a meaningful goal to pursue, and what was more meaningful than her, the wrinkled-lima-bean creature they'd created between the two of them?

• • •

She could tell he wanted to hug her, but more than a continent had separated them for far too long for that. Instead, he stooped to put his arms around Laura, who endured it gamely and stiffly for a few seconds before pulling away.

"I fucked up," Jonah said.

"No shit you did," Blythe replied.

"I'm not here to make it right. I know I can't. But I want to be part of your lives." He shook his head, stray hair coming loose from his ponytail. "You can tell me to fuck off if you want. Or, I don't know, we could get some pizza or something and talk about it."

"Pizza, huh?"

"Yeah. Extra mushrooms."

"You fight dirty."

"Somewhere that's inside and not cold."

The winter had come on so quickly, so viciously, that she hadn't had the time to sort through the closet in search of a pair of gloves. Her hands were dry and chapped. Laura must be colder; her wrists protruded from the sleeves of the coat she'd outgrown. There was no point in lingering here, the wind biting at their faces, arguing a past that couldn't be undone.

"You can have the couch for a month," she said. "After that, find somewhere else to be. Here, out in the woods, on the street, I don't care. A month to get your shit together."

"I can do that," he said. He grinned, all easy charm. He'd had almost forty years to get his shit together; she doubted he was about to start now.

"And you're paying for that pizza out of your big government salary," she said. "Okay. Let's go home."

30

The old bull was ready to die.

Jonah's hunting experience was limited, but he recognized the surrender of something cornered. The animal's great, heavy head drooped on his neck, sniffing through the snow but somehow not summoning the energy to chew any twigs he found. His eyes were filmy, clouded grey where they should have been black. His ribs protruded through a patchy coat.

Jonah's finger twitched where it rested on the trigger of his rifle. The moose's hoof lifted, crunched back down into the crusted snow. He snorted gusts of frosted breath. Jonah squinted through the sights.

"You got a good shot," Neil said. "Take it."

It had been a bad season, and not just for the moose. The last three cycles of near-supersummers had ballooned the moose population, and the plunge into first scorched-earth drought, then barren winter had been sudden, devastating, with rampant disease and famine. The government had extended the hunting season, and besides, this was Neil's land, his people's land, unceded territory, traditional stewardship and all that. Jonah might be an extremely distant cousin to the Coast Salish at best, but he was kin enough for this.

Nothing died easily, whatever Neil said about sacrifice and interconnectedness. Not even a starving geriatric moose whose death would feed the camp blocking the roads into the mine.

Jonah adjusted the rifle butt against his shoulder, and squeezed the trigger, just as the ground first trembled, then turned to liquid underneath his feet. The shot barked out, splintered cedar bark, and the moose, startled, shambled for the protective cage of the trees. Jonah kept the rifle but lost his footing, fell flat in the snow with the earth rattling under him.

Neil, still standing, a gloved hand gripping the tree for support, laughed at him.

"Earthquake?"

"Just a little one." West coasters could afford to be cavalier, had to be lest they go mad, but then, Neil's best friend wasn't a doom-haunted clairvoyant. He held his hand out and Jonah, wincing, clasped it. "Guess it's not your day."

Jonah stared at the heavy tracks where the moose had fled, cracked sideways where the ground had groaned and shifted, already filling in with falling snow.

"Guess it's his," Jonah replied.

• • •

Officially, Jonah was there in solidarity. He split his time between a shabby basement apartment with barely enough room for Laura to pull out a mattress three nights a week, and the blockade on the mainland. He'd promised Blythe and had, in turn, extracted from her a promise to stay in the laboratory. The ceasefire could never repair the family he'd shattered but at least they wouldn't leave their daughter an orphan.

Unofficially, the Elders in charge of the blockade spent a lot of time ensuring that everyone was comfortable with a rifle. It was one thing to fight a pipeline or a mine with the understanding that as hostile as any settler government was to Indigenous sovereignty, Patrice's administration could be brought to heel with the right application of pressure, and quite another to oppose Graves' enthusiastically pro-business agenda. It was another Oka or Unist'ot'en waiting to happen, and they couldn't afford to be naïve. Armed patrols had joined the excursions that went out every night to hit the patches of shriekgrass with flamethrowers.

When he tried to explain Plan B, the lightning rod spell, the words turned to enthusiastic *Night Beats* commentary in his mouth. All he could do was wait to see which came first—the invasion or the Blight.

• • •

"This isn't a thin place," a woman was shouting, hair askew, her face reddened and chapped from the wind. "You fuckers don't know shit."

Jonah gestured to Lorelei, who angled into position amid the trees with her telephoto lens. It made a good shot: the woman, aging, scrawny, her bare fist raised in the face of a hulking Mountie. If they managed to get any photos out, that was. He let her rage for a few minutes, long enough for Lorelei to get the perfect framing, and then, pushing his hair back into some semblance of order, sauntered over to the line of RCMP with his palms facing outwards towards them.

"Hi." He addressed her first, stage whispered: "I think they know, eh?" He turned towards the Mounties. "Officer," accompanied by a smile that had charmed the pants off men and women alike. "There's less than 5% shriekgrass saturation here. We measure it. We're not idiots. It's well under the legal threshold. There are golf courses with more untapped magic, but they conveniently don't have a molybdenum deposit under them, I'm guessing."

"You're not from around here." Fine to be an Indian, if he was a local Indian, but two provinces and three nations away, he was as much an outsider as if he'd stepped off a plane from Pakistan.

"Not so much," Jonah said.

"You shouldn't be here."

The man took a step towards him. He really *was* big, bigger than he'd looked from a distance. They had snipers positioned in the trees, but from the discussion on the scanner, it was a given that the RCMP did too. Still, Jonah stood his ground. If Neil's guys had to start shooting, it was because it was already too late. He was probably not going to get doused in water and marched out into the frigid cold, let alone summarily shot. But he was not so unaware that he could univocally expect that he'd survive the encounter.

Hit me, you stupid fuck. See how that goes for you. He hadn't thrown a first punch since middle school—when he'd spend 20 uncomfortable minutes in the back of a police cruiser listening to the SRO detail the iniquities of the sexual economy of juvie—but he was more than eager to throw the last one. Instead, he endured the Cold War stalemate of a face-off between one side eager to make the news, the other happy to commit crimes against humanity so long as it happened in secret.

He'd promised Blythe. Whatever Ian said about his track record with her, it was all going to change now.

Speaking of Ian—

Jonah pulled up the watermarked assessment map on his phone. "Who do you think came up with the plan to evacuate the thin places?" He enlarged the west coast, with its red zones that were already under evacuation. "That was me." *Involuntarily.*

"You're all gonna die here."

Jonah wasn't; he was due to be back on the Archipelago tomorrow or risk Blythe's wrath. And he'd promised her he wasn't going to do anything stupid. Every muscle in his body hummed with tension. He stood, cowboy-stanced, fists tight at his side, looking for a fuck, or a fight, or both. He ached to collide with another body, to hear the slap of his skin against another's. If it couldn't be in lust, it might as well be hate.

"If we do," he said, picking his way around the words like a minefield, "you're welcome to whatever's left of the land. Until then, come back with an environmental assessment."

• • •

"You're good at what you do," Jade said. "But you don't speak for us. Stay in your lane."

Jonah lit a cigarette off the mouth of the fire barrel, leaned against the polyester back of the lawn chair, and tried not to take it personally. "They're gonna keep coming," he said. "Map or not, they can just declare a thin place and evacuate everyone." Graves didn't have a consultant like Jonah on his team. He gave no shits about consultation.

"With bulldozers, next time," Neil added. "Not just for the forest."

Jade threw another bundle of sticks into the fire. The flames leapt, splashed red and gold across their tired faces. None of them were new at this.

"I know a guy in the city," Jonah admitted. "I've got him working on fake papers for me and my family. I can pass along his info if you want."

Neil shook his head. "You don't think they're just gonna go after us, do you? Just this land?"

"Whether it's magic or molybdenum under our land," Jade said. "They always want the same thing."

Molly, one of the Elders, gestured at Jonah for a smoke, which he tossed in her direction. Lighting it, she said, "The difference is, we've had our apocalypse. Every one of us here because people fought to survive it. What happens when the end comes for them, too?"

• • •

Blythe walked along the pebbled shore, an ethereal music-video dream, her red hair lifted in the wind into a sea of flame around her head. Every so often, she would scoop up a rock and skip it across the thrashing waves. Jonah watched her from a distance, in her weekend clothes, faded jeans and tall rubber boots, considered her beauty, understated to the point of an afterthought, objectively. Aesthetically. They were practically strangers now, but they had been each other's escape, once.

"Hey."

She turned, her mouth almost open to call back to him, before she gasped and clutched her shoulder. He felt it as he ran for her, almost doubled over in shock, the white heat sizzling across his tattoo. She reached him, caught him in her arms before he could fall.

"Joe, look..."

Everything in him screamed not to, but he forced his head up, towards the ocean, towards a sound like a hundred thousand wind chimes, a bone-deep shiver that he felt more than he heard. The waves spat translucent bodies onto the rocks, dozens of corpses of fish turned to blown glass, fragile bones visible through their flesh. He almost nudged one with a boot but Blythe tugged him back.

"Have you seriously never seen a zombie movie?"

He shoved down the momentary flutter of panic. "Fuck."

"I need a photo." She had her scale bar and her phone out, science-jargoning her way out of the fear, pacing, restless while he had all but frozen in place. Jonah knelt, stiffly, on the shore, a safe distance from the closest glass fish, marvelling at the intricacies of its scales, each one preserved in perfect detail. At the tiny labyrinth of veins and organs, the ribcage shielding a heart of ice.

The heart jittered, and the fish convulsed, flapping into the air and back onto the rocks, and he knew the end was coming sooner than any of them, even Blythe, had believed. Molly was right, the end had come before. People had lived through apocalypse, through the plagues and the buffalo slaughter and the dog massacre, through leaders hanged and children murdered and names buried deeper even than his own. Somehow, someone had lived through it, something would survive this, something had to. Laura had to.

Blythe, hesitant, dropped to her knees beside him, the phone falling to the rocks. He felt her hand over his own; he folded his gloved fingers around hers. He couldn't feel her skin, couldn't feel anything but the cold on his face and the burning in his arm.

They watched in silence as the ocean wept glass fish, thrashing and dying all along the beach.

31

Few disasters happen all at once.

There were fissures, this time, cracks in the levies. For Tobias, briefly, the Cascade and the Blight were one long emergency. Cataclysm was a magic trick: the pledge, the turn, and at last, the prestige. He had rarely doubted himself, but now he found himself freezing as he walked down the street, caught in a web of free-floating anxiety, paralyzed by the understanding that he wasn't making the best of the last days he had before everything changed. He would stare for long minutes at shriekgrass budding from gaps in the sidewalk.

To say that he should have seen it coming was to ignore millennia of human evolution and social conditioning.

And yet.

• • •

The revolution, too, took its time.

For that, Tobias—never a revolutionary himself—was grateful. Graves moved slowly, proposing detailed studies for each unravelling of the previous regime's policy. There was work to be done, but no one wanted a misstep, let alone a catastrophe like the SVAR Incident. There were relationships, domestic and foreign, to be repaired. Rampant government spending to rein in. The new government promised to protect Canadians while harnessing the magical resources that gave the country a competitive advantage in the global market. Graves was scouting MAI to investigate the Parliament spell, and while Tobias wasn't short of work, there was nothing photogenic about a balanced, reasonable return to the status quo.

Meanwhile, Tobias had been shortlisted for the World Press Photo of the Year, sending Lucy into a tizzy of planning.

"You know, you can take a vacation. Rest on your laurels."

Had Alycia Curtis just winked at him? Tobias' shudder couldn't have been visible, though for all he knew, she could peer straight into his soul.

Alycia's cheeks seemed rosier these days, skin tighter. Maybe she'd had work done, but it felt like the glow of health, not Botox.

"Not if he wants to keep his job he can't," Reid said with an avuncular chuckle. "The reward for hard work is more work."

They'd won. He'd won. He'd exposed a charlatan with the ear of the most powerful man in the country, he'd begun the delicate work of prying magic's tentacles from their purchase in the nation's politics. There was more to be done but the victory was there, written in headlines and indictments, in the bold red of the flag behind Graves as, smiling, he announced his new cabinet.

Tobias could keep repeating it until it felt true.

He kept the footage of his last private conversation with the Old Man uploaded, a copy of the password-locked recording he would send to Jonah Augustine, in case the truth wasn't what had emerged triumphant.

• • •

Lucy rolled over, arms splayed like a starfish, fingers clenching and unclenching in the Egyptian cotton sheets. She murmured, "not yet, I don't have control over the balloon..."

Tobias chuckled softly and kissed her forehead, then slid from under the covers to pad into the living room. She groaned behind him and yanked the sheets over to her side of the bed.

Moonlight flooded the breakfast nook from the half-opened curtains. The floor was cold, his toes curling with each step. He poured himself a glass of wine and opened his laptop on the glass tabletop, tightened his housecoat around his shoulders.

The interviews didn't change, no matter how many times he watched them, no matter how many new details he noticed. Digital files didn't degrade like analog did. Ian Mallory didn't grow more translucent, spindly, with each rewind. Nothing he said made more sense, or became any more prescient.

Far enough to see what happens to both of you.

Mallory was now a subject for the crime desk, not the federal politics beat, and Tobias had little idea what had become of him, despite playing no small role in his downfall. Surely he must be out on bail by now, but he was keeping a low profile, and the trial would be months away. There wasn't much point, given their crushing defeat, for Patrice Abel to keep him out of the public eye. Perhaps he was hiding out, biding his time until the court case was resolved, conditions granted, and the memoir that would relaunch his career drafted. Still odd, given the degree to which Ottawa was a small town masquerading as a national capital.

"Come to bed." Lucy, a train of sheets wrapped around her shoulders pooling in her wake, came up behind him. "Again?"

"He was trying to tell us something." Tobias pushed the video a few frames back. "This isn't just idle speculation."

"Does it really matter now? Whatever he was trying to do, it didn't work out so well for him, did it?"

"I guess not."

Her arms, graceful and dancer-thin, circled his neck, and she leaned her face into the side of his head. "Consider." Her voice, like a rushing silver creek. "Alycia never had a huge, ambitious scheme. She did her magic to fix what was wrong, and now that it's done, she's stopped."

"And now—what?"

She kissed the top of his ear. She slid her hand down his arm, twining her fingers between his, their gold rings bumping together. "The rest of our lives. And maybe transfer to the sports desk," she added. "No magic there."

"Not the way the Senators are playing this season," he admitted.

"It's okay now," she whispered, half to herself, as the laptop hummed its own private rhythm. "Everything will be okay."

• • •

A red carpet split the steps leading up to the entrance of the Old Man's Laurentian retreat, a razor blade slash cascading bright and bloody along the white marble. Tobias' feet, in polished shoes—the limo had picked him up, avoiding the need for winter boots in the two feet of snow that draped the sprawling property—wanted to avoid stepping on it, breaking the purity of its colour, the perfection of its line. Instead, he forced a smile, Lucy on his arm, beaming at the uniformed waitstaff sweeping them past the tall Ionic columns into the great hall.

Here, they were divested of their coats and separated, Alycia guiding Lucy away to prepare for her performance, Reid slapping him on the back and drawing him into his tuxedoed knot of friends. The journalist in Tobias, if still there was one, ached to set Izzy loose on the crowd, a veritable who's who of Canadian royalty. He spotted three cabinet ministers at a glance, an Alberta oil magnate, and the CEO of a Quebec power company, all clustered around the SVAR ambassador and a former US president. Even Senator Harrison was in attendance, tall and trim and irreproachably dapper.

"Here he is," Reid announced, thrusting Tobias forward. "The man who won the war on magic."

Cal, who had been clustered with the *Post*'s business analyst and a prima ballerina, craned his head toward Tobias and arched an eyebrow at him. The rumours about him and Mallory might have been true after all, hard as it was to picture.

"It was a team effort," Tobias said, though he noticed Cynthia's absence. This was Lucy's night of triumph, Reid and Alycia Curtis'—not his. He'd hoped for small talk and a few choice photos, not the spotlight.

"It was brilliant photojournalism. An old camera, of all weapons!" Reid turned back to one of his companions. "This is what I'm saying, Arthur. It's not enough to be purely reactive anymore. For decades, the left has been on the defensive. Tweak a bit here, pass a forced diversity bill here, but we started winning every major ideological war as soon as we realized how hamstrung they were by their own guilty consciences, their fear of the very change they called for. No man, in his heart, truly wants to yield to the herd. The right has always been the natural home for courageous rebels."

Tobias snagged a glass of champagne, followed by an expertly assembled caviar canapé. He'd say this for his employer: Reid was a lying hypocrite who claimed to be against the use of magic in politics while building immense power through his secret MAI wife, but the man knew how to throw a good party. The animated chatter of deals being finagled, courses being set, almost drowned out the Old Man's torrent of praise for Tobias' integrity, his valour, his stubbornness. Each word was a tiny barb that sat, festering, under his skin.

Cal Harrison, of all people, was the one to rescue him. "I have no interest in talking about politics, I assure you." He flashed a taut smile in Reid's direction, a silent apology for dragging Tobias away. "I'm far more interested in learning all about our evening's diva, and he's the best person to ask."

Freed from his boss' inner circle, he followed Cal through an outer hallway lined with columns. "For a minor celebrity, you're deathly allergic to praise," the senator commented.

"I prefer to do the observing," Tobias said. "Not the other way around. In an ideal world, I'd be in a darkroom with developer on my shirt cuffs."

"Hmm." Cal's own shirt cuffs were blindingly white, and he fiddled with the cufflinks. They were little wizard hats.

Tobias shifted from one foot to the other, scrutinized by the other man. What did Cal want with him? To berate him for his role in the Party's downfall? Oh, Cal was unaffiliated, certainly, but everyone knew the merry chases he'd always led the previous government through were facades before he rubber-stamped even their most radical pieces of legislation. Did he intend to have Tobias quietly murdered and dumped into the frozen lake behind the Old Man's estate?

"I'm intrigued by the work of this Simon Yamashita," Cal said cheerfully. "Had you heard him before? *Opera Canada* had an interesting puff piece on him a few issues ago, but—well, I know you're not a music critic, but I expect you're more than a mere dilettante, given your household."

"Lucy never lets me listen to her practice," Tobias admitted. "I think she met him once. I haven't had much time to listen to new works lately, I'm afraid."

"You certainly have been busy. The *Post*'s white knight, fighting for peace, order, and good government. How's the Pulitzer nomination coming along?"

"World Press, actually." He couldn't rule out murder as Cal's motivation after all. "Is this about Ian Mallory?"

No amount of time served sunning in the SVAR tech enclaves could rob a patrician scion of his ability to turn ice-cold in an instant. "I assure you, Mr. Fletcher, if I had any thoughts at all about Ian Mallory, you would be the last person I'd tell." He watched the former Defence Minister drift by, his cheeks already flushed, chatting to his replacement, Quinn Atherton. If there was bad blood between the two men, no one on the outside would have been able to tell. "And here I promised to be on my best behaviour tonight."

"Promised whom?"

"To the only people I make promises to." He gestured at a geriatric couple in the crowd. "My father went to school with Reid—and your father. Old, old friends, and more importantly, old money. And dark money, at that. Oh don't look so surprised, Tobias. I'm but a grey sheep who attends these soirees for the music, not the company. Present company excepted." Cal caught the attention of one of the waiters and lifted a tarte soleil from the tray. "And the snacks, of course. What better way to greet the end times?"

Tobias blinked at him, and Cal offered a tiny, inscrutable smile in response.

He knew. Or he didn't, and Tobias was grasping at straws, desperate for anyone who could offer him an escape from the corner Alycia Curtis had backed him into. He opened his mouth, almost daring to ask—in this, the Curtises' inner sanctum—when the tintinnabulation of chimes summoned them further into the chateau, to the great dining hall where the tables had been cleared to allow for a stage and rows of white-draped chairs. He took a seat near the front beside Cal as Reid Curtis stepped to the microphone.

"It's an honour to be here, amongst friends—and a few rivals—" Here he winked at the former Defence Minister, who laughed. "—to celebrate the woman who, for the past half-century, has been my companion, my confidante, and my partner in both life and business." Reid held his hand out, bone-white and slender, and Alycia stepped to the stage to take it. He kissed the back of her knuckles, drawing sighs from a crowd Tobias knew to be well beyond the sentimentality of romance. "When I acquired her father's company, back in the early days—oh, some of you remember, I see—she had a controlling interest in the stock. I hadn't realized that she came along with the deal. As it turned out, she proved to be more than a match for me, but in the end it was more of a friendly merger than a hostile takeover." More polite laughter. Cal watched, impassive. Graves, seated between Atherton and the trade minister, looked downright bored. "Together, we have shared ups and downs, failures and triumphs, and above all, a vision for this nation, one of clarity, honour, and glory, of every opportunity for the bold of spirit and faith. And, of course, a love of the arts, to which Alycia has always been a devoted patron. It is with this that I introduce our performer of the evening, singing a new work composed especially for her exquisite voice—Lucy Fletcher!"

The curtain lifted to reveal a modest orchestra, and Lucy, resplendent in a sea of carmine lace and tulle, emerged from some hidden outer room to carefully pick her way up the three steps to the stage. Her gown, its lines traditional and simple, but woven through with iridescent thread that shimmered under the lights, trailed behind her, black hair braided like a Roman noblewoman, a stole of white ermine draped across her shoulders. The strings rose in a rich harmony.

"I see we're capturing the hottest musical trends of the 1750s," Cal murmured under his breath. At Tobias sharp glare, he added, "I'm not complaining."

And then Lucy opened her ruby lips to sing, and Tobias forgot entirely to look at her.

The song filled his veins with sunlight, his heart pumping wildly in his chest, his spirit lifted from the prison of his body to join with every other spirit present, with each molecule of the other's existence, united in purpose, in song. There were phrases amid the tapestry, "*the idle game of the cosmos*," "*life is itself the labyrinth of its path to death*," a verse about a crumbling citadel and an iron sword, but the specifics washed over him. And crashed. His skin prickled. No one else noticed—their eyes, wide and glossy, were fixated on Lucy.

Magic. He wanted to shake the audience out of its stupor, but he was paralyzed by social niceties just as surely as they were by the spell. The gossamer strands of Lucy's song spun together towards their end, and her voice soared up towards the final high note—

—and then. *Then*.

It should have resolved to an E flat, a triumphant final note, but she reached higher, to an E natural. Against the harmony of the orchestra, it was dissonant, oddly modern, and Tobias saw Cal blink, startled out of his own trance. Lucy held it a moment before coming back down to the flat, a strange, if impressive, flourish.

Lucy had been practicing for weeks. Lucy didn't make mistakes. Either the composer had put it in, or she had, and Tobias honestly didn't know which option was more unsettling.

Amid the applause, the standing ovation, he and Cal looked at each other. There were tears brimming in the senator's eyes. Tobias touched his own face to find his cheeks wet.

"You know," Cal said, almost too softly to be heard. "They said Mozart was a magician, too. Well before the Cascade made that a possibility."

Tobias searched for indications in the crowd that anyone else was aware that they'd just been subjected to a spell—whether it was Yamashita's or Alycia's, whether Lucy's high note was its casting or its subversion—but the milling around had already started in anticipation of the evening's feast.

"What do you think it did?" he asked Cal.

The senator shook his head as Lucy emerged, clutching fistfuls of tulle to avoid stumbling over her own dress. Tobias caught her. Beneath the stole, her upper arms were ice cold.

"You were magnificent, my dear," Cal pronounced. "Truly magical."

Tobias wanted to ask her, but her eyes widened and she pressed a finger to his lips, whispered, "Later, we'll talk later," and before he could speak, they were moving again, towards the chateau's pulsing heart.

• • •

He could tell that Lucy was avoiding the subject. She was booked for two afternoon recitals in Toronto that weekend, and he was called back to Ottawa for an early morning press conference. This wasn't a conversation to have over the phone. The talk would have to wait.

• • •

Miriam Atherton was supposed to be at school that day, along with half a dozen other children. Someone in Communications thought that they filled out the frame, provided a humanizing element to the press conference, as Graves announced the *Preserving Our Future Act*, a half-assed magic mitigation policy. At such short notice, it was mainly the kids of party members who could be reliably hauled in for the photo op, which presented a very unfortunate and very pale optic for the cameras. In the interest of fairness and balance, Tobias trained Izzy on Girish Ramasamy and his son as much as possible.

Barring the appointment of an actual Minister of Magic, it was Aaron Murphy, Minister of Natural Resources, standing in front of the podium beside the Prime Minister. Graves being Graves, he'd brought a visual, the official map showing the evacuation and resettlement zones projected on a smart board with a bold graphic branded in party colours. The children looked bored, restless. No one had bothered to explain it to them.

That it would be long-dead Syrian insurgents who ultimately saved him was only the second greatest irony in Tobias Fletcher's life. But he felt the threat before he spotted the blur of movement just outside of his field of vision, reflexively flinching, near-dormant war-zone instincts awakened. He dropped to the ground at the sight of a black balaclava, a hood, what at a glance might have been a black robe, a gauzy burial shroud.

Tobias was not the only survivor. Quinn Atherton, Minister of Defence, was standing behind his daughter, and she absorbed the full force of the blast.

The attacker himself was atomized. He raised his arm to throw what, to Tobias' eyes, looked like a Pokéball, what for all he knew might have been, what else was a basement-dwelling mouthbreather going to use as a case for a magic IED? Maybe he lost his nerve partway through. Maybe the throw that killed the world was just weak. The device didn't make it very far; it bounced once, two metres from his feet, rolled, and exploded in a chrysanthemum of blue particles that devoured him in their light.

According to the Minister of Trade and Immigration—who survived, for a few days, the left half of his body sheared clean from shoulder to hip, the arm and leg turned powder white, dissolving into air—the man shouted "Allahu akbar," shrieked a bold declaration to strike a blow to the puppet client state of the Fascist American Empire in the name of Daesh.

Or—

What he called out, according to Atherton, as he watched his daughter Miriam turn to glass, was instead a call for an MAI insurgency, MAI supremacy, an uprising from the magic underground that would see the mundanes kneel at his feet.

Or—

Perhaps he sobbed to the heavens, "You all destroyed my life!"

Izzy, its casing white hot, burning Tobias' palm, would play back a different version of the corrupted footage each time. Sometimes the attacker murdered in the name of anarchy, for ecology, for all the girls who'd rejected him. What did the motive matter, when reason sputtered and died on the polished wood floor, when the monsters that had lurked in nightmares came alive to play?

For his own part, Tobias remembered only a wordless cry. Sometimes, in his shattered recollection, the man had said nothing at all.

• • •

It wasn't the initial blast that did the most damage, much as Tobias—stunned, as he emerged from the wreckage, the Carrick mat of limbs weaving and twitching behind him, rivers of nacreous light already veining the venerable stone walls—could imagine nothing worse. The leak of weaponized magic moved slowly, but it was uncontainable. One of the Parliamentary pages also survived the explosion, had seemingly outrun the particulate drifting from the Press Gallery, had made it as far as the foyer outside the House of Commons before the blue and green waves in the stained glass had broken free of their moorings and snapped her backwards through the oak doors, her flesh turning to wood where it made contact with the infected building. Kilometres away, shriekgrass erupted in patches, choking out all other life, birds dropped from the sky, human flesh became liquid, bones pushed through skin, branching into antler and claw. Magic obeyed only its own geography, tracing ancient pathways through the earth. His cell was down—everything was down, of course it was—but the crackle of speakers as radio became near-instantaneously relevant again suggested that it was happening all over the country, maybe even all of the world.

He had to find Lucy.

His bike was still on the rack, where he'd left it, but each step towards it, through viscous air, taxed his lungs, and he was choking and coughing by the time he managed, fingers frozen and trembling, to unlock it. Every time he closed his eyes, he saw little Miriam Atherton, who had been so proud of her swimming, crushed and reconstituted into a cobweb of exposed veins and malformed ribs suspended in crystal. His brain refused entirely to dredge up the memory of the thing Graves had become, the howling vortex of hungry mouths, screaming through teeth like broken fenceposts.

He tore off his tie, ripped the stitching so that he could knot the fabric around his nose and lips, maybe it was airborne, maybe it was through skin contact, if so that was better, everyone would be bundled up against the cold...

The Rideau bubbled and rioted, smashing stolons through its shield of ice. He rode past collapsing buildings, around cracks in the earth.

She met him at the door; he dropped the bike, not even bothering to lock it, not thinking about anything except that Lucy was alive, she was still human, she wasn't fighting off a horde of demons with a baseball bat. The street, in fact, was all but silent, the neighbours' lights out, windows boarded with plywood, cardboard, anything that might serve as a barrier between those huddled inside and the encroachment of the bright and vicious morning.

They fell into each other on the threshold, the snow drifting like ash around their heads, and they embraced for those first hours of the end of the world.

32

"I wish we could be doing this in meatspace."

Sujay shifted the pillow under her boobs and adjusted the laptop's monitor in the hope of getting a slightly less unflattering angle on the webcam. The entire tub of Ben & Jerry's wasn't exactly going to help with that long-term situation, but first cursing, and then shredding, the last box of classified documents into non-existence constituted an emotional emergency, goddamn it.

"Cheers." Jamila raised her identical tub to the screen, and Sujay raised her own in response. "Two weeks. You are coming back, right?"

"Yeah." Just...not for good. Probably. "You know what the worst thing is? My place finally looks awesome." She tilted the computer to show a panorama. A string of fairy lights outlined where she hoped one day to have a headboard. She'd had the official Lilith character poster laminated (Ian, to her surprise, had apparently considered it an appropriate use of office resources), and a collection of fan art sent by readers over the years, ranging from awkwardly rendered pencil crayon chibis to a gorgeous, only borderline pornographic graphic piece. Beside it was Patrice's lawn sign and Polaroid of the Broom Closet crew taken shortly after Jonah had been hired. The toner-banded photo of her and Jamila at FanExpo two years ago was tacked on top of the labyrinth that had woven the enchanted PowerPoint, the first and only spell that she and Ian had collaborated on.

It looked like home. It felt like home.

"I don't think that's the *worst* thing," Jamila pointed out.

"This is a virtual unemployment pity party." Sujay shoved another spoonful of Cherry Garcia into her mouth. "I'm allowed to whine about whatever I want. So are you—I can't believe *you* got laid off. It's not like you're overstaffed."

"Apparently the hospital is more efficient—" Jamila rolled the three syllables into four. "—with half the staff working four times as hard. Or something." She was still in work attire, fiddling with the hairpin keeping her hijab in place. Sujay admired her optimism, having gone into permanent sweatpants-and-hoodie mode three days ago.

"Ugh."

"Ugh indeed."

"What do I even put on my resumé? Yearlong internship with a criminal wizard? One of my references is in jail, one's up a tree or something, and if I ask Eric, he'll probably ask me out on a date."

Jamila waggled an eyebrow.

"Oh, *no*. It'd be like dating Xander from *Buffy*. But in a bad way."

"There's a good way?"

"I don't want to join all three of the notches in his bedpost. Eww."

"'Criminal wizard' does sound really badass, though." The corner of Jamila's lips quirked up, a tight, sympathetic smile. "Still ghosting you?"

"Yeah."

"Fuck him. None of those guys deserve you."

"He has his reasons. He always ends up having his reasons."

Jamila said, "Come home. Your parents would be happy."

"Lots of work for sorcerer's apprentices in Toronto?" So much had already been uploaded to the feds, and while Graves himself talked a good game about *utilizing our MAI resources to the benefit of taxpayers*, she was probably looking at work in the private sector. "Anyway. D'you think "communion with eldritch powers" should go before or after "proficiency with Microsoft Excel?"

"Way to pad your resumé by listing the same skill twice," Jamila replied. "I don't care how hardcore a wizard you are. Everyone lies about how proficient they are with Microsoft Excel. If we keep doing it, eventually even the olds are going to catch on, and then what will we do?"

• • •

The website crashed when she'd tried to apply for EI—not an MAI thing, just a system pushed beyond its capacity—so she went down to the Service Canada at City Hall. She hugged herself against the cold, the wind tunnel formed by the California-optimized buildings and the flat expanses of dead grass biting at her face and all but blowing her off her feet.

Next time around, I want to have the power to control the weather.

She sat an hour in a waiting room meant for half the current unemployment rate. It was crowded with the battered and desperate masses, worn faces aglow in the blue light of cell phone screens. She found a three-year-old *Maclean's* with a profile of Patrice's first cabinet, and inset on the second page, Ian, the power behind the throne. She noticed the gap between his teeth, that he'd forbidden her to glamour, and realized she couldn't remember the last time she'd seen him smile. She shut the magazine quickly as her number flashed over the screen.

The clerk watched her with a bored expression as she dutifully hand-wrote the same short employment history that she had failed to upload, and had then printed and carried there carefully in a plastic sheet. She passed the piece of paper through the slot beneath the protective glass. The woman glanced at it, then rattled off questions with a voice that sounded as bored as she looked.

Where was she born? When did she graduate? What did her parents do? What did her grandparents do? When was the last time she'd been back to see her family in Sri Lanka? Had she seen either of her uncles, Bhaswar or Harij, when she'd visited? Sujay could swear EI hadn't known so much about her the last time she'd applied.. She had to correct the woman's assumptions more than once—Bhaswar had died when she was two and she'd never even met Harij for reasons her father wouldn't talk about.

"Am I done?" she asked, clicking Submit.

In the same bored tone, the woman said, "Biomarkers."

She escorted Sujay to a little booth. Unlike the aging terminal, this machine practically shone. The woman picked up her hand, swiftly dipped each finger in ink, and pressed them onto a tablet. She thrust a slide under Sujay's nose. "Spit."

"Seriously?" She did it, though. She loved her family, she really did, but going back home, moving in with them, giving up on everything she'd built here, it felt like a betrayal. Even if Ian *had* told her to run.

The woman inserted the slide into a slot on the machine—Sujay wondered how it could possibly be hygienic—and pressed a button. It beeped once, then repeatedly, the tone growing higher and higher in volume until it became a siren's shriek. The woman rushed to her feet and picked up an in-house phone while Sujay, trying her best not to laugh, watched it billow white smoke.

"Let me guess," she said. "State of the art?"

"You're—"

"Yeah."

"You might have said something."

"You might not make unemployed people jump through demeaning hoops in order to eat." The grief had sat on her, a slick grey weight pressing on her ribcage, for weeks. Just a job, just a city, but she'd caught a glimpse of the things to come. Maybe it was the destiny of all MAI to go mad, to wither away as Ian had, until the grinning man in the three-year-old photo became the crumbling husk she'd seen over her shoulder as, like the coward she was, she'd run.

It still wasn't right to take that out on some civil servant just doing her job, but fuck it, Sujay was over being nice. Or right, for that matter.

"So, does that mean I qualify?" she asked.

"You'll find out in four to six weeks," the woman replied, completely deadpan, as if exploding machines happened all the time.

Sujay gave her a wink and a thumbs up and backed out of the room.

• • •

Sujay sat at the Canadian Firefighters Memorial, the bulk of her heavy winter coat and overstuffed purse taking up most of the space between the anti-homeless armrests on the slate bench. She could feel the cold metal and stone through her clothing, the whistle of the air as it stung her face.

An unemployed sorceress. It was almost funny, if she didn't still have to eat, if her powers had extended to conjuring rent money. She thought of texting Jamila that her magic had broken the dole, but Jamila had her own EI hoops to jump through, made no doubt harder by her refusal to remove her hijab in public in accordance with the new ID rules.

The attempt at foliage in the midst of vast, flat concrete expanses and soulless high-rises was paltry. Some of the trees still had their leaves, crystallized in the cold snap. Others had shed them into congealed wet lumps that dotted the snow. She traced the lines of the Brutalist bulwark, its unforgiving angles signalling violence more than remembrance. She squeezed Panic Pete, now well past the point of replacement, the rubber scuffed and the paint on the eyes and mouth all but worn away.

There was nothing to be gained by self-pity, as her mother would have snapped at her, had she seen Sujay sitting on a bench and feeling sorry for herself. She couldn't help it. The grey wasteland of City Hall, those spent, sunken faces, none of it needed to be. The world they might have made, woven into their last spell, was a peek at a verdant garden through ruins, but no one else would ever see it.

Almost without her bidding, vines crept over the jagged edges of the monument, snaking over the engraved names and the dust of snow. Flowers, moon-pale under the cloud-shrouded sun, burst in tiny explosions though the swaying leaves. Between the white specks emerged a single flame lily, *kanvali kizhangu*, red petals outlined in gold, beautiful and deadly.

A mother, arms sagging under the weight of Christmas shopping, and her small daughter paused at the mouth of the memorial. The girl pointed. Sujay averted her eyes, folded the worn stress toy over and over in her gloved hands.

It was just another parlour trick, after all. What was the point of having power if nothing you did made more than a ripple on the surface of the world?

• • •

The Trenton OnRoute at 4 pm was a refreshingly judgment-free zone, Sujay reflected as she watched a young longboarder devour an entire wrap. She tongued at a sore on the inside of her lip, and pretended to watch the hockey game..

She'd tried to reach Ian. She had no idea if he gave any more of a shit about Christmas than she did—she doubted it, really—but the thought of him suffering through whatever passed for a holiday in prison alone was too sad to contemplate. Just like he'd done with each of her attempts, he'd refused to take her call. She was driving back in his truck, stopping when she could, when the snow became too intense, when the tears threatened to make it impossible to keep her eyes on the road, her cellphone on the passenger seat in case he miraculously changed his mind. Any excuse, even a craving for a pizza slice, was a reason to carve out another delay.

There was only so long she could procrastinate. Her family would be expecting her. Still, her attention flitted between the TV screen and the slowly spreading patch of grease on her napkin, looking for an excuse to turn back, to stay put. The thick cheese and dough was already a solid bezoar in the pit of her stomach. She creased dents in the aluminum Coke can with her chipped fingernails.

The ground blinked. A split second, but she felt it like a flutter at her eyelids, a blip in her memory. It wasn't the earthquake that had hit the West Coast and was now flickering across the bottom of the screen, but she felt it nevertheless, the earth flexing its muscles beneath her, deciding, in a heartbeat, not to break apart and swallow her whole, but reminding her that it could.

Ian never told her where she was supposed to run *to.*

She heard the longboarder outside shout, "Sick!" and her first thought was to be surprised that anyone still said that. Her joints were stiff from sitting too long. She pushed off from the chair, gathering her parka around her, and stumbled outside.

Past the parked cars and the pumps, the highway was on fire.

Distant pockets of unearthly light, poison-green, webbed the curve of the westbound 401 where it met the sky. She stood just behind the young man—still licking tomato sauce from his grimy fingers—watching a backup of cars swerve and slam the brakes through a sea of smoke. Already, the wail of sirens rose and pierced the din of honking horns and screaming. Already, above the noise, the cicada-drone, building to an existential cry of agony, of shriekgrass pushing through the asphalt.

She called her mom first, burst out torrents of *I can't get home* and *are you safe and can you get to somewhere that isn't the 14th floor of a high-rise, no, I don't know, it's going to happen everywhere I think.* She called Jamila next, but it went straight to voicemail. She stood, shivering, beside the longboarder as he live-blogged the beginning of the end of the world.

Pull your shit together, Sujay. This is what a lifetime of reading dystopian YA fiction has trained you for.

She moved through the thickening air as if in a dream, suppressed another wave of panic that rose when, for a split second, she couldn't find her keys. She braced her hands against Bessie's red door, the metal cold under her palms. The truck was warded as fuck, it would get her back, it would get her *away*. It was Ian's last attempt to keep her safe.

She hauled herself into the driver's seat. The kid still stood there, frozen, phone raised against the world as if he was fending off a vampire. Wherever his own car was, he was too stunned to get to it.

You saved people in disasters. Even if you died. Even if the world died.

"Hey," Sujay said. "Get in."

Book 3

Like This, But Worse

The computer was out, and the TV. Most of the electrical grid was still up, just overtaxed, and I remember my mother bringing out the emergency candles, just in case. If the heat went out, we were fucked. It was minus 30 with the windchill, and we heard the storm shaking the thin walls of the apartment.

WHEREAS the safety and security of the individual, the protection of the values of the body politic and the preservation of the sovereignty, security and territorial integrity of the state are fundamental obligations of government;

We listened to CBC Radio 1 instead. We could hear the neighbours on either side of us doing the same. I think it was the last time the country was ever so united.

AND WHEREAS the fulfilment of those obligations in Canada may be seriously threatened by a national emergency and, in order to ensure safety and security during such an emergency, the Governor in Council should be authorized, subject to the supervision of Parliament, to take special temporary measures that may not be appropriate in normal times;

Quinn Atherton had a voice for radio. Not like Patrice Abel, but Abel was already a distant memory. He was calm, and calming, and I remember my mother saying that he sounded like a nice man, and in response, the knowing grief on Teta's face.

AND WHEREAS the Governor in Council, in taking such special temporary measures, would be subject to the Canadian Charter of Rights and Freedoms and the Canadian Bill of Rights and must have regard to the International Covenant on Civil and Political Rights, particularly with respect to those fundamental rights that are not to be limited or abridged even in a national emergency;

"This is a time for mourning, but it is also a time for action. We are faced with a crisis unlike any the nation has ever known, perhaps unlike any in human history. This crisis was brought about through the actions of terrorists who wish to destroy the very freedoms that all of us, as citizens of a free and democratic country, enjoy. This is a crisis that has already claimed hundreds of lives, including that of my seven-year-old daughter, Miriam. And I cannot promise you that the crisis has ended."

"There it is," Teta said, and my mother hissed, "Hush." But they knew. Even I knew, and I hadn't lived through it before like they had.

"The Emergencies Act is bitter medicine," Atherton continued. "It grants the authority for the government, the police, and the military to use extraordinary powers to ensure national security. These powers include authorization to restrict movement of persons both within and outside of our borders, the removal from Canada of persons other than Canadian citizens and permanent residents, to enter and search property and seize possessions, to detain suspects without a warrant, and to detain suspects without bail. These powers allow the government to conscript into national service any MAI who is competent to perform certain

services, or, if necessary, to indefinitely detain any MAI deemed to be acting against national interests and security."

By now, Teta couldn't seem to get comfortable. Her swollen, cracked feet, which she complained about at the best of times, bulging at the top of her house slippers, did a restless dance on the parquet floor.

"Never, since its inception, has any Canadian government been faced with such necessity, such urgency in action. I assure you that it is not a burden I take on lightly. My hand has been forced by the heinous act of a violent MAI extremist who has ensured that of your elected representatives, I am among the few left to make this decision."

They say that in a moment of panic, a person looks to what matters most to them. My mother was staring at me, dishcloth clenched in her thin hands. My grandmother looked to the bedroom closet. That was where the suitcases were, where she still kept the key to her parents' house. She knew, listening to those words, that she was about to become a refugee for the third time in her life.

"Now is a time to stand firm and united in purpose. Make no mistake: These terrorists, be they jihadis or eco-extremists, or MAI, will not prevail. They will not destroy our democracy. They will not rob us of our freedom. We did not choose this fight, but make no mistake, we will win it. And for Miriam's sake, for the sake of all of our children, we will emerge a stronger nation, united in victory."

Teta was clawing her palm so hard that her skin, dried from age and winter, parted under her yellowed nail, drawing a thin line of blood. My mother ran to grab a Band-Aid. I just sat there on the couch like an idiot, twenty years old, with no idea of the hell that was to come.

Teta lowered her head and began to cry, and anyway, for what it's worth, that's how I learned just how many Arabic curse words involve one's sister's genitals.

— Shadi Al-Abdallah

33

Blythe was with Dahlia when she died. Dani and Edgar and the rest of the team came too, but Blythe had known her best—and Blythe had barely known her at all—so Blythe got to hold Dahlia's hand, got to be the one to nod consent and, when a nod was deemed insufficient, to sign a form. As if having it stark on an official form somehow proved that she thought it was the right thing to do. Edgar had tried another round of reaching out to Dahlia's family, but her emergency contact was a former roommate with no landline.

The nurse who administered the two injections was unhappy about it, and not hiding that fact at all. Resources were scarce, and the electrical grid, though still running, was unreliable. She rattled off a list of services that the provincial government had to defund, softening the blow that one of those cutbacks involved not keeping people in inexplicable magic comas on life support.

There were efficiencies to be found, and Dahlia West was one of them.

Cleaning, too, had been cut back. Sitting vigil at the side of a doomed woman was as boring as it was important, and Blythe's attention wandered over the cracks in the wall. Smears of filth streaked across old paint, a eulogy in a language she couldn't translate.

Dahlia's hand was impossibly heavy. Blythe expected something to change as her machine-aided breathing ceased, for it to somehow get lighter as her spirit left her body, but she noticed nothing, even after the nurse said, gently, "She's gone." Blythe touched her own face, expecting tears, and felt nothing.

"We should do something," Dani said. "Maybe go to a bar—did she drink?"

Blythe shrugged, nodded. They'd had a beer once, before the *Love Craft*'s doomed mission. Dani put an arm around her and she realized that she hadn't yet let go of Dahlia's cooling hand.

"Take your time," the nurse said. "I'm just saying that I've got three more of these to do today."

• • •

Sunlight on the archipelago in winter was a rare sight, and should have had half the population out blinking up at the sky, but the street outside the hospital was quiet. No birdsong, no wind, no conversation. An army patrol passed them by, their footsteps unison in the snow. Blythe worried less about the army than she did about the RCMP, which was currently engaged in rooting out "unofficial dwellings and settlements." Her team had issued a report on the prognosis for the West Coast, but the Powers That Be seemed far more interested in routing homeless people and Indigenous settlements than preparing sandbags or distributing supplies. An ill-defined "community" did the dirty work of keeping people alive. Homeless shelters, athletic facilities, the Friendship Centre, and the public libraries opened their doors to bedraggled tech bros and businessmen and punk kids and addicts alike. Schoolteachers rallied their kids to raid Wal-Marts and hardware stores and shore up the buildings where people from the Exclusion Zones had taken shelter.

Dockworkers patrolled the ocean along with grad students from her department, sampling the water, collecting the translucent corpses that dotted the shore.

All of the cops wore ventilator masks. Blythe and her team strapped KN95s over their faces. Even if shriekgrass spores didn't actually turn people into demons, no one was going to risk it, and the infection itself was bad enough.

Meanwhile, the lab was a temporary shelter of sorts, and an emergency headquarters for several city blocks. From here, her team ran shifts to determine the shriekgrass saturation level, studied the various changes and threats—seismological variance, demon sightings, water supply purity—and reported it hourly over a system of shortwave radio that they'd set up at access points throughout the city. She and Jonah relied on pain and unease to determine which objects were safe and what should be tossed beyond the quarantine barriers. Before you got to the cool dirt bikes and studded leather jacket phase of the apocalypse, Blythe thought, you had the incredibly unglamorous one where everyone had a sourdough starter and emptied the big box stores and ensured that produce reached as many people as possible before it rotted. She caught micro sleeps on a cot in the lab, trading off with Jonah so that someone could watch Laura.

Farther from the hospital, she saw a group of teenagers, their makeshift masks fashioned from threadbare bandanas and old t-shirts, leaving a McDonalds with giant gas cans. The leader of the group nodded to her, her friendliness in contrast with her urban guerrilla get-up. Blythe wondered if she recognized one of her own.

"Oil. For the buses."

Gas had been an issue almost immediately after the Blight, with the stations drained dry in a matter of hours. The panicked exodus from the city hadn't lasted long, though. Not once people realized that there was nowhere to flee, the Blight was everywhere, and even if the wilderness wasn't demon-haunted and shriekgrass infested, people who'd lived their whole lives in what was left of Victoria tended to have survival skills that wouldn't last beyond a weekend of camping. The loose neighbourhood collectives that had sprung up from necessity had decided amongst themselves to limit private driving and stockpiled gas and vegetable oil for a fleet of yellow school buses that delivered people and supplies where they needed to go.

Blythe waved back. For exactly one block, it was her youthful vision of an eco-anarchist utopia come to life. It stretched as far as the riot cops at the end of the street and the walled-off Exclusion Zone ahead of them.

"Last Call?" Amrita suggested. There were shortages of nearly everything in the wake of the Blight, but grey-market alcohol was somehow always around. The Last Call had become one of the lab's regular haunts for its proximity and ambiance. It had once been the Woodward & Sons Artisanal Brewing Co. Either Woodward or one of his unknown quantity of sons had gone demon and fled into an Exclusion Zone, and the rest of the family had not seen fit to stick around. Kenny Ocampo, one of the dishwashers, had. He'd nailed a plank of plywood over the reclaimed wood sign with the new name, and decorated the interior with his own extensive collection of zombie movie posters and horror memorabilia. It was in shockingly poor taste and brought in a fire-code challenging number of patrons at all hours of the day.

Blythe nodded. Jonah had Laura for the day, and he could pull his weight for once with childcare. *He* hadn't signed away a colleague's life today.

Kenny himself wore ripped, bloodstained jeans and an antler contraption around his neck and head, repurposed from the old hipster decor. When the light, filtered through the red lampshades, caught him as he moved through the bar to their table, he looked like one of the blurred demon photos himself. The electric spark of fear lasted about as long as it took for Kenny to beam at them and take their order.

"It's all fun and games until someone in here actually *is* a demon," Laith said, as soon as Kenny was out of hearing range.

"If that happens," Blythe replied, "We've all got worse problems."

There wasn't a menu, and Kenny didn't take money. He had a

cupboard full of energy bars and Skittles. Dani had thought ahead and snagged a few bottles of hand sanitizer to trade for shots, which Blythe desperately hoped weren't going to end up in anyone's cocktails.

"They murdered her," Edgar said. "It cost too much, so they just—got rid of her." The lines in his face had deepened, the bags under his eyes a sunset fading to night. He turned his shot glass, idly, in the circle of moisture it had made on the wooden table. "She was a hell of a pilot."

"A hell of a scientist, too. To Dahlia," Blythe said, echoed by the rest of the team, and drained it in one go. "To the end of the fucking world."

• • •

She found Jonah and Laura patrolling the border of the Exclusion Zone to the south of his apartment. The part of Blythe that, through hell and high tide, still remained a semi-competent parent, balked at the proximity between child and flamethrower.

The Exclusion Zones were marked with handmade signs and banners and barbed wire and concrete barriers, a barricade of hope against the encroach of despair. Shriekgrass didn't care much about walls and fences. Like any other organism, it wanted to live. It was simply the ecosystem's tragedy that shriekgrass was better at that task than any other organism.

Her tattoo no longer ached in the presence of magic. The pain was a rotting tooth gone numb, no longer worth the twinge of wiggling with her tongue.

The shriekgrass moaned, squeezing through the cement by the vacant lot. She remembered a corner store there, half-torn down to build a condo that never materialized. Jonah shooed Laura a few feet behind him and, hefting the flamethrower over his shoulder, unleashed a torrent of fire at the ground.

They weren't wrong when they said shriekgrass sounded like someone screaming when it died, just not specific enough.

Dying shriekgrass sounded exactly like a *child* screaming.

"Laura, get over here." Her voice was a dry thing, dusty in her mouth.

Her daughter, still too young to disobey, cast a backward glance at her father and stumbled towards Blythe, backlit by fire. Blythe caught the girl in a hug that would never go on for long enough, until Laura managed to wriggle free. "*Mom*."

"You should be in school," Blythe said, realizing the absurdity of her words even as Laura smirked at them.

"My class is handing out flour rations all afternoon," Laura said. "This is way more awesome."

Jonah slid the backpack from his shoulders and handed the flamethrower off to someone else. He stood, frozen in place, waiting for her slight nod to join them. His eyes were bright in his soot-smudged face.

"It's a lost cause," he said, as much to the ground as to either of them. "A few days more and they'll have to write off the whole block. We can't keep wasting this much gasoline."

The neighbourhood was one of the few habitable areas not under the direct control of one or more law enforcement agencies. Closer to the downtown and a guy with Jonah's complexion could count on being carded every other intersection. Laith had been detained for eight hours after leaving his wallet on his desk during a smoke break. In the wake of the Blight, there was more to be worried about than just shriekgrass and demons.

She blurted, "I like you better like this."

"Like what?"

"Like when you're not being a selfish prick."

Jonah laughed, and that, too, went on longer than was comfortable. He tugged one hand free of a heavy industrial glove and reached into the inner pocket of his parka to remove an envelope. "Speaking of that."

She started to ask, but she knew even before he was opening the envelope and passing her the little book, Bordeaux-red, gold crest.

"How's your French?"

"Joe—"

"The boat tickets should be here tomorrow. I don't know why they're harder to get, they cost half as much..."

"I have a life here."

"And your friend? The one you went to visit today? How's her life coming along?"

He reached for a cigarette, then, apparently remembering where he was, who he was with, stopped himself. His hair had grown even longer in the past month or so, sticking to his forehead under his toque, and he had to keep pushing it out of his eyes.

"I haven't heard from Neil or anyone at the camp. I know there were raids. Worse, maybe. Japan mined its waters, they're not taking any chances. If we're gonna leave, it has to be soon." Jonah looked to Laura, who had moved to balance on a pile of cracked cement blocks forming an inner perimeter a few feet from the fence. His helplessness was twin to Blythe's own.

"Where are people like us supposed to run to?" Blythe punched one glove into the other. Maybe Jonah would reconsider that cigarette. "Where, exactly, did the apocalypse manage to miss?"

"This isn't the time to stand our ground. Not anymore. Atherton has free rein to do whatever he wants now, and you know what he wants, what every goddamned settler government in the history of this mutilated hellscape of a country has ever wanted. No one's watching and he's got a state of emergency. And I'd fight, Blythe, I would, but Laura."

"Fuck," she said. "Just. Fuckdammit all to shitting hell." She turned the passport over in her hands, drew her fingers along the embossing. Another false identity with her face attached, though this time, Ian wasn't around to bury the name of Blythe Augustine. "That's your solution to everything, isn't it? Your career, your marriage, your family? Just cut and run."

He flinched as if struck. Good. She'd quash down any guilt that threatened to bust loose.

Maybe he meant it, about changing. "Think about it, at least. Think about *her*." He waved over at where Laura was standing, crane-footed, and arms outstretched, on the broken concrete. "I'll see you tomorrow, kiddo. Maybe you can have a go at the flamethrower."

"Joe," she said, and walking past her, he stopped. "Did you at least manage to fuck him while you were there?"

His eyes widened, and she had the satisfaction of watching him actually blush.

"It's not like that," he muttered. "Or at least, it's not about that."

"It's always about that."

He shook his head. "I'll have the tickets tomorrow," he said. "We can talk more then."

34

Sujay rolled onto her back on a gym mat, staring up at the ceiling of what had been an elementary school classroom, and reached for her glasses. Just like when she was a little kid, she found herself looking for patterns in the dots, tracing pathways and letters that never managed to coalesce into coherence. The bulletin boards were still intact, large sheets of construction paper with collaged photos from magazines, bubbled letters proclaiming their purpose. The wonders of Egypt. Volcanoes. Climate change. One solitary kid had put together a haphazard collection of blurry demon photos on black paper faded to brown. The edges of the pictures peeled from the backing as if the very mention of demons and magic rendered the glue as ineffective as a state-of-the-art SVAR smartwatch. She'd been that kid once.

It was so quiet here.

The school was technically inside an Exclusion Zone, but only barely. Zach—that was the longboarder's name, because of course it was—was willing to take the risk, so Sujay was willing to take the risk alongside him. The voices sang a shriekgrass chorus in her bloodstream, determined to slide beneath the liminal barrier of skin that separated her from the world, to transform her from the inside out until she was no different than the howling shadows at the periphery of the human race. But if her non-MAI companion wasn't afraid, she refused to be either.

She leaned her face into his bare shoulder. Her nose was cold; his skin, bizarrely warm. He ran hot, the lucky shit. It was one way to survive a superwinter.

Zach wasn't her type, physically or otherwise, despite what any number of well-meaning adults had told her about fat girls not getting to be picky. She doubted that under other circumstances he'd have given her a second glance either. They didn't actually have anything in common besides that they'd both survived and other people hadn't. He must have been more fucked up by the End Times than he let on, and despite being a year or two younger than her, he couldn't keep it up long enough to come. But she could suss out how hot an Exclusion Zone really was and hide them if the apocalypse started to veer in a *Mad Max* direction, and he didn't seem to sleep more than an hour or two at a time and didn't mind keeping watch while she slept. And he didn't ask questions.

She didn't know who Zach was searching for in the wreckage of the 401. Sujay knew in her heart that her own family was dead, that Jamila was dead. Ian, the first person in the entire world to get what she was, to look at her without a hint of fear or disappointment, was gone too, buried under the rubble of CSC Joyceville, or worse. She could have stayed in Belleville, spared herself the crushing pain of closure. She needed to keep moving, and Zach, to his credit, never asked why. It wasn't the makings of a lasting relationship, but at least she wasn't alone.

Bessie had made it twenty-seven minutes on the broken highway before a flash heat fused the tires to the asphalt. Ian had loved that truck. The highway asphalt still smoking beneath her feet, Sujay couldn't even offer it a moment of silence.

"You were headed to Toronto," Zach had reminded her when she'd traced an invisible labyrinth over the cold metal of the truck door. A goodbye. What good were wards now, when the world was awake, thrumming with background magic, carnivorous and malevolent?

"You ready to move?" Zach asked. He had moles on his neck, and one just under his eye, the brown stark against skin that was still soft and pale in the first days after the Blight. She could make a pattern out of them, too.

Her back hurt from sleeping on whatever floor they could find. She hadn't showered, and her skin itched, there were little red bumps on her ankles, hair growing in on her legs and pits. She wanted a coffee. She wiped at the grit that clung to her eyelashes and nodded, tearing open a bag of ketchup chips, mind grown vacant to all but the barest elements of survival.

It wasn't *Mad Max*. It wasn't even the episode of *Night Beats* where they time-travelled into a future zombie apocalypse. People wept. People made shrines, and prayed. They left handwritten notes and photos and baby shoes on the side of the highway, already overgrown with shriekgrass. They piled little rocks and twigs into makeshift crosses, passing on grief and memories and prayers to those who would come after them in the slow-moving caravan. They left clothes or books or scraps of metal they could no longer carry. Others would pick them up, leaving junk of their own that, two days after the Blight, no longer seemed as precious as it had when they'd left their homes.

The few weirdos who still owned battery powered radios were the new town criers of the road, spreading news from the cities where'd they'd restored power. That was how she found out that the Pickering reactor hadn't melted down, that they had lights on in Ottawa and Toronto. That the *Emergencies Act* had painted a target on her back, that her citizenship was revoked. Not to worry, order was in the process of being restored, and everyone should sit tight, close the doors, and not let strangers in. Patrice Abel was missing, on the run, wanted by the RCMP to answer for his absence at Parliament during the MAI terrorist's attack. Quinn Atherton, elevated to the highest office in the country by virtue of being the last guy standing, ended each address with a triumphant *a mari usque ad mare*. He would see them through this crisis—at least, those of them that mattered. She was too tired to summon any kind of ire.

She'd exchanged first names with Zach because she'd saved his life, and then she'd let him fuck her, but she didn't even give as much as that to the endless line of travellers. Names had power. She was supposed to change hers, wasn't she? It didn't seem to matter much—everyone was anonymous out here, dirty-faced and threadbare—and anyway, burying his name hadn't saved Ian.

They gained people daily. Some were fleeing homes and neighbourhoods destroyed, others were unwilling to sit out the quarantine or wait for a rescue that would never arrive. They flitted, shadow-thin, into the line of walkers, heads bowed, speaking less and less the longer they walked.

Those who stuck to the road kept each other safe. Sometimes Sujay saw the soon-to-be-dead peel off from the line, wander into frozen cornfields, into skeleton forests. Considerate, polite suicides, and she was certain there were considerate, polite murders and rapes to go along with them. Who would know? No one who wanted to live strayed far.

Which was why, despite everything else she'd seen, Sujay doubled over and vomited into the ditch when she saw the dead body lying in the middle of the yellow line.

• • •

There was no reason to believe that the old man had died of anything other than what passed for natural causes now that nature had turned on humanity. He lay face down, by one of the stripped-down cars, the highway beside him crushed as if beneath the foot of an angry giant. He had probably been there for several hours. Someone had covered him with a blanket, a half-remembered gesture of empathy, but the wind had blown it mostly off, and Sujay could see the frost flowering at his nostrils, eyes slitted open and glassy.

She spent the next hour or so trying to squeeze flecks of puke out of her hair as they walked, her legs shaking so hard that they barely supported her weight.

She said, "We should have done something."

"The guy's dead."

"Still."

He might have been murdered, Sujay thought. In this endless parade of human misery, who could tell an accidental death from an intentional one? If this were *Night Beats*, she would have turned back. She would have found a telltale knife wound or crumpled letter, she would have searched through this desperate queue of refugees until she found an estranged daughter with a grudge, an old business rival, a scorned ex-wife. She would have hunted down the killer because even if this was the end of the world, even if people died for any reason or none, truth and justice still mattered.

She kept walking, because everyone else kept walking.

Sujay expected the end. She'd grown up on dystopias, played out scenarios in fantasies and visions. No one could say that she didn't see it coming. But the apocalypse never worked like this in movies. She'd been ready for the ground to split open, for everything to get as bad as it was going to get, and just at the moment of irreversible entropy, the good guys sweep in and save the day. The sun would come out through the clearing clouds. She was sure she'd been one of the good guys, and they hadn't saved shit.

What would Lilith do? Sujay straightened, tried to add a self-possessed sway to her step. She was tall, and strong, and immortal. Her ankle twisted with a wrong step over a pile of melting snow, and she winced and swore.

Not Lilith then. Jane. Lilith kicked ass but Jane solved the case, Jane saw the details, the patterns. She played it cautious and safe and kicked in the door, oh, only maybe once per season, but she got the job done. Jane would hide, until she knew the enemy's weak spot, and she would bicker with Lilith over the right course of the action, and they would lean close into each other, hands barely touching, and Lilith would whisper, "We're magic, remember?" But no, that hadn't happened either, not on the screen, that was a story she'd written, before the road, before the corpse, in another life.

Zach interrupted. "You ever seen a dead body before?"

Sujay shook her head. "You?"

"My grandfather. But not—"

"Yeah."

"Do you want to go back?"

The enemy didn't have a weak spot. The enemy was the world itself, waking to consciousness, grown cold and armoured, and birthing nightmares in the wake of its rage.

"No," Sujay said. "What's the fucking point?"

• • •

The forest took Zach. Sujay felt him stir beside her, the rustle of his clothes like the wind through shriekgrass. The atmosphere that lay thick between them and the magic outside was a tattered shroud, and the whispers behind it leaked through its perforations. He stood with his head cocked at the broken window of the farmhouse they'd sheltered in overnight. Shapes moved through the distant barrier of trees. She could see bone twisting through the skin at the back of his neck. He remembered enough of humanity to lope through the door, into the night. His jacket lay on the snow-dusted, rotting floorboards, a discarded beetle carapace.

Sujay left it. The jacket was bigger than hers, but thinner. Someone would be able to use it. She was getting used to the cold.

• • •

Four days after the world had ended, just outside of Oakville, the highway came to life with the roar of an armoured personnel carrier trudging eastbound from the city. Someone tore away from the line to wave at them, wildly, screaming for help. Sujay, plodding ahead, watched him grow small, distant and dusty in the vehicle's wake.

• • •

Panic Pete had barely any elasticity left to him. The grime penetrated every surface; no amount of washing, even if Sujay had regular access to soap and water, would ever get him clean. She pressed him to her chest, the squeezes echoing the anxious thrum of her heart. She tried not to think about what must have happened to Jamila.

Sujay hadn't done magic since the Blight had hit, which seemed absurd even as the air grew brittle and staticky around her. The ward she'd drawn lit up with a low sound like a Tibetan prayer bowl. It all happened much faster, much more physically overwhelming than she was used to, the frail ember of magic she'd so carefully nurtured exploding into a conflagration.

She had no control over the rush of futures that flooded her mind. There was no time to ask questions or to choose one branching pathway of the labyrinth to follow. There were only images, unbidden, tearing each other to shreds in a battle for supremacy.

The vans, lined up outside of a mosque, men, wearing no uniform she knew, dragging old men out of the doors and into the vehicles.

A mother comforting three sobbing children under a white canvas tent.

Patrice, on his knees, as the bullet hit.

A girl she didn't recognize, tugged beneath the ocean's vicious current.

The labyrinth, embroidered in shimmering colours into human skin dotted in blood. Below it, cased within splintered ribs, a gaping absence she felt deep in her own bones.

Sujay gasped, dropped the stress toy, her head jerking up from where it had drooped to her collarbone. Someone across the campfire called out, "Keep it down." She stuffed Panic Pete back in a pocket, hugged her knees, the flames licking heat over one side of her face, and tried to sleep.

• • •

Five days after the world had ended, Sujay knelt beside the highway sign at Toronto's city limits, and touched her hand to the wooden post like an exile at last kissing the soil of her homeland.

35

Eric was so used to the amorphous din of shriekgrass and the hush that otherwise lay in its wake that he all but jumped out of his skin when his phone rang. The chorus of Rihanna's "Umbrella" broke through air stagnant with the dry particulate that the shriekgrass bloom spread. He slid his finger across the screen before the "ella...ella...ella" drew the attention of the two soldiers posted at the corner. He hadn't turned his ringer off before the Blight.

Two months. The Prius had made it all the way back to Toronto. The highways were broken, or choked with shriekgrass, where the black huddle of flapping shreds in the middle of the road ahead might have been a strip of tire, a dead raccoon, a garbage bag, or something worse. Crowded with people desperate to get to, or away from. For all that apocalypse was water-cooler conversation for the Broom Closet crowd, Eric had struggled to envision it, at least until Ian had dropped him a teaser trailer via paperwork spell. Before, he'd pictured the end of the world as *like this, but worse*, with no clearly delineated definition of what *worse* might entail. And he hadn't been completely wrong.

Cell phone towers, wifi, smart devices, anything smarter than a Texas Instruments calculator had gone in the first EMP blast of the Blight. But they'd come spluttering back to life; he'd see the flash of a phone screen here, an LED billboard lazily blink there, long enough only for hope. Cops and soldiers patrolled the streets, but beyond occasionally hassling him for ID, they didn't bother much with people like him. Everyone was still labouring under the assumption that, eventually, life would go back to normal.

It was an orderly, very Canadian kind of apocalypse.

He was so certain that the ringing was a trick of failing tech he almost didn't answer it. But the instinct hadn't quite left, despite the momentary flutter of worry that he'd forgotten how to bump up the volume, forgotten how to speak through an air-filtering mask.

He blurted, "The phones are working!"

"Eric." His mother's voice was shaky. "You need to get home now."

Eric was maybe ten blocks from home—post-Blight blocks, jagged jigsaw puzzles torn from the city's old landscape. Barbed wire and informal markets, here a guard perimeter around an Exclusion Zone, there a man polishing hubcaps to sell for scrap. His parents' neighbourhood, shaded by oak trees and calmed by speed bumps, stood intact and unchanged. A subway stop away, one wall of a high-rise was a gaping wound, exposing concrete bone beneath.

But then, he came from a long line of lucky exceptions who'd kept their heads down and their passports close. Great-grandparents who'd left Poland just soon enough. Ancestors who'd marked lamb's blood on their doorways.

(Eric, eight years old, no longer tasked with asking the Four Questions after changing them: What did the Egyptian babies do to deserve that? Had some compassionate Jewish woman saved her neighbours by telling them what to do? Had some enterprising Egyptian mother figured it out? How did the Israelites manage to wander for forty years in the desert when Google Maps said it was a 6-day walk?)

A line of cop cars sat front to back by the curb along his parents' street.

Well. Fuck.

Eric raked fingers through his dusty hair in a vain attempt to smooth it into something resembling respectable. Straightened his collar. Walked through the front door like he belonged in the place.

His mother was already weeping, draped over the half-wall that led downstairs, her hand across her face like a swooning Victorian heroine. His father stood defiant and blood-splattered beneath a pot light that lit his thinning hair in a halo. No, the thick red trail leading across the polished hardwood floor, crept up the edge of the oriental rug that had belonged to his great-grandmother, wasn't blood. It bled out, not to a heartbeat, but to Jakie smashing his spoon on the floor, screaming and thrashing at the two conductive wires blooming from his chest.

And Abigail?

Abigail didn't move, not even a finger twitch, though the zipties tight around her wrists had to hurt. She was small, round, every feature soft and blunted, and dwarfed by each of the men on either side of her. She was wearing the sweater he'd gotten for her birthday last year.

Jakie howled. He beat his fist, fingers clenched into bulging sausages, into the ground.

"You need to talk him down," Eric's mother said.

Instead, Eric moved between Jakie and the cops. "Let go of him." Aware of the falter in his voice, he stood as straight as he could manage. "Let go of *her*."

"Eric..." His father had never looked so old, or so thin. He flinched as one of the cops on the other end of the taser adjusted his grip.

They were survivors. None of them had ever been brave.

"Please," Eric said. He held up his hands, and when no blast of electricity was forthcoming, moved to Jakie's side. Were you supposed to take the electrodes out? It wasn't like a bullet, except what if it was?

Jakie rallied and flopped to his side. Eric had enough time to see his brother's arm careening towards him, but not enough time to dodge; the spoon slashed cold across his face, knocking his glasses loose. He fell back on his ass, wiping ketchup from his cheek, as the second blast of electricity sent Jakie into convulsions.

"You're gonna kill him." If they could even hear him over his brother's wails. "Abigail—hey! You have to let her go, okay? She's the only one who can talk him down when he's like this."

For the first time, one of the cops spoke. “Mr. Greenglass. We invited you here as a courtesy.”

There was an antique vase—another heirloom from his great-grandmother—on a polished mahogany hall stand that served no other purpose than to hold the vase. He could grab it and smash it into one of the cop’s faces. He could kick, bite. Hell, it worked for Jakie all the time. He could fight.

He did none of these things.

“What did she do?” Eric asked, helpless. “She’s a permanent resident, we checked before we hired her, for fuck’s sake...”

“And now we’re going to check.” The cop probably thought the face he was making looked like a *friendly* smile.

Eric scrambled for purchase, fingernails bending into the quick. His legs were shaking too hard to cooperate. Abigail made a small noise of distress, too terrified even to cry out. Had they hurt her already? “She takes care of my brother. Please, she’s—“

As if she was only an instrument to be used, valuable only because of what she could do for people who were richer than her, whiter than her. As they’d even fucking care.

“We know all about your brother, Mr. Greenglass. We can take the illegal now and leave, or we can section him under Order 204. Your choice.”

Eric was trapped in air like amber, leaden and thick, a nightmare in which he could never outrun the thing chasing him. He sank back on the muddy heels of his boots. Lifted his head only enough to meet Abigail’s wide eyes. One of the two people in what was left of this godforsaken hellscape that he actually liked.

“I have my card.” But there was surrender in Abigail’s voice. He wasn’t going to save her. No one was.

“I’m gonna straighten this out,” he whispered. “I’ll find you. I promise, Abby.” He crawled over to Jakie, whose screams had turned to low moans, and wrapped his arms around his brother. This time, Jakie didn’t fight him. “We’re gonna fix this.”

He didn’t watch as they took her away.

36

The cops wasted no time sending their drones out as soon as there was consistent electricity. Sighting the TIE fighter bob of one above him, Jonah readied a rock, but it was just one of the flyer drops, a confetti of multilingual notices raining like white phosphorus onto the street below, catching in the puddles of slush that clung like limpets to the curb. One landed on his shoulder, and he pulled it free, then jammed it, crumpled, into a pocket.

After less than two weeks, the facade of ceasefire, tolerance, and mutual aid was over. Now it was time for the Shock Doctrine.

Inside Blythe's lab, refugees huddled under sleeping bags, and a row of long tables separated the temporary living quarters from the equipment. Jonah remembered a split second too late that he should have kept his voice down.

"They're declaring this whole neighbourhood an Exclusion Zone." He slapped the flyer down on the worktable, Blythe's forged passport underneath it. "All the way to the lab. Which I'm guessing the feds are taking over."

Blythe, her hair escaping its messy ponytail, rubbed at her red-rimmed eyes. "Technically," she said, "they already own the lab."

Conscious of Laura, scrubbing one of the other tables a few feet away, he dropped his voice. "Is it fucking time *now*?"

"This is our home," Blythe whispered, with all the strength of a balloon rapidly losing air. "We should fight for it."

Jonah had stood at the frontlines of his kin's battles as surely as he'd fled his own. But Victoria had never been *his* home. not even when he'd pretended they were still a family. He wasn't sure if anywhere had ever been, besides the wide snowy expanses by a half-built mine. Besides a rusted pickup truck blaring folk music down a gravel road, and the scent of campfire and sweetgrass clinging to his clothes.

Blythe's face slid down her hands, stray strands of hair a weeping willow over her wrists. Her shoulders, more prominent than they'd been a few weeks ago, shook towards the centre of her spine.

And here he thought it was going to be an argument.

"People need me here," she murmured.

"People will need you wherever you go." He placed a hand on her back. It wasn't permitted, shouldn't have been, he didn't have the right, but she leaned into him anyway, desperate for even this imperfect reassurance.

"I need more time."

She would always need more time. And in the end, he would fail her in that, too.

• • •

"Name and nationality."

The RCMP arrived to relocate the neighbourhood just as the first glass-and-metal scavengers were clearing the streets. Frost hung low in the air, a shimmering veil that caught every breath of the winding queue of cold, miserable people. The sniper, on the roof of a low-rise apartment, probably thought he was being subtle, but Jonah caught a glimpse of a rifle stock as he shifted position.

"Jonah Augustine. *Otipemisiwak.*"

"Joe ..." Blythe started, but one of the men just looked confused, the other only mildly pissed off. "Don't start."

There was too much of a crowd—specifically, there were too many of the white retirees who even these days made up most of the city's population—for the sniper to open fire on him for talking shit. So far, the buses taking people to safe zones were, theoretically, optional. By the end of the week, they wouldn't be.

He did notice, though, that everyone getting on the buses was curdled-milk pale. Skin like crumpled paper. There was maybe one other brown guy in the crowd so sample size would have played a role, but he wondered what would happen if that guy—near the back of the line—asked to get on. Given the new *Emergencies Act* rules, which allowed for deportation for anyone eligible for citizenship elsewhere, he suspected it wouldn't go well.

Atherton didn't seem like the brains behind the policy, but he'd had the visible anguish on his face to sell it.

"So I'm guessing that bomber *wasn't* a lone wolf with a history of mental illness?" Jonah said.

The cop—not nearly as pale as the people he was ushering onto the buses—frowned and turned to his clipboard.

"Relax," Jonah said. "I'm as Canadian as hockey and fetal alcohol syndrome. We're not relocating, shriekgrass or not." He glanced at Blythe, who swallowed hard but nodded, tightening her arm around Laura.

He was handed a slip of paper. It looked official, at least as much as it could be with the government running on bare bones and spite, and laws written and rewritten in the space of a day. Jonah thumbed at the ink, half expecting it to smear.

"You and your family must report back here within three days." The man spoke in a monotone and stared over the top of Jonah's head. Jonah bit back an *Or what?*, deciding that he didn't need to know the answer.

"Give me six hours," Jonah told Blythe.

• • •

There were armed patrols all along Ogden Point, beneath the shadows of the great docked cruise ships. Boats still left the docks, but not without being heavily searched and the passports and tickets of everyone on board scrutinized in detail. Hence the mob scene; hundreds of tired travellers, delayed by the security check.

Jonah was as much a student of history as anyone born under its bootprint. He'd shared Eco's "14 Signs of Fascism" on Facebook after every data-mining scandal, just like every other melodramatic activist kid. If anyone had asked him, he could have predicted that there would be forces that would take advantage of a crisis to enforce their will.

He still reeled from how much it had been. How fast. They hadn't even renamed or reorganized security forces. At least two competing private security firms had sent weedy guys with earpieces who looked like they should be standing by doors at the mall. He'd expected jackboots and snazzy uniforms. But even now, the radio had stories of mass detainment and deportations, businesses smashed, gangs of roving kids beating up anyone darker than a paper bag.

Blythe was already waiting at the pier, leaning on the flank of a tour bus. She had a duffle bag, the bulges in the fabric angular, suggesting instruments and not clothes. Laura had her backpack. It was a few years old; she had mostly grown out of pink, and the idea flickered in him to buy her one that was more her style, before he remembered where he was, and why.

Right away they'd notice that he carried nothing.

He'd never bothered to learn the names of the various sizes and shapes of the ships docked on the pier. The ocean was Blythe's thing. He'd never really trusted it, and all of Ian's stories about his miserable childhood and family friends lost at sea had only hammered in that unease. The profiles of the boats formed a ragged skyline, the high-rise cruise ships, the tilting spears of masts and sails. You could still sail out with the right documentation, but the queues were held up by passport checks.

Make up your mind. Do you want people like us to leave or not?

Blythe, to his shock, threw her arms around him and buried her face against his neck. He held the hug for longer than he should have.

"C'mon," he whispered. They edged along the bus, Laura between them. He peered out at faces cast in sickly orange by the lights of the boats.

"Do we have to?" Laura asked.

Blythe squeezed her shoulder. "Yes."

Laura was too old and too estranged from him for Jonah to gather her into his arms and run his palm over her hair, as much as his arms ached to do it. His hand hovered in the air beside her face, then lowered, searching for the envelope in his jacket. His eyes darted over the pier. There would be eyes and ears; he could only hope that they were too preoccupied to sort signal from noise.

Three French passports. Two tickets, bought in the blood he'd helped shed working for Ian.

Blythe looked at him sharply and shook her head. He raised a finger to his lips.

"Fuck you, Joe," Blythe whispered. At least she knew not to scream at him.

Laura moved between them and this time he did give in, hugged her close despite how she stiffened in surprise, his little girl who was already almost up to his collarbone. "Go get in line," he said.

"What's going on?" Laura asked into his shirt.

"Your father's trying to kill himself because of some stupid alpha male toxic masculinity *bullshit*."

"Get in *line*," Jonah hissed. "Look, I have been an absolute fuckup as a husband and a worse one as a father, but I can do this one thing."

Blythe punched him in the arm, hard. He'd forgotten how hard she could hit. "You stupid shit," she said. "Come with us."

"Yeah, dad." Laura tugged at his other arm. "Why can't you come with?"

"With most of the Pacific countries locked down, and—Australia is still taking people in. If they're white."

"I'm not—" Blythe started, and he snapped his hand around the wrist of the same hand she'd punched him with. Wove his fingers, his brown fingers, still callused from weekends spent on the land, through her pale ones, brushed his thumb over the back of her hand dusted with freckles. She squeezed back, a Morse code of fury, ebbing to acceptance. "You were the one raised by Bible-thumping crackers, dumbass."

"That's not what they're checking."

Blythe's head tilted into her shoulder. Shit. Was she crying? At least this was the last time he'd make her cry. "Asshole." Her voice was thick. She opened the passport, scowled at the mug shot within. "This doesn't fix shit, you know. One big gesture, one sacrifice. It doesn't fix everything else."

He shifted to pull them both close. "You don't need to forgive me," he said. "Either of you. You just need to survive. Nor just for me, but for. You know. Our people. All of that."

Blythe stared up at him, eyes welling. She sniffled. "No pressure or anything."

"None at all." He released them both, tried, ridiculous as it was, to fix their masked faces in his memory, Blythe's sharp geometry echoed in the softer curves of their daughter's face. The awkward knobs of Laura's leggings-clad knees, and the yellow gleam of light shining on her blue-black hair. "It's okay to mourn that the world we knew is gone. Even if that world sucked. I will. I am. But as long as I know you're both safe, I..." His voice cracked. He couldn't do this. Couldn't look at them any longer, beat back the waves of guilt and nausea. He swallowed. "Don't either of you fucking forget me, eh?"

Jonah twisted away from them, pulled his hood up from under his jacket, and fixed it tightly around his head. He thought he could hear Laura calling after him but he kept walking, past the beams of flashlights, until the lights on the masts were tiny pinpricks, fireflies in the night.

37

The demon rummaged through the dumpsters behind the McDonalds. Tobias considered texting the Old Man to remind him that stalking through strip malls to play Crocodile Hunter with monsters wasn't, and had never been, part of his job. He ducked behind the side of the QuicKie and sent Izzy up into the tall ornamental grasses by the curb.

It was rare that they got so close to the truncated habitable zones, at least in the thin grey haze just before dawn. They didn't like the light, or people, which, all things considered, was fortunate for people.

This one was long and spindly, its torso dotted with clusters of swollen tumours. Its upper body was too heavy for its withered legs, its crackling skin clinging to an elongated skull. Its movements were curiously birdlike as it picked its way around the garbage bags. It halted, abruptly, turned its head sidewise, and regarded Tobias out of one glistening black eye.

How much consciousness was in there? What did the thing remember of being human? He thought he saw the glint of intelligence in that oily eye—but that could just as easily have been the kind of anthropomorphism that led to naming your microdrone.

But it *was* watching him. The siding of the QuicKie wall was chalky under his fingers. There was a display of road salt by the sliding doors at the entrance of the building. A limited, non-peer-reviewed study suggested demons were vulnerable to salt. He'd read an article on it before the Blight. They'd abandoned that line of research after the company that had commissioned it determined that demons weren't an immediate enough threat to anyone's bottom line to make it profitable. Tobias wasn't about to improvise in the field. If he got to his bike in time, he might be able to outrun it—that was a better strategy. He edged backwards, summoning Izzy back to him.

The demon opened its long mouth, revealing three layers of tiny yellowed teeth, a rotting tongue rolling from inside its jaw. He braced himself for the ear-piercing shriek, but what came out instead was soft, the sound of wind rushing through dying leaves. There were almost words buried there; if Tobias closed his eyes, and listened, he might make out some semblance of communication.

It watched him, and, deer-in-headlights that he was, Tobias watched it back. Looked for the traces of humanity in it. Then it jittered, lurching on its too-long legs. Its neck cracked as it lumbered towards him. He snatched Izzy out of the air and clambered to his bike, barely balancing on the winterized tires, only to nearly be thrown over by the rush of an army Jeep weaving across the lanes of Walkley Rd.

The demon bolted through the parking lot towards the Leon's. Tobias steadied himself, brushing at his damp knees. He motioned Izzy closer to frame his face against the road, where traffic, though limited to the odd car, mostly army, was beginning to trickle back.

"See?" he said into the lens. "Everything's returning to normal. Everything's fine."

• • •

"That was dangerous," Lucy said.

"More dangerous than fucking up Alycia Curtis' mind-control spell?"

Their house was untouched. They weren't even close to an Exclusion Zone. From inside, they might have been having a perfectly normal breakfast inside a sun-drenched kitchen pulled out of the pages of a home decor magazine. There weren't demons roaming the streets or walled-off regions of the city where magic had sunk its claws into the fabric of reality and tugged hard. The patrols checked for shriekgrass and they didn't have to mask up for fear of breathing in the spores and hearing that scream forever. There was just him, and his beautiful wife, and the steam rising off the top of the eggs she'd found at the informal market, and the lumpy bread that had to be wrestled into the toaster.

"I was trying to show off," Lucy said. She sliced into her egg, yellow pooling over her plate. She'd kept up with makeup, even though most of her students had cancelled, few dedicated enough to keep singing through the greatest paradigm shift the world had ever seen. Her hair, down in a simple ponytail instead of swept into an elaborate up-do, was the only sign that her world had changed. "A flourish."

"Sure." He'd tried to pry her open. Lucy had a lifetime of practice at swimming through waters others drowned in, brushing off conversational topics as too unpleasant to be on the table. No amount of argument would shift it from flourish into deliberate subversion, or tell him why she'd done it, when she'd told him so many times to keep his own head down.

"But Toby. Seriously. A war zone wasn't enough for you?"

"I volunteered." He chewed at the egg, his tongue experimenting with the edge of yolk in his mouth. He wondered if he was losing his sense of taste. The supply lines were still being reestablished, eager as Atherton's government to get business functioning again, which meant that any eggs she'd found were local, some backyard farmer. They should have tasted better. "It was like it recognized me. Who knows, maybe it did. Before it—"

"You didn't need to get that close."

"I don't think it wanted to hurt me."

"I don't think it needs to *want* anything to hurt you."

He should have told her what had been churning in him for days, that there had been too many close calls, too many moments where magic had struck down others and spared him. For days, he'd been tracing the shape of it, the void where it ended and he began. He'd scoured articles about magical immunity without it ever occurring to him that it might have applied to him as well.

It was only late at night, when he might mistake her whisper for a fragment of dream, that she said, "I meant to do it."

The phone, an hour later, jolted him awake. Sgt. Heaver at the Ottawa Police Service.

Scoop of the century, if you want it.

An ellipses, hovering, then:

We got Patrice Abel.

• • •

The former Prime Minister went down without a fight.

Heaver reported, as Tobias navigated his bike around clumps of snow, that Patrice Abel had been picked up in Hull. It didn't seem like much of a run as far as Tobias was concerned. The cops paraded their catch, perp-walked him through the front doors of the Ottawa-Carlton Detention Centre for processing. Tobias expected Cynthia, but instead found Bob Hurst from the business desk.

"Where's Cynthia?" The question hung in the air a moment, and died there.

He led the microdrone in an upwards swoop, being careful to get a close shot of Patrice Abel's hands. The former PM had boxed heavyweight in university, and he'd had a mean left hook. Patrice's face was battered, one eye swollen to squinting, dried blood congealing at his nostrils.

His knuckles, though, were as clean and unmarked as any other politician's. There might have been blood on his hands, but you wouldn't know from looking at them.

There were no witnesses beyond Tobias, Hurst, and Izzy, so Patrice had a clear line of sight to glare balefully at him out of one reddened eye.

"Get the fuck out of here," Patrice snarled.

He'd have to bleep out the obscenity, but the framing couldn't have been better.

One of the cops kicked the back of Patrice's knees. "Keep moving. Traitor."

Heaver grinned at Tobias. "Gonna be a heck of a trial."

• • •

The court hastily assembled to try Patrice Abel was anything but photogenic.

Tobias wasn't even sure what he was doing there. The trial was ponderous, with none of the back-and-forth repartee, the detailed scouring of evidence, the nimble swashbuckling he'd expect from the legal teams. The courtroom—and it was still a courtroom—was half-empty. He spotted none of Patrice's supporters, not even Gaby. Instead, the discussion proceeded quietly, as if all of the participants agreed on the outcome but perhaps differed on the details.

Patrice was silent throughout the entire first day, save for a clearly stated, "not guilty." His hands remained cuffed, the bruises on his face darkened to shades of maroon and black. Impassive as the evidence was laid out: Patrice Abel had access to precognitive data that predicted the terrorist attack, and instead of using it to inform the police, he'd failed to show up at Parliament that day, escaping the fate that had befallen so many of his colleagues.

It was, quite frankly, ridiculous, though Patrice didn't help his case by the startled burst of laughter that forced its way out of his cracked lips.

Tobias couldn't blame him. He had never approved of Patrice's policies. Had found him corrupt, venal, and reckless, his regime marked by an over-dependance on magic and a disdain for fiscal restraint. The last year of Tobias' life had been devoted to ending his misrule. But rampant spending and weakness in the face of special interests did not a traitor make.

There was a snowstorm building as Tobias left the courtroom, howling such that he barely heard his phone ring. He was suddenly glad he'd left his bike at home.

"You're gonna reconsider that pivot to video after you see this," Tobias told Reid. Even Alycia Curtis couldn't have predicted that the next media empire would likely be built on radio after the wifi proved unpredictable.

The Old Man chuckled. "I thought you liked a good scandal."

"I like a spending scandal," Tobias said. "A bribery scandal. A head held down in shame. Not—" Well aware that Reid couldn't see him, he waved his hand loosely in the direction of the courthouse. "—whatever this show trial is."

"The people have spoken," Reid replied, voice light and pleasant as ever. "And the people want blood."

And the actual terrorist responsible vaporized himself into a galaxy of blue sparks, but it wouldn't have mattered. One man's rage, however horrendous his act, wasn't enough to pin an apocalypse on. Wasn't enough to transform a nation into the bright shining fortress that Reid envisioned. Wouldn't justify the new passes, the citizenship tests, the deportations. No, the old order had to die, loudly and publicly. If Patrice Abel had died in the attack, they would have found someone else to sacrifice to the restoration of order and justice.

"There's nothing to shoot, Reid."

There was a long pause on the other end.

"Not yet," the Old Man said.

• • •

"The thing is," Tobias said, halfway through pulling off a sock. "I believe in the rule of law."

His conversation with Reid had wound up too quickly, without commitments from either of them. But the argument hadn't ended.

Lucy groaned. She was sprawled on the bed, her tablet resting on her bare knees and the sheets puddled around her ankles. "No one actually believes in the rule of law, Toby. That's just a thing people say when they don't want to acknowledge the way the world actually is."

"When did you get so cynical?" He slumped on the corner of the bed, staring at his own mismatched feet instead of at his beautiful wife. "An institution being imperfect doesn't mean—they don't need to make an utter *mockery* of it."

"It's early days," Lucy said. "Nothing's going to run like it did before right away."

"I thought we were on the same page," Tobias grumbled. "Reid and I. Sure, he's a bit of a caricature sometimes, and a control freak with his papers, but he doesn't drink champagne distilled from orphan's tears. I didn't think he was...well. Alycia's puppet."

"How do you know that he is?"

"She's an MAI. She could have been controlling him, maybe for years..."

"Or they have a mutually loving and equal partnership." She squeezed his arm, and he at last turned to hold her, permitted her face in the hollow where his neck met his shoulder.

"You know," he said. "I used to look at them and see a future for us."

She laughed, fingers playing lightly over the skin of his bicep.

"I mean it. Married for 50 years, obviously still deeply in love, and he *makes* the news, and she gives so much of herself with her charity work. I thought, maybe, that could be you and me. Fancy restaurants and box seats at the symphony. Well. If she hadn't secretly been an evil witch the whole time."

Lucy wasn't cruel. She didn't tell him how ridiculous he sounded. "What are you going to do about it?" she asked instead.

"I don't have a choice," he replied. "I need to tell the truth."

"Do you?"

He rolled on his side to face her. Parted the streams of black hair that webbed over her face, traced a thumb over the arch of an eyebrow. God, she was gorgeous. "How can I be any less brave than my wife?"

"A flourish," Lucy reminded him. "I'd really rather you weren't brave, this time. Patrice Abel isn't worth bravery."

"He isn't," Tobias agreed. "But the story? That's an entirely different matter."

• • •

Day one of the trial down. Tobias tried to make Reid happy. He couldn't Photoshop Patrice's bruises, but he could focus on the dead gaze straight ahead, the low angles that made him look bigger, more menacing, and avoid showing his hands.

Reid called, sounding jovial, congratulating him on an image already trending on Twitter.

Tobias kept all of the footage.

• • •

They called Patrice to the stand on the last day. His left eye still didn't open all the way. He had none of the swagger or defiance Tobias would have expected from him. If anything, he seemed to have shrunk, the substance drained from his wide shoulders, deep lines carved into his face. They had only one question for him: how early he'd known about the terrorist attack.

Patrice blinked. Tobias had Izzy close in for a closer shot while he looked at Heaver, his arms crossed over his chest by the door, grinning. Just a beat cop, promoted well above his competency, but he had sprouted several new medals on his chest since Atherton had taken over. The prosecutor, too, looked smug. They all did, like they were privy to a secret kept from the defendant, kept from the press. Tobias was twelve years old again, standing on the outside of someone else's joke.

Fuck. They were actually going to *kill* Patrice. Not lambast him in the press, not lock him up in some minimum security luxury spa of a prison with weekend parole, but actually convict him in this Stalinist farce and—

One of Atherton's first acts, roundly applauded by his base, was restoring the death penalty for rape, murder, treason, and terrorism. Tobias had assumed it was a hypothetical—after all, they'd have to have years of appeals, the logistics of sourcing chemicals or electric chairs or whatever means they were planning to appease a people hungering for justice, for resolution—but nothing about this trial suggested a drawn-out process.

"Mr. Abel," the Crown said. "Answer the question."

"I didn't know." For all his passivity, Patrice's voice rang out clear and strong through the courtroom's hollow ribcage. "Isn't that obvious?"

"Would you be here if it was?"

Patrice snorted, shaking his head. "That's not how this works."

"How what works?"

"Precognition. Magic. Politics. Any of it. I barely had an understanding after a two-decade long career; do you think that any of *you*—" His one eye burned in judgment of the mainly youthful faces around him, dressed up in their haphazard uniforms, the accidental and inexperienced enforcers of a new order. "—are going to be able to weigh the tradeoffs and decisions that we had to grapple with after a few minutes of me talking about it?"

The prosecutor blinked. "Are you saying that the lives of nineteen Members of Parliament and citizens, including *children*, are a political tradeoff?"

"Of course not," Abel snapped. "Don't you think I would have warned them if I'd known? What kind of monster do you think I am?"

"Your term," the prosecutor replied lightly.

"You know what they do in China when they have precogs in government? *They listen to them.* They base policy on the most likely outcome. They avert disaster when they can." Abel sounded like a runner at the end of his race, breath coming in short bursts. "If Ian Mallory could have picked that thread out of that rat's nest he sees when he shuts his eyes, he would have warned someone. If you bastards hadn't locked him up. You could ask him yourself but you got him killed under a pile of rubble when he might have prevented all of this." He shook his large bald head, stared down at his cuffed hands. "It doesn't matter. Whatever the truth is, no one in this room cares about it. I've served this country all my life. I have only ever tried to do the right thing for its people. If you want to kill me for it, how could I ever stop you?"

• • •

Tobias had to wait for Lucy to be out of town to make his move, which meant that he had to wait for Patrice Abel to die. There was nothing he could have done to stop it anyway.

She was to fly out the following morning, one of the first flights since the Blight had grounded everything. Her lips traced the outline of the song in the dark as he lay beside her, restive, Izzy's footage replaying on silent on his tablet.

It played backwards, the trial and sentencing, the monsters, the Blight, the attack on Parliament. Reid Curtis' confession, trapped in amber. His conversations with Mallory. The story of every mistake he'd made, every squandered opportunity.

He'd come to Ottawa to slay dragons. And he'd stabbed himself in the foot instead.

Groaning, Tobias turned the tablet off. "It's a beautiful piece," he murmured.

"Isn't it?" Another Yamashita original. Lucy couldn't have angered Alycia that much, unless it was a spell to kill her as she was singing it. His heart lurched at the thought, and he wanted to beg her not to go to Toronto, to run away with him, to abandon his own quixotic battles and find a place where they could be together, safe from the grasping talons of the world.

But there was nowhere safe now.

"I don't tell you enough that I love you," Tobias said.

She laughed, kissed the top of his head. "Don't get too sentimental," she said. "I'll be back Friday."

• • •

Patrice Abel was executed on Wednesday. Four of the prison guards led him to the flooded and frozen Trans-Canada bike trails and made him kneel, ice cracking in a delicate web beneath his knees, and put a gun to the back of his head. His bruises still hadn't healed.

Tobias, shivering in his peacoat, held Izzy steady in the air, the angle oblique so as to afford the dead man some dignity. It was the least he could do.

"What," Patrice asked. "A noose was too on-the-nose?"

The gunshot echoed past the shadow of the factory, rustled the petrified trees and shuddered across the river of ice.

Patrice slumped sideways, and Tobias cut away, to the impassive faces of the guards, depriving his viewership of the catharsis of watching the bulky body tossed into the river, swallowed by the white-foamed current.

• • •

Tobias edited all evening, bleary-eyed into the morning, depositing the files Jonah had given him, the footage, as unadulterated as he could manage without losing coherency, and assembled it all into a .zip file.

The Old Man would block any attempt to publish, but Tobias had contacts elsewhere. Some, certainly, would have been shut down under the new regime, others gone underground. But knowledge was a virus, and his camera had already brought down one government.

His colleagues. His competitors. The fringe press. Wikileaks. Jonah Augustine, if he was even still alive. He made copies on USBs and mailed each one. Someone would find it. Someone would know.

And then he sat back, closed his eyes, and waited until the knock on the door jolted him awake.

• • •

"That was fast." Tobias offered his hands, but the cop had no interest in cuffing him. Another officer collected his laptop, cameras, and Izzy's case.

Tobias was escorted into an unmarked car without violence. He wasn't Patrice Abel; no one was out to make an example of him. Not yet.

In the back seat, Reid Curtis turned to face him.

"I really did expect better from you, son."

Tobias grinned. Still half-asleep, he moved as if in a dream. "I did too," he said. "From you. We're men of principles, I thought."

Reid nodded agreeably. "If only we didn't differ so crucially, in the end, as to what those principles were."

Tobias settled into the seat, into his own captivity. He couldn't tell where they were going, weaving through neighbourhoods lifted up and hammered by the Blight, and rearranged by barbed wire and Exclusion Zones. He didn't recognize much of the shattered jigsaw of a landscape. Here they turned onto a highway, there to a branching gravel road that swerved around places where the highway gapped and broke.

"It's too late anyway. Alycia's secret—your secret—it's all out there in the world. You can take down one source, but another will just pop up like a weed. You can't stop this, Reid."

His boss—former boss—laughed. "Oh Toby," he said. "I never needed to stop anything, any more than your wife's little stunt at the party mattered. Alycia didn't require magic to change anyone's heart. The seeds for the new world were planted there a long time ago."

He'd been through war. There was a time for cringing in the darkness, startling at the distant whiz of a rocket falling, wondering where it would strike. And then there was a time when even fear seemed distant and abstract, when nothing remained beyond pure animal survival.

"So that's it," he said. "All those years working for you, and you're just going to lock me up? Or kill me, like you had Patrice Abel killed?"

"Abel was a symbol," Reid replied. "The old king must lose his head for the revolution to be born from his corpse. I'd hoped you'd have more use than as a martyr for some lost cause. If not for your talents, then perhaps for your—unique gifts."

"Because I'm immune to magic." Saying it out loud formalized it in his head, captured the amorphous sparks of a theory and solidified them into truth. "I get off because of a fluke of genetics?"

Reid turned his attention to the window, to the road carved between great chunks of granite, kilometres of a monument to human intellect and perseverance. Men had blasted civilization through this impassive, hostile country, well before magic had returned to the world. Despite the Cascade, despite the Blight, despite every petty drama of mortals that the flood had unleashed, it was still standing.

"Who said anything about getting off?"

• • •

They drove for hours. Sometimes, unbelievably, Tobias managed to drift off, swallowed by the fog that had engulfed the interior of the car and settled on small, snowblown farmers' fields in the rough, rolling country south of the Shield. He woke as the car took a right up a gravel road, through the dry memory of cornfields and into the mouth of a barbed-wire fence guarded by soldiers.

"I'm afraid this is where we part ways, son."

It wasn't the prison Tobias had expected; the buildings were low brick monstrosities, so recently painted that the graffiti still shadowed through the whitewash, dotted by guard towers, sprawled flat over grounds choked by weeds and scattered lumps of snow. Soldiers paced the trail leading onto the complex, looking bored and restless. A Red Ensign caught in the wind by the entrance, the tattered maple leaf flag below it.

"Classy," Tobias said. The door on his right opened so abruptly that he almost fell out the side of the car.

Adrenaline spiked through him, then, a last gasp of the primordial instincts that had kept alive each of his ancestors. "Reid—"

The Old Man looked up at him, placidly, with the same expression as he had when they sat around a conference table, even as one of the cops maneuvered Tobias' hands behind his back.

"Lucy had nothing to do with this," he said. "Please, whatever you want to do to me—leave her alone. Promise me?"

Impassive, Reid turned away, and Tobias was marched unceremoniously towards the complex.

• • •

They didn't question him. Tobias knew why he was there, and if the guards didn't, they weren't concerned enough to ask. They took his wallet, his cell phone, the watch that Lucy had given him for his birthday a few years ago. Wordlessly, they stripped him and bent him over a table and searched him for contraband. He shut his eyes against the intrusion.

"When do I get to talk to a lawyer?"

The soldier, no older than fifteen, backhanded him across the face.

He was commanded to change into a uniform, white tube socks, and paper slippers. He was led down another long hallway. The institutional grey tiles were new, but mud crept along the edges, and black mold already snaked up the freshly painted walls. The soldiers shoved him into a cell and he barked out a startled laugh as he stumbled onto the single cot with its soggy, blue-and-white striped mattress.

Tobias clambered to his feet and hurled himself against the door. "Hey!" he screamed. "Hey. Don't you think people will come looking for me? I want my fucking phone call."

His voice fell flat, died at the doorstep of his cell.

"Fuck." Tobias collapsed onto the bed, surveying his surroundings. One bed, one sink, something that might have very generously been called a toilet, all in a state of disrepair worse than what he'd seen of the rest of the facility. The smell was choking, the musty damp of the mold in the walls, the relentless assault of urine from somewhere down the hall. There had been a window, but it was boarded from the outside, barely a crack of daylight piercing the gloom. He kicked at the metal frame of the cot.

From the wall to his left, a rattling wet cough that dissolved, incongruously, into laughter.

"What the *fuck*?" He slammed a fist into the brick, shaking loose a shower of white paint flecks.

"Lard thunderin' fuckin' Christ." The dead man's voice rang clear through the vent where the wall met the floor. "Is that you, Fletcher?"

38

Eric had let his schoolboy crush drift into absentminded fantasies often enough that he assumed, at first, that Lucy Fletcher, picking her way over a broken sidewalk in high heels, was a figment of an overtired, overactive imagination. But it was definitely her, in a sharp-cut red duffel coat, black leather gloves gripping a designer purse, a pillbox hat with a veil that covered her face. A few stray strands of hair had come loose, and that was what convinced him that she was real, no matter how incongruous a vision she was.

He'd seen her transform into a demon before his eyes. No, that hadn't happened, that was booby-trapped paperwork, who even knew if it was something that could happen, and no wonder Ian Mallory was bugfuck nuts if that was the kind of shit he'd been seeing for years. It was Lucy, just human, beautiful Lucy, no insect appendages or bony protrusions, a glittering shard of the world that the Blight had all but obliterated.

"Lucy!" He almost tripped. It had snowed again last night, and it had slicked the jagged concrete into sharp teeth. She turned, her face unreadable through the veil.

Eric didn't run, and neither did she, but she was there in front of him nonetheless, her thin arms looped around him. She was a furnace against his chest. He held her longer than he should. They were less than acquaintances, strangers who occasionally bantered at parties.

Or they had been, before, when a familiar face was to be nodded at, not clung to as a fellow survivor, a ray of hope. Lucy didn't exactly pull away either. Eventually, they slid apart, and he forced a self-effacing, nervous giggle.

"Strange times." It was a good enough excuse, but he must have been staring at her, because she ran her gloved hands over her coat where it had made contact with him, as if to dispel all traces of the hug.

"Job interview," she said. "I don't normally dress up for wandering through apocalyptic wastelands."

The top of his grey hoodie was poking out at his neck. He actually had a job interview too, at the Walsingham Institute, that he'd almost certainly get. He wouldn't remain an unemployed embarrassment for long, thanks to his father. "We could die at any time. Why not die in sweatpants?"

She rolled her eyes, and he was sure she'd look gorgeous in sweatpants, anyway.

"Coming or going? From the interview, I mean."

She moved her purse from one shoulder to another. "Going," she said. "Foregone conclusion, really. Did I say a job? I meant a Faustian pact." She glanced around her. One couldn't tell these days who was listening, but Eric was pretty sure the lingering ambient magic levels meant that anything small enough to be easily concealed was also probably too unreliable to be used against them.

"Yeah," he said. "Same, actually."

Lucy's short burst of laughter became a sob almost as soon as it left her lips. The veil concealed her tears but she still turned her face away.

"What's wrong?" He wanted to lift her chin, tuck the loose spiral of hair behind her ear. It felt too intimate, forbidden even now; instead, he patted her upper arm, chastely separated by layers of fabric. "I mean. Other than the obvious."

"It's Tobias," she whispered. "He's—I can't find him. I filed a missing persons but there's so many missing people now, and no one will *do* anything and no one will *tell* me anything and I think..."

"Fuck." Now he did hug her, because what were you supposed to say? "Uh. Someone I know, someone I care about went missing too. I know where she is, well, I—it's different." And Tobias Fletcher wasn't Abigail. He didn't get a bag over his head and shoved into a van heading for the airport, or buried in a mass grave. He was *important*, people would look for him. "Did he—um. Change?" There wasn't a word yet. Not for people who inhaled shriekgrass spores and caught the screaming in their head like a broken record, and not for the people who transformed into monsters.

"They sent him demon-hunting a few weeks ago. But I don't—I don't know." She shifted, lifted a foot and rubbed at the back of her ankle. Shook her head where it rested against his collarbone. "I shouldn't say anything. They've been very kind to me, his employers. But even when the job keeps him away, he always checks in, he always—it's been *days*."

"He'll come back," Eric said, lamely. From what he'd seen, Tobias worshipped Lucy. If she hadn't heard from him, he wasn't going to come waltzing through her front door tomorrow.

"Sure," Lucy replied. "He will." She looked down at the pointed tips of her shoes. "I should go. In case."

"Of course." He slid his hand down her arm to wrap around her wrist. "Hey, it—well, it looks like I'm actually here permanently now. So if you want to talk, about anything at all, if you just want to get a drink and vent, I'm. You know." He fumbled in his jacket pocket, he had to have a pen somewhere.

Lucy produced a pen and tiny notebook from a purse that seemed too small to contain either, and scribbled down a number. "I could use a friend too," she said, pushing it into his hand before she turned and fled.

• • •

Eric's new office was a real office, not a cubicle or the nightmare that had ensued during the Party's brief and tragic experiment with hot-desking. It was a fishbowl of glass; the floor-to-ceiling windows gave no illusions of privacy. His work was the Walsingham Institute's work, transparent and all-encompassing.

As open as it was, his employers had still put eyes on him. He'd been followed here, and yesterday, he'd been followed home. They weren't subtle about it, and probably that was the point. His tail hadn't let him see his face, but he'd seen the man standing, pretending to talk on a cellphone, outside his window.

Eric kept his head down. He had done nothing wrong. He could tell himself that as long as he played the game, they'd make an exception for Jakie. He could tell himself that the moral calculus worked out in the end.

He had a Masters in Poli Sci and five years working for the Party, but they had him plugging numbers into spreadsheets, endless fields of data from phone surveys. It was hard enough to shape the rows and columns into opinions, the fears and anxieties of people huddling in their homes, curled around their suddenly useful landlines, let alone extrapolate policy, to link what he was doing to the roundups of immigrants and noncompliant MAI.

There was a certain reassurance in data. Not truth, Eric had never been so naïve, but a concreteness. If you put a number to something, you could make it real. Each data point was someone's fingers, somewhere in the country, punching in 1 for not concerned at all, 5 for gripped with unholy terror. Even the apocalypse was quantifiable.

His office was as bare and impersonal as he could manage. He had a single family photo, taken when Jakie was an infant. The cactus he'd liberated from the Broom Closet when it had become apparent that Ian wasn't coming back. A Slinky. He didn't know where it had come from. He was familiar enough with the mundane aspects of magic that he wouldn't have been surprised if it had manifested spontaneously on his desk.

He'd always been a cog. The questions were conceived without him, the answers provided by strangers unaware of their design, how the subtleties in phrasing shaped their responses. His manager had promised him that if he worked hard, paid his dues, he could move up.

Twice a week, he made a video call home, and his parents let him talk to Jakie.

Eric was good at complicity, it turned out. Aunt Lydia was right. You could get used to anything, if you did it long enough.

• • •

"The latest," Alcott, his manager, dumped a box of papers on Eric's desk. "Wrangle this into something, will you?"

Like everything that crossed his path, it was a series of opinion questions, tailor-made to gently nudge respondents into support for Atherton's positions. ("How concerned are you about foreign MAI influence?" "Are you worried about the deficit your children will inherit?") Nothing more than a low-grade annoyance, except that the visceral shudder when he touched them came from more than just the ideological bent.

He'd worked with Ian Mallory for five years. He knew what a spell looked like when he saw one. Magic written not in pen scribbles and blue sparks but in numbers entered into a phone to call down the forces wrecking havoc all around them.

They already had the country. What more did they need?

• • •

A block from his apartment, Eric stopped and whirled on his shadow. The sodium halo of a streetlamp caught his glasses, and he flinched. A fat, emboldened raccoon humped its way over the road behind him.

"I know you're there." He kept his voice even, pleased that there was no tremble in it. "You actually suck at this, dude."

Senator Cal Harrison, face covered in a smart Canada Goose mask, stepped out from behind a garage door.

"Don't look so smug," Cal said. "There are at least two people in the office watching you who *aren't* me. I thought it was time we had a chat."

George Smiley would never go for a $6,000 Loro Piana camel coat. At least Eric warranted top-tier surveillance.

"So," Eric said. "Talk. Unless you want to sit on opposite sides of a park bench wearing carnations or something."

"Alcott likes you. He doesn't trust you, but he thinks you'll come around."

"And you?"

"Me? I think you're possessed of slightly more brains and ethics."

"Should I be complimented?"

Cal sighed heavily. He was a long way from the Red Chamber. "I'm not here to flatter you, Eric. I'm here to make you an offer."

It was a trap. Walsingham—or the puppet masters behind it—would want to know that Eric's end of the bargain was being kept. They would test, and keep testing, and they would know that more than anything else, he longed for Cal to have a plan.

"Sorry," Eric said. "I have a family."

"Right. Your brother. For whom you'd let thousands, maybe millions of innocent people die." Cal leaned against the garage door, arms crossed. "They'll kill him anyway. Your family. You. They might have started with the immigrants and Muslims, but don't worry, they'll get around to it. They always do. You have a very short life ahead of you, Eric, but you have an opportunity here. You can choose to make it count."

A very short life. That was what Ian had said, too. "You're wrong," Eric said. "About how ethical I am."

Cal unfolded and clapped Eric on the shoulder. "This isn't a time for heroes. We need traitors. And you'd make a good one."

39

Nothing in Tobias' material circumstances had changed in the seconds since he heard Ian Mallory's voice. He was still in prison—not even a real prison, but some slapdash black site without records or oversight. He had still painted a target on himself, and on Lucy. He'd still blundered into something he didn't understand, fucked it all up beyond belief, done the right thing, certainly, but far too late.

And he still couldn't push down the glimmer of hope.

"Tobias fuckin' Fletcher," Mallory said. "For a guy who hates socialism so much, you really do love gettin' publicly owned." He coughed again, a bloody crunch, his breath coming in short, rapid wheezes. Tobias hadn't heard anything like that since his days in Syria.

"That doesn't sound good," Tobias said. "Broken ribs?"

"Fuck you," Mallory said. His voice, a terrible grey thing in the darkness, was muted by the thick wall between them. "I grew up a skinny gay ginger in a fishing village in Newfoundland. I knows how to take a fuckin' beating, okay?"

Tobias, bunched up by the vent, picked a loose shard of brick free from the wall and turned it over in his hand. The cell had the same dank mold-smell as the processing room and the hallway, the same hasty whitewashing over decades of graffiti. The bare concrete floor was cold through the thin paper soles of his slippers, and felt like if he pushed on it hard enough, it would squish under his foot.

"I heard you were dead," Tobias said. "Buried in some earthquake."

"They'd already dragged me here."

"Where is here?"

"Didn't realize we were doing another interview." Tobias could hear him shifting position, a tight inhale of breath. Trying to cling to some remnant of dignity. There was no point to that now, and Tobias refused to pity him. "Still in Ontario. They were driving west. I could see the sun through the blindfold."

"Patrice Abel is dead," Tobias said.

"And like an idiot, you shot it the way it actually went. So your boss, the cryptofascist pulling the strings behind the scenes for the last fifty years, fucks you over. I knew the ending to this story a long time ago, b'y."

"You could have told someone."

"Who?" Another laugh-cough. Mallory really did sound like shit. "You know the one about the economist and the weatherman?"

"That a joke?" Tobias settled in with the damp wall to his back, stretching out his legs across the floor.

"You could say that. The weatherman says it's gonna rain. The whole day, everyone expects it to rain, but it's bright and sunny. The weather gives no shits about what the weatherman said. He could have said it would be sunny, and it'd have the same effect. But the economist says that it's a bear market and shareholders lose their shit and start sellin'. It matters, what he says."

"And you're an economist, not a weatherman?"

For a while, all he heard of Mallory was the wheeze of his breathing. Tobias waited. He had nothing but time, now.

"I've never really known that for sure."

"How could you not?"

If Mallory had an answer, he wasn't willing to give it.

• • •

Tobias could take four steps in any direction in his cell. There was a sink that ran cold water and a toilet that flushed, sometimes. Metal coils prodded him through the thin mattress, but Tobias didn't sleep much anyway.

He worked at the shadows coming through the whitewash, tracing the letter forms with the pieces of brick he scraped free from the cracks in the wall, scratching at the paint until Mallory shouted at him to stop it.

The paint was cheap, but it clung stubbornly to the walls, uneven. He kept at it. There was one thing left to uncover.

• • •

The guards were new at their job. Everything here was imperfection slathered over with a thin coat of paint. Tobias heard them bantering outside the door, talking about their homes, the girlfriends they had, the girlfriends they wished they had. Most were from small towns, excited to have a steady gig that paid above the now-abolished minimum wage.

They didn't touch Tobias. Maybe they were under orders not to. When they brought Mallory in and out of his cell, there were obvious sounds of struggle, sometimes the quiet gasps of a man trying to rein in his own pained cries, but they opened Tobias' door only to exchange an empty tray for a full one.

Once or twice, he tried to weave a fragile thread of shared humanity, joke with them, prove that he was no threat, that he had even played some bit part in creating the system that had elevated them from schoolyard bullies to uniformed enforcers. He flinched away from the disdain on their faces. Lower than nothing, only the last piece of dirt to be swept under the carpet, after which the room would be clean.

• • •

Reid didn't visit, but Alycia did.

Her coat was white to the point of iridescence, trimmed in ermine, the only clean thing in his squalid cell. She somehow balanced on kitten heels despite the soggy, uneven cement. Her gloved hands stayed clasped behind her back. She practically shone.

"Reid's devastated, of course." She had that habit, beginning a conversation mid-sentence, as if picking up where they'd left off last time. "He wants a big public execution. That's how much you hurt him, Tobias."

"I'm sorry my murder is such an inconvenience to him."

She gave him a pinched smile. "*He* wants an execution. Men are so terribly melodramatic. You're immune to magic. You're special. It's foolhardy to waste the opportunity that you represent. And there's the small matter of Lucy—"

Nothing was real. The days bled together, marked only by the waxing and waning of light from the gaps in the boarded-up window, by his slow progress as he chipped away at the paint on the wall.

Now he sat up. She was drawn in sharp relief, stark white and grey.

"Lucy," Tobias whispered. His only tether to the World Before. "Please, she didn't mean to—"

"The two of you could have coordinated your respective treasons better." If anything, Alycia sounded *amused*. "She's had defiance bred out of her for generations. She's no threat, and if she knows there's a chance of getting you back...well. She's not a stupid girl, is she?"

"You still need her."

"I still want her." Alycia stooped to cup his chin. Her thumb explored the beard that sprouted from days in his cell, unable to shave with anything sharper than the edge of a metal food tray. "I could conquer the country with a few keystrokes and a transfer of imaginary numbers. Or I can do it with a strategically commissioned song sung by a nightingale in a red dress. Both accomplish the same goal, but I would live in a world built on arias before one built on microtransactions. Wouldn't you?"

"I don't think we want to live in the same kind of world after all."

"Hmm." She straightened, brushed imaginary dirt from her perfect coat. "It remains to be seen what kind of world it will be. Don't you want a hand in building it, Tobias?"

Tobias listened to Alycia's footsteps fade down the corridor. Her pace was measured. She had all the time in the world.

Ten minutes later, when they came for Mallory, he tried not to listen.

• • •

The letters, scratch by scratch, took their shape. An archaeologist, he revealed drips of paint, rounded loose letters rendered in a careless hand.

You expect to fall apart like petals falling off flowers
& instead you crack like an abandoned house

He didn't know why he expected it to be something profound.

"Tell me how to fix this," Tobias said to the vent.

40

Blythe was on open waters again, feeling the ocean sway the deck beneath her feet. The *Empress Willow* was a vanity sailboat meant for ten to fit comfortably on a short cruise around the archipelago, not fifty or so desperate refugees crammed together to the railing, crossing the wrathful Pacific in the hopes that Australia might have endured the Blight with a sliver of dignity.

Not everyone on board was accustomed to life on a semi-illegal vessel making its way for international waters. There had been vomit. There was still, every few hours, vomit. Even when there wasn't vomit, the smell hung in the air, molecules of sickness suspended in the salt and spray. Blythe hung over the side of the railing, leaned into the bracing cold in a bid to breathe in the sea and not her fellow desperate, squalid passengers.

She was already half salt herself, the fine grooves in her face, her lips, nostrils encrusted, dusting fragments of sediment onto the back of her hand every time she rubbed her eyes. Lot's wife, but Blythe was the one who hadn't looked back, and Jonah the one as doomed as the home left behind.

"What's gonna happen to Dad?" Laura asked. It wasn't the first time she'd brought up Jonah. She'd mentioned him more in the past day or two than she had in the nearly two years since the divorce.

Blythe almost said that he'd be fine, so inconceivable it was that Jonah could be anything other than fine. The cops wouldn't come crashing in on his humiliating little basement hovel. He wouldn't take to the woods, as he had so many times in the past, and walk straight into the sights of an RCMP sharpshooter. He wouldn't mouth off at exactly the wrong time, to exactly the wrong white man, and die face down on the cracked concrete, too proud to beg for breath.

She wouldn't be left, resenting him, hating him sometimes, indebted to him for their ticket to freedom, and never knowing his fate.

Laura was getting too old for pretty lies.

"There's this type of jellyfish," Blythe said, instead. "*Turritopsis dohrnii*. It's tiny, and, well, it's a jellyfish, so obviously it's very stupid, but when it's hurt, or sick, or very old, it just—changes. Becomes a juvenile again. Grows smaller. Reinvents itself. In theory, it's biologically immortal."

"Yeah?" Laura hadn't inherited either Jonah's knack for escapism, or Blythe's fascination with the sea. "So?"

"So that's what your father is," Blythe said. "Functionally unkillable."

"You're just trying to make me feel better."

"Is it working?" She stretched out an arm to pull Laura close. "I'll get the hang of this parenting thing eventually, I promise."

"We studied Australia last year." Laura's voice was a fragile, trepidatious thing, still feeling out the parameters of what she knew, what was worth fearing. Blythe had almost four decades of watching the life she had built against all odds disrupted. She'd had the first Cascade and the recession and the other recession, had her heart cracked open and sewn clumsily back together. She had watched the way the world shifted and broke and healed, as the new normal became just normal. Laura, a tenth of her young life spent in chaos, had no such context. "They have a lot of fires. And poisonous spiders."

"And kangaroos. Koalas. Schools that are still intact, from what I've heard." And a long coastline. No shortage of work for someone who put numbers to the ocean's fury. Somewhere she wouldn't be Native. Australia had its own ugly racist morass, but the two of them together, her copper hair and olive eyes, even Laura's black hair and skin a shade darker than Blythe's, would be exotic Frenchwomen, their differences rapidly absorbed into a sea of whiteness. It might as well be the moon, but it was a place to start over. Jonah had given them that much.

"Are we ever coming back?"

Blythe tried to picture it. Flights resumed, not just for the sporadic, emergency jaunts of the rich and important—white-knuckled hope that the laws of physics would continue to apply for the duration of their flight—but for everyone. The broken streets paved again, flowers and trees in concrete planters. Universities and chocolate and people walking their dogs and Netflix marathons. The world had been alien for so long that she barely saw what might be left to return home to.

"One day, we'll go home," Blythe promised.

• • •

Laura twitched in her sleep. Little breaths, short and fast, whistled from her lips. Blythe, curled around her, someone's sneaker-clad shoe in her face, couldn't sleep at all. The smell was a military assault, a miasma blanketing the passenger cabin. Worse still were the moans, refugees in the grip of nightmares or sickness. She would drift off, for seconds, only to be jerked awake by someone else's grief.

Someone was singing. She recognized the melody, though she couldn't place it, and she was suffused with rage. It must have been midnight, people were trying to sleep, and someone was singing, not some lullaby to a colicky baby, not some familiar refrain to comfort scared passengers, but an atonal, *antitonal*, locust-buzz drone that flitted just above the surface of her consciousness, just loud enough to keep her from sleep.

The others lay in huddles, families piled together, strangers crammed where they could fit, bent into corners or folded up against the long horizontal oak beams of the cabin. No one's lips moved. No one turned, blinked open reddened eyes to glare in annoyance at the singer. No one else was listening.

She was so tired that, at first, she couldn't even remember where she'd heard it before. Memory skated along her synapses, looking for some revelation. Then—

Oh. For a few long minutes, she'd thought it was some*one* singing.

Laura mumbled and sat up, burrowing into the scratchy army-issue blanket that barely covered them both. Blythe stroked her hair, tried to urge them both down, to at least mimic sleep if she couldn't block out the sea unveiling its horrors. Her daughter's thin wrist was ice cold.

"Go back to sleep," Blythe whispered.

Laura shook her head. "I can't sleep," she said. "Not with the singing."

Laura acquiesced, eventually, the myriad brutalities of the day heaped on top of her until she gave way beneath their weight.

She slept. Blythe, arms goosefleshed and stomach churning, did not. She took a tight breath in and held it until—

The blast tore through the coughing and vomiting, lifted the *Empress Willow* out of the water and twisted her in half. Blythe was able to grab Laura as they were both flung across the cabin, their fall broken by a heap of other fallen bodies, Laura's shrill scream broken by the crack of walls and floors.

Laura's hand clutched hers and she pressed them both into the wall. The ship lurched and people scrambled over each other, scrabbling for the door. A cold tongue of water lapped at her shoe.

"Did we hit something?" Laura asked. "Did someone *hit us*?"

It must have been the latter. Blythe could imagine intent, cruelty. She could not imagine a random accident of fate, the ship a toy in the grip of a storm's tantrum. Couldn't imagine that they would become nameless drowned bodies bobbing face-down in the ocean, barely news against the immense human tragedy grinding forward in slow motion.

The cabin was filling fast. Several of the men bashed into the doorframe, splintering the polished wood of the wall. Blythe held herself and Laura back, the water to her ankles, to Laura's calves. She lifted the girl but she wasn't going to be strong enough to keep them afloat. She waited for a gap in the crowd and pushed them through the gaping wreckage of the door.

Outside, the water was deeper, the passage upstairs a choke point, but she gripped Laura tightly and shoved up, onto the sloping deck. Above the prow, pointed up sharply towards the grey sky, she saw what, at first, she took for a floating city, like Pandora, a grey onslaught welded together from shipping containers and sleek solar panels. Sea foam steamed from the engines at its base, carrying it along in a bed of mist. It dwarfed the *Empress Willow* in its shadow. At either flank, missile launchers like cannons were still smoking, and at its mast, the yellow-and-black of the SVAR flag flapped limply in the wind.

The captain was vainly calling out in at least three languages that they had nothing of value, they were unarmed, refugees, they had papers and passports and just then, the boat lurched and her stomach with it. Her body, smashing into the railing, broke Laura's fall. It'd bruise, if she lived.

Pirates—*privateers*, the pedantic part of her brain refused to shut up, even now—in black dinghies poured fourth in the crashing waves between the *Empress Willow* and their hulking seastead, firing AR-15s in the air, blasting wood into sawdust. Blythe pulled them both down to the deck, seawater choking her mouth.

She braced herself, the ship shuddering under her knees and palms, arched over Laura. She cast out the net of prayer widely, to saints and ancestors, to the Creator, to whatever entity would listen, to not let them die like this, at the mercy of men who'd attack a ship of refugees for whatever scraps they'd carried. She saw the boot-clad feet trampling over bodies, knocking over cargo, tearing off wedding bands and necklaces, strewing the contents of suitcases in their wake.

Then the sea broke apart.

The wave of water that swept over the deck was hot to the point of boiling, scalding her as she grappled for something to cling to as the railing cracked apart. It flung her on her back and she clutched Laura to her chest.

The ocean bubbled and hissed. Her brain didn't entirely process the back-and-forth whip of the spine piercing through the side of the SVAR vessel, thrashing it below the water's surface. The *Empress Willow* kicked upwards, skipping like a stone over the waves. The momentum should have killed them. The gunfire, skimming the surface as the privateers turned their weapons away from the *Empress Willow* and on their attacker, should have hit. The inhuman scream of the creature as it breached should have shattered her ears and driven her to madness.

Another wave, and she was plunged deep into the steaming water. Blythe flailed for purchase, saltwater in her nose, her throat, her eyes burning. You could tell if you were diving deeper or striking up to the surface, something about how the bubbles went, but her heart was a live grenade and she couldn't breathe, couldn't think, and it was only as she drew in that first lungful of copper-laced air that she noticed that she was alone.

"*Laura!*" The screaming, the explosions, the heaving of the *thing* as it loosed itself from the depths swallowed her cry. There were bodies dotting the water, sodden little huddles amongst the wreckage of the two ships. She swam, spluttering, as if she could somehow miraculously pick out one tiny girl in all the carnage.

Somewhere, in the distance, she thought she saw the bright speck of a pink backpack, glossy black hair spilling up along the hollow of the wave. Blythe pinwheeled her arms, kicking forward, only to be dragged under again.

She was going to die here after all, and Laura with her, swallowed in the ocean's teeth.

Her arms and legs went limp. She closed her stinging eyes. Her mouth slackened, let the water throttle her into sleep.

The labyrinth on her shoulder burned incandescent. Her closed lids glowed pink, filled with light. A coil of bone snaked around her ribs, thrust her upwards towards the sky, and she gasped and heaved and puked seawater, life forcing itself back into her lungs.

Blythe slackened in its grasp, but it held her, as securely and as delicately as she might hold a specimen, or child's hand.

Ian, dotting the Pattern into her skin, promised that it would protect her even as he saw into her future, saw all the things he would never tell her, each strike of the needle a prayer to an ocean that would take away everything she ever loved, but would never harm her.

She was going to live after all.

Below her, nothing moved. The waves, calmer now, appeased by blood, wove over their dead. The ocean stretched out as far as she could see, broken by bereft continents of luggage, greasy little islands of human entrails. Somewhere, her daughter's corpse drifted, indistinct from the other bodies turned to flotsam, bashing up against the shore of the sinking ships.

It had claimed Laura, but the sea would always spare Blythe. Would not just let her live but would understand her, love her, as fiercely and coldly as she had loved it all her life. No saint or god would take her prayers, but the sea would answer them.

"Not like this," Blythe whispered, and in the cage of cold bone, slid into unconsciousness.

41

"Tell me," Tobias repeated. "How to fix this."

The silence behind the wall was too long, too deep. Maybe Mallory was already dead. But no, when he strained to listen, Tobias could hear the rattle of his breathing, a crumpled paper caught in the blades of a fan.

Mallory's voice, when at last he spoke, was the creak of a rusted hinge in a condemned house. "The fuck d'you think this is, b'y? Some buddy comedy where we put our differences aside and escape through the air vents?" He banged on the one that bridged their cells for emphasis, the echo of the strike carrying. The register was under a foot in length and the screws holding it in place were fused there by rot and wear. Tobias pried at it experimentally, but it didn't give. "This is where we die."

"I don't accept that," Tobias said.

He was getting sick of Mallory laughing at him, so Tobias waited patiently for him to stop.

"You don't seem like the type to give up."

"Ya cock-wobblin' fuck," Mallory snarled. Impending death hadn't filed down any of his edges. Tobias pictured him bashing against the walls of his cell, thought that the tiny room would be too much to contain the sorcerer's manic energy. "You die first. That's what matters. Means I get to spend my last days without ya yammerin' in my ear."

• • •

Once upon a time.

Once.

There was a castle, and a dungeon, and a wizard. And a knight, who had steadied his lance for the cause of truth, even if it had been too late. Stories that began like that, no matter how badly its heroes had strayed from their path, never ended with the oubliette scene. There was always a chance for redemption.

Tobias didn't believe in fate. He didn't believe in a universe that he couldn't, through hard work and force of will, bend in a better direction. Tobias wouldn't die forgotten in some secret prison, the closest thing he had to an archenemy dying by choking increments on the other side of the wall while Tobias pissed into a toilet with a broken flush handle and reached under the cracked lid to yank the chain with a whispered prayer.

If Mallory had meant to dissuade him from escape, or hope, his words had the opposite effect. When an evil sorcerer tells you that you're doomed, you take up arms against his prophecy. You find an escape, or you meet your end kicking and screaming.

The bed could be disassembled. It was a hollow metal frame. It could be used as a weapon. A crowbar, to force the door open. It had the same deep-set, rusted screws as the register. There were no sheets. Maybe the mold-stained mattress cover? Tobias turned it over, searched for a zipper, a weak patch in the tough fabric. There was always an out. There had to be. His hands, always so strong when they were gripping the handles of his bike, weren't powerful enough to tear it. He ended up hurling it across the room, kicking at it, but his slippered foot had more give than the mattress.

It would have to be diplomacy. Tobias learned the names of the guards. He made sure to address them, to learn their stories. Corey from

Petawawa. Mike from Fergus. Ray, whose parents owned a farm in Leamington, worried about getting the time off to help supervise the spring planting, if spring ever came. They weren't much better company than Mallory. They might have been under orders not to hurt him, but they seemed equally forbidden to talk to him.

He tried not to notice the blood on Ray's knuckles.

Corey talked about his girlfriend, interrupted himself and called her his fiancee. The other guys teased him. Urged him into describing her tits, which he was loathe to do. Tobias thought he sounded sweet when he spoke about her. He wasn't more than twenty, still had baby fat on his cheeks.

Lucy had to be fine. If she wasn't, they would be using her fate against him. But there was nothing from him that they wanted, no trade left for him to give. Alycia hadn't come back, and neither had the Old Man. Tobias had played his role, ensnared their enemy, helped boost their man to power, and now he served no more purpose to them beyond serving as a warning to others.

Tobias punched the mattress again. It didn't help.

"Where is she?" he asked the wall. "Can you see her? Right now?"

Mallory didn't need to ask who Tobias meant. "Yeah," he said. "She's forgotten all about you, b'y. She's moved on with her life, and good for her."

There was no such thing as dignity in a prison cell. The smell alone, decades of shit ground into the walls and floor that no amount of bleach would ever remove, reminded him of that. Someone else's idea of underwear. The pitiful scratches accumulated over time, a history of prisoners marking time. Best to give up the pretences now.

"Please, Mallory. I need to know she's okay."

"Shoulda thought of that before you turned on your boss." With more wince than breath, Mallory said, "I can walk through walls. You think they left my hands free to do magic?"

Tobias arranged himself on the mattress, his ear by the vent. Mallory must have come closer too; the strain and catches in his breathing whistled through the grate. "It's so easy for you to give up," Tobias said. "What do you have to live for now? You don't have anything, no career, no family, no power. No one you love enough to fight for."

Mallory went quiet again. He had been moving around before, the rustle of his clothes over the cement floor audible through the vent. All Tobias could hear of him now was the thick, wet splatter of the occasional cough. A Cheshire cat, dissolving into pained sound before vanishing altogether.

"All that time pinin' after me, Fletcher, followin' me like some stalker after a crush, and you don't knows the slightest fuckin' thing about me."

"Oh?"

"Of course I have a family. Everyone has a family. Everyone's fighting for something, some*one*, even your alt-shite of a boss and his wife."

Tobias supposed that much was true. Reid Curtis might love nothing in the world except Alycia, but mind-controlled or otherwise, he had no doubt that Reid loved Alycia. And whatever the dark motive lay buried within his matryoshka doll of an ideological framework, he believed in it with all his heart.

"So tell me," Tobias said.

"About my personal life?"

"We have the time."

Mallory picked at the words, cautious. It was disconcerting, really, from a man who normally spoke in machine-gun bursts. "Ya don't get love stories when ya sees every possible way for them to end."

"That's it, then? It's all pointless, nothing matters, who gives a fuck?"

"That which doesn't kill me," Mallory said. "Softens me up for that which will."

"You really believe that hard in fate?"

"The Blight was inevitable. There's too many variables, it would take a worldwide effort thirty, forty years ago. One man, one middling power, was never gonna stand in the way of somethin' like that. I saw how it'd all shake out when I was a kid. And by then it was already too late to stop it."

"Why all *this* then?" Tobias waved a hand idly, before he remembered that Mallory couldn't see him. "The politics, the manipulation."

"Had to give it a try, eh? I started seein' the future when I was nineteen years old," Mallory said. "This future. Every other future. Before Vasai raised Pandora City, before they had a name for what was happening to all of us, back when magic was just wakin' up and stretchin' its legs. Every future, as far forward as I could go, right to the heat death of the universe. Until election night, until I finally gots the thing I was workin' at for the better part of my life. That's when the clock started tickin'."

"What clock?" Tobias asked, as Mallory, mockingly, said the exact same words a half-second before they were out of his mouth.

"Four years," Mallory said, answering both their questions. "Give or take. Prophecy isn't poetry. No matter what I changed, what I did, what I told Patrice and the rest."

"Until they brought you here?"

"Until the Great Fuckin' Yawning Void, after which I could see no further."

It took no work to decode what that would mean for an MAI with precognition. "Because you're dead."

"Not in one timeline. In all of them. Whatever I did."

Tobias leaned his head back, tracing a finger over the *e* in *house* marked on the wall. More of the paint and aging brickwork had come loose. He gathered the tiny bits of rubble and arranged them into patterns on the floor. A miniature city. Stonehenge. A cemetery.

"And the Blight too, no matter what? The attack on Parliament, weaponized magic."

"It was always gonna happen, sooner or later. Religion's the opiate of the masses but magic's the amphetamine, and time only goes forward. But I could slow it. We had the Tar Sands pukin' shit into the air, and magic loves us shittin' up the planet, wants us to pick apart the fabric of creation so it can slide through the holes. Cut carbon emissions and the temperature goes up point-zero-something less than if we didn't. Blythe would know, she'd have a number. An amount. A little amount that bought the entire world four months."

All that rhetoric. Crashing the economy, smashing institutions that had stood for a century and change, and for what? "Fuck," Tobias said. "What's four months?"

"Because, you shallow puddle of a man, in those four months some little kid is going to turn five years old and get his first bike, and he's going to ride it up and down his street and feel like a big man. Some family's gonna get to bury their grandmother and cry over her with a funeral instead of dumping her in a mass grave or never knowing what happened to her."

Tobias lined his detritus into a spiral, and tipped them over, hoping for some kind of dramatic domino effect. But the scrap of brick he'd tipped didn't fall right, and the rest stayed up until he swept a hand over the whole thing.

"Enough time," Mallory added, "for my apprentice to escape with everything I taught her."

Tobias, mid-swallow, almost choked. "Your *apprentice*."

"My intern, really. Did ya think I'd leave it up to self-aggrandizing middle-aged white men to save the world?"

"The world *does* get saved?" Tobias asked, hating the brightness in his voice.

"Fucked if I knows, b'y. I can't sees beyond my own death. But she gets time. It's all any of us gets to hope for."

"How do you die, Mallory?"

"As we speak," Mallory said. "There's a girl on a train, headed east. She's lookin' out the window at the prairies, all those miles and miles of flat snow and shriekgrass where there used to be wheat. Bubbling over with magic, so much her skin can hardly contain it. She's making patterns in her head, mapping up the new shape of the world. She's come to take you apart bit by bit to see why magic doesn't work on you. Come to tear my heart out and devour it. I don't sees the actual moment but her face? That's the last thing waiting for my eyes before they close."

"And that's how I die too?"

"Screaming and pissing yourself," Mallory offered. "She isn't cruel, not by nature. It doesn't occur to her that these are acts of cruelty. Your skin, your blood, your very mortality, these are just a veil to be cut aside to reveal her truth."

How many risk assessment reports had Mallory given to Patrice's regime with the same dispassionate, clinical delivery? Tobias was well aware of the irony, but the voice behind the wall had become his sole lifeline. He'd begged, pleaded, rationalized, bargained with it. "One of the ways," Mallory amended. "There's two."

Tobias asked, "What's the other one?"

Without a trace of sympathy or regret, Mallory told him.

• • •

The guards laughed about something outside, unbothered by the damp cold that had settled in Tobias' bones. Of course, they were young, athletic types. They swung their arms when they walked; they had metabolisms that ran hot. He felt ancient and withered in their presence.

Mallory wasn't in a talkative mood today. Maybe he'd overexerted himself with yesterday's Bond villain monologue, maybe, at the end, he shrank from death as surely as any man. Did having years to reconcile yourself to the exact day and time of your death make that final Kubler Ross stage any easier? Tobias' mother died of cancer when he was 14, and she wasn't close to anything like acceptance by the end.

There is no such thing as a good death, Mallory had told him. *None of the paths through the labyrinth lead to the exit. You keep searching for the one with a happy ending. But there isn't the one right policy that everyone agrees is such a good idea that it keeps our guys in power. The path where he both stays and lives. You don't gets that choice. The choice you get to make is between letting a child drown now and letting her die of typhoid fever three months later in a detention centre.*

And maybe you don't even get to choose that.

Corey and Ray both took him out for his daily five minutes of sunlight. Tobias didn't know what made him warrant two guards, but then, the facility was overstaffed for what was so far only a handful of prisoners.

"Nice day," Tobias said. It wasn't. April was almost over, if he'd been counting the days right, but February's weather had sunk its claws in deep and refused to let go. The prison grounds were still powdered with white and shot through with red grass and soggy dead leaves. The cold snow caught the soles of his paper slippers, soaked through in seconds, and he wondered if they'd bother reissuing him new ones.

No, they wouldn't, of course they wouldn't.

Past the main cluster of buildings, workers were unrolling a second layer of barbed wire around the perimeter.

"Do you know why I'm here?" Tobias asked abruptly and then, when there was no answer forthcoming, "Do you know why *you're* here?"

"Beats stocking shelves at Wal-Mart," Corey said, and Ray shot him a nasty glare.

"Because I don't," Tobias went on. "I don't know why any of us are here. Except Mallory, sure, he's a born criminal, but—" He shivered, went to put his hands in his pockets only to remember that he didn't have any. He settled for tucking his hands under his armpits. "This was never supposed to be a revolution, you see. Oh, the Old Man likes his rhetorical flairs."

"Who?" Corey asked.

"They're all nuts here," Ray told him. "And fucking traitors." He kicked at Tobias' heel. "Move. We don't have all day, asshole."

"I came here to fix the system, not smash it to bits. I wanted to root out corruption. I thought I found it, with Mallory. But he's only the ordinary, garden variety type of corrupt. A politician with a few parlour tricks."

Ray said, "Jesus Christ. Do you ever shut up?"

"No," Tobias replied. "That's why I'm here."

He could escape now. Or try. Mallory could be lying, or wrong. Was it even possible for him to be wrong? They hadn't bothered to handcuff

Tobias—he couldn't walk through walls, after all—and he had a clear line through the sparse trees to the fence. Barbed wire, sure. How hard was it to get through barbed wire? The guards were younger than him, but he'd worked out every day of his adult life.

They would shoot him, of course. Well before he reached the fence. You ran zigzag, that was what Specialist—what was that guy's name? Mason? Manson? Something like that—Specialist Mason said in Aleppo, you ran zigzag and you were harder to shoot.

"The men and women you work for," Tobias said, "They already have everything they want. They won, months ago. They ought to be mourning the dead, rebuilding, and instead all of this destruction is just an opportunity to build the world they wanted all along. And it looks like this. Mass deportations. MAI registered and conscripted into service, for some unknown Great Plan. A half-assed gulag waiting to be filled up with anyone who crosses them."

He could only pray that Lucy would be wiser than he had been. Or, if not more sensible, than at least more frightened. That she wouldn't go looking for him, and find this place instead.

"Mallory was right," he muttered. "After all that, he was right."

"Who?" Corey asked.

"Ian Mallory, you know? Douchebag wizard, mouth like a St. John's sewer. Not so much a person as half a dozen personality disorders stuffed in a trench coat. Currently mouldering in the cell next to mine."

"Yeah," Corey said. "This guy's lost it."

Tobias laughed. What else was left? His slipper slid to one side as he took a step that wasn't careful enough. The ground itself felt unsteady, skewed at a Dutch angle. It might have been another earthquake, an aftershock, but it was over too quickly. He released his hands, steadied himself, sucked in a breath of bright, frigid air.

How about you, then? Even if he'd been talking to a wall, the wall had answered back, so what did that say about his mental state? *You're so convinced I should die on my own terms, and you're ready to kick back and get vivisected by the Wicked Witch of the West?*

That had received a snort of amusement from Mallory.

Those are my own terms, b'y. Every future, and I watched them get pared down, one by one. Until. I don't gets to live happily ever after with my devastatingly hot boyfriend and seven fat cats and die an old man surrounded by adorable if biologically improbable redheaded grandchildren. That was never in the cards.

But I gets to look up at my own death and spit right in her fuckin' face.

It was an option, anyway. For two men with few options remaining to them.

"You don't need to do this." Tobias said quietly, to Corey. Not bad guys, those two. Just kids, really, playing at soldiers. Like all soldiers were.

"Do what?" the guard replied, and Tobias swung his fist up and into Corey's face.

He had surprise on his side, and a wild, uncontrollable urge to live. For a few split seconds, as his fingers closed around the grip of the guard's holstered gun, almost gained purchase before Corey recovered and knocked him, sprawling into the snow, he felt more alive than he had in weeks, longer if he were honest—and what, in the moments remaining, was left to him but honesty?—since before he'd come to that festering wound of a city and sold his soul to the Old Man and his ghoulish army, to Alycia and the web she'd woven to ensnare a nation.

Before they both set on him like a pair of rabid dogs, kicking and swinging nightsticks, before the crack that burst too close to his ear, so loud that he thought he'd rolled onto a dry stick and snapped it in half, before he tried to raise his hands to shield his face and *couldn't*, the body that had carried him through war zones and press conferences and had loved a woman with every cell of its being no longer responding to his commands, before he heard Ray shout, "Stop it I think he's—"

Before each one of his possible futures converged to one end, Tobias Fletcher thought he was freer than he'd ever been in all his life.

42

Sujay knew what a gunshot sounded like. She'd grown up in Wildest Scarberia after all, had classmates rumoured to be Gang-Involved, played the late-night game of "Is It Victoria Day Fireworks Or a Shootout?" She had never, though, heard so many, and in such quick succession, little pops in the distance that echoed over the rattling windows. She skulked. She slid through the gaps between buildings, glamour pooled around her like a shroud. It was her only chance now.

She limped onto Morningside Ave. and froze. She had walked all night, and it was early dawn, the pink and orange sunset shot through with veins of crimson and playing across clumps of browning snow. There was no one else on the street, the traffic lights at the intersection gone out, smoke eddying lazily from the windows of the CashMoney. Her twisted ankle throbbed. She could hear what sounded at first like conversation but was only someone's radio, chatter on AM640, an ad for a furniture store, pre-canned and irrelevant when, outside, the world was ending.

Slowly, she let her stiff neck turn sideways. There were police vans, and two armoured personnel carriers, parked in the receiving area of the

No Frills. She blinked, her dry eyes burning, but when she looked again they remained standing sentry, hulking beasts tense and alert and ready to spring. She stood, leaning against the stoplight at the intersection, motionless and alone.

Until she stepped through the door to apartment number 507, she could pretend that the world hadn't changed all that much. Each outrage colliding with the previous atrocity, the travel bans and the kettling of demonstrators and the workplace restrictions and the new ID requirements, all slipping and sliding over each other, until at last the disappearances, Patrice Abel's streamed execution and Ian's decidedly not-public one, and she *knew* this story, knew it and yet there were still ads for furniture stores, there were still furniture stores, and the No Frills at Morningside and Lawrence was still standing, even if it was surrounded by tanks.

She glanced at her phone, down to 20% battery, out of instinct, but this was long past the point where terror could be resolved by a nervously apologetic text. She went for her keys next, placed one between each finger, the one to the front door peeking out from between the knuckles of the index and middle finger, should she need to use it to open the door instead of slashing it across an attacker's face.

Though there were no cars and no traffic lights, she looked both ways before crossing the street.

An electrical wire had fallen and leapt and sparked white-hot on the sidewalk. She skirted around it and dashed for the door, fumbled with the key until she saw that the lock on the inner door had already been smashed open, the vestibule glass cracked in spiderwebs from the frame. She pushed inside, stepping over shell casings, towards the elevator before her higher brain functions kicked in and she headed for the stairwell instead. Her legs had no desire to carry her up five flights of stairs. Each delay bought time against the inevitable discovery, opened the prospect of another, kinder explanation.

Her mother would have told her to stay away. Every painful footfall on the staircase was an aching and leaden betrayal.

Her side cramping and her breath tight in her chest, Sujay stumbled into the beige carpeted tunnel. Her pulse roared too loudly in her ears to hear, but she could smell the blood, and shit, and piss, layered over cigarettes and weed, and onions and garlic, and Axe body spray, and incense, the smells of living and breathing yielding to those of their cessation. There was blood on the carpet, the walls. She could still pretend. It was metres to her family's apartment.

The door to 505 was half open, someone hunched within. Sujay waved, and then remembered that Mrs. Sivasankaran was mostly blind, so she edged closer, whispered, "It's me, it's Sujaya, Kashvi's daughter."

No response. She tried again. "Auntie?"

The old woman wore a stained nightgown and nothing else; the sight of her bare legs, the skin goosefleshed and dry, filled Sujay with vicarious humiliation. Mrs. Sivasankaran had an adult daughter who took care of her, but judging by the state of the apartment, the daughter hadn't been home for days. Fruit flies swarmed over the unwashed dishes in the sink, and something brown and oozing stuck to Sujay's shoe as she stepped onto the parquet floor.

The pop-pop-pop came again, and there was no space for denial anymore. If her parents or her brother could have called, they would have, and there was a furniture ad on the radio because there would be no news of what happened here, not now, not ever again.

A distant, absent part of her mind tried to envision it. Had they gone door-to-door, like Jehovah's Witnesses or canvassers? Knocked, and then opened fire? The sheer scale, the effort to massacre one whole high-rise, when there were so many other high-rises, seemed too vast for even the row of vans across the street to accomplish. But then, did they have to be soldiers, or cops? They likely weren't. She knew from her grandfather's stories how much more convenient it is to have one's neighbours do the actual killing.

"We have to get you out of here," she told Mrs. Sivasankaran. She'd have to run, and the old woman, frail and blind and suffering from dementia, would slow her down, but so many people were *gone*, Jamila and Ian and Jonah and Patrice Abel and Zach, for her to turn her back on someone who was *here*. She tugged at her neighbour's arm, but Mrs. Sivasankaran's head lolled to one side, eyes fixed open. The pops were closer now.

Outside, someone called her name. Her full name. Even knowing better, the voice was young, and male, and she tried to convince herself that it was Anoj, or one of the boys from the neighbourhood.

Sujay peered down the hall and scrambled across to 507. She still had her keys out, but the door was already ajar, the smell even more pungent.

She envied Mrs. Sivasankaran her blindness at the end.

Her father must have died first, still gripping the baseball bat he kept under the bed as defence against home invaders. He was face-down, but she knew the shiny bald spot on the top of his head, the mole under his ear, still visible even through rivulets of dried blood. The grey imprint of a shoe was visible on his white dress shirt. She'd have to step over the corpse to get to the rest of her family, to see how they had died. That was their protection, her father and the baseball bat, and if she closed her eyes, if she listened, if she cast her consciousness wide over the apartment, she knew she would hear no other, hidden heartbeats, no frantic, frightened breathing. His murderers had stepped over him, on him.

Sujay had to know. She stepped over her father's dead body.

Her mother was two meters away, a wide, undignified boulder in front of Anoj's old bedroom. She had a butcher knife and a cellphone, and Sujay forced herself not to look at either. Of every possible world that stemmed from the choice she would make next, there was none in which she opened the bedroom door to find Anoj hidden under the bed. She saw an outstretched hand and bolted for the hallway.

Someone—a man, not her dead father, not her dead brother—called her name again, answered by pops that were now, in no way, anything to be confused with fireworks.

Instinct overriding uncertainty, she pushed herself into the wall.

Two men on opposite ends of the hallway were shooting at *each other*. She squinted to see between the wall's atoms. Sujay knew what a gunshot sounded like but she had never *seen* a gun in her life, not this close. The men were both young and judging from the way they were holding the guns, sideways like they were in *GTA V*, they probably hadn't seen a gun until six weeks ago either. One of the men—boys, he couldn't have been more than 20—was a white kid in jeans and a flak jacket, the clothes giving away his allegiance even if the bloodsplash up the side of the denim didn't already mark him as a murderer. He was sweating, and wide-eyed, and looked just as scared as she was.

The other man held his breath, righted his gun and gripped it with both hands, and blasted. The white kid dropped, abruptly, like Wile E. Coyote realizing he'd gone past the edge of a cliff.

Sujay's breath caught in her lungs and she looked at the crumpled heap of khaki and blue, the spill of blond hair through the bloody crush of brains and skull. The other man, the gun dangling from his fingers like a branch broken off in a storm, picked a careful path around the bloodstains.

He was the single most ridiculous human being she had ever seen in her life. Barely older or less freaked out than the kid he'd just killed, he was a scrawny sack of bones in an oversized Raptors shirt and sagging track pants that showed the waistband of his underwear. He had little wisps of facial hair, black pube curls, dotting his jaw and upper lip. His ears stuck out on the sides of a narrow head. One of his shoelaces was untied. And he'd just saved her life.

"Sujay Krishnamurthy?" he called. She recognized his voice. He was the one who'd been shouting her name.

Sujay stepped out from the wall.

"I'm not here to hurt you," he said. "I have a car waiting outside." As if the sentences had any relation to each other, he added, "I've never killed anyone before." He reached out the hand that wasn't holding a gun.

What she meant to say was that she had an escape plan, and it didn't involve him, or shooting anyone, except that she didn't, and she had to be on fifteen different government databases by now, and her mother and her father and her brother were dead on the parquet floor of her childhood apartment.

Instead, she said, “What kind of car?”

“A Honda Civic.” Sujay’s brain at last kicked into gear and, trembling, too in shock to grieve but her hands moving by rote, she summoned up a Someone Else’s Problem glamour to hide the two of them as best she could.

At the third floor landing, she thought to ask, “Who are you?”

“My name’s Shadi,” he said, and since that wasn’t much of an explanation, added four incongruous words that were so absurd that she had no choice *but* to trust him: “Gaby Abel sent me.”

Epilogue

In the parking lot behind Fort Utopia, Sujay clutched a silicone stress toy between hands sheathed in threadbare acrylic gloves, and buried her name under the frozen concrete.

Shadi stepped from one foot to another, shivering. "Are you sure you don't want someone else here?"

"Like?"

"I don't know. Gaby?" Someone sensitive, Sujay translated. Someone who would look at her with kindness, eyes softening, as if everyone else at Fort Utopia hadn't lost a husband, or a family, or everyone they'd ever known.

The familiar elevator-drop lurch in her stomach swayed her, and she clutched Panic Pete harder. No, Gaby would read the loss in her face, and she couldn't take pity from a woman who'd lost as much as she had. She did want *someone* there. Maybe not Shadi, with his awkward bluster, his too-large parka with holes in the sleeves half covering the Fly Emirates logo on his soccer jersey, but company was in short supply, and at least Shadi wouldn't cry for her.

Fort Utopia had once been Fortune Auto Repair, tucked into the corner of a strip mall off Morningside. Most of the equipment was still there, and some of the cars. There was a beat-up Dodge Ram that the owner had been working on before the Voluntary Relocation came for him. It had a shiny chrome bumper and a star spray of rust across the roof, and it reminded Sujay of Bessie, so much that her heart clenched if she caught a glimpse of it unprepared.

When it was clear that the owner wasn't coming back, that half the neighbourhood had been stripped for parts and abandoned, its residents deported or murdered—*unencumbered*, as they said—Shadi's group had moved in. They'd stuffed old bills and smuggled jewelry under the hoods of cars that would never see a highway again, mementos of dead grandparents that the survivors were not quite desperate enough to sell. Thrown up scavenged wire fencing and stolen signs to warn intruders away from a shriekgrass infestation. Shadi himself had fixed the sign, two of the letters already burned out to give him a head start, and marked the door in the argot of Gaby Abel's Scarborough cell. When they'd grown larger than the four young men who'd initially hidden in the auto shop basement, new arrivals had holed up in the Pakistani bakery and the carpet shop that no one had seen open in years. *Vive la fucking Resistance.*

The alluring smell that still lingered in the bakery aside, Sujay liked the auto shop best. The stain-slicked floor smelled of oil no matter how hard anyone scrubbed it, and there were still, inexplicably, yellowing Sunshine Girls taped to the wall in the office. She lived out of her bag under the desk. It was the perfect place to hit rock bottom.

"Not Gaby," she said. She studied him carefully before returning her attention to the pavement. "If you don't want to stay—"

"I want to stay." He reached out for her wrist, fingers dry and purpled in the cold. "I don't know what the fuck we're doing, but I think I don't love the thought of you having to do it alone."

She bit her bottom lip and squeezed his hand once, only slightly more gently than she squeezed her stress ball, before letting go. She peeled off her gloves. "Thanks."

Deep breaths, as if by force of will she could steady her heartbeat, slow her pulse, reach out to the capricious Pattern of the universe and bring herself into alignment with it, tame the forces that had split the earth and set the cities on fire. As if she could still cosmic forces that cared nothing for humanity, and bend them to her will.

Nothing was happening. She could reach down into its molecules, feel their substance, their slowness. It went against the laws of physics for them to budge. And yet—

The slightest crack, a tiny ripple in the fabric of reality, a quiet violation that almost fell beneath notice. She worried at it like a sore tooth, nudged it apart. The lightning of magic that coursed through her felt less like a feeble current than ambient static these days, but she pried and bent and forced it until it coalesced into a tangible reality.

The parking lot shook and wrenched apart. The crack a few inches from her boots was a deep, yawning void the colour of blood, a hungry mouth.

Shadi grabbed her arm. "Holy *shit.*"

"You wanted to stay," Sujay reminded him, and tugged her name out of her heart.

It didn't want to come easily. It was anchored there by habit and memory, and the first pull felt like a knife through her lungs. Her mother, tucking her in at night. Her father, calling her over to read something he'd seen in the newspaper. Anoj, pulling her hair to make her cry. Every teacher who'd mangled it while calling attendance on the first day of class. Every time she'd carefully corrected the pronunciation. Every card in her wallet, every tax form, every piece of mail.

Jamila, cosplaying as Ms. Marvel at ComicCon with her red hijab loose enough to look like a cowl, *Sujay Sujay we gotta get a picture with Jane the Werewolf, c'mon the line is barely long, Sujay come on—*

Jamila, who was *unencumbered* like her family, like the poor former owner of Fort Utopia, Jamila who on the first day of ninth grade had sat down next to Sujay, admired her careful and awkward drawing of Ryuk from *Death Note* and said, *Nice drawing, what's your name*, and she had said—

She had said—

I'm Sujaya Krishnamurthy, what's yours?

Her name wasn't out of her yet. It clung on by tendons and hooked little claws, a dry, tough burr in her chest. Ian had made it sound so simple, just like unmaking the documents in the Broom Closet.

He'd never said it would *hurt.*

She had graduated that May, almost two years ago, and caught the train to Ottawa because Anoj wanted to see his girlfriend and wouldn't loan her the car. She was rumpled and sweaty when she arrived at the office on Laurier Ave. with no one sitting behind the receptionist's desk and the three chairs against the wall filled with skinny girls with fat resumes. Ian Mallory, the famous sorcerer, had to call her in himself after the last girl scurried out, haunted and pale. The magic roiled off of him, coiling in tangible waves, bumping up against her own glamour. His hand sparked when she shook it.

I'm–

Yeah, he said, tired and irritable. *I know. Come in.*

He had a file on her. He worked for Ottawa, she'd have to pass a security clearance if she got the job, what did she expect? He didn't stumble on her name, or the names of either of her uncles who'd been in the LTTE in Tamil Eelam.

Why do you want this job? You're a bit more Anime Club than Model UN, aren't ya?

I care about politics.

You don't know how to dress or stand properly. You were sweating, back there, when you shook my hand. They'll tear you apart on the ums and the vocal fry, and that's before they find out about the terrorist uncles and the Wellbutrin prescriptions. You're not pretty enough to win at an old white man's game. You don't have a career in Parliament. You won't get far in the civil service, no matter how law-abiding you've been. It's not so much a glass ceiling as a concrete roof.

He waited, expectantly, for her to crumble. His glamour didn't quite disguise a small, mercurial smile.

So what are you doing here, Sujaya Krishnamurthy?

Same thing as you are, she said, as coolly as she could manage.

—that's my secret I'm always insecure—

She'd said, *I'm here, Mr. Mallory, to be a fucking magician. And you can call me—*

you can call me—

I am—

She ripped her name out of her heart and shoved it, screaming and squirming, into the chasm she'd opened in the ground. She stuffed it down, though it fought her all the way, and the pavement rose up, the seam where its ragged edges met an ugly scar no matter how hard she tried to flatten it back down.

When the ground had stopped shivering, she put Panic Pete back inside her jacket pocket and rubbed her hands together. There was a hollow space between her lungs that ached with every inhale. She wiped a trickle of blood from her nose into a streak across her knuckles.

Shadi took a long, shuddering breath. "Okay to talk?"

She nodded.

"You really are a—"

"Yeah." Together, they watched the embers die as they dripped from her fingers. "I really am."

"Cool," he said. "That's really cool—um. What do I call you, exactly?"

Her name danced just off her tongue, her mouth incapable of shaping the syllables into meaning. The name existed, out there, but no longer attached to her.

Instead, she reached into her wallet and made a show of checking her passport. It was useless now; the new brighter blue ones weren't issued to people like her and an old one was cause for suspicion, if not arrest. She flipped it open to the picture, a few years old now, her hair tied back and her face straining so hard to keep a neutral expression that it looked crooked.

A little on the nose, she thought, but it would do, until she could reclaim what she'd lost, or she had burned all that she could in revenge.

"Call me Maya."

She turned from her name, a stillborn child under the lump in the concrete. Each time it shivered was farther apart from the last. Gaby Abel hung in the half-opened back door of Fort Utopia, waiting for them to come back. The city weaved, writhed with magic, behind them. There would be time to grieve later.

"Okay, Maya," Shadi said. It sounded right, somehow, when he said it. "Let's go fix the world."

Acknowledgements

Writing a novel is an inherently socialist endeavour. I am so incredibly grateful to my community of readers, writers, and friends who critiqued, fact-checked, cheerlead, and managed to turn my ridiculous notion of disaster wizards doing politics into an actual novel.

Any errors and omissions can be blamed on pandemic brain and the ongoing trauma of living under the Ontario Tories.

If I crowdsourced your expertise or ranted about my writing process, I owe you a debt. I cannot possibly thank everyone who's had a hand in making this happen. That said ...

Geoffrey Dow, my publisher, took a chance on this weird cross-genre, anti-commercial novel and believed in it, even when I wasn't quite sure if it would have a readership.

Rachel Schwartz-Narbonne fixed my science and spent a remarkable amount of time brainstorming the theoretical feedback loop effects generated by climate catastrophe and eldritch abominations.

Zilla Novikov, my most hardcore beta reader and line editor, consistently encouraged me to lean in and make it darker. If at any point in reading this you felt an emotion, you can blame her.

Romeo Côté provided a necessary voice on Métis representation and I am thankful for his extensive knowledge about the historical and legal details of land title.

The following awesome betas: Tim Whitney, Mary Alexandria Kelly, Jess, Holly Brown, Saevelle, Julian Spurlock, Rohan O'Duill, Dance Harden, Jim Lai, Erica Marques, and Rory Garon. You caught everything from my overuse of semicolons to my appalling lack of knowledge about trucks, and brought your own areas of expertise and experience to the story.

Julian Gunn made a game inspired by Cascade, and our many long conversations about craft and structure have been inspirational.

Noelle Allen talked me through the practicalities of publishing and helped me structure my sprawling first draft into something readable.

Sai Amrita Kaul stayed up late with me to name Maya.

The Aurora Public Library Writers' Group were instrumental in tightening the first few chapters.

My Discord friends in Fantasy Wryters, LGBTQI+ Critique Group, Cats and Eldritch Horrors, The Spicy Pepper, and Night Beats Discord. Particular shoutouts to Sun, Marten Norr, Emily Dawn Kelly, Vorpal, Eagan, Wing Hang, Renee, and Elyzabeth for their support, memes, brainstorming, and sprinting. I have loved getting to know your worlds and characters as you've helped me create mine. I am not quite sure how people got novels finished before Discord existed but you weirdos have been my enablers and my joy.

And finally, to you, dear reader. You have picked up a massive tome by a first time author and read it all the way to the end. While you await the sequel, get out there and use your magic to fix the world.

Publisher's Acknowledgements

If writing a novel is an inherently socialist endeavour, publishing a novel is, at very least, a collective one.

The BumblePuppy Press gratefully acknowledges the following people for their support, which allowed us to *publish* this book, and not just print it.

L.J. LaForest, Reccia Mandelcorn, Sai Amrita Kaul, Dominick Bruno, Erys Purmoar, Troy Parker, Jason Pinkney, April Goodwin-Smith, Nathanael Vaprin, Joel Troster, Rick Innis, Mary Kelly, Leah Marcus, Caitlyn Pascal, Van Lepthien, Jonathan Culp, Meagan Harris, François Villeneuve, Moira Russell, Nicole Bezanson, Timothy John Whitney, Stephanie Saroiberry, Mark W, Isabella Bosetti, Robin Frolic, Nicholas Dziedzic, Mick Sweetman, Chris Bowman, Julian, Mathieu Brule, Bunny McCabe, Jordan Smith Carroll, Heather Savage, Raye Clemente, David Neil Lee, Wesley Williams, Lisa Lai, Lynna Landstreet, Barbara Kaye, Caro Moffatt, Ellen Kaye-Cheveldayoff, Kirsti Hart-negrich, Sarah Palmer, CJ Mantel, Midnight Andrews

About the Author

Rachel A. Rosen is an activist, graphic designer, and for her sins, a high school teacher. In a previous life, she published two long-running anarchist 'zines and designed the uniform for the Christie Pits Hardball League. She has written for *Atlas Obscura, The Humanist In Canada, Culture and the State*, and *Exit Device*, not to mention the book you're holding right now. She lives in Toronto, where she is the harried personal assistant to two cats.

Also published by
The BumblePuppy Press

www.bppress.ca

Rachel A. Rosen

• *Cascade: The Sleep of Reason, Book I*

• *Blight: The Sleep of Reason, Book II* (forthcoming)

Carl Dow

• *The Old Man's Last Sauna*

• *Black Grass*

• *Wildflowers: The Women Who Made McCord Chronicle* (forthcoming)

• *Beyond the Blood* (forthcoming)

Zilla Novikov

• *Reprise* (forthcoming)

Jules Paivio

• *Life Is Good: A Memoir* (forthcoming)

A. A. Milne

• *The Woke Winnie the Pooh*

(Forthcoming: Edited and with commentary by Geoffrey Dow)

Manufactured by Amazon.ca
Bolton, ON

26824917R00243